Life's handicap : being stories of mi

Kipling, Rudyard, 1865-1936

THE

LIFE'S HANDICAP

In Northern India stood a monastery called The Chubara of Dhunni Bhagat. No one remembered who or whatDhunni Bhagat had been. He had lived his Hfe, made alittle money and spent it all, as every good Hindu shoulddo, on a work of piety—the Chubara. That was full ofbrick cells, gaily painted with the figures of Gods andkings and elephants, where worn-out priests could sit andmeditate on the latter end of things; the paths were brickpaved, and the naked feet of thousands had worn theminto gutters. Clumps of mangoes sprouted from betweenthe bricks; great pipal trees overhung the well-windlassthat whined all day; and hosts of parrots tore through thetrees. Crows and §quirrels were tame in that place, forthey knew that never a priest would touch them.

The wandering mendicants, charm-sellers, and holyvagabonds for a hundred miles round used to make theChubara their place of call and rest. Mahomedan, Sikh,and Hindu mixed equally under the trees. They were oldmen, and when man has come to the turnstiles of Nightall the creeds in the world seem to him wonderfully alikeand colourless.

Gobind the one-eyed told me this. He was a holy manwho lived on an island in the middle of a river and fed thefishes with little bread pellets twice a day. In flood-time,when swollen corpses stranded themselves at the foot ofthe island, Gobind would cause them to be piously burned,for the sake of the honour of mankind, and having regard

to his own account with God hereafter. But when two-thirds of the island was torn away m a spate, Gobindcame across the river to Dhunni Bhagat's Chubira, heand his brass drinking vessel with the well-cord roundthe neck, his short arm-rest crutch studded with brassnails, his roll of bedding, his big pipe, his umbrella, andhis tall sugar-loaf hat with the nodding peacock feathersin it. He wrapped himself up in his patched quilt madeof every colour and material in the world, sat down in asunny corner of the very quiet Chubara, and, resting hisarm on his short-handled crutch, waited for death. Thepeople brought him food and little clumps of marigoldflowers, and he gave his blessing in return. He wasnearly blind, and his face was seamed and lined andwrinkled beyond behef, for he had lived in his time whichwas before the English came within five hundred milesof Dhunni Bhagat's Chubira.

When we grew to know each other well, Gobind wouldtell me tales in a voice most like the rumbling of heavyguns over a wooden bridge. His tales were true, but notone in twenty could be printed in an English book, be-cause the English do not think as natives do. Theybrood over matters that a native would dismiss till afitting occasion; and what they would not think twiceabout a native will brood over till a fitting occasion: thennative and English stare at each other hopelessly acrossgreat gulfs of miscomprehension.

'And what,' said Gobind one Sunday evening, yourhonoured craft, and by what manner of means earn youyour daily bread?'

I am,' said I, 'a kerani—one who writes with a penupon paper, not being in the service of the Government.'

Then what do you write?' said Gobind. Come nearer,for I cannot see your countenance, and the light fails.'

I write of all matters that lie within my understand-ing, and of many that do not. But chiefly I write of Lifeand Death, and men and women, and Love and Fateaccording to the measure of my abiHty, telling the talethrough the mouths of one, two, or more people. Thenby the favour of God the tales are sold and money accruesto me that I may keep alive.'

'Even so,' said Gobind. 'That is the work of thebazar story-teller; but he speaks straight to men andwomen and does not write anything at all. Only whenthe tale has aroused expectation, and calamities are aboutto befall the virtuous, he stops suddenly and demandspayment ere he continues the narration. Is it so in yourcraft, my son?'

'I have heard of such things when a tale is of greatlength, and is sold as a cucumber, in small pieces.'

'Ay, I was once a famed teller of stories when I wasbegging on the road between Koshin and Etra; before thelast pilgrimage that ever I took to Orissa. I told manytales and heard many more at the rest-houses in theevening when we were merry at the end of the march.It is in my heart that grown men are but as little childrenin the matter of tales, and the oldest tale is the most be-loved.'

'With your people that is truth,' said I. 'But in re-gard to our people they desire new tales, and when all iswritten they rise up and declare that the tale were bettertold in such and such a manner, and doubt either thetruth or the invention thereof.'

'But what folly is theirs!' said Gobind, throwing outhis knotted hand. 'A tale that is told is a true tale aslong as the telHng lasts. And of their talk upon it—youknow how Bilas Khan, that was the prince of tale-tellers, said to one who mocked him in the great rest'

house on the Jhelum road: "Go on, my brother, andfinish that I have begun," and he who mocked took upthe tale, but having neither voice nor manner for the taskcame to a standstill, and the pilgrims at supper madehim eat abuse and stick half that night.'

'Nay, but with our people, money having passed, it istheir right; as we should turn against a shoeseller inregard to shoes if those wore out. If ever I make a bookyou shall see and judge.'

'And the parrot said to the falhng tree. Wait, brother,till I fetch a prop I' said Gobind with a grim chuckle.' God has given me eighty years, and it may be some over.I cannot look for more than day granted by day and as afavour at this tide. Be swift.'

'In what manner is it best to set about the task,'said I, '0 chief est of those who string pearls with^ theirtongue?'

'How do I know? Yet'—he thought for a little—'how should I not know? God has made very manyheads, but there is only one heart in all the world amongyour people or my people. They are children in thematter of tales.'

'But none are so terrible as the Uttle ones, if a manmisplace a word, or in a second teUing vary events by somuch as one small devil.'

'Ay, I also have told tales to the little ones, but do
thou this ' His old eyes fell on the gaudy paintings
of the wall, the blue and red dome, and the flames of thepomsettias beyond. 'Tell them first of those things thatthou hast i 3n and they have seen together. Thus theirknowledge will piece out thy imperfections. Tell themof what thou alone hast seen, then what thou hast heard,and

since they be children tell them of battles and kings,horses, devils, elephants, and angels, but omit not to tell

them of love and suchlike. All the earth is full of talesto him who listens and does not drive away the poorfrom his door. The poor are the best of tale-tellers; forthey must lay their ear to the ground every night.

After this conversation the idea grew in my head, andGobind was pressing in his inquiries as to the health ofthe book.

Later, when we had been parted for months, it hap-pened that I was to go away and far off, and I came tobid Gobind good-bye.

It is farewell between us now, for I go a very longjourney, I said.

'And I also. A longer one than thou. But what ofthe book?   said he.

It will be bom in due season if it is so ordained.'

I would I could see it,' said the old man, huddlingbeneath his quilt. 'But that will not be. I die threedays hence, in the night, a little before the dawn. Theterm of my years is accomplished.'

In nine cases out of ten a native makes no miscalcula-tion as to the day of his death. He has the foreknowl-edge of the beasts in this respect.

'Then thou wilt depart in peace, and it is good talk,for thou hast said that life is no deHght to thee.'

'But it is a pity that our book is not born. Howshall I know that there is any record of my name?'

'Because I promise, in the forepart of the book, pre-ceding everything else, that it shall be written, Gobind,sadhu, of the island in the river and awaiting God inDhuimi Bhagat's Chubara, first spoke of the book,' saidI.

'And gave counsel—an old man's counsel. Gobind,son of Gobind of the Chumi village in the Karaon tehsil,in the district of Mooltan. Will that be written also?'

'That wdll be written also

'And the book will go across the Black Water to thehouses of your people, and all the Sahibs will know ofme who am eighty years old?'

'All who read the book shall know. I cannot promisefor the rest.'

'That is good talk. Call aloud to all who are in themonastery, and I will tell them this thing.'

They trooped up, faquirSj sadhus^ sunnyasis, byragis^nihangs, and mullahs, priests of all faiths and everydegree of raggedness, and Gobind, leaning upon hiscrutch, spoke so that they were visibly filled with envy,and a white-haired senior bade Gobind think of hislatter end instead of transitory repute in the mouthsof strangers. Then Gobind gave me his blessing andI came away.

These tales have been collected from all places, and allsorts of people, from priests in the Chubara, from AlaYar the carver, Jiwun Singh the carpenter, namelessmen on steamers and trains round the world, womenspinning outside their cottages in the twilight, officersand gentlemen now dead and buried, and a few, butthese are the very best, my father gave me. The greaterpart of them have been published in magazines and news-papers, to whose editors I am indebted; but some are newon this side of the water, and some have not seen thelight before.

The most remarkable stories are, of course, those whichdo not appear—for obvious reasons.

CONTENTS

xili

jjiv CONTENTS

\

LIFE'S HANDICAP

The Chief Engineer's sleeping suit was of yellow stripedwith blue, and his speech was the speech of Aberdeen.They sluiced the deck under him, and he hopped on tothe ornamental capstan, a black pipe between his teeth,though the hour was not seven of the morn.

*Did you ever hear o' the Lang Men o' Larut?' heasked when the Man from Orizava had finished a storyof an aboriginal giant discovered in the wilds of Brazil.There was never story yet passed the lips of teller, butthe Man from Orizava could cap it.

*No, we never did,' we responded with one voice. TheMan from Orizava watched the Chief keenly, as a possiblerival.

*I'm not telling the story for the sake of talkingmerely,' said the Chief, 'but as a warning against bet-ting, unless you bet on a perrfect certainty. The LangMen o' Larut were just a certainty. I have hadtalk wi' them. Now Larut, you will understand, is adependency, or it may be an outlying possession, o' theisland o' Penang, and there they will get you tin andmanganese, an' it mayhap mica, and all manner o'meenerals. Larut is a great place.'

*But what about the population?' said the Man fromOrizava.

'The population,' said the Chief slowly, 'were fewbut enorrmous. You must understand that, exceptin*

the tin-mines, there is no special inducement to Euro-peans to reside in Larut. The climate is warm andremarkably like the climate o' Calcutta; and in regardto Calcutta, it cannot have escaped your obsairvationthat—'

'Calcutta isn't Larut; and we've only just comefrom it,' protested the Man from Orizava. 'There's ameteorological department in Calcutta, too.'

'Ay, but there's no meteorological department inLarut. Each man is a law to himself. Some drinkwhisky, and some drink brandipanee, and some drinkcocktails—vara bad for the coats o' the stomach is acocktail—and some drink sangaree, so I have beencredibly informed; but one and all they sweat like thepacking of a piston-head on a fourrteen-days' voyagewith the screw racing half her time. But, as I was say-ing, the population o' Larut was five all told of EngUsh—that is to say, Scotch—an' I'm Scotch, ye know,' saidthe Chief.

The Man from Orizava lit another cigarette, andwaited patiently. It was hopeless to hurry the ChiefEngineer.

' I am not pretending to account for the population o'Larut being laid down according to such fabulous dimen-sions. O' the five white men engaged upon the extrac-tion o' tin ore and mercantile pursuits, there were threeo' the sons o' Anak. Wait while I remember. Lammit-ter was the first by two inches—a giant in the land, an' aterreefic man to cross in his ways. From heel to head hewas six feet nine inches, and proportionately built acrossand through the thickness of his body. Six good feetnine inches—an overbearin' man. Next to him, and Ihave forgotten his precise business, was Sandy Vowle.And he was six feet seven, but lean and lathy, and it

was more in the elasteecity of liis neck that the heightlay than in any honesty o' bone and sinew. Five feetand a few odd inches may have been his real height.The remainder came out when he held up his head, andsix feet seven he was upon the door-siUs. I took hismeasure in chalk standin' on a chair. And next to him,but a proportionately made man, ruddy and of a faircountenance, was Jock Coan—that they called the FirCone. He was but six feet five, and a child besideLammitter and Vowle. When the three walked outtogether, they made a scunner run through the colony o*tarut. The Malays ran round them as though they hadbeen the giant trees in the Yosemite Valley—these threeLang Men o' Larut. It was perfectly ridiculous—a licsusnakir(B—tha.t one little place should have containedmaybe the three tallest ordinar' men upon the face o'the earth.

'Obsairve now the order o' things. For it led to thefinest big drink in Larut, and six sore heads the mornthat endured for a week. I am against immoderateliquor, but the event to follow was a justification. Youmust understand that many coasting steamers call atLarut wi' strangers o' the mercantile profession. In thespring time, when the young cocoanuts were ripening,and the trees o' the forests were putting forth theirleaves, there came an American man to Larut, and hewas six foot three, or it may have been four, in hisstockings. He came on business from Sacramento, buthe stayed for pleasure wi' the Lang Men o' Larut.Less than a half o' the population were ordinar' in theirgirth and stature, ye will understand—Howson andNailor, merchants, five feet nine or thereabouts. Hehad business with those two, and he stood above themfrom the six feet threedom o' his height till they went

5 LIFE'S HANDICAP

to drink. In the course o conversation he said, as taBmen will, things about his height, and the trouble of it tohim. That was his pride o' the flesh.

'"As the longest man in the island " he said, but

there they took him up and asked if he were sure.

'"I say I am the longest man in the island," he said,"and on that I'll bet my substance."

'They laid down the bed-plates of a big drink then andthere, and put it aside while they called Jock Coan fromhis house, near by among the fireflies' winking.

'*'How's a' wi' you?" said Jock, and came in by theside o' the Sacramento profligate, two inches, or it mayhave been one, taller than he.

" "You're long," said the man, opening his eyes. "ButI am longer." An' they sent a whistle through the nightan' howkit out Sandy Vowle from his bit bungalow, andhe came in an' stood by the side o' Jock, an' the pair justflllit the room to the ceiling-cloth.

'The Sacramento man was a euchre-player and a mostprofane sweerer. "You hold both Bowers," he said,"but the Joker is with me."

'"Fair an' softly," says Nailor. "Jock, whaur's LangLammitter?"

'"Here," says that man, putting his leg through thewindow and coming in like an anaconda o' the desertfurlong by furlong, one foot in Penang and one in Batavia,and a hand in North Borneo it may be.

'"Are you suited?" said Nailor, when the hinder endo' Lang Lammitter was slidden through the sill an' thehead of Lammitter was lost in the smoke away above.

'The American man took out his card and put it onthe table. "Esdras B. Longer is my name, America ismy nation, 'Frisco is my resting-place, but this here beatsCreation," said he. "Boys, giants—side-show giants—I

THE LANG MEN O' LARUT 7

minded to slide out of my bet if I had been overtopped,on the strength of the riddle on this paste-board. Iwould have done it if you had topped me even by threeinches, but when it comes to feet—yards—miles, I amnot the man to shirk the biggest drink that ever madethe travellers'-joy palm blush with virginal indignation,or the orang-outang and the perambulating dyak howlwith envy. Set them up and continue till the final con-clusion."

'O mon, I tell you 'twas an awful sight to see thosefour giants threshing about the house and the island, andtearin' down the pillars thereof an' throwing palm-treesbroadcast, and currhng their long legs round the hills o*Larut. An awfu' sight! I was there. I did not meanto tell you, but it's out now. I was not overcome, for Ie'en sat me down under the pieces o' the table at four themom an' meditated upon the strangeness of things.

'Losh, yon's the breakfast-bell!'

REINGELDER AND THE GERMAN FLAG^

Hans Breitmann paddled across the deck in his pinkpyjamas, a cup of tea in one hand and a cheroot in theother, when the steamer was sweltering down the coast onher way to Singapur. He drank beer all day and allnight, and played a game called 'Scairt' with threecompatriots.

'I haf washed,' said he in a voice of thunder, 'butdere is no use washing on these hell-seas. Look at me—Iam still all wet and schweatin'. It is der tea dot makesme so. Boy, bring me Bilsener on ice.'

'You will die if you drink beer before breakfast,'said one man. 'Beer is the worst thing in the worldfor '

'Ya, I know~der liver. I haf no Hver, und I shallnot die. At least I will not die obon dese benny sdeamersdot haf no beer fit to trink. If I should haf died, I willhaf don so a hoondert dimes before now—in Shermany,in New York, in Japon, in Assam, und all over der insidebarts of South Amerique. Also in Shamaica should I hafdied or in Siam, but I am here; und der are my orchitsdot I have drafelled all the world round to find.'

He pointed towards the wheel, where, in two roughwooden boxes, lay a mass of shrivelled vegetation, sup-posed by all the ship to represent Assam orchids of fabu-lous value.

Now, orchids do not grow in the main streets of towns,

and Hans Breitmann had gone far to get his. Therewas nothing that he had not collected that year, fromking-crabs to white kangaroos.

'Lisden now/ said he, after he had been speaking fornot much more than ten minutes without a pause; 'Lisdenund I will dell you a sdory to show how bad und worseit is to go goUectin' und belief vot anoder fool haf said.Dis was in Uraguay which was in Amerique—North orSout' you would not know—und I was hoontin' orchitsund aferydings else dot I could back in my kanasters—dot is drafelling sbecimen-gaces. Dere vas den mit meanoder man—Reingelder, dot vas his name—und he vashoontin' also but only coral-snakes—joost Uraguay coral-snakes—aferykind you could imagine. I dell you acoral-snake is a peauty—all red und white like coral dothas been gestrung in bands upon der neck of a girl. Dereis one snake howefer dot we who gollect know ash derSherman Flag, pecause id is red und plack und white,joost Hke a sausage mit druffles. Reingelder he wasnaturalist—goot man—goot trinker—better as me! "ByGott," said Reingelder, "I will get a Sherman Flag snakeor I will die." Und we toorned all Uraguay upside-behint all pecause of dot Sherman Flag.

'Von day when we was in none knows where—shwingin' in our hummocks among der woods, oop comesa natif woman mit a Sherman Flag in a bickle-bottle—my bickle-bottle—und we both fell from our hummocksflat ubon our pot—what you call stomach—mit shoy atdis thing. Now I was gollectin' orchits also, und Iknowed dot der idee of life to Reingelder vas dis Sher-man Flag. Derefore I bicked myselfs oop und I said,"Reingelder, dot is your find."—"Heart's true friend, douart a goot man," said Reingelder, und mit dot he obensder bickle-bottle, und der natif woman she shqueals:

*'Herr Gott! It will bite." I said—pecause in Uraguaya man must be careful of der insects—"Reingelder,shpifligate her in der alcohol und den she will be allright."—"Nein/' said Reingelder, "I will der shnakealife examine. Dere is no fear. Der coral-shnakes aremitout shting-apparatus brofided." Boot I looked ather het, und she vas der het of a boison-shnake—dertrue viper cranium, narrow und contract. "It is notgoot," said I, "she may bite und den—we are treehoondert mile from aferywheres. Broduce der alcoholund bickle him alife." Reingelder he had him in hishand—grawlin' und grawlin' as slow as a woorm unddwice as guiet. "Nonsense," says Reingelder. "Yateshaf said dot not von of der coral-shnakes haf der sack ofboison." Yates vas der crate authority ubon der reptiliaof Sout' Amerique. He haf written a book. You donot know, of course, but he vas a crate authorite.

'I gum my eye upon der Sherman Flag, grawlin' undgrawlin' in Reingelder's fist, und der het vas not der hetof innocence. "Mein Gott," I said. "It is you dot vvil)get der sack—der sack from dis Ufe here pelow!"

'"Denyoumay haf der shnake," says Reingelder, pat-tin' it ubon her het. "See now, I will show you vatYates haf written!"

'Und mit dot he went indo his dent, unt brung outhis big book of Yates; der Sherman Flag grawlin' in hisfist. "Yates haf said," said Reingelder, und he throwedoben der book in der fork of his fist und read der passage,proofin' conglusivement dot nefer coral-shnake bite vasboison. Den he shut der book mit a bang, und dotshqueeze der Sherman Flag, und she nip once und dwice.

' "Der liddle fool he haf bit me," says Reingelder.

'Dese things was before we know apout der perman-ganat-pota^ iniection. I was discomfordable.

REINGELDER AND THE GERMAN FLAG ii

'"Die oop der arm, Reingelder," said I, "und trinkwhisky on til you can no more trink."

'"Trink ten tousand tevils! I will go to dinner," saidReingelder, und he put her afay und it vsis very red mitemotion.

'We lifed upon soup, horse-flesh, und beans for dinner,but before we vas eaten der soup, Reingelder he haf holdof his arm und cry, "It is genumben to der clavicle. Iam a dead man; und Yates he haf lied in brintl"

'I dell you it vas most sad, for der symbtoms dotcame vas all dose of strychnine. He vas doubled intobig knots, und den undoubled, und den redoubled moochworse dan pefore, und he frothed. I vas mit him, saying,"Reingelder, dost dou know me?" but he himself, derinward gonsciousness part, was peyond knowledge, undso I know he vas not in bain. Den he wrop himself oopin von dremendous knot und den he died—all alone mitme in Uraguay. I was sorry, for I lofed Reingelder, undI puried him, und den I took der coral-shnake—dot Sher-man Flag—so bad und dreacherous und I bickled himalife.

'So I got him: und so I lost Reingelder.'

THE WANDERING

'If you go once round the world in an easterly direction,you gain one day,' said the men of science to JohnHay. In after years John Hay went east, west, north,and south, transacted business, made love, and begat afamily, as have done many men, and the scientific infor-mation above recorded lay neglected in the deeps of hismind with a thousand other matters of equal importance.When a rich relative died, he found himself wealthybeyond any reasonable expectation that he had enter-tained in his previous career, which had been a chequeredand evil one. Indeed, long before the legacy came tohim, there existed in the brain of John Hay a Httle cloud—a momentary obscuration of thought that came andwent almost before he could realize that there was anysolution of continuity. So do the bats flit round theeaves of a house to show that the darkness is falling. Heentered upon great possessions, in money, land, and houses;but behind his delight stood a ghost that cried out thathis enjoyment of these things should not be of long dura-tion. It was the ghost of the rich relative, who had beenpermitted to return to earth to torture his nephew intothe grave. Wherefore, under the spur of this constantreminder, John Hay, always preserving the air of heavybusiness-like stohdity that hid the shadow on his mind,turned investments, houses, and lands into sovereigns—rich, round, red, EngHsh sovereigns, each one worth

twenty shillings. Lands may become valueless, andhouses fly heavenward on the wings of red flame, but tillthe Day of Judgment a sovereign will always be a sov-ereign—that is to say, a king of pleasures.

Possessed of his sovereigns, John Hay would fain havespent them one by one on such coarse amusements as hissoul loved; but he was haunted by the instant fear ofDeath; for the ghost of his relative stood in the hall ofhis house close to the hat-rack, shouting up the stairwaythat hfe was short, that there was no hope of increase ofdays, and that the undertakers were already roughingout his nephew's coffin. John Hay was generally alonein the house, and even when he had company, his friendscould not hear the clamorous uncle. The shadow insidehis brain grew larger and blacker. His fear of death wasdriving John Hay mad.

Then, from the deeps of his mind, where he had stowedaway all his discarded information, rose to Hght thescientific fact of the Easterly journey. On the nextoccasion that his uncle shouted up the stairway urginghim to make haste and live, a shriller voice cried, 'Whogoes round the world once easterly, gains one day.'

His growing diffidence and distrust of mankind madeJohn Hay unwilling to give this precious message of hopeto his friends. They might take it up and analyse it.He was sure it was true, but it would pain him acutelywere rough hands to examine it too closely. To himalone of all the toiling generations of mankind had thesecret of immortality been vouchsafed. It would beimpious—against all the designs of the Creator—to setmankind hurrying eastward. Besides, tliis would crowdthe steamers inconveniently, and John Hay wished of allthings to be alone. If he could get round the world intwo months—some one of whom he had read, he could

not remember the name, had covered the passage ineighty days—he would gain a clear day; and by steadilycontinuing to do it for thirty years, would gain onehundred and eighty days, or nearly the half of a year.It would not be much, but in course of time, as civilisa-tion advanced, and the Euphrates Valley Railway wasopened, he could improve the pace.

Armed with many sovereigns, Jolm Hay, in thetliirty-fifth year of his age, set forth on his travels,two voices bearing him company from Dover as hesailed to Calais. Fortune favoured him. The EuphratesValley Railway was newly opened, and he was thefirst man who took ticket direct from Calais to Calcutta—thirteen days in the train. Thirteen days in the trainare not good for the nerves; but he covered the worldand returned to Calais from America in twelve days overthe two months, and started afresh with four and twentyhours of precious time to his credit. Three years passed,and John Hay rehgiously went round this earth seekingfor more time wherein to enjoy the remainder of hissovereigns. He became known on many lines as theman who wanted to go on; when people asked him whathe was and what he did, he answered—

'I'm the person who intends to live, and I am tryingto do it now.'

His days were divided between watching the whitewake spinning behind the stern of the swiftest steamers,or the brown earth flashing past the windows of thefastest trains; and he noted in a pocket-book everyminute that he had railed or screwed out of remorselesseternity.

'This is better than praying for long Hfe,' quoth JohnHay as he turned his face eastward for his twentieth trip.The years had done more for him than he dared to hope.

THE WANDERING JEW 15

By the extension of the Brahmaputra Valley line to meetthe newly-developed China Midland, the Calais railwayticket held good ma Karachi and Calcutta to Hongkong.The round trip could be managed in a fraction over forty-seven days, and, filled with fatal exultation, John Haytold the secret of his longevity to his only friend, thehouse-keeper of his rooms in London. He spoke andpassed; but the woman was one of resource, and im-mediately took counsel with the lawyers who had firstinformed John Hay of his golden legacy. Very manysovereigns still remained, and another Hay longed tospend them on things more sensible than railway ticketsand steamer accommodation.

The chase was long, for when a man is journeyingliterally for the dear life, he does not tarry upon theroad. Round the world Hay swept anew, and overtookthe wearied Doctor, who had been sent out to lookfor him, in Madras. It was there that he found thereward of his toil and the assurance of a blessed im-mortality. In half an hour the Doctor, watching alwaysthe parched lips, the shaking hands, and the eye thatturned eternally to the east, won John Hay to rest ina little house close to the Madras surf. All that Hayneed do was to hang by ropes from the roof of the roomand let the round earth swing free beneath him. Thiswas better than steamer or train, for he gained a day ina day, and was thus the equal of the undying sun. Theother Hay would pay his expenses throughout eternity.

It is true that we cannot yet take tickets from Calaisto Hongkong, though that will come about in fifteenyears; but men say that if you wander along the southerncoast of India you shall find in a neatly whitewashed

little bungalow, sitting in a chair swung from the roof,over a sheet of thin steel which he knows so well destroysthe attraction of the earth, an old and worn man whofor ever faces the rising sun, a stop-watch in his hand,racing against eternity. He cannot drink, he does notsmoke, and his Hving expenses amount to perhapstwenty-five rupees a month, but he is John Hay, theImmortal. Without, he hears the thunder of the wheel-ing world with which he is careful to explain he has noconnection whatever; but if you say that it is only thenoise of the surf, he will cry bitterly, for the shadow onhis brain is passing away as the brain ceases to work, andhe doubts sometimes whether the doctor spoke the truth.'Why does not the sun always remain over my head?'asks John Hay.

The Policeman rode through the Himalayan forest, underthe moss-draped oaks, and his orderly trotted after him.

'It's an ugly business, Bhere Singh,' said the Police-man. 'Where are they?'

'It is a very ugly business,' said Bhere Singh; 'and asfor them, they are, doubtless, now frying in a hotter firethan was ever made of spruce-branches.'

'Let us hope not,' said the PoHceman, 'for, allowing forthe difference between race and race, it's the story ofFrancesca da Rimini, Bhere Singh.'

Bhere Singh knew nothing about Francesca da Rimini,so he held his peace until they came to the charcoal-burners' clearing where the dying flames said whit, whit,whit* as they fluttered and whispered over the whiteashes. It must have been a great fire when at fullheight. Men had seen it at Donga Pa across the valleywinking and blazing through the night, and said that thecharcoal-burners of Kodru were getting drunk. But itwas only Suket Singh, Sepoy of the i02d Punjab NativeInfantry, and Athira, a woman, burning—burning—burning.

This was how things befell; and the PoHceman's Diarywill bear me out.

Athira was the wife of Madu, who was a charcoal-burner, one-eyed and of a maHgnant disposition. Aweek after their marriage, he beat Athira with a heavy

stick. A month later, Suket Singh, Sepoy, came thatway to the cool hills on leave from his regiment, andelectrified the villagers of Kodru with tales of serviceand glory under the Government, and the honour inwhich he, Suket Singh, was held by the Colonel SahibBahadur. And Desdemona listened to Othello as Des-demonas have done all the world over, and, as she lis-tened, she loved.

'I've a wife of my own,' said Suket Singh, 'thoughthat is no matter when you come to think of it. I amalso due to return to my regiment after a time, and Icannot be a deserter—I who intend to be Havildar.'There is no Himalayan version of 'I could not love thee,dear, as much. Loved I not Honour more;' but SuketSingh came near to making one.

'Never mind,' said Athira, 'stay with me, and, ifMadu tries to beat me, you beat him.'

'Very good,' said Suket Singh; and he beat Maduseverely, to the deHght of all the charcoal-burners ofKodru.

'That is enough,' said Suket Singh, as he rolled Madudown the hillside. 'Now we shall have peace.' ButMadu crawled up the grass slope again, and hoveredround his hut with angry eyes.

'He'll kill me dead,' said Athira to Suket Singh.* You must take me away.'

'There'll be a trouble in the Lines. My wife will pullout my beard; but never mind,' said Suket Singh, 'I willtake you.'

There was loud trouble in the Lines, and SuketSingh's beard was pulled, and Suket Singh's wife went tolive with her mother and took away the children. ' That'sall right,' said Athira; and Suket Singh said, 'Yes, that'sall right'

So there was only Madu left in the hut that looksacross the valley to Donga Pa; and, since the beginningof time, no one has had any s>Tnpathy for husbands sounfortunate as Madu.

He went to Juseen Daze, the wizard-man who keepsthe Talking Monkey's Head.

*Get me back my wife,' said Madu.

'I can't,' said Juseen Daze, 'until you have made theSutlej in the valley run up the Donga Pa.'

*No riddles/ said Madu, and he shook his hatchetabove Juseen Daze's wliite head.

'Give all your money to the headmen of the village,'said Juseen Daze; 'and they will hold a communalCouncil, and the Council will send a message that yourwife must come back.'

So Madu gave up all his worldly wealth, amountingto twenty-seven rupees, eight annas, three pice, and asilver chain, to the Council of Kodru. And it fell asJuseen Daze foretold.

They sent Athira's brother down into Suket Singh'sregiment to call Athira home. Suket Singh kickedhim once round the Lines, and then handed him over tothe Havildar, who beat him with a belt.

' Come back,' yelled Athira's brother.

'Where to?' said Athira.

'To Madu,' said he.

'Never,' said she.

'Then Juseen Daze will send a curse, and you willwither away like a barked tree in the springtime,' saidAthira's brother. Athira slept over these things.

Next morning she had rheumatism. 'I am beginningto wither away Hke a barked tree in the springtime,' shesaid. ' That is the curse of Juseen Daze.'

And she really began to wither away because her

heart was dried up with fear, and those who beKeve incurses die from curses. Suket Singh, too, was afraidbecause he loved Athira better than his very life. Twomonths passed, and Athira's brother stood outside theregimental Lines again and yelped, *Aha! You arewithering away. Come back.'

'I will come back,' said Athira.

' Say rather that we will come back,' said Suket Singh.

'Ai; but when?' said Athira's brother.

*Upon a day very early in the morning,' said SuketSingh; and he tramped off to apply to the Colonel SahibBahadur for one week's leave.

'I am withering away like a barked tree in the spring,'moaned Athira.

'You will be better soon,' said Suket Singh; and hetold her what was in his heart, and the two laughedtogether softly, for they loved each other. But Athiragrew better from that hour.

They went away together, travelling third-class bytrain as the regulations provided, and then in a cart tothe low hills, and on foot to the high ones. Athirasniffed the scent of the pines of her own hills, the wetHimalayan hills. 'It is good to be alive,' said Athira.

'Hah!' said Suket Singh. 'Where is the Kodru roadand where is the Forest Ranger's house?'

. . .

'It cost forty rupees twelve years ago,' said the ForestRanger, handing the gun.

'Here are twenty,' said Suket Singh, 'and you mustgive me the best bullets.'

'It is very good to be alive,' said Athira wistfully,sniiling the scent of the pine-mould; and they waitedtiii the night had fallen upon Kodru and the Donga Pa.Madu had stacked the dry wood for the next day'scharcoal-burning on the SDur above his house. 'It is

THROUGH THE FIRE 21

courteous in Madu to save us this trouble,' said SuketSingh as he stumbled on the pile, which was twelve footsquare and four high. 'We must wait till the mooi,rises.'

When the moon rose, Athira knelt upon the pile. ' Ifit were only a Government Snider,' said Suket Singhruefully, squinting down the wire-bound barrel of theForest Ranger's gun.

'Be quick,' said Athira; and Suket Singh w^as quick;but Athira was quick no longer. Then he lit the pileat the four corners and climbed on to it, re-k>ading thegun.

The little flames began to peer up between the b:-!,,logs atop of the brushwood. 'The Government shouldteach us to pull the triggers with our toes,' said SuketSingh grimly to the moon. That was the last publi."observation of Sepoy Suket Singh.

Upon a day, early in the morning, Madu came to thepyre and shrieked very grievously, and ran away to catchthe Policeman who was on tour in the district.

'The base-bom has ruined four rupees' worth ofcharcoal wood,' Madu gasped. 'He has also killed mywife, and he has left a letter which I cannot read, dad toa pine bough.'

In the stiff, formal hand taught in the regimentalschool. Sepoy Suket Singh had written—

'Let us be burned together, if anything remain over,for we have made the necessary prayers. We have alsocursed Madu, and Malak the brother of Athira—bothevil men. Send my service to the Colonel Sahib Baha-dur,'

The Policemaii looked long and curiously at the

marriage bed of red and white ashes on which lay, dullblack, the barrel of the Ranger's gun. He drove hisspurred heel absently into a half-charred log, and thechattering sparks flew upwards. 'Most extraordinarypeople,' said the Policeman.

' Whe-w, whew, ouiou,' said the little flames.

The PoUceman entered the dry bones of the case, forthe Punjab Government does not approve of romancing,in his Diary.

^But who will pay me those four rupees?' said Madu.

The evening meal was ended in Dhunni Bhagat's Chu-bara and the old priests were smoking or counting theirbeads. A little naked child pattered in, with its mouthwide open, a handful of marigold flowers in one hand, anda lump of conserved tobacco in the other. It tried tokneel and make obeisance to Gobind, but it was so fatthat it fell forward on its shaven head, and rolled on itsside, kicking and gasping, while the marigolds tumbledone way and the tobacco the other. Gobind laughed,set it up again, and blessed the marigold flowers as hereceived the tobacco.

'From my father,' said the child. 'He has the fever,and cannot come. Wilt thou pray for him, father?^

'Surely, Httlest; but the smoke is on the ground, andthe night-chill is in the air, and it is not good to goabroad naked in the autumn/

'I have no clothes,' said the child, 'and all to-day Ihave been carrying cow-dung cakes to the bazar. It wasvery hot, and I am very tired.' It shivered a little, forthe twilight was cool.

Gobind hfted an arm under his vast tattered quilt ofmany colours, and made an inviting little nest by hisside. The child crept in, and Gobind filled his brass-studded leather waterpipe with the new tobacco. WhenI came to the Chubara the shaven head with the tuftatop, and the beady black eyes looked out of the folds

of the quilt as a squirrel looks out from his nest, andGobind was smiling while the child played with hisbeard.

I would have said something friendly, but rememberedin time that if the child fell ill afterwards I should becredited with the Evil Eye, and that is a horrible pos-session.

' Sit thou still, Thumbling,' I said as it made to get upand run away. 'Where is thy slate, and why has theteacher let such an evil character loose on the streetswhen there are no poHce to protect us weaklings? Inwhich ward dost thou try to break thy neck with flyingkites from the house-tops?'

'Nay, Sahib, nay,' said the child, burrowing its faceinto Gobind's beard, and twisting uneasily. 'There wasa holiday to-day among the schools, and I do not alwaysfly kites. I play ker-li-kit Hke the rest.'

Cricket is the national game among the schoolboys ofthe Punjab, from the naked hedge-school children, whouse an old kerosene-tin for wicket, to the B.A.'s of theUniversity, who compete for the Championship belt.

'Thou play kerlikit! Thou art half the height of thebat!' I said.

The child nodded resolutely. ' Yea, I do play. Perlay-hall, Ow-atI Ran, ran, ran J I know it all.'

'But thou must not forget with all this to pray to theGods according to custom,' said Gobind, who did notaltogether approve of cricket and western innovations.

'I do not forget,' said the child in a hushed voice.

'Also to give reverence to thy teacher, and'—Gobind'svoice softened—' to abstain from pulling holy men by thebeard, Httle badling. Eh, eh, eh?'

The child's face was altogether hidden in the greatwhite beard, and it began to whimper till Gobind soothed

it as children are soothed all the world over, with thepromise of a story.

*I did not think to frighten thee, senseless little one.Look up! Am I angry? Are, are, are! Shall I weeptoo, and of our tears make a great pond and drown usboth, and then thy father will never get well, lacking theeto pull his beard? Peace, peace, and I will tell thee ofthe Gods. Thou hast heard many tales?'

* Very many, father.'

*Now, this is a new one which thou hast not heard.Long and long ago when the Gods walked with men asthey do to-day, but that we have not faith to see, Shiv,the greatest of Gods, and Parbati his wife, were walkingin the garden of a temple.'

^Which temple? That in the Nandgaon ward?' saidthe child.

^ Nay, very far away. Maybe at Trimbak or Hurdwar,whither thou must make pilgrimage when thou art aman. Now, there was sitting in the garden under thejujube trees, a mendicant that had worshipped Shiv forforty years, and he Uved on the offerings of the pious, andmeditated holiness night and day.'

*Oh father, was it thou?' said the child, looking upwith large eyes.

'Nay, I have said it was long ago, and, moreover, thismendicant was married.'

*Did they put him on a horse with flowers on his head,and forbid him to go to sleep all night long? Thus theydid to me when they made my wedding,' said the child,who had been married a few months before.

*And what didst thou do?' said I.

'I wept, and they called me evil names, and then Ismote her, and we wept together.'

'Thus did not the mendicant,' said Gobind; 'for he

was a holy man, and very poor. Parbati perceived himsitting naked by the temple steps where all went up anddown, and she said to Shiv, "What shall men think of theGods when the Gods thus scorn their worshippers? Forforty years yonder man' has prayed to us, and yet therebe only a few grains of rice and some broken cowriesbefore him after all. Men's hearts will be hardened bythis thing." And Shiv said, "It shall be looked to," andso he called to the temple which was the temple of hisson, Ganesh of the elephant head, saying, "Son, there isa mendicant without who is very poor. What wilt thoudo for him?" Then that great elephant-headed Oneawoke in the dark and answered, "In three days, if it bethy will, he shall have one lakh of rupees." Then Shivand Parbati went away.

^But there was a money-lender in the garden hiddenamong the marigolds'—the child looked at the ball ofcrumpled blossoms in its hands—'ay, among the yellowmarigolds, and he heard the Gods talking. He was acovetous man, and of a black heart, and he desired thatlakh of rupees for himself. So he went to the mendicantand said, "0 brother, how much do the pious give theedaily?" The mendicant said, "I cannot tell. Some-times a little rice, sometimes a Httle pulse, and a fewcowries and, it has been, pickled mangoes, and dried fish."'

'That is good,' said the child, smacking its Hps.

'Then said the money-lender, "Because I have longwatched thee, and learned to love thee and thy patience,I will give thee now five rupees for all thy earnings ofthe three days to come. There is only a bond to sign onthe matter." But the mendicant said, "Thou art mad.In two months I do not receive the worth of five rupees,"and he told the thing to his wife that evening. She, beinga woman, said, "When did money-lender ever make a bad

THE FINANCES OF THE GODS 27

bargain? The wolf runs through the corn for the sake ofthe fat deer. Our fate is in the hands of the Gods.Pledge it not even for three days."

' So the mendicant returned to the money-lender, andwould not sell. Then that wicked man sat all day beforehim offering more and more for those three days' earnings.First, ten, fifty, and a hundred rupees; and then, for hedid not know when the Gods would pour down theirgifts, rupees by the thousand, till he had offered half alakh of rupees. Upon this sum the mendicant's wifeshifted her counsel, and the mendicant signed the bond,and the money was paid in silver; great white bullocksbringing it by the cartload. But saving only all thatmoney, the mendicant received nothing from the Gods atall, and the heart of the money-lender was uneasy onaccount of expectation. Therefore at noon of the thirdday the money-lender went into the temple to spy uponthe councils of the Gods, and to learn in what mannerthat gift might arrive. Even as he was making hisprayers, a crack between the stones of the floor gaped,and, closing, caught him by the heel. Then he heard theGods walking in the temple in the darkness of the columns,and Shiv called to his son Ganesh, saying, "Son, whathast thou done in regard to the lakh of rupees for themendicant?" And Ganesh woke, for the money-lenderheard the dry rustle of his trunk uncoihng, and heanswered, "Father, one half of the money has been paid,and the debtor for the other half I hold here fast by theheel."'

The child bubbled with laughter. 'And the money-lender paid the mendicant?' it said.

' Surely, for he whom the Gods hold by the heel mustpay to the uttermost. The money was paid at evening,all silver, in great carts, and thus Ganesh did his work.'

'Nathu! OheNathu!^

A woman was calling in the dusk by the door of thecourtyard.

The child began to wriggle. 'That is my mother/it said.

'Go then, littlest,' answered Gobind; 'but stay amoment.'

He ripped a generous yard from his patchwork-quilt,put it over the child's shoulders, and the child ranaway.

His Royal Highness Abdur Rahman, Amir of Afghanis-tan, G.C.S.I., and trusted ally of Her Imperial Majestythe Queen of England and Empress of India, is a gentle-man for whom all right-thinking people should have aprofound regard. Like most other rulers, he governs notas he would but as he can, and the mantle of his author-ity covers the most turbulent race under the stars. Tothe Afghan neither life, property, law, nor kingship aresacred when his own lusts prompt him to rebel. He isa thief by instinct, a murderer by heredity and training,and frankly and bestially immoral by all three. Nonethe less he has his own crooked notions of honour, andhis character is fascinating to study. On occasion hewill fight without reason given till he is hacked in pieces;on other occasions he will refuse to show fight till he isdriven into a comer. Herein he is as unaccountable asthe gray wolf, who is his blood-brother.

And these men His Higlmess rules by the only weaponthat they understand—the fear of death, which amongsome Orientals is the beginning of wisdom. Some saythat the Amir's authority reaches no farther than a riflebullet can range; but as none are quite certain whentheir king may be in their midst, and as he alone hold?every one of the threads of Government, his respect isincreased among men. Gholam Hyder, the Commander-in-chief of the Afghan army, is feared reasonably, for he

can impale; all Kabul city fears the Governor of Kabul,who has power of life and death through all the wards;but the Amir of Afghanistan, though outlying tribes pre-tend otherwise when his back is turned, is dreaded beyondchief and governor together. His word is red law; bythe gust of his passion falls the leaf of man's life, and hisfavour is terrible. He has suffered many things, andbeen a hunted fugitive before he came to the throne, andhe imderstands all the classes of his people. By thecustom of the East any man or woman having a com-plaint to make, or an enemy against whom to be avenged,has the right of speaking face to face with the king atthe daily pubHc audience. This is personal government,as it was in the days of Harun al Raschid of blessedmemory, whose times exist still and will exist long afterthe Enghsh have passed away.

The privilege of open speech is of course exercised atcertain personal risk. The king may be pleased, andraise the speaker to honour for that very bluntness ofspeech which three minutes later brings a too imitativepetitioner to the edge of the ever ready blade. And thepeople love to have it so, for it is their right.

It happened upon a day in Kabul that the Amirchose to do his day's work in the Baber Gardens, whichlie a short distance from the city of Kabul. A lighttable stood before him, and round the table in the openair were grouped generals and finance ministers accord-ing to their degree. The Court and the long tail of feudalchiefs—men of blood, fed and cowed by blood— stood inan irregular semicircle round the table, and the windfrom the Kabul orchards blew among them. All daylong sweating couriers dashed in with letters from theoutlying districts with rumours of rebellion, intrigue,famine, failure of pa)rments, or announcements of treas-

ure on the road; and all day long the Amir would readthe dockets, and pass such of these as were less privateto the officials whom they directly concerned, or call up awaiting chief for a word of explanation. It is well tospeak clearly to the ruler of Afghanistan. Then the grimhead, under the black astrachan cap with the diamondstar in front, would nod gravely, and that chief wouldreturn to his fellows. Once that afternoon a womanclamoured for divorce against her husband, who wasbald, and the Amir, hearing both sides of the case, badeher pour curds over the bare scalp, and lick them off, thatthe hair might grown again, and she be contented. Herethe Court laughed, and the woman withdrew, cursing herking under her breath.

But when twilight was falling, and the order of theCourt was a little relaxed, there came before the king, incustody, a trembling haggard wretch, sore with muchbufifeting, but of stout enough build, who had stolenthree rupees—of such small matters does His Highnesstake cognisance.

^Why did you steal?' said he; and when the kingasks questions they do themselves service who answerdirectly.

*I was poor, and no one gave. Hungry, and therewas no food.'

* Why did you not work?'

'I could find no work, Protector of the Poor, and Iwas starving.'

*You lie. You stole for drink, for lust, for idleness,for anything but hunger, since any man who will mayfind work and daily bread.'

The prisoner dropped his eyes. He had attended theCourt before, and he knew the ring of the death-tone.

*Any man may get work. Who knows this so well

as I do? for I too have been hungered—not like you,bastard scum, but as any honest man may be, by theturn of Fate and the will of God.'

Growing warm, the Amir turned to his nobles all arowand thrust the hilt of his sabre aside with his elbow.

*You have heard this Son of Lies? Hear me tell atrue tale. I also was once starved, and tightened mybelt on the sharp belly-pinch. Nor was I alone, forwith me was another, who did not fail me in my evildays, when I was hunted, before ever I came to thisthrone. And wandering like a houseless dog by Kanda-har, my money melted, melted, melted til\'7d——' Heflung out a bare palm before the audience. 'And dayupon day, faint and sick, I went back to that one whowaited, and God knows how we Hved, till on a day I tookour best lihaf—silk it was, fine work of Iran, such as noneedle now^ works, warm, and a coverlet for two, and allthat we had. I brought it to a money-lender in a by-iane, and I asked for three rupees upon it. He said tome, who am now the King, ^'You are a thief. This isw^ortb three hundred." I am no thief," I answered,"but a prince of good blood, and I am hungry."—"Princeof wandering beggars," said that money-lender, "I haveno money with me, but go to my house with my clerkand he will give you two rupees eight annas, for that iaall I will lend." So I went wath the clerk to the house,and we talked on the way, and he gave me the money.We lived on it till it was spent, and we fared hard. Andthen that clerk said, being a young man of a good heart,"Surely the money-lender will lend yet more on thatlihaf,^^ and he offered me two rupees. These I refused,saying, *'Nay; but get me some work." And he gotme work, and I, even I, Abdur Rahman.^ Amir of Afghanis-tan, wrought day by d^y as a coolif bearing burdens,

THE AMIR HOMILY

33

and labouring of my hands, receiving four annas wagea day for my sweat and backache. But he, this bastardson of naught, must steal! For a year and four months Iworked, and none dare say that I lie, for I have a wit-ness, even that clerk who is now my friend.'

Then there rose in his place among the Sirdars andthe nobles one clad in silk, who folded his hands andaaid, ' This is the truth of God, for I, who, by the favourof God and the Amir, am such as you know, was onceclerk to that money-lender.'

There was a pause, and the Amir cried hoarsely tothe prisoner, throwing scorn upon him, till he ended withthe dread 'Dar arid/ which clinches justice.

So they led the thief away, and the whole of him wasseen no more together; and the Court rustled out ofits silence, whispering, 'Before God and the Prophet, butthis is a man!'

JEWS IN SHUSHAN*

My newly purchased house furniture was, at the least,insecure; the legs parted from the chairs, and the topsfrom the tables, on the slightest provocation. But suchas it was, it was to be paid for, and Ephraim, agent andcollector for the local auctioneer, waited in the verandahwith the receipt. He was announced by the Mahomedanservant as 'Ephraim, Yahudi'—Ephraim the Jew. Hewho beheves in the Brotherhood of Man should hear myElahi Bukhsh grinding the second word through hiswhite teeth with all the scorn he dare show before hismaster. Ephraim was, personally, meek in manner—someek indeed that one could not understand how he hadfallen into the profession of bill-collecting. He resembledan over-fed sheep, and his voice suited his figure. Therewas a fixed, unvarying mask of childish wonder upon hisface. If you paid him, he was as one marveUing at yourwealth; if you sent him away, he seemed puzzled at yourhard-heartedness. Never was Jew more unlike his dreadbreed.

Ephraim wore list slippers and coats of duster-cloth,so preposterously patterned that the most brazen ofBritish subalterns would have shied from them in fear.Very slow and deliberate was his speech, and carefullyguarded to give offence to no one. After many weeks,Ephraim was induced to speak to me of his friends.

'There be eight of us in Shushan, and we are waiting

till there are ten. Then we shall apply for a synagogue,and get leave from Calcutta. To-day we have no syna-gogue; and I, only I, am Priest and Butcher to our people.I am of the tribe of Judah—I think, but I am not sure.My father was of the tribe of Judah, and we wish muchto get our synagogue. I shall be a priest of that syna-gogue.'

Shushan is a big city in the North of India, countingits dwellers by the ten thousand; and these eight ofthe Chosen People were shut up in its midst, waiting tilltime or chance sent them their full congregation.

Miriam the wife of Ephraim, two Httle children, anorphan boy of their people, Epraim's uncle JackraelIsrael, a white-haired old man, his wife Hester, a Jewfrom Cutch, one Hyem Benjamin, and Ephraim, Priestand Butcher, made up the list of the Jews in Shushan.They lived in one house, on the outskirts of the greatcity, amid heaps of saltpetre, rotten bricks, herds of kine,and a fixed pillar of dust caused by the incessant passingof the beasts to the river to drink. In the evening thechildren of the City came to the waste place to fly theirkites, and Ephraim's sons held aloof, watching the sportfrom the roof, but never descending to take part in them,At the back of the house stood a small brick enclosure,in which Ephraim prepared the daily meat for his peopleafter the custom of the Jews. Once the rude door of thesquare was suddenly smashed open by a struggle frominside, and showed the meek bill-collector at his work,nostrils dilated, lips drawn back over his teeth, and hishands upon a half-maddened sheep. He was attired instrange raiment, having no relation whatever to dustercoats or hst slippers, and a knife was in his mouth.As he struggled with the animal between the walls, thebreath came from him in thick sobs, and the nature of

the man seemed changed. When the ordained slaughterwas ended, he saw that the door was open and shut ithastily, his hand leaving a red mark on the timber, whilehis children from the neighbouring house-top looked downawe-stricken and open-eyed. A glimpse of Ephraimbusied in one of his religious capacities was no thingto be desired twice.

Summer came upon Shushan, turning the troddenwaste-ground to iron, and bringing sickness to the city.

'It mil not touch us,' said Ephraim confidently.'Before tlie winter we shall have our synagogue. Mybrother and his wife and children are comJng up fromCalcutta, and then I shall be the priest of the synagogue.'

Jackrael Israel, the old m.an, would crawl out in thestifling evenings to sit on the rubbish-heap and watch thecorpses being borne down to the river.

*It will not come near us,' said Jackrael Israel feebly,*for we are the People of God, and my nephew will bepriest of our synagogue. Let them die.' He creptback to his house again and barred the door to shut him-self off from the world of the Gentile.

But Miriam, the wife of Ephraim, looked out of thewindow at the dead as the biers passed and said that shewas afraid. Ephraim comforted her with hopes of thesynagogue to be, and collected bills as was his custom.

In one night, the two children died and were buriedearly in the morning by Ephraim. The deaths neverappeared in the City returns. 'The sorrow is my sor-row,' said Ephraim; and this to him seemed a sufficientreason for setting at naught the sanitary regulations of alarge, flourishing, and remarkably well-governed Empire.

The orphan boy, dependent on the charity of Ephraimand his wife, could have felt no gratitude, and must havebeen a ruffian. He begged for whatever money his pro-

lectors would give him, and with that fled down-countryfor his life. A week after the death of her childrenMiriam left her bed at night and wandered over thecountry to find them. She heard them cr\'7ddng behindevery bush, or drowning in every pool of water in thefields, and she begged the cartmen on the Grand TrunkRoad not to steal her little ones from her. In the morn-ing the sun rose and beat upon her bare head, and sheturned into the cool wet crops to lie down and never Came back; though Hyem Benjamin and Ephraim soughther for two nights.

The look of patient wonder on Ephraim's face deep-ened, but he presently found an explanation. 'Thereare so few of us here, and these people are so many/ saidhe,' that, it may be, our God has forgotten ua.'

In ihe house on the outskirts of the dty old JackradIsrael and Hester grumbled that there was no one towait on them, and that Miriam had been untrue to herrace. Ephraim went out and collected bills, and in theevenings smoked with Hyem Benjamin till, one dawning,Hyem Benjamin died, having first paid all his debts toEphraim. Jackrael Israel and Hester sat alone in theempty house all day, and, when Ephraim returned,wept the easy tears of age tiU they cried themselvesasleep.

A week later Ephraim, staggering under a hugebundle of clothes and cooking-pots, led the old man anc!woman to the railway station, where the bustle and con-fusion made them whimper.

'We are going back to Calcutta,' said Ephraim, towhose sleeve Hester was clinging. 'There are more ofus there, and here my house is empty/

He helped Hester into the carriage and, turning back,said to me, ' I should have been priest of the synagogue

if there had been ten of us. Surely we must have beenforgotten by our God.'

The remnant of the broken colony passed out of thestation on their journey south; while a subaltern, turningover the books on the bookstall, was whistling to himself'The Ten Little Nigger Boys.'

But the tune sounded as solemn as the Dead March,

It was the dirge of the Jews in Shushan.

If you consider the circumstances of the case, it was theonly thing that he could do. But Pambe Serang hasbeen hanged by the neck till he is dead, and Nurkeedis dead also.

Three years ago, when the Elsass-Lothringen steamerSaarbruck was coaling at Aden and the weather was veryhot indeed, Nurkeed, the big fat Zanzibar stoker who fedthe second right furnace thirty feet down in the hold, gotleave to go ashore. He departed a' Seedee boy,' as theycall the stokers; he returned the full-blooded Sultan ofZanzibar—His Highness Sayyid Burgash, with a bottlein each hand. Then he sat on the fore-hatch grating,eating salt fish and onions, and singing the songs of a farcountry. The fogd belonged to Pambe, the Serang or headman of the lascar sailors. He had just cooked it for him-self, turned to borrow some salt, and when he came backNurkeed's dirty black fingers were spading into the rice.

A serang is a person of importance, far above a stoker,though the stoker draws better pay. He sets the chorusof 'Hya! Hulla! Hee-ah! Heh!' when the captain'sgig is pulled up to the davits; he heaves the lead too; andsometimes, when all the ship is lazy, he puts on hiswhitest muslin and a big red sash, and plays with thepassengers' children on the quarter-deck. Then thepassengers give him money, and he saves it all up foran orgie at Bombay or Calcutta, or Pulu Penang.

'Ho! you fat black barrel, you're eating my food!'said Pambe, in the Other Lingua Franca that beginswhere the Levant tongue stops, and runs from Port Saideastward till east is west, and the sealing-brigs of theKurile Islands gossip with the strayed Hakodate junks.

'Son of Eblis, monkey-face, dried shark's liver, pig-man, I am the Sultan Sayyid Burgash, and the com-mander of all this ship. Take away your garbage;'and Nurkeed thrust the empty pewter rice-plate intoPambe's hand.

Pambe beat it into a basin over Nurkeed's woollyhead. Nurkeed drew his sheath-knife and stabbedPamb6 in the leg. Pambe drew his sheath-knife; butNurkeed dropped down into the darkness of the holdand spat through the grating at Pambe, who was stainingthe clean fore-deck with his blood.

Only the white moon saw these things; for the oflScerswere looking after the coaHng, and the passengers weretossing in their close cabins. 'All right,' said Pambe—and went forward to tie up his leg—'we will settlethe account later on.'

He was a Malay born in India: married once in Burma,where his wife had a cigar-shop on the Shwe Dagonroad; once in Singapore, to a Chinese girl; and once inMadras, to a Mahomedan woman who sold fowls. TheEnglish sailor cannot, owing to postal and telegraphfacilities, marry as profusely as he used to do; but nativesailors can, being uninfluenced by the barbarous inventions of the Western savage. Pambe was a good hus-band when he happened to remember the existence of awife; but he was also a very good Malay; and it is notwise to offend a Malay, because he does not forget any-thing. Moreover, in Pambe's case blood had been drawnand food spoiled.

Next morning Nurkeed rose with a blank mind. Hewas no longer Sultan of Zanzibar, but a very hot stoker.So he went on deck and opened his jacket to the morningbreeze, till a sheath-knife came like a flying-fish andstuck into the woodwork of the cook's galley half aninch from his right armpit. He ran down below beforehis time, trying to remember what he could have said tothe owner of the weapon. At noon, when all the ship'slascars were feeding, Nurkeed advanced into their midst,and, being a placid man with a large regard for his ownskin, he opened negotiations, saying, 'Men of the ship,last night I was drunk, and this morning I know that Ibehaved unseemly to some one or another of you. Whowas that man, that I may meet him face to face and saythat I was drunk?'

Pambe measured the distance to Nurkeed's nakedbreast. If he sprang at him he might be tripped up,and a blind blow at the chest sometimes only meansa gash on the breast-bone. Ribs are difficult to thrustbetween unless the subject be adeep. So he saidnothing; nor did the other lascars. Their faces im-mediately dropped all expression, as is the custom ofthe Oriental when there is killing on the carpet orany chance of trouble. Nurkeed looked long at thewhite eyeballs. He was only an African, and couldnot read characters. A big sigh—almost a groan—broke from him, and he went back to the furnaces.The lascars took up the conversation where he hadinterrupted it. They talked of the best methods ofcooking rice.

Nurkeed suffered considerably from lack of freshair during the run to Bombay. He only came on deckto breathe when all the world was about; and even then aheavy block once dropped from a derrick within a foot

of his head, and an apparently firm-lashed grating onwhich he set his foot, began to turn over with the inten-tion of dropping him on the cased cargo fifteen feet below;and one insupportable night the sheath-knife droppedfrom the fo'c's'le, and this time it drew blood. SoNurkeed made complaint; and, when the Saarhruckreached Bombay, fled and buried himself among eighthundred thousand people, and did not sign articles tillthe ship had been a month gone from the port. Pambewaited too; but his Bombay wife grew clamorous, andhe was forced to sign in the Spicheren to Hongkong, be-cause he realised that all play and no work gives Jack aragged shirt. In the foggy China seas he thought a greatdeal of Nurkeed, and, when Elsass-Lothringen steamerslay in port with the Spicheren, inquired after him andfound he had gone to England via the Cape, on theGravelotte. Pambe came to England on the Worth,The Spicheren met her by the Nore Light. Nurkeedwas going out with the Spicheren to the Calicut coast.

'Want to find a friend, my trap-mouthed coal-scuttle?'said a gentleman in the mercantile service. 'Nothingeasier. Wait at the Nyanza Docks till he comes. Everyone comes to the Nyanza Docks. Wait, you poorheathen.' The gentleman spoke truth. There arethree great doors in the world where, if you stand longenough, you shall meet any one you wish. The headof the Suez

Canal is one, but there Death comes also;Charing Cross Station is the second—for inland work;and the Nyanza Docks is the third. At each of theseplaces are men and women looking eternally for those whowill surely come. So Pambe waited at the docks. Timewas no object to him; and the wives could wait, as hedid from day to day, week to week, and month to month,by the Blue Diamond funnels, the Red Dot smoke-stacks,

the Yellow Streaks, and the nameless dingy gypsies ofthe sea that loaded and unloaded, jostled, whistled, androared in the everlasting fog. When money failed, akind gentleman told Pambe to become a Christian; andPambe became one with great speed, getting his rehgiousteachings between ship and ship's arrival, and six orseven shillings a week for distributing tracts to mariners.What the faith was Pambe did not in the least care; buthe knew if he said 'Native Ki-lis-ti-an, Sar' to men withlong black coats he might get a few coppers; and thetracts were vendible at a little public-house that soldshag by the 'dottel,' which is even smaller weight thanthe 'half-screw,' which is less than the half-ounce, and amost profitable retail trade.

But after eight months Pambe fell sick with pneu-monia, contracted from long standing still in slush; andmuch against his will he was forced to lie down in histwo-and-sixpenny room raging against Fate.

The kind gentleman sat by his bedside, and grievedto find that Pambe talked in strange tongues, instead ofHstening to good books, and almost seemed to become abenighted heathen again—till one day he was roused fromsemi-stupor by a voice in the street by the dock-head.'My friend—he,' whispered Pambe. 'Call now—callNurkeed. Quick! God has sent him!'

'He wanted one of his own race,' said the kind gentle-man; and, going out, he called 'Nurkeed!' at the top ofhis voice. An excessively coloured man in a raspingwhite shirt and brand-new slops, a shining hat, and abreastpin, turned round. Many voyages had taughtNurkeed how to spend his money and made him a citizenof the world.

'Hi! Yes!' said he, when the situation was ex-plained. 'Command him—black nigger—when I was

in the Saarhruck. Ole Pambe, good ole Pamb6. Damlascar. Show him up, Sar;' and he followed into theroom. One glance told the stoker what the kind gentle-man had overlooked. Pambe was desperately poor.Nurkeed drove his hands deep into his pockets, thenadvanced with clenched fists on the sick, shouting,'Hya, Pambe. Hya! Hee-ah! HuUa! Heh! Takilo!Takilo! Make fast aft, Pambe. You know, Pambe.You know me. Dekho, jee! Look! Dam big fat lazylascar!'

Pamb6 beckoned with his left hand. His rightwas under his pillow. Nurkeed removed his gorgeoushat and stooped over Pambe till he could catch a faintwhisper. 'How beautiful!' said the kind gentleman.*How these Orientals love like children!'

* Spit him out,' said Nurkeed, leaning over Pambe yetmore closely.

'Touching the matter of that fish and onions ^

said Pambe—and sent the knife home under the edge ofthe rib-bone upwards and forwards.

There was a thick sick cough, and the body of theAfrican slid slowly from the bed, his clutching handsletting fall a shower of silver pieces that ran across theroom.

^Now I can die!' said Pambe.

But he did not die. He was nursed back to life withall the skill that money could buy, for the Law wantedhim; and in the end he grew sufi&ciently healthy to behanged in due and proper form.

Pambe did not care particularly; but it was a sadblow to the kind gentleman.

'Prisoner's head did not reach to the top of the dock/as the English newspapers say. This case, however, wasnot reported because nobody cared by so much as ahempen rope for the life or death of Little Tobrah. Theassessors in the red court-house sat upon him all throughthe long hot afternoon, and whenever they asked him aquestion he salaamed and whined. Their verdict wasthat the evidence was inconclusive, and the Judge con-curred. It was true that the dead body of Little To-brah's sister had been found at the bottom of the well, andLittle Tobrah was the only human being within a halfmile radius at the time; but the child might have fallenin by accident. Therefore Little Tobrah was acquitted,and told to go where he pleased. This permission wasnot so generous as it sounds, for he had nowhere to goto, nothing in particular to eat, and nothing whatever towear.

He trotted into the court-compound, and sat upon thewell-kerb, wondering whether an unsuccessful dive intothe black water below would end in a forced voyageacross the other Black Water. A groom put down anemptied nose-bag on the bricks, and Little Tobrah, beinghungry, set himself to scrape out what wet grain thehorse had overlooked.

'O Tliief—-and but newly set free from the terror ofthe Law! Come along!' said the groom, and Little To-Copyright, 1891, by Macmillan & Co.45

brah was led by the ear to a large and fat Englishman,who heard the tale of the theft.

' Hah!' said the Englishman three times (only he saida stronger word). 'Put him into the net and take himhome.' So Little Tobrah was thrown into the net of thecart, and, nothing doubting that he should be stuck likea pig, was driven to the EngKshman's house. 'Hah!'said the Englishman as before. 'Wet grain, by Jove!Feed the little beggar, some of you, and we'll make ariding-boy of him! See? Wet grain, good Lord!'

'Give an account of yourself,' said the Head of theGrooms, to Little Tobrah after the meal had been eaten,and the servants lay at ease in their quarters behind thehouse. 'You are not of the groom caste, unless it be forthe stomach's sake. How came you into the court, andwhy? Answer, little devil's spawn!'

'There was not enough to eat,' said Little Tobrahcalmly. 'This is a good place.'

'Talk straight talk,' said the Head Groom, 'or I willmake you clean out the stable of that large red stallionv/ho bites like a camel.'

'We be Telis, oil-pressers,' said Little Tobrah, scrach-ing his toes in the dust. 'We were Telis—my father,my mother, my brother, the elder by four years, myself,and the sister.'

'She who was found dead in the well?' said one whohad heard something of the trial.

'Even so,' said Little Tobrah gravely. 'She who wasfound dead in the well. It befel upon a time, which isnot in my memory, that the sickness came to the villagewhere our oil-press stood, and first my sister was smittenas to her eyes, and went without sight, for it was mata—the smallpox. Thereafter, my father and my motherdied of that same sickness, so we were alone—my brother

LITTLE TOBRAH 47

who had twelve years, I who had eight, and the sisterwho could not see. Yet were there the bullock and theoil-press remaining, and we made shift to press the oil asbefore. But Surjun Dass, the grain-seller, cheated us inhis dealings; and it was always a stubborn bullock todrive. We put marigold flowers for the Gods upon theneck of the bullock, and upon the great grinding-beamthat rose through the roof; but we gained nothing thereby,and Surjun Dass was a hard man.'

' Bapri-bap/ muttered the grooms' wives, Ho cheat achild so! But we know what the bunnia-io\k sue,sisters.'

'The press was an old press, and we were not strongmen—my brother and I; nor could we fix the neck ofthe beam firmly in the shackle.'

*Nay, indeed,' said the gorgeously-clad wife of theHead Groom, joining the circle. 'That is a strong man'swork. When I was a maid in my father's house '

'Peace, woman,' said the Head Groom. 'Go on, boy.'

'It is nothing,' said Little Tobrah. 'The big beamtore down the roof upon a day which is not in my mem-ory, and with the roof fell much of the hinder wall, andboth together upon our bullock, whose back was broken.Thus we had neither home, nor press, nor bullock—mybrother, myself, and the sister who was blind. Wewent crying away from that place, hand-in-hand, acrossthe fields; and our money was seven annas and six pie.There was a famine in the land. I do not know thename of the land. So, on a night when we were sleep-ing, my brother took the five annas that remained to usand ran away. I do not know wliither he went. Thecurse of my father be upon him. But I and the sisterbegged food in the villages, and there was none to give.Only all men said—"Go to the Englishmen and they

will give." I did not know what the Englishmen were;but they said that they were white, living in tents. Iwent forward; but I cannot say whither I went, and therewas no more food for myself or the sister. And upon ahot night, she weeping and calling for food, we came to awell, and I bade her sit upon the kerb, and thrust her in,for, in truth, she could not see; and it is better to diethan to starve.'

*Ai! Ahi!' wailed the grooms' wives in chorus; 'hethrust her in, for it is better to die than to starve!'

'I would have thrown myself in also, but that shewas not dead and called to me from the bottom of thewell, and I was afraid and ran. And one came out ofthe crops saying that I had killed her and defiled thewell, and they took me before an Englishman, white andterrible, living in a tent, and me he sent here. Butthere were no witnesses, and it is better to die than tostarve. She, furthermore, could not see with her eyes,and was but a little child.'

'Was but a little child,' echoed the Head Groom'swife. 'But who art thou, weak as a fowl and small asa day-old colt, what art thou ?'

'I who was empty am now full,' said Little Tobrah,stretching himself upon the dust. 'And I would sleep.'

The groom's wife spread a doth over him while LittleTobrah slept the sleep of the just.

Look out on a large scale map the place where theChenab river falls into the Indus fifteen miles or so abovethe hamlet of Chachuran. Five miles west of Chachuranlies Bubbling Well Road, and the house of the gosain orpriest of Arti-goth. It was the priest who showed methe road, but it is no thanks to him that I am able totell this story.

Five miles west of Chachuran is a patch of the plumedjungle-grass, that turns over in silver when the windblows, from ten to twenty feet high and from threeto four miles square. In the heart of the patch hides thegosain of Bubbling Well Road. The villagers stone himwhen he peers into the dayUght, although he is a priest,and he runs back again as a strayed wolf turns into tallcrops. He is a one-eyed man and carries, burnt betweenhis brows, the impress of two copper coins. Some saythat he was tortured by a native prince in the old days;for he is so old that he must have been capable of mis-chief in the days of Runjit Singh. His most pressingneed at present is a halter, and the care of the BritishGovernment.

These things happened when the jungle-grass wastall; and the villagers of Chachuran told me that asounder of pig had gone into the Arti-goth patch. Toenter jungle-grass is always an unwise proceeding, but Iwent, partly because I knew nothing of pig-hunting, and

partly because the villagers said that the big boar of thesounder owned foot long tushes. Therefore I wished toshoot him, in order to produce the tushes in after years,and say that I had ridden him down in fair chase. Itook a gun and went into the hot, close patch, behevingthat it would be an easy thing to unearth one pig in tensquare miles of jungle. Mr. Wardle, the terrier, wentwith me because he believed that I was incapable ofexisting for an hour without his advice and countenance.He managed to slip in and out between the grass clumps,but I had to force my way, and in twenty minutes wasas completely lost as though I had been in the heart ofCentral Africa. I did not notice this at first till I hadgrown wearied of stumbKng and pushing through thegrass, and Mr. Wardle was beginning to sit down veryoften and hang out his tongue very far. There wasnothing but grass ever\'7d^where, and it was impossible tosee two yards in any direction. The grass-stems heldthe heat exactly as boiler-tubes do.

In half-an-hour, when I was devoutly wishing that Ihad left the big boar alone, I came to a narrow pathwhich seemed to be a compromise between a native foot-path and a pig-run. It was barely six inches wide, but Icould sidle along it in comfort. The grass was extremelythick here, and where the path was ill defined it wasnecessary to crush into the tussocks either with bothhands before the face, or to back into it, leaving bothhands free to manage the rifle. None the less it was apath, and valuable because it might lead to a place.

At the end of nearly fifty yards of fair way, just whenI was preparing to back into an unusually stiff tussock, Imissed Mr. Wardle, who for his girth is an unusuallyfrivolous dog and never keeps to heel. I called him threetimes and said aloud, 'Where has the little beast gone

to? ^ Then I stepped backwards several paces, for almostunder my feet a deep voice repeated, * Where has thelittle beast gone?' To appreciate an unseen voicethoroughly you should hear it when you are lost instifling jungle-grass. I called JMr. Wardle again and theunderground echo assisted me. At that I ceased callingand hstened very attentively, because I thought I hearda man laughing in a peculiarly offensive manner. Theheat made me sweat, but the laughter made me shake.There is no earthly need for laughter in high grass. It isindecent, as well as impoHte. The chuckling stopped,and I took courage and continued to call till I thoughtthat I had located the echo somewhere behind and belowthe tussock into which I was preparing to back just beforeI lost Mr. Wardle. I drove my rifle up to the triggers,between the grass-stems in a downward and forwarddirection. Then I waggled it to and fro, but it did notseem to touch ground on the far side of the tussock asit should have done. Every time that I grunted withthe exertion of driving a heavy rifle through thick grass,the grunt was faithfully repeated from below, and whenI stopped to wipe my face the sound of low laughter wasdistinct beyond doubting.

I went into the tussock, face first, an inch at a time,my mouth open and my eyes fine, full, and prominent.When I had overcome the resistance of the grass I foundthat I was looking straight across a black gap in theground—that I was actually lying on my chest leaningover the mouth of a well so deep I could scarcely see thewater in it.

There v^ere things in the water,—black things,—andthe water was as black as pitch with blue scum atop.The laughing sound came from the noise of a Httle spring,spouting half-way down one side of the well. Some-

times as the black things circled round, the trickle fromthe spring fell upon their tightly-stretched skins, andthen the laughter changed into a sputter of mirth. Onething turned over on its back, as I watched, and driftedround and round the circle of the mossy brickwork witha hand and half an arm held clear of the water in a stiffand horrible flourish, as though it were a very weariedguide paid to exhibit the beauties of the place.

I did not spend more than half-an-hour in creepinground that well and finding the path on the other side.The remainder of the journey I accomphshed by feelingevery foot of ground in front of me, and crawHng like asnail through every tussock. I carried Mr. Wardle inmy arms and he licked my nose. He was not frightenedin the least, nor was I, but we wished to reach openground in order to enjoy the view. My knees wereloose, and the apple in my throat refused to sHde up anddown. The path on the far side of the well was a verygood one, though boxed in on all sides by grass, and itled me in time to a priest's hut in the centre of a littleclearing. When that priest saw my very white facecoming through the grass he howled with terror and em-braced my boots; but when I reached the bedstead setoutside his door I sat down quickly and Mr. Wardlemounted guard over me. I was not in a condition totake care of myself.

When I awoke I told the priest to lead me into theopen, out of the Arti-goth patch, and to walk slowly infront of me. Mr. Wardle hates natives, and the priestwas more afraid of Mr. Wardle than of me, though wewere both angry. He walked very slowly down a narrowlittle path from his hut. That path crossed three paths,such as the one I had come by in the first instance, andevery one of the three headed towards the Bubbling

BUBBLING WELL ROAD S3

Well. Once when we stopped to draw breath, I heardthe Well laughing to itself alone in the thick grass, andonly my need for his services prevented my firing bothbarrels into the priest's back.

When we came to the open the priest crashed backinto cover, and I went to the village of Arti-goth for adrink. It was pleasant to be able to see the horizon allround, as well as the ground underfoot.

The villagers told me that tlie patch of grass was fullof devils and ghosts, all in the service of the priest, andthat men and women and children had entered it and hadnever returned. They said the priest used their liversfor purposes of witchcraft. When I asked why they hadviot told me of this at the outset, they said that they wereafraid they would lose their reward for bringing news ofthe pig.

Before I left I did my best to set the patch alight,but the grass was too green. Some fine summer day,however, if the wind is favourable, a file of old newspapersand a box of matches will make clear the mystery ©fBubbling Well Road.

'THE CITY OF DREADFUL NIGHT'^

The dense wet heat that hung over the face of land, likea blanket, prevented all hope of sleep in the first instance.The cicalas helped the heat; and the yelling jackals thecicalas. It was impossible to sit still in the dark, empty,echoing house and watch the punkah beat the dead air.So, at ten o'clock of the night, I set my walking-stick onend in the middle of the garden, and waited to see howit would fall. It pointed directly down the moonHt roadthat leads to the City of Dreadful Night. The sound ofits fall disturbed a hare. She limped from her form andran across to a disused Mahomedan burial-ground, wherethe jawless skulls and rough-butted shank-bones, heart-lessly exposed by the July rains, glimmered Hke mothero' pearl on the rain-channelled soil. The heated air andthe heavy earth had driven the very dead upward forcoolness' sake. The hare limped on; snuffed curiouslyat a fragment of a smoke-stained lamp-shard, and diedout, in the shadow of a clump of tamarisk trees.

The mat-weaver's hut under the lee of the Hindutemple was full of sleeping men who lay Hke sheetedcorpses. Overhead blazed the unwinking eye of theMoon. Darkness gives at least a false impression ofcoolness. It was hard not to believe that the floodof light from above was warm. Not so hot as the Sun,but still sickly warm, and heating the heavy air beyondwhat was our due. Straight as a bar of polished steel

iCopyright, 1891, by Macmillan & Co.54

mn the road to the City of Dreadful Night; and oneither side of the road lay corpses disposed on beds infantastic attitudes—one hundred and seventy bodiesof men. Some shrouded all in white with bound-upmouths; some naked and black as ebony in the stronglight; and one—that lay face upwards with dropped jaw^far away from the others—silvery white and ashen gray.

'A leper asleep; and the remainder wearied cooHes,servants, small shopkeepers, and drivers from the hack-stand hard by. The scene—a main approach to Lahorecity, and the night a warm one in August.' This was allthat there was to be seen; but by no means all that onecould see. The witchery of the moonlight was every-where; and the world was horribly changed. The longline of the naked dead, flanked by the rigid silver statue,was not pleasant to look upon. It was made up ofmen alone. Were the womenkind, then, forced to sleepin the shelter of the stifling mud-huts as best theymight? The fretful wail of a child from a low mud-roofansv/ered the question. Where the children are themothers must be also to look after them. They needcare on these sweltering nights. A black Uttle bullet-head peeped over the coping, and a thin—a painfullythin—brown leg was slid over on to the gutter pipe.There was a sharp cluik of glass bracelets; a woman'sarm showed for an instant above the parapet, twineditself round the lean Httle neck, and the child wasdragged back, protesting, to the shelter of the bedstead.His thin, high-pitched shriek died out in the thick airalmost as soon as it was raised; for even the children o^the soil found it too hot to weep.

More corpses; more stretches of moonht, white road,a string of sleeping camels at rest by the wayside; avis-ion of scudding jackals; ekka-ponies asleep—the

harness still on their backs, and the brass-studdedcountry carts, winking in the moonlight—and againmore corpses. Wherever a grain cart atilt, a treetrunk, a sawn log, a couple of bamboos and a few handfulsof thatch cast a shadow, the ground is covered with them.They lie—some face downwards, arms folded, in the dust;some with clasped hands flung up above their heads;some curled up dog-wise; some thrown like limp gunny-bags over the side of the grain carts; and some bowedwith their brows on their knees in the full glare of theMoon. It would be a comfort if they were only given tosnoring; but they are not, and the likeness to corpses isunbroken in all respects save one. The lean dogs snuffat them and turn away. Here and there a tiny childlies on his father's bedstead, and a protecting arm isthrown round it in every instance. But, for the mostpart, the children sleep with their mothers on the house-tops. Yellow-skinned white-toothed pariahs are not tobe trusted within reach of brown bodies.

A stifling hot blast from the mouth of the DelhiGate nearly ends my resolution of entering the Cityof Dreadful Night at this hour. It is a compound of allevil savours, animal and vegetable, that a walled citycan brew in a day and a night. The temperature withinthe motionless groves of plantain and orange-treesoutside the city walls seems chilly by comparison.Heaven help all sick persons and young children withinthe city to-night! The high house-walls are still radiatingheat savagely, and from obscure side gullies fetid breezeseddy that ought to poison a buffalo. But the buffaloesdo not heed. A drove of them are parading the vacantmain street; stopping now and then to lay their pon-derous muzzles against the closed shutters of a graindealer's shop^ and to blow thereon like grampuses.

Then silence follows—the silence that is full of thenight noises of a great city. A stringed mstrument ofsome kind is just, and only just, audible. High over-head some one throws open a window, and the rattleof the wood-work echoes down the empty street. Onone of the roofs, a hookah is in full blast; and the menare talking softly as the pipe gutters. A Httle fartheron, the noise of conversation is more distinct. A sKt ofHght shows itself between the sliding shutters of a shop.Inside, a stubble-bearded, weary-eyed trader is balancinghis account-books among the bales of cotton prints thatsurround him. Three sheeted figures bear him company,and throw in a remark from time to time. First hemakes an entry, then a remark; then passes the back ofhis hand across his streaming forehead. The heat in thebuilt-in street is fearful. Inside the shops it must bealmost unendurable. But the work goes on steadily;entry, guttural growl, and upHfted hand-stroke succeed-ing each other with the precision of clock-work.

A poUceman—turbanless and fast asleep—lies acrossthe road on the way to the Mosque of Wazir Khan. Abar of moonhght falls across the forehead and eyes of thesleeper, but he never stirs. It is close upon midnight,and the heat seems to be increasing. The open squarein front of the Mosque is crowded with corpses; and aman must pick his way carefully for fear of treading onthem. The moonlight stripes the Mosque's high front ofcoloured enamel work in broad diagonal bands; and eachseparate dreaming pigeon in the niches and corners of themasonry throws a squab little shadow. Sheeted ghostsrise up wearily from their pallets, and flit into the darkdepths of the building. Is it possible to climb to thetop of the great Minars, and thence to look down on thecity? At all events the attempt is worth making, and

the chances are that the door of the staircase will beunlocked. Unlocked it is; but a deeply sleeping janitorlies across the threshold, face turned to the Moon. Arat dashes out of his turban at the sound of approachingfootsteps. The man grunts, opens his eyes for a minute,turns round, and goes to sleep again. All the heato-f a decade of fierce Indian summers is stored in thepitch-black, polished walls of the corkscrew staircase.Half-way up, there is something alive, warm, andfeathery; and it snores. Driven from step to step asit catches the sound of my advance, it flutters to thetop and reveals itself as a yellow-eyed, angry kite.Dozens of kites are asleep on this and the other Minars,and on the domes below. There is the shadow of a cool,or at least a less sultry breeze at this height; and, re-freshed thereby, turn to look on the City of DreadfulNight.

Dore might have drawn it! Zola could describe it—this spectacle of sleeping thousands in the moonlight andin the shadow of the Moon. The roof-tops are crammedwith men, women, and children; and the air is full ofundistinguishable noises. They are restless in the Cityof Dreadful Night; and small wonder. The marvelis that they can even breathe. If you gaze intentlyat the multitude, you can see that they are almostas uneasy as a daylight crowd; but the. tumult is sub-dued. Everywhere, in the strong light, you can watchthe sleepers turning to and fro; shifting their beds andagain resettling them. In the pit-like court-yards of thehouses there is the same movement.

Hie pitiless Moon shows it all. Shows, too, the plainsoutside the city, and here and there a hand's-breadth ofthe Ravee without the walls. Shows lastly, a splash ofglittering silver on a house-top almost directly below the

mosque Minar. Some poor soul has risen to throw ajar of water over his fevered body; the tinkle of the fall-ing water strikes faintly on the ear. Two or three othermen, in far-off corners of the City of Dreadful Night,follow his example, and the water flashes like hehographicsignals. A small cloud passes over the face of the Moon,and the city and its inhabitants—clear drawn in blackand white before—fade into masses of black and deeperblack. Still the unrestful noise contmues, the sigh of agreat city overwhehned with the heat, and of a peopleseeking in vain for rest. It is only the lower-classwomen who sleep on the house-tops. What must thetorment be in the latticed zenanas, where a few lampsare still twinkling? There are footfalls in the courtbelow. It is the Muezzin—faithful minister; but heought to have been here an hour ago to tell the Faithfulthat prayer is better than sleep—the sleep that will notcome to the city.

The Muezzin fumbles for a moment with the door ofone of the Minars, disappears awhile, and a bull-likeroar—a magnificent bass thunder—tells that he hasreached the top of the Minar. They must hear the cryto the banks of the shrunken Ravee itself! Even acrossthe courtyard it is almost overpowering. The clouddrifts by and shows him outlined in black against thesky, hands laid upon his ears, and broad chest heavingwith the play of his lungs—'Allah ho Akbar'; then apause while another Muezzin somewhere in the directionof the Golden Temple takes up the call—' Allah ho Akbar/Again and again; four times in all; and from the bed-steads a dozen men have risen up already.—'I bearwitness that there is no God but God.' What a splendidcry it is, the proclamation of the creed that brings mencut of their beds by scores at midnight! Once again he

thunders through the same phrase, shaking with thevehemence of his own voice; and then, far and near, thenight air rings with 'Mahomed is the Prophet of God/It is as though he were flinging his defiance to the far-offhorizon, where the summer Ughtning plays and leapslike a bared sword. Every Muezzin in the city is in fullcry, and some men on the roof-tops are beginning tokneel. A long pause precedes the last cry, 'La ilahaIllallah/ and the silence closes up on it, as the ram on thehead of a cotton-bale.

The Muezzin stumbles down the dark stairwaygrumbHng in his beard. He passes the arch of theentrance and disappears. Then the stifling silence settlesdown over the City of Dreadful Night. The kites on theMinar sleep again, snoring more loudly, the hot breezecomes up in puffs and lazy eddies, and the Moon slidesdown towards the horizon. Seated with both elbows onthe parapet of the tower, one can watch and wonder overthat heat-tortured hive till the dawn. 'How do theylive down there? What do they think of? When willthey awake?']\Iore tinkling of sluiced water-pots; faintjarring of wooden bedsteads moved into or out of theshadows; uncouth music of stringed instruments softenedby distance into a plaintive wail, and one low grumble offar-off thunder. In the courtyard of the mosque thejanitor, who lay across the threshold of the Minar whenI came up, starts wildly in his sleep, throws his handsabove his head, mutters something, and falls back again.Lulled by the snoring of the kites—they snore like over-gorged humans—I drop off into an uneasy doze, consciousthat three o'clock has struck, and that there is a slight—a very slight—coolness in the atmosphere. The city is^absolutely quiet now, but for some vagrant dog's love-song. Nothing save dead heavy sleep.

Several weeks of darkness pass after this. For thexVEoon has gone out. The very dogs are still, and Iwatch for the first Hght of the dawn before making myway homeward. Again the noise of shuMng feet.The morning call is about to begin, and my night watchis over. 'Allah ho Akbar! Allah ho Akbar!' Theeast grows gray, and presently saffron; the dawn windcomes up as though the Muezzin had summoned it; and,as one man, the City of Dreadful Night rises from itsbed and turns its face towards the dawning day. Withreturn of Kfe comes return of sound. First a low whis-per, then a deep bass hum; for it must be rememberedthat the entire city is on the house-tops. My eyehdsweighed down with the arrears of long deferred sleep, Iescape from the Minar through the courtyard and outinto the square beyond, where the sleepers have risen,stowed away the bedsteads, and are discussing the morn-ing hookah. The minute's freshness of the air hasgone, and it is as hot as at first.

'Will the Sahib, out of his kindness, make room?'What is it? Something borne on men's shoulders comesby in th,^ half-Hght, and I stand back. A woman'scorpse g'An down to the burning-ghat, and a bystandersays, 'She died at midnight from the heat.' So the citywas of Death as well as Night after all.

GEORGIE PORGIE

Georgie Porgie, pudding and pie,Kissed the girls and made them cry.When the girls came out to playGeorgie Porgie ran away.

If you will admit that a man has no right to enter hisdrawing-room early in the morning, when the housemaidis setting things right and clearing away the dust, youwill concede that civiKsed people who eat out of chinaand own card-cases have no right to apply their standardof right and wrong to an unsettled land. When theplace is made fit for their reception, by those men whoare told off to the work, they can come up, bringing intheir trunks their own society and the Decalogue, andall the other apparatus. Where the Queen's Law doesnot carry, it is irrational to expect an observance of otherand weaker rules. The men who run ahead of the carsof Decency and Propriety, and make the jungle waysstraight, cannot be judged in the same manner as thestay-at-home folk of the ranks of the regular TcJiin.

Not many months ago the Queen's Law stopped a fewmiles north of Thayetmyo on the Irrawaddy. There wasno very strong PubKc Opinion up to that limit, but itexisted to keep men in order. When the Governmxentsaid that the Queen's Law must carry up to Bhamo andthe Chinese border the order was given, and some menwhose desire was to be ever a little in advance of the

rush of Respectability flocked forward with the troops.These were the men who could never pass examinations,and would have been too pronounced in their ideas forthe administration of bureau-worked Provuices. TheSupreme Government stepped in as soon as might be,with codes and regulations, and all but reduced NewBurma to the dead Indian level; but there was a shorttime during which strong men were necessary andploughed a field for themselves.

Among the fore-runners of Civilisation was GeorgiePorgie, reckoned by all who knew him a strong man.He held an appointment in Lower Burma when the ordercame to break the Frontier, and his friends called himGeorgie Porgie because of the singularly Burmese-likemanner in which he sang a song whose first Hne is some-thmg like the words 'Georgie Porgie.' Most men whohave been m Burma will know the song. It means:'Puff, puff, puff, puff, great steamboat!' Georgie sangit to his banjo, and his friends shouted with delight,so that you could hear them far away in the teak-forest.

When he went to Upper Burma he had no specialregard for God or Man, but he knew how to make him-self respected, and to carry out the mixed Mihtary-Civilduties that fell to most men's share in those months.He did his office work and entertained, now and again,the detachments of fever-shaken soldiers who blunderedthrough his part of the world in search of a flying partyof dacoits. Sometimes he turned out and dressed downdacoits on his own account; for the country was stillsmouldering and would blaze when least expected. Heenjoyed these charivaris, but the dacoits were not soamused. All the officials who came in contact with himdeparted with the idea that Georgie Porgie was a valuable

person, well able to take care of himself, and, on thatbelief, he was left to his own devices.

At the end of a few months he wearied of his solitude,and cast about for company and refinement. TheQueen's Law had hardly begun to be felt in the country,and Public Opinion, which is more powerful than theQueen's Law, had yet to come. Also, there was a cus-tom in the country which allowed a white man to take tohimself a wife of the Daughters of Heth upon due pay-ment. The marriage was not quite so bindmg as is thenikkah ceremony among Mahomedans, but the Vvdfe wasvery pleasant.

When all our troops are back from Burma there ml\be a proverb in their mouths, 'As thrifty as a Burmesewife,' and pretty English ladies will wonder what in theworld it means.

The headman of the village next to Georgie Porgie'spost had a fair daughter who had seen Georgie Porgieand loved him from afar. WTien news went abroad thatthe Englishman with the heavy hand who hved in thestockade was looking for a housekeeper, the headmancame in and explained that, for five hundred rupeesdown, he would entrust his daughter to Georgie Porgie'skeeping, to be maintained in all honour, respect, andcomfort, viith pretty dresses, according to the custom ofthe country. This thing was done, and Georgie Porgienever repented it.

He found his rough-and-tumble house put straightand made comfortable, his hitherto unchecked expensescut down by one half, and himself petted and made muchof by his new acquisition, who sat at the head of histable and sang songs to him and ordered his Madrasseeservants about, and was in every way as sweet and merryand honest and winning a little woman as the most

exacting of bachelors could have desired. No race, mensay who know, produces such good wives and heads ofhouseholds as the Burmese. When the next detachmenttramped by on the war-path the Subaltern in Commandfound at Georgie Porgie's table a hostess to be deferentialto, a woman to be treated in every way as one occupyingan assured position. When he gathered his men togethernext dawn and replunged into the jungle he thought re-gretfully of the nice little dinner and the pretty face, andenvied Georgie Porgie from the bottom of his heart. Yethe was engaged to a girl at Home, and that is how somemen are constructed.

The Burmese girl's name was not a pretty one; but asshe was promptly christened Georgina by Georgie Porgie,the blemish did not matter. Georgie Porgie thought wellof the petting and the general comfort, and vowed thathe had never spent five hundred rupees to a better end.

After three months of domestic life, a great ideastruck him. Matrimony—English matrimony—couldnot be such a bad thing after all. If he were so thor-oughly comfortable at the Back of Beyond mth thisBurmese girl who smoked cheroots, how much morecomfortable would he be with a sweet EngHsh maidenwho would not smoke cheroots, and would play upon apiano instead of a banjo? Also he had a desire to returnto his kind, to hear a Band once more, and to feel howit felt to wear a dress-suit again. Decidedly, Matrimonywould be a very good thing. He thought the matterout at length of evenings, while Georgina sang to him,or asked him why he was so silent, and whether she haddone anything to offend him. As he thought, he smoked,and as he smoked he looked at Georgina, and in hisfancy turned her into a fair, thrifty, amusing, merry,little English girl, with hair coming low down on hei

forehead, and perhaps a cigarette between her lips.Certainly, not a big, thick, Burma cheroot, of the brandthat Georgina smoked. He would wed a girl withGeorgina's eyes and most of her ways. But not all.She could be improved upon. Then he blew thicksmoke-wreaths through his nostrils and stretched himself.He would taste marriage. Georgina had helped him tosave money, and there were six months' leave due to him.

'See here, Httle woman,' he said, 'we must put bymore money for these next three months. I want it.'That was a direct slur on Georgina's housekeeping; forshe prided herself on her thrift; but since her God wantedmoney she would do her best.

'You want money?' she said with a Httle laugh. '1have money. Look!' She ran to her own room andfetched out a small bag of rupees. 'Of all that you giveme, I keep back some. See! One hundred and sevenrupees. Can you want miore money than that? Takeit. It is my pleasure if you use it.' She spread out themoney on the table and pushed it towards him, mth herquick, httle, pale yellow fingers.

Georgie Porgie never referred to economy in the house-hold again.

Three months later, after the dispatch and receipt of•several mysterious letters v/hich Georgina could notunderstand, and hated for that reason, Georgie Porgiesaid that he was going away and she must return to herfather's house and stay there.

Georgina wept. She would go with her God from theworld's end to the world's end. Why should she leavehim? She loved him.

'I am only going to Rangoon,' said Georgie Porgie.'I shall be back in a month, but it is safer to stay withyour father. I will leave you two hundred rupees.'

'If you go for a month, what need of two hundred?Fifty are more than enough. There is some evil here.Do not go, or at least let me go with you.'

Georgie Porgie does not like to remember that sceneeven at this date. In the end he got rid of Georgina bya compromise of seventy-five rupees. She would nottake more. Then he went by steamer and rail to Ran-goon.

The mysterious letters had granted him six months'leave. The actual flight and an idea that he might havebeen treacherous hurt severely at the time, but as soon asthe big steamer was well out into the blue, things wereeasier, and Georgina's face, and the queer little stockadedhouse, and the memory of the rushes of shouting dacoitsby night, the cry and struggle of the first man that he hadever killed with his own hand, and a hundred other moreintimate things, faded and faded out of Georgie Porgie'sheart, and the vision of approaching England took itsplace. The steamer was full of men on leave, all ram-pantly jovial souls who had shaken off the dust and sweatof Upper Burma and were as merry as schoolboys. Theyhelped Georgie Porgie to forget.

Then came England with its luxuries and decenciesand comforts, and Georgie Porgie walked in a pleasantdream upon pavements of which he had nearly forgottenthe ring, wondering why men in their senses ever leftTown. He accepted his keen dehght in his furlough asthe reward of his services. Providence further arrangedfor him another and greater dehght—all the pleasuresof a quiet EngKsh wooing, quite different from the brazenbusinesses of the East, when half the community standback and bet on the result, and the other half wonderwhat Mrs. So-and-So will say to it.

It was a pleasant girl and a perfect summer, and a big

country-house near Petworth where there are acres andacres of purple heather and high-grassed water-meadowsto wander through. Georgie Porgie felt that he had atlast found something worth the living for, and naturallyassumed that the next thing to do was to ask the girl toshare his life in India. She, in her ignorance, was wiUingto go. On this occasion there was no bartering with avillage headman. There was a line middle-class weddingin the country, with a stout Papa and a weeping Mamma,and a best-man in purple and fine linen, and six snub-nosed girls from the Sunday School to throw roses on thepath between the tombstones up to the Church door.The local paper described the affair at great length, evendown to giving the hymns in full. But that was becausethe Direction were starving for want of material.

Then came a honeymoon at Arundel, and the Mammawept copiously before she allowed her one daughter tosail away to India under the care of Georgie Porgie theBridegroom. Beyond any question, Georgie Porgie wasimmensely fond of his wife, and she was devoted to himas the best and greatest man in the world. When he re-ported himself at Bombay he felt justified in demandinga good station for his wife's sake; and, because he hadmade a httle mark in Burma and was beginning to beappreciated, they allowed him nearly all that he askedfor, and posted him to a station which we will callSutrain. It stood upon several hills, and was styledofficially a 'Sanitarium,' for the good reason that thedrainage was utterly neglected. Here Georgie Porgiesettled down, and found married life come very naturallyto him. He did not rave, as do m.any bridegrooms, overthe strangeness and delight of seeing his own true lovesitting down to breakfast vdth. him every morning 'as\hous:h it were the most natural thing in the world.'

'He had been there before/ as the Americans say, and,checking the merits of his own present Grace by those ofGeorgina, he was more and more incHned to think thathe had done well.

But there was no peace or comfort across the Bay ofBengal, under the teak-trees where Georgina lived withher father, waiting for Georgie Porgie to return. Theheadman was old, and remembered the war of ^51. Hehad been to Rangoon, and knew something of the ways ofthe Kidlalts. Sitting in front of his door in the evenings,he taught Georgina a dry philosophy which did not con-sole her in the least.

The trouble was that she loved Georgie Porgie just asmuch as the French girl in the English History booksloved the priest whose head was broken by the king'sbullies. One day she disappeared from the village withall the rupees that Georgie Porgie had given her, and aver>^ small smattering of English—also gained fromGeorgie Porgie.

The headman was angry at first, but lit a fresh cherootand said something uncompUmentary about the sex ingeneral. Georgina had started on a search for GeorgiePorgie, who might be in Rangoon, or across the BlackWater, or dead, for aught that she knew. Chancefavoured her. An old Sikh policeman told her thatGeorgie Porgie had crossed the Black Water. She took asteerage-passage from Rangoon and went to Calcutta;keeping the secret of her search to herself.

In India every trace of her was lost for six weeks,and no one knows what trouble of heart she must haveundergone.

She reappeared, four hundred miles north of Calcutta,heading northwards, very worn and liaggard, but in her determination to find Georgie Porgie.

She could not understand the language of the people;but India is infinitely charitable, and the women-folkalong the Grand Trunk gave her food. Something madeher believe that Georgie Porgie was to be found at theend of that pitiless road. She may have seen a sepoy whoknew him in Burma, but of this no one can be certain.At last, she found a regiment on the line of march, andmet there one of the many subalterns whom GeorgiePorgie had invited to dinner in the far-off, old days of thedacoit-hunting. There was a certain amount of amuse-ment among the tents when Georgina threw herself at theman's feet and began to cry. There was no amusementwhen her story was told; but a collection was made, andthat was more to the point. One of the subalterns knewof Georgie Porgie's whereabouts, but not of his marriage.So he told Georgina and she went her way joyfully to thenorth, in a railway carriage where there was rest for tiredfeet and shade for a dusty Httle head. The marchesfrom the train through the hills into Sutrain were trying,but Georgina had money, and families journeying inbullock-carts gave her help. It was an ahnost miraculousjourney, and Georgina felt sure that the good spirits ofBurma were looking after her. The hill-road to Sutrainis a chilly stretch, and Georgina caught a bad cold. Stillthere was Georgie Porgie at the end of all the trouble totake her up in his arms and pet her, as he used to do inthe old days when the stockade was shut for the night andhe had approved of the evening meal. Georgina wentforward as fast as she could; and her good spirits did herone last favour.

An Englishman stopped her, in the twilight, just atthe turn of the road into Sutrain, saying,' Good Heavens!What are you doing here?'

He was Gillis, the man who had been Georgie Porgie's

GEORGIE PORGIE It

assistant in Upper Burma, and who occupied the nextpost to Georgie Porgie's in the jungle. Georgie Porgiehad apphed to have him to work with at Sutram becausehe hked him.

'I have come/ said Georgina simply. 'It was such along way, and I have been months in coming. Where ishis house?'

Gillis gasped. He had seen enough of Georgina inthe old times to know that explanations would be use-less. You cannot explain things to the Oriental. Youmust show.

'I'll take you there,' said Gillis, and he led Georginaoff the road, up the cUff, by a Httle pathway, to the backof a house set on a platform cut into the hillside.

The lamps were just Ht, but the curtains were notdrawn. 'Now look,' said Gillis, stopping in front of thedrawing-room window. Georgina looked and saw GeorgiePorgie and the Bride.

She put her hand up to her hair, which had comeout of its top-knot and was stragghng about her face.She tried to set her ragged dress in order, but the dresswas past pulling straight, and she coughed a queer Httlecough, for she really had taken a very bad cold. Gilhslooked, too, but while Georgina only looked at the Brideonce, turning her eyes always on Georgie Porgie, Gillislooked at the Bride all the time.

'What are you going to do?' said Gillis, who heldGeorgina by the wrist, in case of any unexpected rushinto the lamplight. 'Will you go in and tell that Englishwoman that you Hved with her husband?'

' No,' said Georgina faintly. ' Let me go. I am goingaway. I swear that I am going away.' She twistedherself free and ran off into the dark.

'Poor little beast!' said Gillis, droppmg on to the main

road. ' I'd ha' given her something to get back to Burmawith. What a narrow shave though! And that angelwould never have forgiven it.'

This seems to prove that the devotion of Gillis wasnot entirely due to his affection for Georgia Porgie.

The Bride and the Bridegroom came out into theverandah after dinner, in order that the smoke of GeorgiePorgie's cheroots might not hang in the new drawing-room curtains.

'What is that noise down there?' said the Bride.Both Hstened.

'Oh/ said Georgie Porgie, 'I suppose some brute of ahillman has been beating his wife.'

'Beating—his—wife! How ghastly!' said the Bride.'Fancy your beating met' She shpped an arm roundher husband's waist, and, leaning her head against hisshoulder, looked out across the cloud-filled valley in deepcontent and security.

But it was Georgina crying, all by herself, down thehillside, among the stones of the water-course where thewashermen wash the clothes.

NABOTH'

This was how it happened; and the truth is also anallegory of Empire.

I met him at the comer of my garden, an emptybasket on his head, and an unclean cloth round his loins.That was all the property to which Naboth had theshadow of a claim when I first saw Mm. He openedour acquaintance by begging. He was very thin andshowed nearly as many ribs as his basket; and he toldme a long story about fever and a lawsuit, and an ironcauldron that had been seized by the court in executionof a decree. I put my hand into my pocket to helpNaboth, as kings of the East have helped aHen adven-turers to the loss of their kingdoms. A rupee hadhidden in my waistcoat lining. I never knew it wasthere, and gave the trove to Naboth as a direct gift fromHeaven. He replied that I was the only legitimateProtector of the Poor he had ever known.

Next morning he reappeared, a little fatter in theround, and curled himself into knots in the front ve-randah. He said I was his father and his mother, andthe direct descendant of all the gods in his Pantheon,besides controlling the destinies of the universe. Hehimself was but a sweetmeat-seller, and m.uch lessimportant than the dirt under my feet. I had heardthis sort of thing before, so I asked him what he wanted.My rupee, quoth Naboth, had raised him to the ever-

lasting heavens, and he wished to prefer a request. Hewished to establish a sweetmeat-pitch near the house ofliis benefactor, to gaze on my revered countenance as Iwent to and fro illumining the world. I was graciouslypleased to give permission, and he went away with liishead between his knees.

Now at the far end of my garden, the ground slopestoward the pubHc road, and the slope is crowned with athick shrubbery. There is a short carriage-road fromthe house to the Mall, which passes close to the shrub-bery. Next afternoon I saw that Naboth had seatedhimself at the bottom of the slope, down in the dust of thepublic road, and in the full glare of the sun, with a starvedbasket of greasy sweets in front of him. He had gone intotrade once more on the strength of my munificent dona-tion, and the ground was as Paradise by my honouredfavour. Remember, there was only Naboth, his basket,the sunshine, and the gray dust when the sap of my Em-pire first began.

Next day he had moved himself up the slope nearerto my shrubbery, and waved a palm-leaf fan to keep theflies off the sweets. So I judged that he must have donea fair trade.

Four days later I noticed that he had backed himselfand his basket under the shadow of the shrubbery, and hadtied an Isabella-coloured rag betv/een two branches in orderto make more shade. There were plenty of sweets in hisbasket. I thought that trade must certainly be looking up.

Seven weeks later the Government took up a plot ofground for a Chief Court close to the end of my com-pound, and employed nearly four hundred coolies on thefoundations. Naboth bought a blue and white stripedblanket, a brass lamp-stand, and a small boy, t@ eopewith the rush of trade, which was tremendous.

Five days later he bought a huge, fat, red-backedaccount-book, and a glass inkstand. Thus I saw thatthe coolies had been getting into his debt, and that com-merce was increasing on legitimate lines of credit. AlsoI saw that the one basket had grown into three, and thatKfaboth had backed and hacked into the shrubbery, andmade himself a nice little clearing for the proper displayof the basket, the blanket, the books, and the boy.

One week and five days later he had built a mud fire-place in the clearing, and the fat account-book was over-flowing. He said that God created few EngUshmen ofmy kind, and that I was the incarnation of all humanvirtues. He offered me some of his sweets as tribute,and by accepting these I acknowledged him as my feuda-tory under the skirt of my protection.

Three weeks later I noticed that the boy was in thehabit of cooking Naboth's mid-day meal for him, andN'aboth was beginning to grow a stomach. He hadhacked away more of my shrubbery and owned anotherand a fatter account-book.

Eleven weeks later Naboth had eaten his way nearlyJirough that shrubbery, and there was a reed hut with aoedstead outside it, standing in the little glade that hehad eroded. Two dogs and a baby slept on the bedstead.So I fancied Naboth had taken a wife. He said that hehad, by my favour, done this thing, and that I wasseveral times finer than Krishna.

Six weeks and two days later a mud wall had grownup at the back of the hut. There were fowls in frontand it smelt a little. The Municipal Secretary said thata cess-pool was forming in the public road from thedrainage of my compound, and that I must take steps toclear it away. I spoke to Naboth. He said I was LordParamount of his earthly concerns, and the p;arden was

all my own property, and sent me some more sweets in asecond-hand duster.

Two months later a coolie bricklayer was killed in ascuffle that took place opposite Naboth's Vineyard. TheInspector of Police said it was a serious case; went intomy servants' quarters; insulted my butler's wife, andwanted to arrest my butler. The curious thing about themurder was that most of the coolies were drunk at thetime. Naboth pointed out that my name was a strongshield between him and his enemies, and he expected thatanother baby would be bom to him shortly.

Four months later the hut was all mud walls, verysolidly built, and Naboth had used most of my shrubberyfor his five goats. A silver watch and an aluminiumchain shone upon his very round stomach. My servantswere alarmingly drunk several times, and used to wastethe day with Naboth when they got the chance. I spoketo Naboth. He said, by my favour and the glory of m)'coimtenance, he would make all his women-folk ladies,and that if any one hinted that he was running an illicitstill under the shadow of the tamarisks, why, I, hisSuzerain, was to prosecute.

A week later he hired a man to make several dozensquare yards of trellis-work to put around the back of hishut, that his women-folk might be screened from thepubHc gaze. The man went away in the evening, andleft his day's work to pave the short cut from the publicroad to my house. I was driving home in the dusk, andturned the corner by Naboth's Vineyard quickly. Thenext thing I knew was that the horses of the phaetonwere stamping and plunging in the strongest sort ofbamboo net-work. Both beasts came down. One rosewith nothing more than chipped knees. The other wasso badly kicked that I was forced to shoot him.

NABOTH 77

Naboth is gone now, and his hut is ploughed into itsnative mud with sweetmeats instead of salt for a signthat the place is accursed. I have built a summer-houseto overlook the end of the garden, and it is as a fort onmy frontier whence I guard my Empire.

I know exactly how Ahab felt. He has been shame-fully misrepresented in the Scriptures.

THE DREAM OF DUNCAN PARRENNESS*

Like Mr. Bunyan of old, I, Duncan Parrenness, Writerto the Most Honourable the East India Company, in thisGod-forgotten city of Calcutta, have dreamed a dream,and never since that Kitty my mare fell lame have Ibeen so troubled. Therefore, lest I should forget mydream, I have made shift to set it down here. ThoughHeaven knows how unhandy the pen is to me who wasalways readier with sword than ink-horn when I leftLondon two long years since.

When the Governor-General's great dance (that hegives yearly at the latter end of November)was finisht,I had gone to mine own room which looks over thatsullen, un-EngKsh stream, the Hoogly, scarce so sober asI might have been. Now, roaring drunk in the West isbut fuddled in the East, and I was drunk Nor'-Nor'Easterly as Mr. Shakespeare might have said. Yet, inspite of my liquor, the cool night winds (though I haveheard that they breed chills and fluxes innumerable)sobered me somewhat; and I remembered that I hadbeen but a Httle wrung and wasted by all the sicknessesof the past four months, whereas those young bloods thatcame eastward with me in the same ship had been all, amonth back, planted to Eternity in the foul soil north ofWriters' Buildings. So then, I thanked God mistily(though, to my shame, I never kneeled down to do so) forlicense to live, at least till March should be upon us again,

^Copyright, 1891, by Macmtllan & Co.78

Indeed, we that were alive (and our number was less by-far than those who had gone to their last account in thehot weather late past) had made very merry that evening,by the ramparts of the Fort, over this kindness of Provi-dence; though our jests were neither witty nor such as Ishould have liked my Mother to hear.

When I had lain down (or rather thrown me on mybed) and the fumes of my drink had a little cleared away,I found that I could get no sleep for thinking of a thou-sand things that were better left alone. First, and itwas a long time since I had thought of her, the sweet faceof Kitty Somerset, drifted, as it might have been drawn ina picture, across the foot of my bed, so plainly, that Ialmost thought she had been present in the body. ThenI remembered how she drove me to this accursed countryto get rich, that I might the more quickly marry her, ourparents on both sides giving their consent; and then howshe thought better (or worse may be) of her troth, andwed Tom Sanderson but a short three months after I hadsailed. From Kitty I fell a-musing on Mrs.

Vansuythen,a tall pale woman with violet eyes that had come to Cal-cutta from the Dutch Factory at Chinsura, and had setall our young men, and not a few of the factors, by theears. Some of our ladies, it is true, said that she hadnever a husband or marriage-lines at all; but women, andspecially those who have led only indifferent good livesthemselves, are cruel hard one on another. Besides,Mrs. Vansuythen was far prettier than them all. Shehad been most gracious to me at the Governor-General'srout, and indeed I was looked upon by all as her preuxchevalier— which is French for a much worse word. Now,whether I cared so much as the scratch of a pin for thissame Mrs. Vansuythen (albeit I had vowed eternal lovethree days after we met) I knew not then nor did till

later on; but mine own pride, and a skill in the smaHsword that no man in Calcutta could equal, kept me inher affections. So that I believed I worshipt her.

When I had dismist her violet eyes from my thoughts,my reason reproacht me for ever having followed her atall; and I saw how the one year that I had lived in thisland had so burnt and seared my mind with the flamesof a thousand bad passions and desires, that I had agedten months for each one in the Devil's school. WhereatI thought of my Mother for a while, and was verypenitent: making in my sinful tipsy mood a thousandvows of reformation—all since broken, I fear me, againand again. To-morrow, says I to myself, I will livecleanly for ever. And I smiled dizzily (the liquor beingstill strong in me) to think of the dangers I had escaped;and built all manner of fine Castles in Spain, whereof ashadowy Kitty Somerset that had the violet eyes and thesweet slow speech of Mrs. Vansuy then, was always Queen,

Lastly, a very fine and magnificent courage (thatdoubtless had its birth in Mr. Hastings' Madeira) grewupon me, till it seemed that I could become Governor-General, Nawab, Prince, ay, even the Great Mogul him-self, by the mere wishing of it. Wherefore, taking myfirst steps, random and unstable enough, towards my newkingdom, I kickt my servants sleeping without till theyhowled and ran from me, and called Heaven and Earthto witness that I, Duncan Parrenness, was a Writer inthe service of the Company and afraid of no man. Then,seeing that neither the Moon nor the Great Bear wereminded to accept my challenge, I lay down again andmust have fallen asleep.

I was waked presently by my last words repeated tw«or three times, and I saw that there had come into theroom a drunken man, as I thought, from Mr. Hastings

rout. He sate down at the foot of my bed in all theworld as it belonged to him, and I took note, as well asi could, that his face was somewhat like mine own grown' Ider, save when it changed to the face of the Governor-General or my father, dead these six months. But thisseemed to me only natural, and the due result of too muchwine; and I was so angered at his entry all unannounced,that I told him, not over civilly, to go. To all my wordshe made no answer whatever, only saying slowly, asthough it were some sweet morsel: 'Writer in the Com-pany's service and afraid of no man.' Then he stopsshort, and turning round sharp upon me, says that one ofmy kidney need fear neither man nor devil; that I was abrave young man, and like enough, should I live so long,to be Governor-General. But for all these things (and Isuppose that he meant thereby the changes and chancesof our shifty life in these parts) I must pay my price.By this time I had sobered somewhat, and being wellwaked out of my first sleep, was disposed to look uponthe matter as a tipsy man's jest. So, says I merrily:'And what price shall I pay for this palace of mine, whichis but twelve feet square, and my five poor pagodas amonth? The Devil take you and your jesting: I haveDaid my price twice over in sickness.' At that momentmy man turns full towards me: so that by the moonlightI could see every line and wrinkle of his face. Then mydrunken mirth died out of me, as I have seen the watersof our great rivers die away in one night; and I, DuncanParrenness, who was afraid of no man, was taken with amore deadly terror than I hold it has ever been the lotof mortal man to know. For I saw that his face wasmy very own, but marked and lined and scarred with thefurrows of disease and much evil living—as I once, whenI was (Lord help me) very dnmk ir.deed, have seen mine

own face, all white and drawn and grown old, in a mirror.I take it that any man would have been even moregreatly feared than I. For I am in no way wanting incourage.

After I had lain still for a little, sweating in my agonyand waiting until I should awake from this terrible dream(for dream I knew it to be) he says again, that I must paymy price, and a little after, as though it were to be givenin pagodas and sicca rupees: ' What price will you pay?'Says I, very softly: 'For God's sake let me be, whoeveryou are, and I will mend my ways from to-night.' Sayshe, laughing a little at my words, but otherwise makingno motion of having heard them: 'Nay, I would onlyrid so brave a young rufHer as yourself of much that willbe a great hindrance to you on your way through life inthe Indies; for believe me,' and here he looks full onme once more,' there is no return.' At all this rigmarole,which I could not then understand, I was a good dealput aback and waited for what should come next. Sayshe very calmly, ' Give me your trust in man.' At that Isaw how heavy would be my price, for I never doubtedbut that he could take from me all that he asked, and myhead was, through terror and wakefulness, altogethercleared of the wine I had drunk. So I takes him upvery short, cr\'7ddng that I was not so wholly bad as hewould make beUeve, and that I trusted my fellows to thefull as much as they were worthy of it. ' It was none ofmy fault,' says I, 'if one half of them were liars and theother half deserved to be burnt in the hand, and I wouldonce more ask him to have done with his questions.*'Hien I stopped, a Httle afraid, it is true, to have let mytongue so run away with me, but he took no notice ofthis, and only laid his hand lightly on my left breast andI felt very cold there for a while. Then he says, laughing

more: ' Give me your faith in women.' At that I startedin my bed as though I had been stung, for I thought ofmy sweet mother in England, and for a while fancied thatmy faith in God's best creatures could neither be shakennor stolen from me. But later, Myself's hard eyes beingupon me, I fell to thinking, for the second time thatnight, of Kitty (she that jilted me and married TomSanderson) and of Mistress Vansuythen, whom only mydevilish pride made me follow, and how she was even worsethan Kitty, and I worst of them all—seeing that with mylife's work to be done, I must needs go dancing down theDevil's swept and garnished causeway, because, forsooth,there was a light woman's smile at the end of it. And Ithought that all women in the world were either likeKitty ®r Mistress Vansuythen (as indeed they have eversince been to me) and this put me to such an extremityof rage and sorrow, that I was beyond word glad whenMyself's hand fell again on my left breast, and I was nomore troubled by these follies.

After this he was silent for a little, and I made surethat he must go or I awake ere long: but presently hespeaks again (and very softly) that I was a fool to carefor such follies as those he had taken from me, and thatere he went he would only ask me for a few other triflessuch as no man, or for matter of that boy either, wouldkeep about him in this country. And so it happenedthat h-e took from out of my very heart as it were,looking all the time into my face with my own eyes, asmuch as remained to me of my boy's soul and conscience.This was to me a far more terrible loss than the two thatI had suffered before. For though, Lord help me, I hadtravelled far enough from all paths of decent or godlyliving, yet there was in me, though I myself write it, acertaim goodness of heart which, whep T was sober (or

sick) made me very sorry of all that I had done beforethe fit came on me. And this I lost wholly: having inplace thereof another deadly coldness at the heart. I amnot, as I have before said, ready with my pen, so I fearthat what I have just written may not be readily under-stood.

Yet there be certain times in a young man's life,when, through great sorrow or sin, all the boy in him isburnt and seared away so that he passes at one step to themore sorrowful state of manhood: as our staring Indianday changes into night witli never so much as the gray oftwilight to temper the two extremes. This shall perhapsmake my state more clear, if it be remembered that mytorment was ten times as great as comes in the naturalcourse of nature to any man. At that time I dared notthink of the change that had come over me, and all inone night: though I have often thought of it since. 4have paid the price,' says I, my teeth chattering, for I wasdeadly cold, 'and what is my return?' At this time itwas nearly dawn, and Myself had begun to grow paleand thin against the white light in the east, as my motherused to tell me is the custom of ghosts and devils andthe like. He made as if he would go, but my wordsstopt him and he laughed—as I remember that I laughedwhen I ran Angus Macalister through the sword-arm lastAugust, because he said that Mrs. Vansuythen was nobetter than she should be. 'What return?'—says he,catching up my last words—'Why, strength to live aslong as God or the Devil pleases, and so long as you livemy young master, my gift.' With that he puts some-thing into my hand, though it was still too dark to seewhat it v/as, and when next I lookt up he was gone.

When the light came I made shift to behold his gift,and saw that \'7dt was a Httle piece of dry bread.

Wohl auf, my bully cavaliers,
We ride to church to-day,The man that hasn't got a horse
Must steal one straight away.
Be reverent, men, remember
This is a Gottes hau§.Du, Conrad, cut along der aisle
And schenck der whiskey aus.
Hans Breitmann^s Ride to Church.

Once upon a time, very far from England, there livedthree men who loved each other so greatly that neitherman nor woman could come between them. They werein no sense refined, nor to be admitted to the outer-door mats of decent folk, because they happened to beprivate soldiers in Her Majesty's Army; and privatesoldiers of our service have small time for self-culture.Their duty is to keep themselves and their accoutre-ments specklessly clean, to refrain from getting drunkmore often than is necessary, to obey their superiors, andto pray for a war. All these things my friends accom.-plished; and of their own motion threw in some fighting-work for which the Army Regulations did not call.Their fate sent them to serve in India, which is nota golden country, though poets have sung otherwise.There men die with great swiftness, and those who liv*:?

85

suffer many and curious things. I do not think that myfriends concerned themselves much with the social orpolitical aspects of the East. They attended a not un-important war on the northern frontier, another one onour western boundary, and a third in Upper Burma.Then their regiment sat still to recruit, and the boundlessmonotony of cantonment Hfe was their portion. Theywere drilled morning and evening on the same dustyparade-ground. They wandered up and down the samestretch of dusty white road, attended the same churchand the same grog-shop, and slept in the same lime-washed barn of a barrack for two long years. There wasMulvaney, the father in the craft, who had served withvarious regiments from Bermuda to Halifax, old in war,scarred, reckless, resourceful, and in his pious hours anunequalled soldier. To him turned for help and comfortsix and a half feet of slow-moving, heavy-footed York-shireman, born on the wolds, bred in the dales, andeducated chiefly among the carriers' carts at the back ofYork railway-station. His name was Learoyd, and hischief virtue an unmitigated patience which helped himto win fights. How Ortheris, a fox-terrier of a Cockney,ever came to be one of the trio, is a mystery which evento-day I cannot explain. ^ There was always three av us,'Mulvaney used to say. 'An' by the grace av God, solong as our service lasts, three av us they'll always be.'Tis betther so.'

They desired no companionship beyond their own,and it was evil for any man of the regiment who at-tempted dispute with them. Physical argument wasout of the question as regarded Mulvaney and the York-shireman; and assault on Ortheris meant a combinedattack from these twain—a business which no five menwere anxious to have on their hands. Therefore they

flourished, sharing their drinks, their tobacco, and theirmoney; good luck and evil; battle and the chances ofdeath; Hfe and the chances of happiness from Calicut insouthern, to Peshawur in northern India.

Through no merit of my own it was my good fortuneto be in a measure admitted to their friendship—franklyby Mulvaney from the beginning, sullenly and with re-luctance by Learoyd, and suspiciously by Ortheris, whoheld to it that no man not in the Army could fraternisewith a red-coat. ' Like to Hke,' said he. ' I'm a bloomin'sodger—he's a bloomin' civilian. 'Tain't natural—that's all'

But that was not all. They thawed progressively,and in the thawing told me more of their lives and ad-ventures than I am ever Hkely to write.

Omitting all else, this tale begins with the LamentableThirst that was at the beginnmg of First Causes. Neverwas such a thirst—Mulvaney told me so. They kickedagainst their compulsory virtue, but the attempt wasonly successful in the case of Ortheris. He, whosetalents were many, went forth into the highways andstole a dog from a 'civilian'—videlicet, some one, he knewnot who, not in the Army. Now that civiHan wasbut newly connected by marriage with the colonel of theregiment, and outcry was made from quarters leastanticipated by Ortheris, and, in the end, he was forced,lest a worse thing should happen, to dispose at ridicu-lously unremunerative rates of as promising a smallterrier as ever graced one end of a leading string. Thepurchase-money was barely sufficient for one small out-break which led him to the guard-room. He escaped,however, with nothing worse than a severe reprimand,and a few hours of punishment drill. Not for nothinghad he acquired the reputation of being ' the best soldier

of his inches' in the regiment. Mulvaney had taughtpersonal cleanHness and efficiency as the first articlesof his companions' creed. 'A dhirty man,' he was usedto say, in the speech of his kind, 'goes to Clink for aweakness in the knees, an' is coort-martialled for a pairav socks missin'; but a clane man, such as is an orna-ment to his service—a man whose buttons are gold,whose coat is wax upon him, an' whose 'coutrements arewidout a speck—that man may, spakin' in reason, dofwhat he likes an' dhrink from day to divil. That's thepride av bein' dacint.'

We sat together, upon a day, in the shade of a ravinefar from the barracks, where a watercourse used to runin rainy weather. Behind us was the scrub jungle, inwhich jackals, peacocks, the gray wolves of the North-western Provinces, and occasionally a tiger estrayedfrom Central India, were supposed to dwell. In frontlay the cantonment, glaring white under a glaring sun;and on either side ran the broad road that led to Delhi.

It was the scrub that suggested to my mind thewisdom of Mulvaney taking a day's leave and going upona shooting-tour. The peacock is a holy bird throughoutIndia, and he who slays one is in danger of being mobbedby the nearest villagers; but on the last occasion thatMulvaney had gone forth, he had contrived, without inthe least offending local rehgious susceptibihties, to returnwith six beautiful peacock skins which he sold to profit.It seemed just possible then

'But fwhat manner av use is ut to me goin' outwddout a dhrink? The ground's powdher-dhry under-foot, an' ut gets unto the throat fit to kill,' wailedMulvaney, looking at me reproachfully. 'An' a peacockis not a bird you can catch the tail av onless ye run.Can a man run on wather—an' jungle-wather too?'

Ortheris had considered the question in all its bearings.He spoke, chewing his pipe-stem meditatively the while:

* Go forth, return in glory,To Clusium's royal 'ome:An' round these bloomin' temples 'angThe bloomin' shields o' Rome.

Vou better go. You ain't Hke to shoot yourself—notwhile there's a chanst of Uquor. Me an' Learoyd '11 stayat 'ome an' keep shop—'case o' anythin' turnin' up. Butyou go out with a gas-pipe gun an' ketch the little pea-cockses or some thin'. You kin get one day's leave easyas winkin'. Go along an' get it, an' get peacockses orsome thin'.'

' Jock,' said Mulvaney, turning to Learoyd, who was halfasleep under the shadow of the bank. He roused slowly.

'Sitha, Mulvaaney, go,' said he.

And Mulvaney went; cursing his allies with Irishfluency and barrack-room point.

'Take note,' said he, when he had won his holiday,and appeared dressed in his roughest clothes with theonly other regimental fowling-piece in his hand. 'Takenote, Jock, an' you Orth'ris, I am goin' in the face avmy own will—all for to please you. I misdoubt any-thin' will come av permiscuous huntin' afther peacocksesin a desolit Ian'; an' I know that I will He down an' diewid thirrrst. Me catch peacockses for you, ye lazy scutts—an' be sacrificed by the peasanthry—Ugh!'

He waved a huge paw and went away.

At twilight, long before the appointed hour, he re-turned empty-handed, much begrimed with dirt.

'Peacockses?' queried Ortheris from the safe restof a barrack-room table whereon he was smoking cross-legged, Learoyd fast asleep on a bench.

'Jock/ said Mulvaney without answering, as he stirredup the sleeper. 'Jock, can ye fight? Will ye fight?'

Very slowly the meaning of the words communicateditself to the half-roused man. He understood—andagain—what might these things mean? Mulvaney wasshaking him savagely. Meantime the men in the roomhowled with delight. There was war in the confederacyat last—war and the breaking of bonds.

Barrack-room etiquette is stringent. On the directchallenge must follow the direct reply. This is morebinding than the ties of tried friendship. Once againMulvaney repeated the question. Learoyd answered bythe only means in his power, and so swiftly that theIrishman had barely time to avoid the blow. Thelaughter around increased. Learoyd looked bewilderedlyat his friend—himself as greatly bewildered. Ortherisdropped from the table because his world was falling.

' Come outside,' said Mulvaney, and as the occupantsof the barrack-room prepared joyously to follow, heturned and said furiously, 'There will be no fight thisnight—onless any wan av you is wishful to assist. Theman that does, follows on.'

No man moved. The three passed out into the moon-light, Learoyd fumbling with the buttons of his coat.The parade-ground was deserted except for the scurryingjackals. Mulvaney's impetuous rush carried his com-panions far into the open ere Learoyd attempted to turnround and continue the discussion.

'Be still now. 'Twas my fault for beginnin' thingsin the middle av an end, Jock. I should ha' comminstwid an explanation; but Jock, dear, on your sowl areye fit, think you, for the finest fight that iver was—betther than fightin' me? Considher before ye ansv/er.'

More than ever puzzled, Learoyd turned round tv/o or

three times, felt an arm, kicked tentatively, and an-swered, 'Ah'm fit.' He was accustomed to fight blindly at the bidding of the superior mind.

They sat them down, the men looking on from afar, and Mulvaney untangled himself in mighty words.

'Followin' your fools' scheme I wint out into the thrackless desert beyond the barricks. An' there I met a pious Hindu dhriving a bullock-kyart. I tuk ut for granted he wud be delighted for to convoy me a piece, an' I jumped in '

'You long, lazy, black-haired swine,' drawled Ortheris, who would have done the same tiling under similar circumstances.

* 'Twas the height av policy. That naygur-man dhruv miles an' miles—as far as the new railway line they're buildin' now back av the Tavi river. ^' 'Tis a kyart for dhirt only," says he now an' again timoreously, to get me out av ut. "Dhirt I am," sez I, "an' the dhryest that you iver kyarted. Dhrive on, me son, an glory be wid you." At that I wint to slape, an' took no heed till he pulled up on the embankmint av the line where the cooHes were pilin' mud. There was a matther av two thousand coolies on that line—you remimber that. Prisintly a bell rang, an' they throops off to a big pay-shed. "Where's the white man in charge?" sez I to my kyart-dhriver. "In the shed," sez he, "engaged on a rifle."—"A fwhat?" sez I. "Riffle," sez he. "You take ticket. He take money. You get no thin'."—"Oho!" sez I, "that's fwhat the shuperior an' cultivated man calls a raffle, me misbeguided child a^^ darkness an' sin. Lead on to that raffle, though fwhat the mischief 'tis doin' so far away from uts home—which is the charity-bazaar at Christmas, an' the colonel's wife grinnin' behind the tea-table—is more than I know." Wid that

I wint to the shed an' found 'twas pay-day among the coolies. Their wages was on a table forninst a big, fine, red buck av a man—sivun fut high, four fut wide, an' three fut thick, wid a fist on him like a corn-sack. He was payin' the cooHes fair an' easy, but he wud ask each man if he wud raffie that month, an' each man sez, *'Yes," av course. Tliin he wud deduct from their wages accordin'. Whin all was paid, he filled an ould cigar-box full av gun-wads an' scatthered ut among the coolies. They did not take much joy av that per-formince, an' small wondher. A man close to me picks up a black gun-wad an' sings out, *'I have ut."—"Good may ut do you," sez I. The cooHe wint forward to this big, fine, red man, who threw a cloth off av the most sumpshus, jooled, enamelled an' variously bedivilled sedan-chair I iver saw.'

'Sedan-chair! Put your 'ead in a bag. That "was a palanquin. Don't yer know a palanquin when you see it?' said Ortheris with great scorn.

*I chuse to call ut sedan-chair, an' chair ut shall be, Uttle man,' continued the Irishman. ' 'Twas a most amazin' chair—all fined wid pink silk an' fitted wid red silk curtains. "Here ut is," sez the red man. "Here ut is," sez the cooHe, an' he grinned weakly-ways. "I? ut any use to you?" sez the red man. "No," sez the coolie; "I'd like to make a presint av ut to you."—"I am graciously pleased to accept that same," sez the red man; an' at that all the coohes cried aloud in fwhat was mint for cheerful notes, an' wint back to their diggin', lavin' me alone in the shed. The red man saw me, an' his face grew blue on his big, fat neck. "Fwhat d'you want here?" sez he. "Standin'-room an' no more," sez I, "onless it may be fwhat ye niver had, an' that's manners, ye raflain' ruffian," fo r J. was not ^oin' to have the Service

throd upon. *'Out of this," sez he. *'I'm in charge av this section av construction."—"I'm in charge av mesilf," sez I, "an' it's like I will stay a while. D'yer raffle much in these parts?"—'^Fwhat's that to you?'*sez he. "Nothin'," sez I, "but a great dale to you, for begad I'm thinkin' you get the full half av your revenue from that sedan-chair. Is ut always raffled so?" I sez, an' wid that I wint to a coohe to ask questions. Bhoys, that man's name is Dearsley, an' he's been rafflin' that ould sedan-chair monthly this matther av nine months. Ivry coohe on the section takes a ticket—or he gives 'emthe go—^wanst a month on pay-day. Ivry coohe thatwins ut gives ut back to him, for 'tis too big to carryaway, an' he'd sack the man that thried to sell ut. ThatDearsley has been makin' the rowlin' wealth av Roshusby nefarious rafflin'. Think av the burnin' shame to thesufferin' coolie-man that the army in Injia are bound toprotect an' nourish in their bosoms! Two thousandcooHes defrauded wanst a month!'

*Dom t' coolies. Has't gotten t' cheer, man?' saidLearoyd.

' Hould on. Havin' onearthed this amazin' an' stupen-jus fraud committed by the man Dearsley, I hild a councilav wat; he thryin' all the time to sejuce me into afight with opprobrious language. That sedan-chairniver belonged by right to any foreman av coohes. 'Tisa king's chair or a quane's. There's gold on ut an' silkan' all manner av trapesemints. Bhoys, 'tis not for meto countenance any sort av wrong-doin'—me bein' the

ould man—but anyway he has had ut nine months,

an' he dare not make throuble av ut was taken from him.Five miles away, or ut may be six

'

There was a long pause, and the jackals howled mer-rily. Learoyd bared one arm, and contemplated it in

the moonlight. Then he nodded partly to himself andpartly to his friends. Ortheris wriggled with suppressedemotion.

'I thought ye wud see the reasonableness av ut,' saidIMulvaney. 'I made bould to say as much to the manbefore. He was for a direct front attack—fut, horse, an' guns an' all for nothin', seein' that I had no thrans-

port to convey the machine away. *'I will not arguewid you," sez I, *'this day, but subsequintly, MisterDearsley, me rafflin' jool, we talk ut out lengthways.'Tis no good poHcy to swindle the naygur av his hard-earned emolumints, an' by presint informashin'"—'twas the kyart man that tould me—"ye've been per-pethrating that same for nine months. But I'm a justman," sez I, *'an' overlookin' the presumpshin thatyondher settee wid the gilt top was not come by honust"—at that he turned sky-green, so I knew things was morethrue than tellable—"not come by honust, I'm willin'to compound the felony for this month's winnin's.'"

'Ah! Ho!' from Learoyd and Ortheris.

*That man Dearsley's rushin' on his fate,' continuedMulvaney, solemnly w^agging his head. 'AH Hell had noname bad enough for me that tide. Faith, he called mea robber! Me! that was savin' him from continuin' inhis evil w^ays widout a remonstrince—an' to a man avconscience a remonstrince may change the chune av hislife. " 'Tis not for me to argue," sez I, "fwhatever yeare. Mister Dearsley, but, by my hand, I'll take away thetemptation for you that Hes in that sedan-chair."—"Youwill have to fight me for ut," sez he, "for well I know youwill never dare make report to any one."—"Fight I will,"sez I, "but not this day, for I'm rejuced for want avnourishment."—"Ye're an ould bould hand," sez he,sizin' me up an' down; "an' a jool av a fight we will have.

Eat now an' dhrink, an' go your way." Wid that he gaveme some hump an' whisky—good whisky—an' we talkedav this an' that the while. "It goes hard on me now,"sez I, wipin' my mouth, "to confiscate that piece avfurniture, but justice is justice."—"Ye've not got ut yet,"sez he; "there's the fight between."—"There is," sez I,"an' a good fight. Ye shall have the pick av the bestquality in my rigimint for the dinner you have given thisday." Thin I came hot-foot to you two. Hould yourtongue, the both. 'Tis this way. To-morrow we threewill go there an' he shall have his pick betune me an'Jock. Jock's a deceivin' fighter, for he is all fat to theeye, an' he moves slov/. Now, I'm all beef to the look,an' I move quick. By my reckonin' the Dearsley manwon't take me; so me an' Orth'ris '11 see fair play. Jock,I tell you, 'twill be big fightin'—whipped, wid the creamabove the jam. Afther the business 'twill take a goodthree av us—Jock '11 be very hurt—to haul away thatsedan-chair.'

* Palanquin.' This from Ortheris.

'Fwhatever ut is, we must have ut. 'Tis the onlyseUin' piece av property widin reach that we can get socheap. An' fwhat's a fight afther all? He has robbedthe naygur-man, dishonust. We rob him honust for thesake av the whisky he gave me.'

*But wot'll we do with the bloomin' article when we'vegot it? Them palanquins are as big as 'ouses, an'uncommon 'ard to sell, as McCleary said when ye stolethe sentry-box from the Curragh.'

'Wlio's goin' to do t' fightin'?' said Learoyd, andOrtheris subsided. The three returned to barracks with-out a word. Mulvaney's last argument clinched thematter. This palanquin was property, vendible, andt© be attained in the simplest and least embarrassing

fashion. It would eventually become beer. Great wasMulvaney.

Next afternoon a procession of three formed itself anddisappeared into the scrub in the direction of the newrailway line. Learoyd alone was without care, for Mul-vaney dived darkly into the future, and little Ortherisfeared the unknown. What befell at that interview inthe lonely pay-shed by the side of the half-built embank-ment, only a few hundred coolies know, and their tale isa confusing one, running thus—

'We were at work. Three men in red coats came.They saw the Sahib—Dearsley Sahib. They madeoration; and noticeably the small man among the red-coats. Dearsley Sahib also made oration, and usedmany very strong words. Upon this talk they departedtogether to an open space, and there the fat man in thered coat fought with Dearsley Sahib after the custom ofwhite men—with his hands, making no noise, and neverat all pulling Dearsley Sahib's hair. Such of us as werenot afraid beheld these things for just so long a time as aman needs to cook the mid-day meal. The small manin the red coat had possessed himself of Dearsley Sahib'swatch. No, he did not steal that watch. He held it inhis hand, and at certain seasons made outcry, and thetwain ceased their combat, which was like the combat ofyoung bulls in spring. Both men were soon all red, butDearsley Sahib was much more red than the other.Seeing this, and fearing for his life—because we greatlyloved him—some fifty of us made shift to rush upon thered-coats. But a certain man—very black as to the hair,and in no way to be confused with the small man, or thefat man who fought—that man, we affirm, ran upon us,and of us he embraced some ten or fifty in both arms,and b«at our heads together, so that our livers turned to

water, and we ran away. It is not good to interfere inthe fightings of white men. After that Dearsley Sahibfell and did not rise, these men jumped upon his stomachand despoiled him of all his money, and attempted tofire the pay-shed, and departed. Is it true that DearsleySahib makes no complaint of these latter things ha\ingbeen done? We were senseless with fear, and do notat all remember. There was no palanquin near the pa\'7d-shed. What do we know about palanquins? Is it truethat Dearsley Sahib docs not return to this place, onaccount of his sickness, for ten days? This is the faultof those bad men in the red coats, who should be severelypunished; for Dearsley Sahib is both our father andmother, and we love him much. Yet, if Dearsley Sahibdoes not return to this place at all, we will speak thetruth. There was a palanquin, for the up-keep of whichwe were forced to pay nine-tenths of our monthly wage.On such mulctings Dearsley Sahib allowed us to makeobeisance to him before the palanquin. What could wedo? We were poor men. He took a full half of ourwages. WiU the Government repay us those moneys?Those three men in red coats bore the palanquin upontheir shoulders and departed. All the money thatDearsley Sahib had taken from us was in the cushions ofthat palanquin. Therefore they stole it. Thousands ofrupees were there—all our money. It was our bank-box,to fill which we cheerfully contributed to

Dearsley Sahibthree-sevenths of our monthly wage. Why does thewhite man look upon us with the eye of disfavour?Before God, there was a palanquin, and now there is nopalanquin; and if they send the police here to make in-quisition, we can only say that there never has been anypalanquin. Why should a palanquin be near theseworks? We are poor men, ard we know nothing.'

Such is the simplest version of the simplest storyconnected with the descent upon Dearsley. From thelips of the coolies I received it. Dearsley himself was inno condition to say anything, and Mulvaney preserveda massive silence, broken only by the occasional lickingof the lips. He had seen a fight so gorgeous that evenliis power of speech was taken from him. I respectedthat reserve until, three days after the ajffair, I discoveredin a disused stable in my quarters a palanquin of unchas-tened splendour—evidently in past days the Htter of aqueen. The pole whereby it swung between the shouldersof the bearers was rich with the painted papier-macheof Cashmere. The shoulder-pads were of yellow silk.The panels of the litter itself were ablaze with the lovesof all the gods and goddesses of the Hindu Pantheon—lacquer on eedar. The cedar sliding doors were fittedwith hasps of translucent Jaipur enamel and ran ingrooves shod with silver. The cushions were of brocadedDelhi silk, and the curtains which once hid any glimpseof the beauty of the king's palace were stiff with gold.Closer investigation showed that the entire fabric waseverywhere rubbed and discoloured by time and wear;but even thus it was sufi&ciently gorgeous to deservehousing on the threshold of a royal zenana. I found nofault with.it, except that it was in my stable. Then,trying to Hft it by the silver-shod shoulder-pole, I laughed.The road from Dearsley's pay-shed to the cantonmentwas a narrow and uneven one, and, traversed by three veryinexperienced palanquin-bearers, one of whom was sorelybattered about the head, must have been a path of tor-ment. Still I did not quite recognise the right of the threemusketeers to turn me into a 'fence' for stolen property.

'I'm askin' you to warehouse ut,' said Mulvaney whenhe was brought to consider the question. * There's no

steal in ut. Dearsley tould us we cud have ut if wefought. Jock fought—an', oh, sorr, when the throublewas at uts finest an' Jock was bleedin' Hke a stuck pig,an' Httle Orth'ris was shquealin' on one leg chewin' bigbites out av Dearsley's watch, I wud ha' given my placeat the fight to have had you see wan round. He tukJock, as I suspicioned he would, an' Jock was deceptive.

Nine roun's they were even matched, an' at the tenth

About that palanquui now. There's not the leastthrouble in the world, or we wud not ha' brought uthere. You will ondherstand that the Queen—God blessher!—does not reckon for a privit soldier to kape ele-phints an' palanquins an' sich in barricks. Afther wehad dhragged ut down from Dearsley's through thatcruel scrub that near broke Orth'ris's heart, we set ut inthe ravine for a night; an' a thief av a porcupine an' acivet-cat av a jackal roosted in ut, as well we knew in themornin'. I put ut to you, sorr, is an elegint palanquin,fit for the princess, the natural abidin' place av all thevermin m cantonmints? We brought ut to you, afth11erdhark, and put ut in your shtable. Do not let yourconsciense prick. Think av the rejoicin' men in thepay-shed yonder—lookin' at Dearsley wid his headtied up in a towel—an' well knowin' that they can dhrawtheir pay ivry month widout stoppages for rifHes. In-directly, sorr, you have rescued from an onprincipledson av a night-hawk the peasanthry av a numerous vil-lage. An' besides, will I let that sedan-chair rot on ourhands? Not I. 'Tis not every day a piece av purejoolry comes into the market. There's not a king widinthese forty miles'—he waved his hand round the dustyhorizon—'not a king wud not be glad to buy ut. Someday meself, whin I have leisure, I'll take ut up along theroad an' dishpose av ut.'

UFE'S HANDICAP

'How?' said I, for I knew the man was capable ofanything.

'Get mto ut, av coorse, and keep wan eye openthrough the curtains. Whin I see a likely man av thenative persuasion, I will descind blushin' from my canopyand say, "Buy a palanquin, ye black scutt?" I willhave to hire four men to carry me first, though; and that'simpossible till next pay-day.'

Curiously enough, Learoyd, who had fought for theprize, and in the wiiming secured the highest pleasurelife had to offer him, was altogether disposed to under-value it, while Ortheris openly said it would be better tobreak the thing up. Dearsley, he argued, might be amany-sided man, capable, despite his magnificent fightingquahties, of setting in motion the machinery of the civillaw—a thing much abhorred by the soldier. Under anycircumstances their fun had come and passed, the nextpay-day was close at hand, when there would be beer forall. Wherefore longer conserve the painted palanquin?

'A first-class rifle-shot an' a good Httle man av yourinches you are,' said Mulvaney. 'But you niver hada head worth a soft-boiled egg. 'Tis me has to lie awakeav nights schamin' an' plottin' for the three av us.Orth'ris, me son, 'tis no matther av a few gallons av beer—no, nor twenty gallons—but tubs an' vats an' firkinsin that sedan-chair. Who ut was, an' what ut was, an'how ut got there, we do not know; but I know in mybones tliat you an' me an' Jock wid his sprained thumbwill get a fortune thereby. Lave me alone, an' let methink.'

Meantime the palanquin stayed in my stall, the keyof which was in Mulvaney's hands.

Pay-day came, and with it beer. It was not in experi-ence to hope that Muivaney, dried by four weeks'
drought, would avoid excess. Next morning he and thepalanquin had disappeared. He had taken the precau-tion of getting three days' leave 'to see a friend on therailway/ and the colonel, well knowing that the seasonaloutburst was near, and hoping it would spend its forcebeyond the limits of his jurisdiction, cheerfully gave himall he demanded. At this point Mulvaney's history, asrecorded in the mess-room, stopped.

Ortheris carried it not much further. 'No, 'e wasn'tdrunk,' said the little man loyally, 'tht hquor was nomore than feelin' its way round inside of 'im; but 'ewent an' filled that 'ole bloomin' palanquin with bottles'fore 'e went off. 'E's gone an' 'ired six men to carry'im, an' I 'ad to 'elp 'im into 'is nupshal couch, 'cause 'ewouldn't 'ear reason. 'E's gone off in 'is shirt an' trousies,swearin' tremenjus—gone down the road in the palanquin,wavin' 'is legs oiit o' windy.'

'Yes,'said I,'but where?'

'Now you arx me a question. 'E said 'e was goin'to sell tiiat palanquin, but from observations whathappened when I was stufhn' 'im through the door, Ifancy 'e's gone to the new embankment to mock atDearsley. 'Soon as Jock's off duty I'm goin' there tosee if 'e's safe—not Mulvaney, but t'other man. Mysaints, but I pity 'im as 'elps Terence out o' the palanquinwhen 'e's once fair drunk!'

'He'll come back without harm,' I said.

' 'Corse 'e will. On'y question is, what '11 'e be doin'on the road? Killing Dearsley, like as not. 'E shouldn't'a gone without Jock or me.'

Reinforced by Learoyd, Ortheris sought the foremanof the coolie-gang. Dearsley's head was still embellishedwith towels. Mulvaney, drunk or sober, would havestruck no man in that condition, and Dearsley indig-
nantly denied that he would have taken advantage of theintoxicated brave.

'I had my pick o' you two/ he explained to Learoyd,'and you got my palanquin—not before I'd made myprofit on it. Why'd I do harm when everything's settled?Your man did come here—drunk as Davy's sow on afrosty night—came a-purpose to mock me—stuck hishead out of the door an' called me a crucified hodman.I made him drunker, an' sent him along. But I nevertouched him.'

To these things, Learoyd, slow to perceive the evi-dences of sincerity, answered only,' If owt comes to Mul-vaaney 'long o' you, I'll gripple you, clouts or no cloutson your ugly head,an'I'll draw t' throat twistyways, man.See there now.'

The embassy removed itself, and Dearsley, the bat-tered, laughed alone over his supper that evening.

Three days passed—a fourth and a fifth. The weekdrew to a close and Mulvaney did not return. He, hisroyal palanquin, and his six attendants, had vanishedinto air. A very large and very tipsy soldier, his feetsticking out of the fitter of a reigning princess, is not athing to travel along the ways without comment. Yetno man of aU the country round had seen any such won-der. He was, and he was not; and Learoyd suggestedthe immediate smashment of Dearsley as a sacrifice to hisghost. Ortheris insisted that all was well, and in thelight of past experience his hopes seemed reasonable.

'When Mulvaney goes up the road,' said he, "e'slike to go a very long ways up, specially when 'e's so bluedrunk as 'e is now. But what gits me is 'is not bein"eard of pulfin' wool off the niggers somewheres about.That don't look good. The drink must ha' died out in'im by this, unless 'e's broke a bank, an' then—Why

don't 'e come back? 'E didn't ought to ha' gone offwithout us.'

Even Ortheris's heart sank at the end of the seventhday, for half the regiment were out scouring the country-side, and Learoyd had been forced to fight two men whohinted openly that Mulvaney had deserted. To do himjustice, the colonel laughed at the notion, even when itwas put forward by his much-trusted adjutant.

'Mulvaney would as soon think of deserting as youwould,' said he. 'No; he's either fallen into a mischiefamong the villagers—and yet that isn't likely, for he'dblarney himself out of the Pit; or else he is engaged onurgent private affairs—some stupendous devilment thatwe shall hear of at mess after it has been the round ofthe barrack-rooms. The worst of it is that I shall haveto give him twenty-eight days' confinement at least forbeing absent without leave, just when I most want him tolick the new batch of recruits into shape. I never knewa man who could put a polish on young soldiers asquickly as Mulvaney can. How does he do it?'

'With blarney and the buckle-end of a belt, sir,' saidthe adjutant. 'He is worth a couple of non-commis-sioned officers when we are dealing with an Irish draft,and the London lads seem to adore him. The worst ofit is that if he goes to the cells the other two are neitherto hold nor to bind till he comes out again. I believeOrtheris preaches mutiny on those occasions, and I knowthat the mere presence of Learoyd mourning for Mul-vaney kills all the cheerfulness of his room. The ser-geants tell me that he allows no man to laugh when hefeels unhappy. They are a queer gang.'

'For all that, I wish we had a few more of them. Ilike a well-conducted regiment, but these pasty-faced,shifty-eyed, mealy-mouthed young slouchers from the

depot worry me sometimes with their offensive virtue.They don't seem to have backbone enough to do any-thing but play cards and prowl round the marriedquarters. I beheve I'd forgive that old villain onthe spot if he turned up with any sort of explanationthat I could in decency accept.'

'Not hkely to be much difficulty about that, sir/said the adjutant. 'Mulvaney's explanations are onlyone degree less wonderful than his performances. Theysay that when he was in the Black Tyrone, before hecame to us, he was discovered on the banks of the Liffeytrying to sell his colonel's charger to a Donegal dealeras a perfect lady's hack. Shackbolt commanded theTyrone then.'

'Shackbolt must have had apoplexy at the thoughtof his ramping war-horses answering to that description.He used to buy unbacked devils, and tame them onsome pet theory of starvation. What did Mulvaneysay?'

'That he was a member of the Society for the Pre-vention of Cruelty to Animals, anxious to "sell the poorbaste where he would get something to fill out his dim-ples." Shackbolt laughed, but I fancy that was whyMulvaney exchanged to ours.'

'I w^sh he were back,' said the colonel; 'for I likehim and beHeve he likes me.'

That evening, to cheer our souls, Learoyd, Ortheris,and I went into the waste to smoke out a porcupine.All the dogs attended, but even their clamour—andthey began to discuss the shortcomings of porcupinesbefore they left cantonments—could not take us outof ourselves. A large, low moon turned the tops ofthe plume-grass to silver, and the stunted camelthombushes and sour tamarisks into the likenesses of trooping

devils. The smell of the sun had not left the earth,and little aimless winds blowing across the rose-gardensto the southward brought the scent of dried roses andwater. Our fire once started, and the dogs craftilydisposed to wait the dash of the porcupine, we climbedto the top of a rain-scarred hillock of earth, and lookedacross the scrub seamed with cattle paths, white withthe long grass, and dotted with spots of level pond-bottom, where the snipe would gather in winter.

'This,' said Ortheris, with a sigh, as he took in theunkempt desolation of it all, 'this is sanguinary. Thisis unusually sanguinary. Sort o' mad country. Like agrate when the fire's put out by the sun.' He shadedhis eyes against the moonhght. 'An' there's a loonydancin' in the middle of it all. Quite right. I'd dancetoo if I wasn't so downheart.'

There pranced a Portent in the face of the moon—ahuge and ragged spirit of the waste, that flapped itswings from afar. It had risen out of the earth; it wascoming towards us, and its outline was never twice thesame. The toga, table-cloth, or dressing-gown, what-ever the creature wore, took a hundred shapes. Once itstopped on a neighbouring mound and flung all its legsand arms to the winds.

'My, but that scarecrow 'as got 'em bad!'said Ortheris.'Seems like if 'e comes any furder we'll 'ave to argifywith 'im.'

Learoyd raised liimself from the dirt as a bull clearshis flanks of the wallow. And as a bull bellows, so he,after a short minute at gaze, gave tongue to the stars. ,

'MulvaaneyI Mulv.aaney! A-hoo!'

Oh then it was that we yelled, and the figure dippedinto the hollow, till, with a crash of rending grass, theiost one strode up to the light of the fire and disappeared to the waist in a wave of joyous dogs! Then Learoydand Ortheris gave greeting, bass and falsetto together,both swallowing a lump in the throat.

'You damned fool!' said they, and severally poundedhim with their fists.

'Go easy!' he answered; wrapping a huge arm roundeach. 'I would have you to know that I am a god, to betreated as such—tho', by my faith, I fancy I've got to goto the guard-room just like a privit soldier.'

The latter part of the sentence destroyed the sus-picions raised by the former. Any one would havebeen justified in regarding Mulvaney as mad. He washatless and shoeless, and his shirt and trousers weredropping off him. But he wore one wondrous garment—a gigantic cloak that fell from collar-bone to heel—ofpale pink silk, wTought all over in cunningest needleworkof hands long since dead, with the loves of the Hindugods. The monstrous figures leaped in and out of thelight of the fire as he settled the folds round him.

Ortheris handled the stuff respectfully for a moment while I was trying to remember w^here I had seen it before. Then he screamed, 'What ^ave you done with the palanquin? You're wearin' the linin'.'

'I am,' said the Irishman, 'an' by the same token the 'broidery is scrapin' my hide off. I've lived in this sumpshus counterpane for four days. Me son, I begin to ondherstand why the naygur is no use. Widout me boots, an' me trousies like an openwork stocking on a gyurl's leg at a dance, I begin to feel like a naygur-man—all fearful an' timoreous. Give me a pipe an' I'll tell on.'

He lit a pipe, resumed his grip of his two friends, and rocked to and fro in a gale of laughter.

'^ulvaney,' said Ortheris sternly, ' 'tain't no time for

kughin'. You've given Jock an' me more trouble than you're worth. You 'ave been absent without leave an' you'll go into cells for that; an' you 'ave come back disgustin'ly dressed an' most improper in the linin' o' that bloomm' palanquin. Instid of which you laugh. An' we thought you was dead all the time.'

'Bhoys,' said the culprit, still shaking gently, 'wliin I've done my tale you may cry if you like, an' littleOrth'ris here can thrample my inside out. Ha' done an' listen. My performinces have been stupenjus: my luck has been the blessed luck av the British Army—an' there's no betther than that. I went out dhrunk an' dhrinkin' in the palanquin, and I have come back a pink god. Did any of you go to Dearslcy afther my time was up? He was at the bottom of ut all.'

'Ah said so,' murmured Learoyd. 'To-morrow ah'Hsmash t' face in upon his heead.'

'Ye will not. Dearsley's a jool av a man. Afther Ortheris had put me into the palanquin an' the six bearer-men were gruntin' down the road, I tuk thought to mock Dearsley for that fight. So I tould thim, "Goto the embankmint," and there, bein' most amazin' full, I shtuck my head out av the concern an' passed compli-ments wid Dearsley. I must ha' miscalled him out-rageous, for whin I am that way the power av the tongue comes on me. I can bare remimber tellin' him that his mouth opened endways like the mouth av a skate, which was thrue afther Learoyd had handled ut; an' I clear remimber his takin' no manner nor matter av offence, but givin' me a big dhrink of beer. 'Twas the beer did the thrick, for I crawled back into the palanquin, step-pin' on me right ear wid me left foot, an' thin I slept hke the dead. Wanst I half-roused, an' begad the noise in my head was tremenjus—roarin' and rattlin' an' poundin'

such as was quite new to me. "Mother av Mercy," thinks I, "phwat a concertina I will have on my shoulders whin I wake!" An' wici that I curls mysilf up to sleep before ut sliould get hould on me. Bhoys, that noise was not dhrink, 'twas the rattle av a thrain!'

There followed an impressive pause.

'Yes, he had put me on a thrain—put me, palanquin an' all, an' six black assassins av his own coohes that was in his nefarious confidence, on the flat av a ballast-thruck, and we were rowlin' an' bowhn' along to Benares. Glory be that I did not wake up thin an' introjuce mysilf to the coolies. As I was sayin', I slept for the betther part av a day an' a night. But remimber you, that that man Dearsley had packed me off on wan av his material-thrains to Benares, all for to make me overstay my leave an' get me into the cells.'

The explanation v/as an eminently rational one Benares lay at least ten hours by rail from the canton-ments, and nothing in the world could have saved Mulvaney from arrest as a deserter had he appeared there in the apparel of has orgies. Dearsley had not for-gotten to take revenge. Learoyd, drawing back a little, began to place soft blows over selected portions of Mul-vaney's body. His thoughts were away on the embank-ment, and they meditated evil for Dearsley. Mulvaney continued—

'Whin I was full awake the palanquin was set down in a street, I suspicioned, for I cud hear people passin' an'talkin'. But I knev/ well I was far from home. Thereis a queer smell upon our cantonments—a smell av driedearth and brick-kilns wid whiffs av cavalry stable-litter. This place smelt marigold flowers an' bad water,an' wanst somethin' alive came an' blew heavy mth hismuzzle at the chink av t^e shutter. "It's in a village

I am," thinks I to mysilf, "an' the parochial buffalo Isinvestigatin' the palanquin." But anyways I had nodesire to move. Only lie still whin you're in foreignparts an' the standin' luck av the British Army willcarry ye through. That is an epigram. I made ut.

'Thin a lot av whishperin' divils surrounded thepalanquin. "Take ut up," sez wan man. "But who'llpay us?" sez another. "The Maharanee's minister, avcoorse," sez the man. "Oho!" sez I to mysilf, "I'm aquane in me own right, wid a minister to pay me ex-penses. I'll be an emperor if I he still long enough; butthis is no village I've found." I lay quiet, but I gummedme right eye to a crack av the shutters, an' I saw thatthe whole street was crammed wid palanquins an' horses,an' a sprinklin' av naked priests all yellow powder an'tigers' tails. But I may tell you, Orth'ris, an' you,Learoyd, that av all the palanquins ours was the mostimperial an' magnificent. Now a palanquin means anative lady all the world over, except whin a soldier avthe Quane happens to be takin' a ride. "Women an'priests!" sez I. "Your father's son is in the right pewthis time, Terence. There will be proceedin's." Sixblack divils in pink mushn tuk up the palanquin, an' oh!but the rowlin' an' the rockin' made me sick. Thin wegot fair jammed among the palanquins—not more thanfifty av them—an' we grated an' bumped like Queens-town potato-smacks in a runnin' tide. I cud hear thewomen gigglin' and squirkin' in their palanquins, butmine was the royal equipage. They made way for ut,an', begad, the pink muslin men o' mine were howlin',"Room for the Maharanee av Gokral-Seetarun." Doyou know aught av the lady, sorr?'

'Yes,' said I. 'She is a very estimable old queenof the Central Indian States, and they say she is fat.

How on earth could she go to Benares without all the
city knowing her palanquin?'

* 'Twas the eternal foolishness av the naygur-man.They saw the palanquin l3dng loneful an' forlornsome,an' the beauty av ut, after Dearsley's men had dhroppedut and gone away, an' they gave ut the best name thatoccurred to thim. Quite right too. For aught we knowthe ould lady was thravellin' incog—like me. I'm gladto hear she's fat. I was no Kght weight mysilf, an' mymen were mortial anxious to dhrop me under a great bigarchway promiscuously ornamented wid the most im-proper car\'in's an' cuttin's I iver saw. Begad! theymade me blush—like a—like a Maharanee.'

'The temple of Prithi-Devi,' I murmured, remember-ing the monstrous horrors of that sculptured archway atBenares.

'Pretty Devilskins, savin' your presence, sorr! Therewas nothin' pretty about ut, except me. 'Twas all halfdhark, an' whin the coolies left they shut a big blackgate behind av us, an' half a company av fat yellowpriests began puUy-haulin' the palanquins into a dharkerplace yet—a big stone hall full av pillars, an' gods, an'incense, an' all manner av similar thruck. The gate dis-concerted me, for I perceived I wud have to go forwardto get out, my retreat bein' cut off. By the same tokena good priest makes a bad palanquin-coolie. Begad!they nearly turned me inside out draggin' the palanquinto the temple. Now the disposishin av the forces insidewas this way. The Maharanee av Gokral-Seetarun—that was me—lay by the favour av Providence on thefar left flank behind the dhark av a pillar carved withelephints' heads. The remainder av the palanquins wasin a big half circle facing in to the biggest, fattest, an'most amazin' she-god that iver I dreamed av. Her head
ran up into the black above us, an' her feet stuck outin the light av a little fire av melted

butter that a priest was feedin' out av a butter-dish. Thin a man began tosing an' play on somethin' back in the dhark, an' 'twas a queer song. Ut made my hair Hft on the back av my neck. Thin the doors av all the palanquins sKd back, an' the women bundled out. I saw what I'll niver see again. 'Twas more glorious than thransformations at a pantomime, for they was in pink an' blue an' silver an' red an' grass green, wid di'monds an' im'ralds an' great red rubies all over thim. But that was the least part av the glory. O bhoys, they were more lovely than the like av any loveliness in hiven; ay, their little bare feet were betther than the white hands av a lord's lady, an' their mouths were like puckered roses, an' their eyes were bigger an' dharker than the eyes av any livin' women I've seen. Ye may laugh, but I'm speakin' truth. I niver saw the like, an' niver I will again.'

* Seeing that in all probability you were watching the wives and daughters of most of the kings of India, the chances are that you won't,' I said, for it was dawning on me that Mulvaney had stumbled upon a big Queens' Praying at Benares.

'I niver will,' he said mournfully. 'That sight doesn't come twist to any man. It made me ashamed to watch. A fat priest knocked at my door. I didn't think he'd have the insolince to disturb the Maharanee av Gokral-Seetarun, so I lay still. "The old cow's asleep," sez he to another. "Let her be," sez that. "'Twill be long before she has a calf!" I might ha^known before he spoke that all a woman prays for in Injia—an' for matter o' that in England too—is childher. That made me more sorry I'd come, me bein', as you weHknow, a childless man.'

He was silent for a moment, thinking of his little son, dead many years ago.

'They prayed, an' the butter-iires blazed up an' the incense turned everything blue, an' between that an' the fires the women looked as tho' they were all ablaze an' twinklin'. They took hold av the she-god's knees, they cried out an' they threw themselves about, an' that world-without-end-amen music was dhrivin' thim mad. Mother av Hiven! how they cried, an' the ould she-god grinnin' above thim all so scornful! The dhrink was dyin' out in me fast, an' I was thinkin' harder than the thoughts wud go through my head—thinkin' how to get out, an' all manner of nonsense as well. The women were rockin' in rows, their di'mond belts dickin', an' the tears runnin' out betune their hands, an' the lights were goin' lower an' dharker. Thin there was a blaze Hkelightnin' from the roof, an' that showed me the inside av the palanquin, an' at the end where my foot was, stood the Hvin' spit an' image o' mysilf v/orked on the linin'. This man here, ut was.'

He hunted in the folds of his pink cloak, ran a hand under one, and thrust into the firelight a foot-long em-broidered presentment of the great god Krishna, play-ing on a flute. The heavy jowl, the staring eye, and the blue-black moustache of the god made up a far-olf resemblance to Mulvaney.

'The blaze was gone in a wink, but the whole schame came to me thin. I believe I was mad too. I slid the off-shutter open an' rowled out into the dhark behind the elephint-head pillar, tucked up my trousies to my knees, sKpped oft* my boots an' tuk a general hould av all the pink Hnin' av the palanquin. Glory be, ut ripped out Hke a woman's dhriss whin you tread on ut at a sergeants' ball, an' a bottle came with ut. I tuk the

bottle an' the next minut I was out av the dhark av the pillar, the pink linin' wrapped round me most grace-ful, the music thunderin' like kettledrums, an' a could draft blowin' round my bare legs. By this hand that did ut, I was Khrislma tootHn' on the flute—the god that the rig'mental chaplain talks about. A sweet sight I must ha' looked. I knew my eyes were big, and my face was wax-white, an' at the worst I must ha' looked like a ghost. But they took me for the li\in' god. The music stopped, and the women were dead dumb an' I crooked my legs like a shepherd on a china basin, an' I did the ghost-waggle with my feet as I had done ut at the rig'mental theatre many times, an' I slid acrost the width av that temple in front av the she-god tootlin' on the beer bottle.'

*Wot did you toot?' demanded Ortheris the prac-tical.

' Me? Oh!' Mulvaney sprang up, suiting the action tothe word, and sHding gravely in front of us, a dilapidatedbut imposing deity in the half Ught. ' I sang—

'Only say

You'll be Mrs. Brallaghan.

Don't say nay,Charmin' Judy Callaghan.

I didn't know me own voice when I sang. An' oh!'twas pitiful to see the women. The darlin's were downon their faces. Whin I passed the last wan I cud seeher poor little fingers workin' one in another as if shewanted to touch my feet. So I dhrew the tail av tLispink overcoat over her head for the greater honour, an'I sHd into the dhark on the other side av the temple,and fetched up in the arms av a big fat priest. All iwanted was to ge,t away clear. So I tuk him by his

greasy throat an' shut the speech out av him. "Out!"sez I. "Which way, ye fat heathen?"— "Oh!" sez he."Man," sez I. "White man, soldier man, commonsoldier man. Where in the name av confusion is theback door?" The women in the temple were still ontheir faces, an' a young priest was holdin' out his armsabove their heads.

'"This way," sez my fat friend, duckin' behind a bigbull-god an' divin' into a passage. Thin I remimberedthat I must ha' made the miraculous reputation av thattem_ple for the next fifty years. "Not so fast," I sez, an'I held out both my hands wid a wink. That ould thiefsmiled like a father. I tuk him by the back av theneck in case he should be wishful to put a knife intome unbeknownst, an' I ran him up an' down the passagetwice to collect his sensibilities! "Be quiet," sez he, inEnglish. "Now you talk sense," I sez. "Fwhat '11 yougive me for the use av that most iligant palanquin Ihave no time to take away?"—"Don't tell," sez he."Is ut like?" sez I. "But ye might give me my rail-way fare. I'm far from my home an' I've done you aservice." Bhoys, 'tis a good thing to be a priest. Theould man niver throubled himself to dhraw from a bank.As I will prove to you subsequint, he philandered allround the slack av his clothes an' began dribblin' ten-rupee notes, old gold mohurs, and rupees into my handtill I could hould no more.'

'You lie!' said Ortheris. 'You're mad or sunstrook.A native don't give coin unless you cut it out o' 'im.'Tain't nature.'

'Then my lie an' my sunstroke is concealed underthat lump av sod yonder,' retorted Mulvaney unruffled,nodding across the scrub. 'An' there's a dale more innature than your squidgy little legs have iver tak^i yc«\

THE INCARNATION OF KRISHNA MULVANEY 115

to, Orth'ris, me son. Four hundred an' thirty-four rupeesby my reckonin', an^ a big fat gold necklace that I tookfrom him as a remimbrancer, was our share in thatbusiness.'

^An' 'e give it you for love?' said Ortheris.

*We were alone in that passage. Maybe I was atrifle too pressin', but considher fwhat I had done for thegood av the temple and the iverlastin' joy av thosewomen. 'Twas cheap at the price. I wud ha' takenmore if I cud ha' found ut. I turned the ould man up-side down at the last, but he was milked dhry. Thin heopened a door in another passage an' I found mysilf upto my knees in Benares river-water, an' bad smellin' utis. More by token I had come out on the river-lineclose to the burnin' ghat and contagious to a cracklin'corpse. This was in the heart av the night, for I hadbeen four hours in the temple. There was a crowd avboats tied up, so I tuk wan an' wint across the river.Thin I came home acrost country, lyin' up by day.'

*How on earth did you manage?' I said.

^How did Sir Frederick Roberts get from Cabul toCandahar? He marched an' he niver tould how near hewas to breakin' down. That's why he is fwhat he is.An' now—' Mulvaney yawned portentously. *Now Iwill go an' give myself up for absince widout leave. It'seight an' twenty days an' the rough end of the colonel'stongue in orderly room, any way you look at ut.

But'tis cheap at the price.'

*Mulvaney,' said I softly. *If there happens to beany sort of excuse that the colonel can in any wayaccept, I have a notion that you'll get nothing more thanthe dressing-gown. The new recruits are in, and '

'Not a word more, sorr. Is ut excuses the old manwants? 'Tis not my way, but he shall have them. I'll

tell him I was engaged in financial operations connectedwid a church,' and he flapped his way to cantonments andthe cells, singing lustily—

' So they sent a corp'ril's file,And they put me in the gyard-roomFor conduck unbecomin' of a soldier.'

And when he was lost in the midst of the moonlight wecould hear the refrain—

Bang upon the big drum, bash upon the cymbals,

As we go marchin' along, boys, oh!

For although in this campaign

There's no whisky nor champagne,

We'll keep our spirits goin' with a song, boys!'

Therewith he surrendered himself to the joyful andalmost weeping guard, and was made much of by hisfellows. But to the colonel he said that he had beensmitten with sunstroke and had lain insensible on avillager's cot for untold hours; and between laughterand goodwill the affair was smoothed over, so that hecould, next day, teach the new recruits how to 'FearGod, Honour the Queen, Shoot Straight, and KeepClean.'

What did the colonel's lady thmk?

Nobody never knew.Somebody asked the sergeant's wife

An' she told 'em true.When you git to a man in the case

They're like a row o' pins,For the colonel's lady an' Judy O'Grady

Arc sisters under their skins.

Barrack-Room Ball^nd.

All day I had followed at the heels of a pursuing annyengaged on one of the finest battles that ever camp ofexercise beheld. Thirty thousand troops had by thewisdom of the Government of India been turned looseover a few thousand square miles of country to practisein peace what they would never attempt in war. Con-sequently cavalry charged unshaken infantry at the trot.Infantry captured artillery by frontal attacks deKveredin line of quarter columns, and mounted infantry skir-mished up to the wheels of an armoured train whichcarried nothing more deadly than a twenty-five pounderArmstrong, two Nordenfeldts, and a few score/volunteersall cased in three-eighths-inch boiler-plate. Yet it wasa very lifelike camp. Operations did not cease at sun-down; nobody knew the country and nobody sparedman or horse. There was unending cavalry scoutingand almost unending forced work over broken ground.The Army of the South had finally pierced the centre ofthe Army of the North, and was pouring through the gap

117

hot-foot to capture a city of strategic importance. Itsfront extended fanwise, the sticks being represented byregiments strung out along the line of route backwards tothe divisional transport columns and all the lumber thattrails behind an army on the move. On its right thebroken left of the Army of the North was flying inmass, chased by the Southern horse and hammered bythe Southern guns till these had been pushed far beyondthe limits of their last support. Then the flying satdown to rest, while the elated commandant of the pur-suing force telegraphed that he held all in check andobservation.

Unluckily he did not observe that three miles to hisright flank a flying column of Northern horse with adetachment of Ghoorkhas and British troops had beenpushed round, as fast as the failing Kght allowed, tocut across the entire rear of the Southern Army, tobreak, as it were, all the ribs of the fan where theyconverged by striking at the transport, reserve ammuni-tion, and artillery suppHes. Their instructions wereto go in, avoiding the few scouts who might not havebeen drawn off by the pursuit, and create sufficientexcitement to impress the Southern Army with thewisdom of guarding their own flank and rear beforethey captured cities. It was a pretty manoeuvre, neatlycarried out.

Speaking for the second division of the SouthernArmy, our first intimation of the attack was at twilight,when the artillery were labouring in deep sand, most ofthe escort were trying to help them out, and the mainbody of the infantry had gone on. A Noah's Ark ofelephants, camels, and the mixed menagerie of an Indiantransport-train bubbled and squealed behind the gunswhen there appeared from nowhere in particular British

infantry to the extent of three companies, who sprang tothe heads of the gun-horses and brought all to a stand-still amid oaths and cheers.

^How's that, umpire?' said the major commandingthe attack, and with one voice the drivers and limbergunners answered 'Hout!' while the colonel of artillerysputtered.

*ALL your scouts are charging our main body,' saidthe major. ' Your flanks are unprotected for two miles.I think we've broken the back of this division. Andlisten,—there go the Ghoorkhas!'

A weak fire broke from the rear-guard more thana mile away, and was answered by cheerful bowlings.The Ghoorkhas, who should have swung clear of thesecond division, had stepped on its tail in the dark,but drawing off hastened to reach the next line of attack,which lay almost parallel to us five or six miles away.

Our column swayed and surged irresolutely,—threebatteries, the divisional ammunition reserve, the baggage,and a section of the hospital and bearer corps. Thecommandant ruefully promised to report himself 'cutup' to the nearest umpire, and commending his cavalryand all other cavalry to the special care of Eblis, toiledon to resume touch with the rest of the division.

* We'll bivouac here to-night,' said the major, 'I havea notion that the Ghoorkhas will get caught. They maywant us to re-form on. Stand easy till the transportgets away.'

A hand caught my beast's bridle and led him out ofthe choking dust; a larger hand deftly canted me out ofthe saddle; and two of the hugest hands in the worldreceived me sliding. Pleasant is the lot of the specialcorrespondent who falls into such hands as those ofPrivates Mulvaney, Ortheris, and Learoyd.

'An' that's all right,' said the Irishman calmly. 'Wethought we'd find you somewheres here by. Is thereanything av yours in the transport? Orth'ris '11 fetch utout'

Ortheris did 'fetch ut out,' from under the trunk of anelephant, in the shape of a servant and an animal bothladen with medical comforts. The little man's eyessparkled.

'If the brutil an' Hcentious soldiery av these partsgets sight av the thruck,' said Mulvaney, making prac-tised investigations, 'they'll loot ev'rything. They'rebein' fed on iron-filin's an' dog-biscuit these days, butglory's no compensation for a belly-ache. Praise be,we're here to protect you, sorr. Beer, sausage, bread(soft an' that's a cur'osity), soup in a tin, whisky by thesmell av ut, an' fowls! Mother av Moses, but ye takethe field like a confectioner! 'Tis scand'lus.'

 Ere's a officer,' said Ortheris significantly. 'Whenthe sergent's done lushin' the privit may clean the pot.'

I bundled several things into Mulvaney's haversackbefore the major's hand fell on my shoulder and he saidtenderly, 'Requisitioned for the Queen's service. Wolse-ley was quite wrong about special correspondents: theyare the soldier's best friends. Come and take pot-luckwith us to-night.'

And so it happened amid laughter and shoutings thatmy well-considered commissariat melted away to reap-pear later at the mess-table, which was a waterproofsheet spread on the ground. The flying column hadtaken three days' rations with it, and there be few thingsnastier than government rations—especially when govern-ment is experimenting with German toys. Erbsenwurst,tinned beef of surpassing tinniness, compressed vegetables,ana meat-biscuits may be nourishing, but what Thomas

Atkins needs is bulk in his inside. The major, assistedby his brother officers, purchased goats for the camp andso made the experiment of no effect. Long before thefatigue-party sent to collect brushwood had returned, themen were settled down by their valises, kettles and potshad appeared from the surrounding country and weredangUng over fires as the kid and the compressed vege-table bubbled together; there rose a cheerful clinking ofmess-tins; outrageous demands for *a little more stuffin'with that there Uver-wing;* and gust on gust of chaff aspointed as a bayonet and as delicate as a gun-butt.

'The boys are in a good temper,' said the major.' They'll be singing presently. Well, a night like this isenough to keep them happy.'

Over our heads burned the wonderful Indian stars,which are not all pricked in on one plane, but, preservingan orderly perspective, draw the eye through the velvetdarkness of the void up to the barred doors of heavenitself. The earth was a gray shadow more unreal thanthe sky. We could hear her breathing Hghtly in thepauses between the howHng of the jackals, the movementof the wind in the tamarisks, and the fitful mutter ofmusketry-fire leagues away to the left. A native womanfrom some unseen hut began to sing, the mail-trainthundered past on its way to Delhi, and a roosting crowcawed drowsily. Then there was a belt-loosening silenceabout the fires, and the even breathing of the crowdedearth took up the story.

The men, full fed, turned to tobacco and song,—theirofficers with them. The subaltern is happy who canwin the approval of the musical critics in his regiment,and is honoured among the more intricate step-dancers.By him, as by him who plays cricket cleverly, ThomasAtkins will stand in time of need, when he will let a

better officer go on alone. The ruined tombs of forgottenMussulman saints heard the ballad of Agra Town, TheBuffalo Battery, Marching to Kabul, The long, long IndianDay, The Place where the Punkah-coolie died, and thatcrashing chorus which announces,

Youth's daring spirit, manhood's fire,
Firm hand and eagle eye,Must he acquire who would aspire
To see the gray boar die.

To-day, of all those jovial thieves who appropriatedmy commissariat and lay and laughed roimd that water-proof sheet, not one remains. They went to campsthat were not of exercise and battles without umpires.Burmah, the Soudan, and the frontier,—fever and fight,—took them in their time.

I drifted across to the men's fires in search of Mul-vaney, whom I found strategically greasing his feet bythe blaze. There is nothing particularly lovely in thesight of a private thus engaged after a long day's march,but when you reflect on the exact proportion of the* might, majesty, dominion, and power' of the BritishEmpire which stands on those feet you take an interest inthe proceedings.

'There's a blister, bad luck to ut, on the heel,' saidMulvaney. 'I can't touch ut. Prick ut out, little man.'

Ortheris took out his house-wife, eased the troublewith a needle, stabbed Mulvaney in the calf with thesame weapon, and was swiftly kicked into the fire.

*I've bruk the best av my toes over you, ye grinnin'child av disruption,' said Mulvaney, sitting cross-leggedand nursing his feet; then seeing me, 'Oh, ut's you,son! Be welkim, an' take that maraudin' scutt's place.Jock, hold him down on the cindhers for a bit.'

But Ortheris escaped and went elsewhere, as I tookpossession of the hollow he had scraped for himself andlined with his greatcoat. Learoyd on the other side ofthe fire grinned affably and in a minute fell fast asleep.

'There's the height av politeness for you/ said Mul-vaney, Ugh ting his pipe with a flaming branch. 'ButJock's eaten half a box av your sardines at wan gulp,an' I think the tin too. What's the best wid you, sorr,an' how did you happen to be on the losin' side this daywhin we captured you?'

'The Army of the South is winning all along theline,' I said.

'Then that Ime's the hangman's rope, savin' yourpresence. You'll learn to-morrow how we rethreated todhraw thim on before we made thim trouble, an' that'swhat a woman does. By the same tokin, we'll beattacked before the dawnin' an' ut would be betther notto slip your boots. How do I know that? By thelight av pure reason. Here are three companies av usever so far inside av the enemy's flank an' a crowd avroarin', tarin', squealin' cavalry gone on just to turn outthe whole hornet's nest av them. Av course the enemywill pursue, by brigades like as not, an' thin we'll haveto run for ut. Mark my words. I am av the opinionav Polonius whin he said, "Don't fight wid ivry scuttfor the pure joy av fightin', but if you do, knock thenose av him first an' frequint." We ought to ha' goneon an' helped the Ghoorkhas.'

'But what do you know about Polonius?' I demanded.This was a new side of Mulvaney's character.

'AH that Shakespeare iver wrote an' a dale more thatthe gallery shouted,' said the man of war, carefully lacinghis boots. 'Did I not tell you av Silver's theatre inDublin, whin I was younger than I am now an' a patron

av the drama? Ould Silver wud never pay actor-man orwoman their just dues, an' by consequince his comp'nies^as collapsible at the last minut. Thin the bhoys wuddamour to take a part, an' oft as not ould Silver madethem pay for the fun. Faith, I've seen Hamlut playedwid a new black eye an' the queen as full as a cornu-copia. I remimber wanst Hogin that 'Ksted in the BlackTyrone an' was shot in South Africa, he sejuced ouldSilver into givin' him Hamlut's part instid av me thathad a fine fancy for rhetoric in those days. Av courseI wint into the gallery an' began to fill the pit wid otherpeople's hats, an' I passed the time av day to Hoginwalkin' through Denmark like a hamstrung mule wid apall on his back. ^"Hamlut," sez I, "there's a hole inyour heel. Pull up your shtockin's, Hamlut," sez I."Hamlut, Hamlut, for the love av decincy dhrop thatskull an' pull up your shtockin's." The whole housebegun to tell him that. He stopped his soliloquishmsmid-between. "My shtockin's may be comin' down orthey may not," sez he, screwin' his eye into the gallery,for well he knew who I was. "But afther this per-formince is over me an' the Ghost '11 trample the tripesout av you, Terence, wid your ass's bray!" An' that'show I come to know about Hamlut. Eyah! Thosedays, those days! Did you iver have onendin' devilmintan' nothin' to pay for it in your life, sorr?'

'Never, without having to pay,' I said.

'That's thrue! 'Tis mane whin you considher on ut;but ut's the same wid horse or fut. A headache if youdhrink, an' a belly-ache if you eat too much, an' a heart-ache to kape all down. Faith, the beast only gets thecolic, an' he's the lucky man.'

He dropped his head and stared into the fire, finger-ing his moustache the while. From the far side of

the bivouac the voice of Corbet-Nolan, senior subalternof B company, uplifted itself in an ancient and muchappreciated song of sentiment, the men moaning me-lodiously behind him.

The north wind blew coldly, she drooped from that hour,My own little Katlileen, my sweet little Kathleen,Kathleen, my Kathleen, Kathleen O'Moore!

With forty-five O's in the last word: even at thatdistance you might have cut the soft South Irish accentwith a shovel.

'For all we take we must pay, but the price is cruelhigh,' murmured Mulvaney when the chorus hadceased.

'What's the trouble?' I said gently, for I knew thathe was a man of an inextinguishable sorrow.

'Hear now,' said he. 'Ye know what I am now. 1know what I mint to be at the beginnin' av my service.I've tould you time an' again, an' what I have not DinahShadd has. An' what am I ? Oh, Mary Mother avHiven, an ould dhrunken, untrustable baste av a privitthat l:a5 :een the reg'ment change out from colonel todrumme:-boy, n©t wanst or twice, but scores av times!Ay, scores! An' me not so near gettin' promotion asin the first! An' me livin' on an' kapin' clear av clink,not by my own good conduck, but the kindness av someorf'cer-bhoy young enough to be son to me! Do I notknow ut? Can I not tell whin I'm passed over atp'rade, tho' I'm rockin' full av liquor an' ready to fall allin wan piece, such as even a suckin' child might see,bekaze, "Oh, 'tis only ould Mulvaney!" An' whin I'mlet off in ord'ly-room through some thrick of the tonguean' a ready answer an' the ould man's mercy, is ut smilin'I feel whin I fall away an'go back to Dinah Shadd, thryin'

to carry ut all off as a joke? Not I! Tis hell to me,dumb hell through ut all; an' next time whin the fitcomes I will be as bad again. Good cause the reg'menthas to know me for the best soldier in ut. Better causehave I to know mesilf for the worst man. I'm only fit totache the new drafts what I'll niver learn mesilf; an'I am sure, as tho' I heard ut, that the minut wan avthese pink-eyed recruities gets away from my "Mind yenow," an' "Listen to tliis, Jim, bhoy,"—sure I am thatthe sergint houlds me up to him for a warnin'. So Itache, as they say at musketry-instruction, by directand ricochet fire. Lord be good to me, for I have studsome throuble!'

'Lie down and go to sleep,' said I, not being able tocomfort or advise. 'You're the best man in the regi-ment, and, next to Ortheris, the biggest fool. Lie downand wait till we're attacked. What force will they turnout? Guns, think you?'

'Try that wid your lorrds an' ladies, twistin' an' turnin'the talk, tho' you mint ut well. Ye cud say nothin' tohelp me, an' yet ye niver knew what cause I had to bewhat I am.'

'Begin at the beginning and go on to the end,' I saidroyally. 'But rake up the fire a bit first.'

I passed Ortheris's bayonet for a poker.

'That shows how little we know what we do,' saidMulvaney, putting it aside. 'Fire takes all the heartout av the steel, an' the next time, may be, that our littleman is fighting for his life his bradawl'11 break, an' soyou'll ha' killed him, manin' no more than to kape your-self warm. 'Tis a recruity's thrick that. Pass theclanin'-rod, sorr.'

I snuggled down abased; and after an interval thevoice of Mulvaney began.

'Did I iver tell you how Dinah Shadd came to bewife av mine?'

I dissembled a burning anxiety that I had felt forsome months—ever since Dinah Shadd, the strong, thepatient, and the infinitely tender, had of her own goodlove and free will washed a shirt for me, moving in abarren land where washing was not.

'I can't remember,' I said casually. ^Was it beforeor after you made love to Annie Bragin, and got nosatisfaction?'

The story of Annie Bragin is written in another place.It is one of the many less respectable episodes in Mul-vaney's chequered career.

'Before—before—long before, was that business avAnnie Bragin an' the corp'ril's ghost.

Niver woman wasthe worse for me whin I had married Dinah. There's atime for all things, an' I know how to kape all things inplace—barrin' the dhrink, that kapes me in my place widno hope av comin' to be aught else.'

'Begin at the beginning,' I insisted. 'Mrs. Mulvaneytold me that you married her when you were quarteredin Krab Bokhar barracks.'

'An' the same is a cess-pit,' said Mulvaney piously.' She spoke thrue, did Dinah. 'Twas this way. Talkin'av that, have ye iver fallen in love, sorr?'

I preserved the silence of the damned. Mulvaneycontinued—

'Thin I will assume that ye have not. / did. Inthe days av my youth, as I have more than wanst touldyou, I was a man that filled the eye an' delighted thesowl av women. Niver man was hated as I have bin.Niver man was loved as I—no, not within half a day'smarch av ut! For the first five years av m.y service,whin I was what I wud give my sowl to be now, I tuk

whatever was within my reach an' digested ut—an that'smore than most men can say. Dhrink I tuk, an' ut didme no harm. By the Hollow av Hiven, I cud play widfour women at wanst, an' kape them from lindin' outanythin' about the other three, an' smile like a full-blownmarigold through ut all. Dick Coulhan, av the batterywe'll have down on us to-night, could drive his team nobetther than I mine, an' I hild the worser cattle! An' soI lived, an' so I wa^ happy till afther that business widAnnie Bragin—she that turned me off as cool as a meat-safe, an' taught me where I stud in the mind av an honestwoman. 'Twas no sweet dose to swallow.

'.Afther that I sickened awhile an' tuk thought to myreg'mental work; conceiting mesilf I wud study an' be asergint, an' a major-gineral twinty minutes afther that.But on top av my ambitiousness there was an emptyplace in my sowl, an' me own opinion av mesilf cud notfiU ut. Sez I to mesilf, " Terence, you're a great man an'the best set-up in the reg'mint. Go on an' get promo-tion." Sez mesilf to me, ^'What for?" Sez I to mesUf,"For the glory av ut!" Sez mesilf to me, "Will thatfill these two strong arrums av yours, Terence?" "Goto the devil," sez I to mesilf. " Go to the married Knes,"sez mesilf to me. " 'Tis the same thing," sez I to mesilf."Av you're the same man, ut is," said mesilf to me; an'wid that I considhered on ut a long while. Did youiver feel that way, sorr?'

I snored gently, knowing that if Mulvaney were un-interrupted he would go on. The clamour from thebivouac fires beat up to the stars, as the rival singers ofthe companies were pitted against each other.

'So I felt that way an' a bad time ut was. Wanst,bein' a fool, I wint into the married lines more for thesake av spakin' to our ould colour-sergint Shadd than for any thruck wid women-folk. I was a corp'ril then—rejuced aftherwards, but a corp'ril then. I've got aphotograft av mesilf to prove ut. "You'll take a cupav tay wid us?" sez Shadd. "I will that," I sez, "tho'tay is not my divarsion."

'" 'Twud be better for you if ut were," sez ould MotherShadd, an' she had ought to know, for Shadd, in the indav his service, dhrank bung-full each night.

'Wid that I tuk off my gloves—there was pipe-clay in thim, so that they stud alone—an' pulled upmy chair, lookin' round at the china ornaments an' bits avthings in the Shadds' quarters. They were things thatbelonged to a man, an' no camp-kit, here to-day an' dishi-pated next. "You're comfortable in this place, sergint,"sez I. " 'Tis the wife that did ut, boy," sez he, pointin'the stem av his pipe to ould Mother Shadd, an' shesmacked the top av his bald head apon the compliment.**That manes you want money," sez she.

'An' thin—an' thin whin the kettle was to be filled,Dinah came in—my Dinah—her sleeves rowled up tothe elbow an' her hair in a winkin' glory over her fore-head, the big blue eyes beneath twinklin' like stars on afrosty night, an' the tread av her two feet lighter thanwaste-paper from the colonel's basket in ord'ly-roomwhin ut's emptied. Bein' but a shhp av a girl she wentpink at seein' me, an' I twisted me moustache an' lookedat a picture forninst the wall. Niver show a woman thatye care the snap av a finger for her, an' begad she'll comebleatin' to 3^our boot-heels!'

'I suppose that's why you followed Annie Bragin tilleverybody in the married quarters laughed at you,' saidI, remembering that unhallowed Vv'^ooing and casting offthe disguise of drowsiness.

'I'm layin' down the sdn'ral theory av the attack,' said

Mulvaney, driving his boot into the dying fire. *Iiyou read the Soldier's Pocket Book, which niver any sol-dier reads, you'll see that there are exceptions. WhinDinah was out av the door (an' 'twas as tho' the sun-light had shut too)—'^Mother av Hiven, sergint," sezI, *'but is that your daughter?"—"I've believed thatway these eighteen years," sez ould Shadd, his eyes twinklin'; "but Mrs. Shadd has her own opinion, like iv'rywoman."—" 'Tis wid yours this time, for a mericle," sezMother Shadd. "Thin why in the name av fortune did Iniver see her before?" sez I. "Bekaze youVe beenthrapesin' round wid the married women these threeyears past. She was a bit av a child till last year, an'she shot up wid the spring," sez ould Mother Shadd."I'll thrapese no more," sez I. "D'you mane that?"sez ould Mother Shadd, lookin' at me side-ways like ahen looks at a hawk whin the chickens are runnin' free."Try me, an' tell," sez I. Wid that I pulled on my gloveS;dhrank off the tay, an' went out av the house as stiff asat gin'ral p'rade, for well I knew that Dinah Shadd'3eyes were in the small av my back out av the scullerywindow. Faith! that was the only time I mourned Iwas not a cav'lry-man for the pride av the spurs tojingle.

'I wint out to think, an' I did a powerful lot avthinkin', but ut all came round to that shlip av a girlin the dotted blue dhress, wid the blue eyes an' the spar-kil in them. Thin I kept off canteen, an' I kept to themarried quarthers, or near by, on the chanst av meetin'Dinah. Did I meet her? Oh, my time past, did I not;wid a lump in my throat as big as my valise an' myheart goin' like a farrier's forge on a Saturday morning?Twas "Good day to ye. Miss Dinah," an' "Good dayt'you, corp'ril," for a week or two, and divil a bit further

could I get bekaze av the respect I had to that girl thatI cud ha' broken be tune finger an' thumb.'

Here I giggled as I recalled the gigantic figure ofDinah Shadd when she handed me my shirt.

' Ye may laugh,' grunted Mulvaney. ' But Tm spcakin'the trut', an' 'tis you that are m fault. Dinah was a girlthat wud ha' taken the imperiousness out av the Duchessav Clonmel in those days. Flower hand, foot av shodair, an' the eyes av the livin' m.ornin' she had that ismy wife to-day—ould Dinah, and niver aught else thanDinah Shadd to me.

' 'Twas after three weeks standin' off an' on, an' nivermakin' headway excipt through the eyes, that a littledrummer-boy grinned in me face whin I had admonishedhim wid the buckle av my belt for riotin' all over theplace. "An' I'm not the only wan that doesn't kape tobarricks," sez he. I tuk him by the scruff av his neck,—my heart was hung on a hair-thrigger those days, youwill onderstand—an' "Out wid ut," sez I, "or I'll laveno bone av you unbreakable."—"Speak to Dempsey,"sez he howlin'. "Dempsey which?" sez I, "ye unwashedlimb av Satan."—"Av the Bob-tailed Dhragoons," sezhe. "He's seen her home from her aunt's house in thecivil lines four times this fortnight."—"Child!" sez I,dhroppin' him, "your tongue's stronger than your body.Go to your quarters. I'm sorry I dhressed you down."

'At that I went four ways to wanst huntin' Dempsey.I was mad to think that wid all my airs among womenI shud ha' been chated by a basin-faced fool av a cav'lry-man not fit to trust on a trunk. Presently I found himin our lines—the Bobtails was quartered next us—an' atallowy, topheavy son av a she-mule he was wid his bigbrass spurs an' his plastrons on his epigastrons an' all. But he niver flinched a hair.

"'A word widyou, Dempsey," sez I. "You've walkedwid Dinah Shadd four times this fortnight gone."

'*'What's that to you?" sez he. "I'll walk fortytimes more, an' forty on top av that, ye shovel-futtedclod-breakin' infantry lance-corp'ril."

' Before I cud gyard he had his gloved fist home on mycheek an' down I went full-sprawl. "Will that contentyou?" sez he, blowin' on his knuckles for all the worldlike a Scots Greys orf'cer. "Content!" sez I. "Foryour own sake, man, take off your spurs, peel your jackut,an' onglove. 'Tis the beginnin' av the overture; standup!"

'He stud all he know, but he niver peeled his jackut,an' his shoulders had no fair play. I was fightin' forDinah Shadd an' that cut on my cheek. What hope hadhe forninst me? "Stand up," sez I, time an' again whinhe was beginnin' to quarter the ground an' gyard high an'go large. "This isn't ridin'-school," I sez. "0 man,stand up an' let me get in at ye." But whin I sawhe wud be runnin' about, I grup his shtock in my left an'his waist-belt in my right an' swung him clear to myright front, head undher, he hammerin' my nose till thewind was knocked out av him on the bare ground. "Stand up," sez I, "or I'll kick your head into yourchest!" and I wud ha' done ut too, so ragin' mad I was.

"'My collar-bone's bruk," sez he. "Help m.e backto lines. I'll walk wid her no more." So I helped himback.'

'And was his collar-bone broken?' I asked, for Ifancied that only Learoyd could neatly accomplish thatterrible throw.

' He pitched on his left shoulder-point. Ut was. Nextday the news was in both barricks, an' whin I met DinahShadd wid a cheek on me like all the reg'mintal tailor's samples there was no "Good mornin', corp'ril," or aughtelse. ^'An' what have I done, Miss Shadd," sez I, verybould, plan tin' mesilf forninst her, "that ye should notpass the time of day?"

"'Ye've half-killed rough-rider Dempsey/' sez she,her dear blue eyes fillin' up.

"'May be," sez I. "Was he a friend av yours thatsaw ye home four times in the fortnight?"

"'Yes," sez she, but her mouth was down at thecorners. "An'—an' what's that to you?" she sez.

"'Ask Dempsey," sez I, purtendin' to go away.

"'Did you fight for me then, ye silly man?" she sez,tho' she knew ut all along.

"'Who else?" sez I, an' I tuk wan pace to the front.

"'I wasn't worth ut," sez she, fingerin' in her apron.

"'That's for me to say," sez I. "Shall I say ut?"

"'Yes," sez she in a saint's whisper, an' at that Iexplained mesilf; and she tould me what ivry man thatis a man, an' many that is a woman, hears wanst in hisHfe.

"'But what made ye cry at startin', Dinah, darlin'?"sez I.

"'Your—your bloody cheek," sez she, duckin' herlittle head down on my sash (I was on duty for the day)an' whimperin' like a sorrowful angil.

'Now a man cud take that two ways. I tuk ut aspleased me best an' my first kiss wid ut. Mother avInnocence! but I kissed her on the tip av the nose an'undher the eye; an' a girl that let's a kiss come tumble-ways like that has never been kissed before. Take noteav that, sorr. Thin we wint hand in hand to ould MotherShadd like two little childher, an' she said 'twas no badthing, an' ould Shadd nodded beliind his pipe, an' Dinahran away to her own room. That day I throd on rollin'

clouds. All earth was too small to hould me. Begad, Icud ha* hiked the sun out av the sky for a live coalto my pipe, so magnificent I was. But I tuk recruitiesat squad-drill instid, an' began wid general battalionadvance whin I shud ha' been balance-steppin' them.Eyah! that day! that day!'

A very long pause. 'Well?' said I.

* 'Twas all wrong,' said Mulvaney, with an enormoussigh. *An' I know that ev'ry bit av ut was my ownfoolishness. That night I tuk maybe the half av threepints—not enough to turn the hair of a man in hisnatural senses. But I was more than half drunk wid purejoy, an' that canteen beer was so much whisky to me. Ican't tell how it came about, but bekaze I had no thoughtfor anywan except Dinah, bekaze I hadn't slipped herlittle white arms from my neck five minuts, bekaze thebreath of her kiss was not gone from my mouth, I mustgo through the married lines on my way to quarters an'I must stay tall^in' to a red-headed Mullingar heifer av agirl, Judy Sheehy, that was daughter to Mother Sheehy,the wife of Nick Sheehy, the canteen-sergint—the BlackCurse av Shielygh be on the v/hole brood that are abovegroun' this day!

'"An' what are ye houldin' your head that high for,corp'ril?" sez Judy. "Come in an' thry a cup av tay,'*she sez, standin' in the doorway. Bein' an ontrustablefool, an' thinkin' av anything but tay, I wint.

'"Mother's at canteen," sez Judy, smoothin' the hairav hers that was like red snakes, an' lookin' at me corner-ways out av her green cats' eyes. " Ye will not mind,corp'ril?"

'"I can endure," sez I; ould Mother Sheehy bein' nodivarsion av mine, nor her daughter too. Judy fetchedthe tea things an' put thim on the tablcj leanin' over me

very close to get thim square. I dhrew back, thinkin'av Dinah.

'"Is ut afraid you are av a girl alone?" sez Judy.

'"No," sez I. "Why should I be?"

'"That rests wid the girl," sez Judy, dhrawin' herchair next to mine.

'"Thin there let ut rest," sez I; an' thinkin' I'd beena triiSe onpolite, I sez, "The tay's not quite sweet enoughfor my taste. Put your httle finger in the cup, Judy.'Twill make ut necthar."

'"What's necthar?" sez she.

'"Somethin' very sweet," sez I; an' for the sinful lifeav me I cud not help lookin' at her out av the comer avmy eye, as I was used to look at a woman.

'"Go on wid ye, corp'ril," sez she. "You're a flirrt."

'"On me sowl I'm not," sez I.

'"Then you're a cruel handsome man, an' that'sworse," sez she, heaving big sighs an' lookin' crossways.

'"You know your own mind," sez I.

'" 'Twud be better for me if I did not," she sez.

'"There's a dale to be said on both sides av that," sezI, unthinkin'.

'"Say your own part av ut, then, Terence, darlin',"sez she; "for begad I'm thinkin' I've said too much ortoo Httle for an honest girl," an' wid that she put herarms round my neck an' kissed me.

'"There's no more to be said afther that," sez I, kissin'her back again—Oh the mane scutt that I was, my headringin' wid Dinah Shadd! How does ut come about,sorr, that when a man has put the comether on wan wo-man, he's sure bound to put it on another? 'Tis thesame thing at musketry. Wan day ivry shot goes wideor into the bank, an' the next, lay high lay low, sight orsnap, ye can't get off the bull's-eye for ten shots rumiin'.'

'That only happens to a man who has had a gooddeal of experience. He does it without thinking/ Ireplied.

'Thankin' you for the complimint, sorr, ut may be so.But I'm doubtful whether you mint ut for a complimint.Hear now; I sat there wid Judy on my knee tellin' meall manner av nonsinse an' only sa>in' "yes" an' "no,"when I'd much better ha' kept tongue betune teeth. An'that was not an hour afther I had left Dinah! What Iwas thinkin' av I cannot say. Presintly, quiet as a cat,ould Mother Sheehy came in velvet-dhrunk. She hadher daughter's red hair, but 'twas bald in patches, an' Icud see in her wicked ould face, clear as lightnin', whatJudy wud be twenty years to come. I was for jumpin'up, but Judy niver moved.

"'Terence has promust, mother,' sez she, an' the couWsweat bruk out all over me. Ould Mother Sheehy satdown of a heap an' began playin' wid the cups. "Thinyou're a well-miatched pair," she sez very thick. "Forhe's the biggest rogue that iver spoiled the queen's shoe-leather" an'——

"'I'm off, Judy," sez I. "Ye should not talk nonsinseto your mother. Get her to bed, girl."

"'Nonsinse!" sez the ould woman, prickin' up herears like a cat an' grippin' the table-edge. " 'Twill bethe most nonsinsical nonsinse for you, ye grinnin' badger,if nonsinse 'tis. Git clear, you. I'm goin' to bed."

'I ran out into the dhark, my head in a stew an' rnyheart sick, but I had sinse enough to see that I'd broughtut all on mysilf. "It's this to pass the time av day to apanjandhrum av hell-cats," sez I. "What I've said, an'*what I've not said do not matther. Judy an' her damwill hould me for a promust man, an' Dinah will give methe go, an' I desarve ut. I will ^o an' get dhrunk," sez I,

"an' forget about ut, for 'tis plain I'm not a marrin'man."

' On my way to canteen I ran against Lascelles, colour-sergint that was av E Comp'ny, a hard, hard man, wida torment av a wife. "You've the head av a drownedman on your shoulders," sez he; "an' you're goin' whereyou'll get a worse wan. Come back," sez he. "Let mego," sez I. "I've thrown my luck over the wall widmy own hand!"—"Then that's not the way to get utback again," sez he. "Have out wid your throuble, yefool-bhoy." An' I tould him how the matther was.

'He sucked in his lower lip. "You've been thrapped,"sez he. "Ju Sheehy wud be the betther for a man'sname to hers as soon as can. An' ye thought ye'd putthe comether on her,—that's the natural vanity of thebaste. Terence, you're a big born fool, but you're notbad enough to marry into that comp'ny. If you saidany thin', an' for all your protestations I'm sure ye did or did not, which is worse,—eat ut all—lie like the fatherof all lies, but come out av ut free av Judy. Do I notknow what ut is to marry a woman that was the veryspit an' image av Judy whin she was young? I'mgettin' old an' I've larnt patience, but you, Terence,you'd raise hand on Judy an' Idll her in a year. Nevermind if Dinah gives you the go, you've desarved ut;never mind if the whole reg'mint laughs you all day.Get shut av Judy an' her mother. They can't dhragyou to church, but if they do, they'll dhrag you tohell. Go back to your quarters and lie down," sez he.Thin over his shoulder, "You must ha' done with thim."

'Next day I wint to see Dinah, but there was notucker in me as I walked. I knew the throuble wudcome soon enough widout any handlin' av mine, an'I dreaded ut sore.

'I heard Judy callin* me, but I hild straight on tothe Shadds' quarthers, an' Dinah wud ha' kissed me butI put her back.

'*'WMn all's said, darlin'," sez I, "you can give ut meif ye will, tho' I misdoubt 'twill be so easy to come bythen/'

' I had scarce begun to put the explanation into shapebefore Judy an' her mother came to the door. I thinkthere was a verandah, but I'm forget tin'.

"'Will ye not step in?" sez Dinah, pretty and polite,though the Shadds had no deahn's with the Sheehys.Ould Mother Shadd looked up quick, an' she was the fustto see the throuble; for Dinah was her daughter.

"'I'm pressed for time to-day," sez Judy as bouldas brass; "an' I've only come for Terence,—^my promustman. 'Tis strange to find him here the day afther theday."

'Dinah looked at me as though I had hit her, an' I answered straight.

"'There was some nonsinse last night at the Sheehys' quarthers, an' Judy's carryin' on the joke, darhn'," sez I.

"'At the Sheehys' quarthers?" sez Dinah very slow, an' Judy cut in wid: "He was there from nine till ten, Dinah Shadd, an' the betther half av that time I was sittin' on his knee, Dinah Shadd. Ye may look and ye may look an' ye may look me up an' down, but ye won't look away that Terence is my promust man. Terence, darlin', 'tis time for us to be comin' home."

'Dinah Shadd niver said word to Judy. "Ye left meat half-past eight," she sez to me, "an I niver thought that ye'd leave me for Judy,—promises or no promises. Go back wid her, you that have to be fetched by a girl! I'm done with you," sez she, and she ran into her own

room, her mother foll?win*. So I was alone wid those two women and at liberty to spake my sentiments.

"'Judy Sheehy," sez I, '*if you made a fool av me betune the lights you shall not do ut in the day. I niver promised you words or lines."

"'You He," sez ould Mother Sheehy, "an' may ut choke you where you stand!" She was far gone in dhrink.

' "An' tho' ut choked me where I stud I'd not change," sez I. "Go home, Judy. I take shame for a decent girl like you dhraggin' your mother out bare-headed on this errand. Hear now, and have ut for an answer. I gave my word to Dinah Shadd yesterday, an', more blame to me, I was wid you last night talkin' nonsinse but nothin' more. You've chosen to thry to hould me on ut. I will not be held thereby for anythin' in the world. Is that enough? "

'Judy wint pink all over. "An' I wish you joy av the perjury," sez she, duckin' a curtsey. "You've lost a woman that would ha' wore her hand to the bone for your pleasure; an' 'deed, Terence, ye were not thrapped.. . ." Lascelles must ha' spoken plain to her. "I am such as Dinah is—'deed I am! Ye've lost a fool av a girl that'll niver look at you again, an' ye've lost what he niver had,—your common honesty. If you manage your men as you manage your love-makin', small won-dher they call you the worst corp'ril in the comp'ny. Come away, mother," sez she.

' But divil a fut would the ould woman budge! " D'you hould by that?" sez she, peerin' up under her thick gray eyebrows.

"'Ay, an' wud," sez I, "tho' Dinah give me the go twinty times. I'll have no thruck with you or yours," sez I. " Take your child away, ye shameless woman."

**'An' am I shameless?" sez she, bringin' her hands up above her head. "Thin what are you, ye lyin', schamin', weak-kneed, dhirty-souled son av a sutler? Am / shameless? Who put the open shame on me an' my child that we shud go beggin' through the lines in the broad daylight for the broken word of a man? Double portion of my shame be on you, Terence Mul-vaney, that think yourself so strong! By Mary and the saints, by blood and water an' by ivry sorrow that came into the world since the beginnin', the black blight fall on you and yours, so that you may niver be free from pain for another when ut's not your own! May your heart bleed in your breast drop by drop wid all your friends laughin' at the bleedin'! Strong you think yourself? May your strength be a curse to you to dhrive you into the divil's hands against your own will! Clear-eyed you are? May your eyes see clear ivry step av the dark path you take till the hot cindhers av hell put thim out! May the ragin' dry thirst in my own ould bones go to you that you shall niver pass bottle full nor glass empty. God preserve the light av your onder-standin' to you, my jewel av a bhoy, that ye may niver forget what you mint to be an' do, whin you're wallowin' in the muck! May ye see the betther and follow the worse as long as there's breath in your body; an' may ye die quick in a strange land, watchin' your death before ut takes you, an' onable to stir hand or foot!"

*I heard a scufllSin' in the room behind, and thin Dinah Shadd's hand dhropped into mine like a rose-leaf into a muddy road.

'"The half av that I'll take," sez she, "an' more too ifI can. Go home, ye silly talkin' woman,—go home an'confess."

'"Come away! Come away!" sez Judy, pullin' her

mother by the shawl. " Twas none av Terence^s fault.For the love av Mary stop the talkin'!"

**'An' you!" said ould Mother Sheehy, spinnin' roundforninst Dinah. "Will ye take the half av that man'sload? Stand off from him, Dinah Shadd, before he takesyou down too—you that look to be a quarther-master-sergeant's wife in five years. You look too high, child.You shall wash for the quarther-master-sergeant, whin heplases to give you the job out av charity; but a privit'swife you shall be to the end, an' ivry sorrow of a privit'swife you shall know and niver a joy but wan, that shallgo from you like the running tide from a rock. The painav bearin' you shall know but niver the pleasure avgiving the breast; an' you shall put away a man-childinto the common ground wid niver a priest to say aprayer over him, an' on that man-child ye shall thinkivry day av your life. Think long, Dinah Shadd, foryou'll niver have another tho' you pray till your kneesare bleedin'. The mothers av childher shall mock youbehind your back when you're wringfaig over the wash-tub. You shall know what ut is to help a dhrunkenhusband home an' see him go to the gyard-room. WiDthat plase you, Dinah Shadd, that won't be seen talkin'to my daughter? You shall talk to worse than Judybefore all's over. The sergints' wives shall look down onyou contemptuous, daughter av a sergint, an' you shallcover ut all up wid a smiling face when your heart'sburstin'. Stand off av him, Dinah Shadd, for I've putthe Black Curse of Shielygh upon him an' his own mouthshall make ut good."

' She pitched forward on her head an' began foamin' atthe mouth. Dinah Shadd ran out wid water, an' Judydhragged the ould woman into the verandah till she satup.

*"I'm old an' forlore," she sez, thremblin' an' cryin','and 'tis like I say a dale more than I mane."

'"When you're able to walk,—go," says ould MotherShadd. "This house has no place for the likes av youthat have cursed my daughter."

'"Eyah!" said the ould woman. "Hard wordsbreak no bones, an' Dinah Shadd'll kape the loveav her husband till my bones are green corn. JudydarUn', I misremember what I came here for. Canyou lend us the bottom av a taycup av tay, Mrs. Shadd? "

'But Judy dhragged her off cryin' as tho' her heartwud break. An' Dinah Shadd an' I, in ten minutes wehad forgot ut all.'

'Then why do you remember it now?' said I.

'Is ut lilve I'd forget? Ivry word that wicked ouldwoman spoke fell thrue in my Hfe aftherwards, an' I cudha' stud ut all—stud ut all—excipt when my Httle Shaddwas born. That was on the line av march three monthsafther the regiment was taken with cholera. We werebetune Umballa an' Kalka thin, an' I was on picket.Whin I came off duty the women showed me the child,an' ut turned on uts side an' died as I looked. Weburied hun by the road, an' Father Victor was a day'smarch behind wid the heavy baggage, so the comp'nycaptain read a prayer. An' since dien I've been achildless man, an' all else that ould Mother Sheehy putupon me an' Dinah Shadd. W^at do you think, sorr?'

I thought a good deal, but it seemed better then toreach out for Mulvaney's hand. The demonstrationnearly cost me the use of three fingers. Whatever heknows of his weaknesses, Mulvaney is entirely igno-rant of his strength.

'But what do you think?' he repeated, as I wasstraightening out the crushed fingers.

My reply was drowned in yells and outcries fromthe next fire, where ten men were shouting for 'Orth'ris,"Privit Orth'ris/ 'Mistah Or—ther—ris!' 'Deah boy,'Xap'n Orth'ris/ Tield-Marshal Orth'ris/ 'Stanley, youpen'north o' pop, come 'ere to your own comp'ny!' Andthe cockney, who had been delighting another audiencewith recondite and Rabelaisian yarns, was shot downamong his admirers by the major force.

'You've crumpled my dress-shirt 'orrid,' said he, ^an*I shan't sing no more to this 'ere bloomin' drawin'-room_.'

Learoyd, roused by the confusion, uncoiled himself,crept behind Ortheris, and slung him aloft on his shoul-ders.

'Sing, ye bloomin' hummin' bird!' said he, andOrtheris, beating time on Learoyd's skull, deKveredhimself, in the raucous voice of the Ratcliffe Highway, ofthis song:—

My girl she give me the go onst,
When I was a London lad,An' I went on the drink for a fortnight,
An' then I went to the bad.The Queen she give me a shillin'
To fight for 'er over the seas;But Guv'ment built me a fever-trap,
An' Injia give me disease.
Chorus.Ho! don't you 'eed what a girl says,
An' don't you go for the beer;But I was an ass when I was at grass,
An' that is why I'm 'ere.
I fired a shot at a Afghan,
The beggar 'e fired again,An' I lay on my bed with a 'ole in my 'cd;
An' missed the next campaign!

144 LIFE'S HANDICAP

I up with my gun at a Burman
Who carried a bloomin' dah,But the cartridge stuck and the bay'nit bruk,
An' all I got was the scar.
Chorus.Ho! don't you aim at a Afghan
When you stand on the sky-line clear;An' don't you go for a Burman
If none o' your friends is near.
I served my time for a corp'ral,
An' wetted my stripes with pop,For I went on the bend with a intimate friend
An' finished the night in the 'shop.'I served my time for a sergeant;
Thecolonel'esez'No!The most you'll see is a full C. B.'*
An' , . . very next night 'tw»s so.
Chorus.Ho! don't you go for a corp'ral
Unless your 'ed is clear;But I was an ass when I was at grass,
An' that is why I'm 'ere.
I've tasted the luck o' the army
In barrack an' camp an' clink,An' I lost my tip through the bloomin' trip
Along o' the women an' drink.I'm down at the heel o' my service
An' when I am laid on the shelf,' M\'7d'- very wust friend from beginning to end
By the blood of a mouse was myself!
Chorus.Ho! don't you 'eed what a girl says,
An' don't you go for the beer;But I was an ass when I was at grass
An' that is why I'm 'ere.
^ Confined to barracks.

THE COURTING OF DINAH SHADD 145

'Ay, listen to our little man now, singin' an' shoutin*as tho' trouble had niver touched him.

D'you rememberwhen he went mad with the home-sickness?' said Mul-vaney, recalling a never-to-be-forgotten season whenOrtheris waded through the deep waters of afHiction andbehaved abominably. 'But he's talkin' bitter truth,though. Eyah!

'My very worst frind from beginnin' to indBy the blood av a mouse was mesilf!'

When I woke I saw Mulvaney, the night-dew gem-ming his moustache, leaning on his rifle at picket, lonelyas Prometheus on his rock, with I know not what vulturestearing his liver.

ON GREENHOW HILL

To Love's low voice she lent a careless ear;
Her hand within his rosy fingers lay,
A chilling weight. She would not turn or hear;
But with averted face went on her way.
But when pale Death, all featureless and grim,
Lifted his bony hand, and beckoning
Held out his 'press-wreath, she followed bin,
And Love was left forlorn and wondering,
That she who for his bidding would not stay,
At Death's first whisper rose and went away.
Rivals.

' Ore , A hmed Din I Shafiz Ullah alwo ! Bahadur Khan,where are you? Come out of the tents, as I have done,and fight against the English. Don't kill your own kinlCome out to me!'

The deserter from a native corps was crawling roundthe outskirts of the camp, firing at intervals, and shout-ing invitations to his old comrades. Misled by the rainand the darkness, he came to the EngHsh wing of thecamp, and with his yelping and rifle-practice disturbedthe men. They had been making roads all day, andwere tired.

Ortheris was sleeping at Learoyd's feet. 'Wot's allthat?' he said thickly. Learoyd snored, and a Sniderbullet ripped its way through the tent wall. The menswore. 'It's that bloomin' deserter from the Auranga-badis,' said Ortheris. 'Git up, some one, an' tell 'im'e's come to the wrong shop.'

146

'Go to sleep, little man/ said Mulvaney, who wassteaming nearest the door. ' I can't arise an' expaytiatewith him. 'Tis rainin' entrenchin' tools outside.'

' 'Tain't because you bloomin' can't. It's 'cause youbloomin' won't, ye long, limp, lousy, lazy beggar, you.'Arkto'im 'owHnM'

'Wot's the good of argifying? Put a bullet into theswine! 'E's keepin' us awake!' said another voice.

A subaltern shouted angrily, and a dripping sentrywhined from the darkness—

* 'Tain't no good, sir. I can't see 'im. 'E's 'idin'somewhere down 'ill.'

Ortheris tumbled out of his blanket. 'Shall I try toget 'im, sir?' said he.

*No,' was the answer. 'Lie down. I won't have thewhole camp shooting all round the clock. Tell him to goand pot his friends.'

Ortheris considered for a moment. Then, putting hishead under the tent wall, he called, as a 'bus conductorcalls in a block,' Tgher up, there! 'Igher up!'

The men laughed, and the laughter was carried downwind to the deserter, who, hearing that he had made amistake, went off to worry his ovm regiment half a mileaway. He was received with shots; the Aurangabadiswere very angry with him for disgracing their colours.

'An' that's all right,' said Ortheris, withdrawing hishead as he heard the hiccough of the Sniders in the dis-tance. 'S'elp me Gawd, tho', that man's not fit to live—messin' with my beauty-sleep this way.'

'Go out and shoot him in the morning, then,' said the subaltern incautiously. 'Silence in the tents now. Get your rest, men.'

Ortheris lay down with a happy little sigh, and in two minutes there was no sound except the rain on the

canvas and the all-embracing and elemental snoring of Learoyd.

The camp lay on a bare ridge of the Himalayas, and for a week had been waiting for a flying colmnn to make connection. The nightly rounds of the deserter and his friends had become a nuisance.

In the morning the men dried themselves in hot sun-shine and cleaned their grimy accoutrements. The native regiment was to take its turn of road-making that day while the Old Regiment loafed.

'I'm goin' to lay for a shot at that man/ said Ortheris, w^hen he had finished washing out his rifle. ' 'E comes up the watercourse every evenin' about five o'clock. If we go and lie out on the north 'ill a bit this afternoon we'll get 'im.'

'You're a bloodthirsty little mosquito/ said Mulvaney, blowing blue clouds into the air. 'But I suppose I will have to come wid you. Fwhere's Jock?'

'Gone out with the Mixed Pickles, 'cause 'e thinks 'isself a bloomin' marksman,' said Ortheris with scorn.

The 'iMixed Pickles' were a detachment of picked shots, generally employed in clearing spurs of hills when the enemy were too impertinent. This taught the young officers how to handle men, and did not do the enemy much harm. Mulvaney and Ortheris strolled out of camp, and passed the Aurangabadis going to their road-making.

'You've got to sweat to-day,' said Ortheris genially. 'We're going to get your man. You didn't knock 'im out last night by any chance, any of you?'

'No. The pig went away mocking us. I had one shot at him,' said a private. 'He's my cousin, and /ought to have cleared our dishonour. But good luck to you.'

They went cautiously to the north hill, Ortheris leading, because, as he explained, 'this is a long-range show, an^ I've got to do it.' His was an almost pas-sionate devotion to his rifle, wliich, by barrack-room report, he was supposed to kiss every night before turn-ing in. Charges and scuffles he held in contempt, and, when they were inevitable, shpped between Mulvaney and Learoyd, bidding them to fight for his skin as well as their own. They never failed him. He trotted along, questing like a hound on a broken trail, through the wood of the north hill. At last he was satisfied, and threw himself down on the soft pine-needled slope that commanded a clear view of the watercourse and a brown, bare hillside beyond it. The trees made a scented dark-ness in which an army corps could have hidden from the sun-glare without.

' 'Ere's the tail o' the wood,' said Ortheris. ' 'E's eot to come up the watercourse, 'cause it gives 'im cover. We'll lay 'ere. 'Tain't not arf so bloomin' dusty neither.'

He buried his nose in a clump of scentless white violets. No one had come to tell the flowers that the season of their strength was long past, and they had bloomed merrily in the twilight of the pines.

'This is something like,* he said luxuriously. *Wota 'evinly clear drop for a bullet acrost! How much d'you make it, Mulvaney?'

'Seven hunder. Maybe a trifle less, bekaze the air's so thin.'

Wop! wop! wop! went a volley of musketry on the rear face of the north hill.

'Curse them Mixed Pickles firin' at nothin'! They'll scare arf the country,'

*Thry a sigh tin' shot in the middle of the row,' said

Mulvaney, the man of many wiles. 'There's a red rock yonder he'll be sure to pass. Quick!'

Ortheris ran his sight up to six hundred yards and fired. The bullet threw up a feather of dust by a clump of gentians at the base of the rock.

' Good enough!' said Ortheris, snapping the scale down. 'You snick your sights to mine or a little lower. You're always firin' high. But remember, first shot to me. O Lordy! but it's a lovely afternoon.'

The noise of the firing grew louder, and there was a tramping of men in the wood. The two lay very quiet, for they knew that the British soldier is desperately prone to fire at anything that moves or calls. Then Learoyd appeared, his tunic ripped across the breast by a bullet, looking ashamed of himself. He flung down on the pine-needles, breathing in snorts.

'One o' them damned gardeners o' th' Pickles,' said he, fingering the rent. 'Firin' to th' right flank, when he knowed I was there. If I knew who he was I'd 'a' rippen the hide offan him. Look at ma tunic!'

' That's the spishil trustability av a marksman. Train him to hit a fly wid a stiddy rest at seven hunder, an' he loose on any thin' he sees or hears up to th' mile. You're well out av that fancy-firin' gang, Jock. Stay here.'

'Bin firin' at the bloomin' wind in the bloomin' tree-tops,' said Ortheris with a chuckle. 'I'll show you some firin' later on.'

They wallowed in the pine-needles, and the sun warmed them where they lay. The Mixed Pickles ceased firing, and returned to camp, and left the wood to a few scared apes. The watercourse lifted up its voice in the silence, and talked foolishly to the rocks. Now and again the dull thump of a blasting charge three miles away told

that the Aurangabadis were in difficulties with their road-making. The men smiled as they listened and lay still, soaking in the warm leisure. Presently Learoyd, between the whiffs of his pipe—

'Seems queer—about 'im yonder—desertin' at all.'

^ 'E'll be a bloomin' side queerer when I've done with 'im,' said Ortheris. They were talking in whispers, for the stillness of the wood and the desire of slaughter lay heavy upon them.

'I make no doubt he had his reasons for desertin'; but, my faith! I make less doubt ivry man has good reason for killin' him,' said Mulvaney.

'Happen there was a lass tewed up m' it. Men do more than more for th' sake of a lass.'

'They make most av us 'list. They've no manner av right to make us desert.'

'Ah; they make us 'list, or their fathers do,' said Learoyd softly, his helmet over his eyes.

Ortheris's brows contracted savagely. He was watch-ing the valley. ' If it's a girl I'll shoot the beggar twice over, an' second time for bein' a fool. You're blasted sentimental all of a sudden. Thinkin' o' your last near shave?'

'Nay, lad; ah was but thinkin' o' what had hap-pened.'

'An' fwhat has happened, ye lumberin' child av calamity, that you're lowing like a cow-calf at the back av the pasture, an' suggestin' invidious excuses for the man Stanley's goin' to kill. Ye'll have to wait another hour yet, little man. Spit it out, Jock, an' bellow melojus to the moon. It takes an earthquake or a bullet graze to fetch aught out av you. Discourse, Don Juan! The a-moors av Lotharius Learoyd! Stanley, kape a rowlin' rig'mental eye on the valley.'

'It's along o' yon hill there,' said Learoyd, watching the bare sub-Himalayan spur that reminded him of his Yorkshire moors. He was speaking more to himself than his fellows. 'Ay,' said he, 'Rumbolds Moor stands up ower Skipton town, an' Greenhow Hill stands up ower Pately Brig. I reckon you've never heeard tell o' Greenhow Hill, but yon bit o' bare stuff if there was nobbut a white road windin' is like ut; strangely like. Moors an' moors an' moors, wi' never a tree for shelter, an' gray houses wi' flagstone rooves, and pewits cryin', an' a windhover goin' to and fro just Hke these kites.And cold! A wind that cuts you Hke a knife. You couldtell Greenhow Hill folk by the red-apple colour o' theircheeks an' nose tips, and their blue eyes, driven into pin-points by the wind. Miners mostly, burro win' for leadi' th' hillsides, followin' the trail of th' ore vein same as afield-rat. It was the roughest minin' I ever seen. Yo'dcome on a bit o' creakin' wood windlass like a well-head,an' you was let down i' th' bight of a rope, fendin' yoursenoff the side wi' one hand, carryin' a candle stuck in aLamp o' clay with t'other, an' clickin' hold of a rope witht'other hand.'

'An' that's three of them,' said Mulvaney. 'Must bea good cHmate in those parts.'

Learoyd took no heed.

'An' then yo' came to a level, where you crept onyour hands and knees through a mile o' windin' drift, an'you come out into a cave-place as big as Leeds Town-hall, with a engine pumpin' water from workin's 'at wentdeeper still. It's a queer country, let alone mining forthe hill is full of those natural caves, an' the rivers an'the becks drops into what they call pot-holes, an' comeout again miles away.'

'Wot was you doin' there?' said Ortheris.

'I was a young chap then, an' mostly went wi' 'osses,leadin' coal and lead ore; but at th' time I'm tellin' on Iwas drivin' the waggon-team i' th' big sumph. I didn'tbelong to that country-side by rights. I went therebecause'of a little difference at home, an' at fust I tookup wi' a rough lot. One night we'd been drinkin', an' Imust ha' hed more than I could stand, or happen th' alewas none so good. Though i' them days, By for God, Inever seed bad ale.' He flung his arms over his head, andgripped a vast handful of white violets. 'Nah,' saidhe, 'I never seed the ale I could not drink, the bacca Icould not smoke, nor the lass I could not kiss. Well,we mun have a race home, the lot on us. I lost all th'others, an' when I was climbin' ower one of them wallsbuilt o' loose stones, I comes down into the ditch, stones!and all, an' broke my arm. Not as I knawed much aboutit, for I fell on th' back of my head, an' was knockedstupid like. An' when I come to my sen it were mornin',an' I were lyin' on the settle i' Jesse Roantree's house-place, an' 'Liza Roan tree was settin' sewin'. I ached allower, and my mouth were like a lime-kiln. She gaveme a drink out of a china mug wi' gold letters—^'A Pres-ent from Leeds"—as I looked at many and many a timeat after. "Yo're to lie still while Dr. Warbottom comes,because your arm's broken, and father has sent a lad tofetch him. He found yo' when he w\as goin' to work,an' carried you here on his back," sez she. "Oa!" sezI; an' I shet my eyes, for I felt ashamed o' mysen."Father's gone to his work these three hours, an' hesaid he'd tell 'em to get somebody to drive the tram."The clock ticked, an' a bee comed in the house, an' theyrung i' my head like mill-wheels. An' she give meanother drink an' settled the pillow. "Eh, but yo'reyoung to be getten drunk an' such like, but yo' won't do

154 LIFE'S HANDICAP

it again, will yo'?"—"Noa/' sez I, "I wouldn't if she'dnot but stop they mill-wheels clatterin'.'"

'Faith, it's a good thing to be nursed by a womanwhen you're sick!' said Mulvaney. 'Dir' cheap at theprice av tv/enty broken heads.'

Ortheris turned to frown across the valley. He hadnot been nursed by many women in his life.

'An' then Dr. Warbottom comes ridin' up, an' JesseRoantree along with 'im. He was a high-lamed doctor,but he talked wi' poor folk same as theirsens. "What'sta big agaate on naa?" he sings out "Brekkin' thathick head?" An' he felt me all ower. "That's nonebroken. Tha' nobbut knocked a bit sillier than ordi-nary, an' that's daaft eneaf." An' soa he went on, callin'me all the names he could think on, but settin' my arm,wi' Jesse's help, as careful as could be. "Yo' mun letthe big oaf bide here a bit, Jesse," he says, when he hedstrapped me up an' given me a dose o' physic; "an' youan' Liza will tend him, though he's scarcelins worth thetrouble. An' tha'll lose tha work," sez he, "an' tha'U beupon th' Sick Club for a couple o' months an' more.Doesn't tha think tha's a fool?"'

'But whin was a young man, high or low, the otherav a fool, I'd like to know?' said Mulvaney. 'Sure,folly's the only safe way to wisdom, for I've thriedit.'

'Wisdom!' grinned Ortheris, scanning his comradeswith uplifted chin. 'You're bloomin' Solomons, youtwo, ain't you?'

Learoyd went calmly on, with a steady eye like an oxchewing the cud.

'And that was how I come to know 'Liza Roantree.There's some tunes as she used to sing—aw, she werealways singin'—that fetches Greenhow Hill before my

eyes as fair as yon brow across there. And she wouldlearn me to sing bass, an' I was to go to th' chapel wi"em where Jesse and she led the singin', th' old man play-in' the fiddle. He was a strange chap, old Jesse, fair madwi' music, an' he made me promise to learn the big fiddlewhen my arm was better. It belonged to him, and itstood up in a big case alongside o' th' eight-day clock, butWillie Satterthwaite, as played it in the chapel, had gettendeaf as a door-post, and it vexed Jesse, as he had to raphim ower his head wi' th' fiddle-stick to make him giveower sawin' at th' right time.

'But there was a black drop in it all, an' it was a manin a black coat that brought it. When th' PrimitiveMethodist preacher came to Greenhow, he would alwaysstop wi' Jesse Roantree, an' he laid hold of me from th'beginning. It seemed I wor a soul to be saved, and hemeaned to do it. At th' same time I jealoused 'at he werekeen o' savin' 'Liza Roantree's soul as well, and I couldha' killed him many a time. An' this went on till oneday I broke out, an' borrowed th' brass for a drink from'Liza. After fower days I come back, wi' my tail be-tween my legs, just to see 'Liza again. But Jesse wereat home an' th' preacher—th' Reverend Amos Barra-clough. 'Liza said naught, but a bit o' red come intoher face as were white of a regular thing. Says Jesse,tryin' his best to be civil, *' Nay, lad, it's Hke this. You'vegetten to choose which way it's goin' to be. I'll ha*nobody across ma doorstep as goes a-drinkin', an' bor-rows my lass's money to spend i' their drink. Ho'dtha tongue, 'Liza," sez he, when she wanted to put in aword 'at I were welcome to th' brass, and she were noneafraid that I wouldn't pay it back. Then the Reverendcuts in, seein' as Jesse were losin' his temper, an' theyfair beat me among them. But it were 'Liza, as looked

iS6 LUFE'5 HANDICAP

an' said naught, as did more than either o' their tongues,an' soa I concluded to get converted.'

*Fwhat?' shouted Mulvaney. Then, checking him-self, he said softly, 'Let be! Let be! Sure the BlessedVirgin is the mother of all reHgion an' most women; an'there's a dale av piety in a girl if the men would only letut stay there. I'd ha' been converted myself under thecircumstances.'

'Nay, but,' pursued Learoyd with a blush, *I meanedit.'

Ortheris laughed as loudly as he dared, having regardto his business at the time.

*Ay, Ortheris, you may laugh, but you didn't knowyon preacher Barraclough—a Httle white-faced chap, wi'a voice as 'ud wile a bird off an a bush, and a way o'layin' hold of folks as made them think they'd neverhad a live man for a friend before. You never saw him,an'—an'—you never seed 'Liza Roantree—never seed'Liza Roantree. . . . Happen it was as much 'Lizaas th' preacher and her father, but anyways they allmeaned it, an' I was fair shamed o' mysen, an' so I be-come what they call a changed character. And when Ithink on, it's hard to believe as yon chap going to prayer-meetin's, chapel, and class-meetin's were me. But Inever had naught to say for mysen, though there was adeal o' shoutin', and old Sammy Strother, as were almostclemmed to death and doubled up with the rheumatics,would sing out, "Joyful! Joyful!" and 'at it were betterto go up to heaven in a coal-basket than dowTi to hell i'a coach an' six. And he would put his poor old claw onmy shoulder, sayin', "Doesn't tha feel it, tha great lump?Doesn't tha feel it?" An' sometimes I thought I did,and then again I thought I didn't, an' how was that?'

'The iverlastin' nature av mankind,' said Mulvaney.

*An^ furthermore, I misdoubt you were built for thePrimitive Methodians. They're a new corps anjrways. Ihold by the Ould Church, for she's the mother of themall—ay, an' the father, too. I like her bekaze she's mostremarkable regimental in her fittings. I may die inHonolulu, Nova Zambra, or Cape Cayenne, but whereverI die, me bein' fwhat I am, an' a priest handy, I go underthe same orders an' the same words an' the same unctionas tho' the Pope himself come down from the roof avSt. Peter's to see me off. There's neither high nor low,nor broad nor deep, nor betwixt nor between wid her, an'that's what I like. But mark you, she's no manner avChurch for a wake man, bekaze she takes the body andthe soul av him, onless he has his proper work to do. Iremember when my father died that was three monthscomin' to his grave; begad he'd ha' sold the shebeenabove our heads for ten minutes' quittance of purgathory.An' he did all he could. That's why I say. ut takes astrong man to deal with the Ould Church, an' for thatreason you'll find so many women go there. An' thatsame's a conundrum.'

*Wot's the use o' worritin' 'bout these things?' saidOrtheris. ' You're bound to find all out quicker nor youwant to, any'ow.' He jerked the cartridge out of thebreech-block into the palm of his hand. ' 'Ere's mychaplain,' he said, and made the venomous black-headedbullet bow like a marionette. ' 'E's goin' to teach a manall about which is which, an' wot's true, after all, beforesundown. But wot 'appened after that, Jock?'

' There was one thing they boggled at, and almost shutth' gate i' my face for, and that were my dog Blast, th'only one saved out o' a Htter o' pups as was blowed upwhen a keg o' minin' powder loosed off in th' store-keeper's hut. They liked his name no better than his

business, which were fightin' every dog he corned across;a rare good dog, wi' spots o' black and pink on his face,one ear gone, and lame o' one side wi' being driven in abasket through an iron roof, a matter of half a mile.

'They said I mun give him up 'cause he were worldlyand low; and would I let mysen be shut out of heavenfor the sake on a dog? "Nay," says I, "if th' door isn'twide enough for th' pair on us, we'll stop outside, forwe'll none be parted." And th' preacher spoke up forBlast, as had a Kkin' for him from th' first—I reckonthat was why I come to like th' preacher—and wouldn'thear o' changin' his name to Bless, as some o' themwanted. So th' pair on us became reg'lar chapel-members. But it's hard for a young chap o' my buildto cut traces from the world, th' flesh, an' the devil alluv a heap. Yet I stuck to it for a long time, while th'lads as used to stand about th' town-end an' lean owerth' bridge, spittin' into th' beck o' a Sunday, would callafter me, "Sitha, Learoyd, when's ta bean to preach,'cause we're comin' to hear tha."—"Ho'd tha jaw. Hehasn't getten th' white choaker on ta morn," anotherlad would say, and I had to double my fists hard i' th'bottom of my Sunday coat, and say to mysen, "If 'twereMonday and I warn't a member o' the Primitive Metho-dists, I'd leather all th' lot of yond'." That was th'hardest of all—to know that I could fight and I mustn'tfight.'

Sympathetic grunts from Mulvaney.

'So what wi' singin', practisin', and class-meetin's, andth' big fiddle, as he made me take between my knees, Ispent a deal o' time i' Jesse Roantree's house-place. Butoften as I was there, th' preacher fared to me to go oftener,and both th' old man an' th' young woman were pleasedto have him. He lived i' Pately Brig, as were a goodish

step off, but he come. He come all the same. I likedhim as well or better as any man I'd ever seen i' oneway, and yet I hated him wi' all my heart i' t'other, andwe watched each other Hke cat and mouse, but civil asyou please, for I was on my best behaviour, and he wasthat fair and open that I was bound to be fair with him.Rare good company he was, if I hadn't wanted to wringhis cHver Httle neck half of the time. Often and oftenwhen he was goin' from Jesse's I'd set him a bit onthe road.'

'See 'im 'ome, you mean?' said Ortheris.

'Ay. It's a way we have i' Yorkshire o' seein' friendsoff. You was a friend as I didn't want to come back, andhe didn't want me to come back neither, and so we'dwalk together towards Pately, and then he'd set me backagain, and there we'd be wal two o'clock i' the mornin'settin' each other to an' fro like a blasted pair o' pen-dulums twLxt hill and valley, long after th' hght had goneout i' 'Liza's window, as both on us had been looking at,pretending to watch the moon.'

'Ah!' broke in Mulvaney, 'ye'd no chanst against themaraudin' psalm-singer. They'll take the airs an' thegraces instid av the man nine times out av ten, an'they only find the blunder later—the wimmen.'

'That's just where yo're wrong,' said Learoyd, red-dening under the freckled tan of his cheeks. ' I was th'first wi' 'Liza, an' yo'd think that were enough. Butth' parson were a steady-gaited sort o' chap, and Jessewere strong o' his side, and all th' women i' the congre-gation dinned it to 'Liza 'at she were fair fond to take upwi' a wastrel ne'er-do-weel like me, as was scarcelinsrespectable an' a fighting dog at his heels. It was allvery well for her to be doing me good and saving mysoul, but she must mind as she didn't do herself harm.

They talk o' rich folk bein' stuck up an' genteel, but forcast-iron pride o' respectability there's naught like poorchapel folk. It's as cold as th' wind o' Greenhow Hill-ay, and colder, for 'twill never change. And now Icome to think on it, one at strangest things I know is 'atthey couldn't abide th' thought o' soldiering. There's avast o' fightin' i' th' Bible, and there's a deal of Metho-dists i' th' army; but to hear chapel folk talk yo'd thinkthat soldierin' were next door, an' t'other side, to hangin'.I' their meetin's all their talk is o' fightin'. When SammyStrother were stuck for sum mat to say in his prayers,he'd sing out, *'Th' sword o' th' Lord and o' Gideon."They were alius at it about puttin' on th' whole armouro' righteousness, an' fightin' the good fight o' faith. Andthen, atop o' 't all, they held a prayer-meetin' ower ayoung chap as wanted to 'list, and nearly deafened him,till he picked up his hat and fair ran away. And they'dtell tales in th' Sunday-school o' bad lads as had beenthumped and brayed for bird-nesting o' Sundays andplayin' truant o' week-days, and how they took towrestlin', dog-fightin', rabbit-runnin', and drinkin',till at last, as if 'twere a hepitaph on a gravestone, theydamned him across th' moors wi', "an' then he went and'listed for a soldier," an' they'd all fetch a deep breath,and throw up their eyes lilie a hen drinkin'.'

Twhy is ut?' said Mulvaney, bringing down hishand on his thigh with a crack. 'In the name av God.fwhy is ut? I've seen ut, tu. They cheat an' theyswindle an' they lie an' they slander, an' fifty thingsfifty times worse; but the last an' the worst by theirreckonin' is to serve the Widdy honest. It's like thetalk av childher—seein' things all round.'

'Plucky lot of fightin' good fights of whatsernamethey'd do if wc didn't sec tbey had a quJet pla<:e to fight

in. And such fightin' as theirs is! Cats on the tiles.T'other callin' to which to come on. I'd give a month'spay to get some o' them broad-backed beggars in Londonsweatin' through a day's road-makin' an' a night's rain.They'd carry on a deal afterv/ards—same as we're sup-posed to carry on. I've bin turned out of a measly arf-license pub down Lambeth way, full o' greasy kebmen,'fore now,' said Ortheris with an oath.

'Maybe you were dhrunk,' said Mulvaney soothingly.

'Worse nor that. The Forders were drunk. I waswearin' the Queen's uniform.'

'I'd no particular thought to be a soldier i' themdays,' said Learoyd, still keeping his eye on the bare hillopposite, 'but this sort o' talk put it i' my head. Theywas so good, th' chapel folk, that they tumbled owert'other side. But I stuck to it for 'Liza's sake, speciallyas she was learning me to sing the bass part in a horo-torio as Jesse were gettin' up. She sung hke a throstlehersen, and we had practisin's night after night for amatter of three months.'

'I know what a horotorio is,' said Ortheris pertly.'It's a sort of chaplain's suig-song—words all out of theBible, and hullabaloojah choruses.'

'Most Greenhow Hill folks played some instrumentor t'other, an' they all sung so you might have heard themmiles away, and they were so pleased wi' the noise theymade they didn't fair to want anybody to listen. Thepreacher sung high seconds when he wasn't pla\in' theflute, an' they set me, as hadn't got far with big fiddle,agam WiUie Satterthwaite, to jog his elbow when he hadto get a' gate playin'. Old Jesse was happy if ever aman was, for he were th' conductor an' th' first fiddle an'th' leadin' smger, beatin' time wi' his fiddle-stick, till attimes he'd rap with it on the table, and cry out, "Now,

you mun all stop; it's my turn." And he'd face roundto his front, fair sweating wd' pride, to sing th' tenorsolos. But he were grandest i' th' choruses, v/aggin' hishead, flinging his arms round like a windmill, and singin'hisself black in the face. A rare singer were Jesse.

*Yo' see, I was not o' much account wi' 'em all ex-ceptin' to 'Liza Roantree, and I had a deal o' time settin'quiet at meetings and horotorio practises to hearken theirtalk, and if it were strange to me at beginnin', it gotstranger still at after, when I was shut on it, and couldstudy what it meaned.

'Just after th' horotorios come off, 'Liza, as had aliusbeen weakly like, was took very bad. I v/alked Dr.Warbottom's horse up and down a deal of times while hewere inside, where they wouldn't let me go, though I fairached to see her.

"'She'll be better i' noo, lad—better i' noo," he usedto say. "Tha mun ha' patience." Then they said if Iwas quiet I might go in, and th' Reverend Amos Barra-clough used to read to her lyin' propped up among th'pillows. Then she began to mend a bit, and they letme carry her on to th' settle, and when it got warm againshe went about same as afore. Th' preacher and me andBlast was a deal together i' them days, and i' one waywe was rare good comrades. But I could ha' stretchedhim time and again with a good will. I mind one da\'7d^he said he would hke to go down into th' bowels o' th'earth, and see how th' Lord had built th' framework o'th' everlastin' hills. He were one of them chaps as hada gift o' sayin' things. They rolled off the tip of hisclever tongue, same as Mulvaney here, as would ha' madea rare good preacher if he had nobbut given his mindto it. I lent him a suit o' miner's kit as almost buriedth' little man, and his white face down i' th' coat-collar

and hat-flap looked like the face of a boggart, and hecowered down i' th' bottom o' the waggon. I was drivin'a tram as led up a bit of an incline up to th' cave wherethe engine was pumpin', and where th' ore was broughtup and put into th' waggons as went down o' themselves,me puttin' th' brake on and th' horses a-trottin' after.Long as it was daylight we were good friends, but whenwe got fair into th' dark, and could nobbut see th' dayshinin' at the hole like a lamp at a street-end, I feeleddownright wicked. Ma religion dropped all away fromme when I looked back at him as were always comin'between me and 'Liza. The talk was 'at they were to bewed when she got better, an' I couldn't get her to sayyes or nay to it. He began to sing a hymn in his thinvoice, and I came out wi' a chorus that was all cussin'an' swearin' at my horses, an' I began to know how Ihated him. He were such a little chap, too. I coulddrop him wi' one hand down Garstang's Copper-hole—a place where th' beck slithered ower th' edge on a rock,and fell wi' a bit of a whisper into a pit as no rope i'Greenhow could plumb.'

Again Learoyd rooted up the innocent violets. *Ay,he should see th' bowels o' th' earth an' never naughtelse. I could take him a mile or two along th' drift, andleave him wi' his candle doused to cry hallelujah, wi'none to hear him and say amen. I was to lead himdown th' ladder-way to th' drift where Jesse Roantreewas workin', and why shouldn't he sHp on th' ladder, wi'my feet on his fingers till they loosed grip, and I put himdown wi' my heel? If I went fust down th' ladder Icould click hold on him and chuck him over my head,so as he should go squshin' down the shaft, breakin' hisbones at ev'ry timberin' as Bill Appleton did when he wasfresh, and hadn't a bone left when he wrought to th'

bottom. Niver a blasted leg to walk from Pately. Niveran arm to put round 'Liza Roantree's waist. Niver nomore—niver no more.'

The thick lips curled back over the yellow teeth, andthat flushed face was not pretty to look upon. Mulvaneynodded sympathy, and Ortheris, moved by his comrade'spassion, brought up the rifle to his shoulder, and searchedthe hillside for his quarry, muttering ribaldry about asparrow, a spout, and a thunder-storm. The voice ofthe watercourse supplied the necessary small talk tillLearoyd picked up his story.

'But it's none so easy to kiU a man like yon. WhenI'd given up my horses to th' lad as took my placeand I was showin' th' preacher th' workin's, shoutin'into his ear across th' clang o' th' pumphi' engines, I sawhe were afraid o' naught; and when the lampHght showedhis black eyes, I could feel as he was masterin' me again.I were no better nor Blast chained up short and growlin'i' the depths of him while a strange dog went safe past.

""Th'art a coward and a fool," I said to mysen; an'I wrestled i' my mind again' him till, when we come toGarstang's Copper-hole, I laid hold o' the preacher andlifted him up over my head and held him into the darkeston it. "Now, lad," I says "it's to be one or t'other onus—thee or me—for 'Liza Roantree. Why, isn't theeafraid for thysen?" I says, for he were still i' my arms asa sack. "Nay; I'm but afraid for thee, my poor lad, asknows naught," says he. I set him down on th' edge,an' th' beck run stifler, an' there was no more buzzin'in my head like when th' bee come through th' windowo' Jesse's house. "What dost tha mean?" says I.

*"I've often thought as thou ought to know," says he,"but 'twas hard to tell thee. 'Liza Roantree's for nei-ther on us, nor for nobody o' this earth. Dr. Warbottom

says—and he knows her, and her mother before her that she is in a decline, and she cannot Hve sLx monthslonger. He's known it for many a day. Steady, John!Steady!" says he. And that weak little man pulledme further back and set me again' him, and talked it allover quiet and still, me tumin' a bunch o' candles in myhand, and counting them ower and ower again as I Hs-tened. A deal on it were th' regular preachin' talk, butthere were a vast lot as made me begin to think as hewere more of a m'an than I'd ever given him credit for,till I were cut as deep for him as I were for mysen.

*Six candles wx had, and we crawled and dimbed aUthat day while they lasted, and I said to mysen, " XizaRoan tree hasn't six months to Uve." And when we cameinto th' daylight again we were like dead men to look at,an' Blast come behind us without so much as waggin' histail. When I saw 'Liza again she looked at me a minuteand says, *^ Who's telledtha? For I see tha knows." Andshe tried to smile as she kissed me, and I fair broke down.

^Yo' see, I was a young chap i' them days, and hadseen naught o' hfe, let alone death, as is alius a-waitin'.She told me as Dr. Warbottom said as Greenhow airwas too keen, and they were goin' to Bradford, to Jesse'sbrother David, as worked i' a mill, and I mun hold uplike a man and a Christian, and she'd pray for me. Well,and they went away, and the preacher that same backend o' th' year were appointed to another circuit, as theycall it, and I were left alone on Greenhow Hill.

'I tried, and I tried hard, to stick to th' chapel, but'tweren't th' same thing at after. I hadn't 'Liza's voiceto follow i' th' singin', nor her eyes a-shinin' acrost theirheads. And i' th' class-meetings they said as I mun have]some experiences to tell, and I hadn't a word to say for'mysen.

^ Blast and me moped a good deal, and happen wedidn't behave ourselves over well, for they dropped usand wondered however they'd come to take us up. Ican't tell how we got through th' time, while i' th' winterI gave up my job and went to Bradford. Old Jesse wereat th' door o' th' house, in a long street o' little houses.He'd been sendin' th' children 'way as were clatterin'their clogs in th' causeway, for she were asleep.

'^'Is it thee?" he says; "but you're not to see her.I'll none have her wakened for a nowt like thee. She'sgoin' fast, and she mun go in peace. Thou'lt never begood for naught i' th' world, and as long as thou livesthou'U never play the big fiddle. Get away, lad, getaway!" So he shut the door softly i' my face.

* Nobody never made Jesse my m_aster, but it seemedto me he was about right, and I went away into the townand knocked up against a recruiting sergeant. The oldtales o' th' chapel folk came buzzin' into my head. Iwas to get away, and this were th' regular road for thelikes o' me. I 'listed there and then, took th' Widow'sshillin', and had a bunch o' ribbons pinned i' my hat.

'But next day I found my way to David Roan tree'sdoor, and Jesse came to open it. Says he, "Thou's comeback again wi' th' devil's colours flyin'—thy true colours,as I always telled thee."

'But I begged and prayed of him to let me see hernobbut to say good-bye, till a woman calls down th'stairway, "She says John Learoyd's to come up." Th*old man shifts aside in a flash, and lays his hand on myarm, quite gentle Kke. "But thou'lt be quiet, John,"says he, "for she's rare and weak. Thou was alius agood lad."

'Her eyes were all alive wi' light, and her hair wasthick on the pillow round her, but her cheeks were thin

—thin to frighten a man that's strong. "Nay, father,yo mayn't say th' devil's colours. Them ribbons ispretty." An' she held out her hands for th' hat, an' sheput all straight as a woman will wi' ribbons. "Nay, butwhat they're pretty," she says. "Eh, but I'd ha' liked tosee thee i' thy red coat, John, for thou was alius my ownlad—my very own lad, and none else."

'She hfted up her arms, and they come round myneck i' a gentle grip, and they slacked away, and sheseemed fainting. "Now yo' mun get away, lad," saysJesse, and I picked up my hat and I came downstairs.

'Th' recruiting sergeant were waitin' for me at th'corner pubUc-house. "Yo've seen your sweetheart?"says he. "Yes, I've seen her," says I. "Well, we'llhave a quart now, and you'll do your best to forget her,"says he, bein' one o' them smart, bustlin' chaps. "Ay,sergeant," says I. "Forget her." And I've been for-gettin' her ever since.'

He threw away the wilted clump of white violets ashe spoke. Ortheris suddenly rose to his knees, his rifleat his shoulder, and peered across the valley in the clearafternoon Hght. His chin cuddled the stock, and therewas a twitching of the muscles of the right cheek as hesighted; Private Stanley Ortheris was engaged on hisbusiness. A speck of white crawled up the watercourse.

'See that beggar? . . . Got'im.'

Seven hundred yards away, and a full two hundreddown the hillside, the deserter of the Aurangabadispitched forward, rolled down a red rock, and lay verystill, with his face in a clump of blue gentians, while a bigraven flapped out of the pine wood to make investiga-tion.

'That's a clean shot, little man,' said Mulvaney.

Learoyd thoughtfully watched the smoke clear away.

'Happen there was a lass tewed up wi'him, too/ saidhe.

Ortheris did not reply. He was staring across thevalley, with the smile of the artist who looks on thecompleted worko

The Earth gave up her dead that tide,

Into our camp he came,And said his say, and went his way,

And left our hearts aflame.

Keep tally—on the gun-butt score

The vengeance we must take.When God shall bring full reckoning,

For our dead comrade's sake.

Ballad.

Let it be clearly understood that the Russian is a delight-ful person till he tucks in his shirt. As an Oriental heis charming. It is only when he insists upon beingtreated as the most easterly of western peoples instead ofthe most westerly of easterns that he becomes a racialanomaly extremely difficult to handle. The host neverknows which side of his nature is going to turn up next.

Dirkovitch was a Russian—a Russian of the Russians—who appeared to get his bread by serving the Czar asan officer in a Cossack regiment, and corresponding for aRussian newspaper with a name that was never twicealike. He was a handsome young Oriental, fond of wan-dering through unexplored portions of the earth, and hearrived in India from nowhere in particular. At leastno living man could ascertain whether it was by way ofBalkh, Badakshan, Chitral, Beluchistan, or Nepaul, oranywhere else. The Indian Government, being in anunusually affable mood, gave orders that he was to be

169

civilly treated and shown everything that was to be seen.So he drifted, talking bad English and worse French, fromone cit\'7d^ to another, till he foregathered with Her Maj-esty's White Hussars in the city of Peshawur, whichstands at the mouth of that narrow swordcut in the hillsthat men call the Khyber Pass. He was undoubtedlyan oflScer, and he was decorated after the manner of theRussians with little enamelled crosses, and he could talk,and (though this has nothing to do with his merits) hehad been given up as a hopeless task, or cask, by theBlack Tyrone, who individually and collectively, withhot whisky and honey, mulled brandy, and mixed spiritsof every kind, had striven in all hospitality to make himdrunk. And when the Black Tyrone, who are exclu-sively Irish, fail to disturb the peace of head of a foreigner—that foreigner is certain to be a superior man.

The White Hussars were as conscientious in choosingtheir wine as in charging the enemy. All that theypossessed, including some wondrous brandy, was placed atthe absolute disposition of Dirkovitch, and he enjoyed him-self hugely—even more than among the Black Tyrones.

But he remained distressingly European through it all.The White Hussars were 'My dear true friends/ 'Fellow-soldiers glorious,' and 'Brothers inseparable.' He wouldunburden himself by the hour on the glorious future thatawaited the combined arms of England and Russia whentheir hearts and their territories should run side by sideand the great mission of civilising Asia should begin.That was unsatisfactory, because Asia is not going to beciviUsed after the methods of the West. There is toomuch Asia and she is too old. You cannot reform alady of many lovers, and Asia has been insatiable in herflirtations aforetime. She will never attend Sunday-school or learn to vote save with swords for tickets.

Dirkovitch knew this as well as any one else, but itsuited him to talk specialcorrespondently and to makehimself as genial as he could. Now and then he volun-teered a little, a very Httle, information about his ownsotnia of Cossacks, left apparently to look after them-selves somewhere at the back of beyond. He had donerough work in Central Asia, and had seen rather morehelp-yourself fighting than most men of his years. Buthe was careful never to betray his superiority, and morethan careful to praise on all occasions the appearance,drill, uniform, and organisation of Her Majesty's WhiteHussars. And indeed they were a regiment to be ad-mired. When Lady Durgan, widow of the late Sir JohnDurgan, arrived in their station, and after a short timehad been proposed to by every single man at mess, sheput the public senthnent very neatly when she explainedthat they were all so nice that unless she could marrythem all, including the colonel and some majors alreadymarried, she was not going to content herself with onehussar. Wherefore she wedded a Httle man in a rifleregiment, being by nature contradictious; and the WhiteHussars were going to wear crape on their arms, butcompromised by attending the wedding in full force,and lining the aisle with unutterable reproach. Shehad jilted them all—from Basset-Holmer the seniorcaptain to Httle Mildred the junior subaltern, whocould have given her four thousand a year and atitle.

The only persons who did not share the general regardfor the White Hussars were a few thousand gentlemen ofJewish extraction who lived across the border, andanswered to the name of Pa than. They had once metthe regiment officially and for something less than twentyminutes, but the interview, which was complicated with

many casualties, had filled them with prejudice. Theyeven called the White Hussars children of the devil andsons of persons whom it would be perfectly impossible tomeet in decent society. Yet they were not above makingtheir aversion fill their money-belts. The regimentpossessed carbines—beautiful Martini-Henri carbinesthat would lob a bullet into an enemy's camp at onethousand yards, and were even handier than the longrifle. Therefore they were coveted all along the border,and since demand inevitably breeds supply, they weresupplied at the risk of life and limb for exactly theirweight in coined silver—seven and one-half poundsweight of rupees, or sixteen pounds sterling reckoningthe rupee at par. They were stolen at night by snaky-haired thieves who crawled on their stomachs under thenose of the sentries; they disappeared mysteriously fromlocked arm-racks, and in the hot weather, when all thebarrack doors and windows were open, they vanished likepuffs of their own smoke. The border people desiredthem for family vendettas and contingencies. But inthe long cold nights of the northern Indian winter theywere stolen most extensively. The traffic of murderwas liveliest among the hills at that season, and pricesruled high. The regimental guards were first doubledand then trebled. A trooper does not much care if heloses a weapon—Government must make it good—buthe deeply resents the loss of his sleep. The regimentgrew very angry, and one rifle-thief bears the visiblemarks of their anger upon him to this hour. Thatincident stopped the burglaries for a time, and the guardswere reduced accordingly, and the regiment devoted itselfto polo with unexpected results; for it beat by two goalsto one that very terrible polo corps the Lushkar LightHorse, though the latter had four ponies apiece for a

short hour's fight, as well as a native officer who playedlike a lambent flame across the ground.

They gave a dinner to celebrate the event. TheLushkar team came, and Dirkovitch came, in the fullestfull uniform of a Cossack officer, which is as full as adressing-gown, and was introduced to the Lushkars, andopened his eyes as he regarded. They were fightermen than the Hussars, and they carried themselveswith the swing that is the pecuHar right of the PunjabFrontier Force and all Irregular Horse. Like every-thing else in the Service it has to be learnt, but, unlikemany things, it is never forgotten, and remains on thebody tin death.

The great beam-roofed mess-room of the WhiteHussars was a sight to be remembered. All the messplate was out on the long table—the same table that hadserved up the bodies of five ofiicers after a forgottenfight long and long ago—the dingy, battered standardsfaced the door of entrance, clumps of winter-roses laybetween the silver candlesticks, and the portraits ofeminent ©flacers deceased looked down on their suc-cessors from between the heads of sambhur, nilghai,markhor, and, pride of all the mess, two grinning snow-leopards that had cost Basset-Holmer four months'leave that he might have spent in England, instead of onthe road to Thibet and the daily risk of his fife by ledge,snow-slide, and grassy slope.

The servants in spotless white musKn and the crestof their regiments on the brow of their turbans waitedbehind their masters, who were clad in the scarlet andgold of the White Hussars, and the cream and silver ofthe Lushkar Light Horse. Dirkovitch's dull greenuniform was the only dark spot at the board, but hisbig onyx eyes made up for it. He was fraternising ef-fusively with the captain of the Lushkar team, who waswondering how many of Dirkovitch's Cossacks his owndark wiry down-countrymen could account for in a faircharge. But one does not speak of these things openly.

The talk rose higher and higher, and the regimentalband played between the courses, as is the immemorialcustom, till all tongues ceased for a moment with theremoval of the dinner-slips and the first toast of obli-gation, when an officer rising said, 'Mr. Vice, the Queen,*and little Mildred from the bottom of the table answered,'The Queen, God bless her,' and the big spurs clanked a?the big men heaved themselves up and drank the Queenupon whose pay they were falsely supposed to settletheir mess-bills. That Sacrament of the Mess nevergrows old, and never ceases to bring a lump into thethroat of the Hstener wherever he be by sea or by land.Dirkovitch rose with his 'brothers glorious/ but he couldnot understand. No one but an officer can tell what thetoast means; and the bulk have more sentiment thancomprehension. Immediately after the Httle silence thatfollows on the ceremony there entered the native officerwho had played for the Lushkar team. He could not,of course, eat with the mess, but he came in at dessert,all six feet of him, with the blue and silver turban atop,and the big black boots below. The mess rose joyouslyas he thrust forward the hilt of his sabre in token offealty for the colonel of the White Hussars to touch,and dropped into a vacant chair amid shouts of: ^Rungho, Hira Singh!' (wliich being translated means 'Go inand win'). 'Did I whack you over the knee, old man?"Ressaidar Sahib, what the devil made you play thatkicking pig of a pony in the last ten minutes?' 'Shabash,Ressaidar Sahib!' Then the voice of the colonel, 'Thehealth of Ressaidar Hira Singh!*

After the shouting had died away Hira Singh roseto reply, for he was the cadet of a royal house, the sonof a king's son, and knew what was due on these oc-casions. Thus he spoke in the vernacular:—'ColonelSahib and officers of this regiment. Much honourhave you done me. This will I remember. We camedown from afar to play you. But we were beaten.'(*No fault of yours, Ressaidar Sahib. Played on ourown ground y'know. Your ponies were cramped fromthe railway. Don't apologise!') 'Therefore perhapswe will come again if it be so ordained.' ('Hear! Hear!Hear, indeed! Bravo! Hsh!') 'Then we will playyou afresh' ('Happy to meet you.') 'till there are leftno feet upon our ponies. Thus far for sport.' Hedropped one hand on his sword-hilt and his eye wanderedto Dirkovitch lolling back in his chair. 'But if by thewill of God there arises any other game which is notthe polo game, then be assured. Colonel Sahib andofficers, that we will play it out side by side, thoughthey,^ again his eye sought Dirkovitch, 'though theyI say have fifty ponies to our one horse.' And witha deep-mouthed Rung ho! that sounded like a mus-ket-butt on flagstones he sat down amid leapingglasses.

Dirkovitch, who had devoted himself steadily to thebrandy—the terrible brandy aforementioned—did notunderstand, nor did the expurgated translations offeredto him at all convey the pomt. Decidedly Hira Singh'swas the speech of the evening, and the clamour mighthave contiiiued to the dawn had it not been broken bythe noise of a shot without that sent every man feelingat his defenceless left side. Then there was a scuffle anda yell of pain.

'Carbine-stealing again!' said the adjutant, calmly

sinking back in his chair. 'This comes of reducing theguards. I hope the sentries have killed him.'

The feet of armed men pounded on the verandah flags,and it was as though something was being dragged.

'Why don't they put him in the cells till the morn-ing?' said the colonel testily. 'See if they've damagedhim, sergeant.'

The mess sergeant fled out into the darkness andreturned with tv/o troopers and a corporal, all very muchperplexed.

'Caught a man stealin' carbines, sir,' said the corporal.'Leastways 'e was crawlin' towards the barricks, sir, pastthe main road sentries, an' the sentry 'e sez, sir '

The limp heap of rags upheld by the three mengroaned. Never was seen so destitute and demoralisedan Afghan. He was turbanless, shoeless, caked withdirt, and all but dead with rough handling. Hira Singhstarted slightly at the sound of the man's pain. Dirko-vitch took another glass of brandy.

' What does the sentry say?' said the colonel.

'Sez 'e speaks English, sir,' said the corporal.

'So you brought him into mess instead of handinghim over to the sergeant! If he spoke all the Tongues ofthe Pentecost you've no business '

Again the bundle groaned and muttered. LittleMildred had risen from his place to inspect. He jumpedback as though he had been shot.

'Perhaps it would be better, sir, to send the menaway,' said he to the colonel, for he was a much privilegedsubaltern. He put his arms round the ragbound horroras he spoke, and dropped him into a chair. It may nothave been explained that the Httleness of Mildred layin his being six feet four and big in proportion. Thecorporal seeing that an officer was disposed to look after

the capture, and that the colonel's eye was beginning toblaze, promptly removed himself and his men. Themess was left alone \dth tlae carbine-thief, who laid hishead on the table and wept bitterly, hopelessly, andinconsolably, as Uttle children weep.

Hira Singh leapt to his feet. 'Colonel Sahib,' saidhe, 'that man is no Afghan, for they weep At! At!Nor is he of Hindustan, for they weep Oh ! Ho ! Heweeps after the fashion of the white men, who say Ow l

Owr

'Now where the dickens did you get that knowl-edge, Hira Singh?' said the captain of the Lushkarteam.

'Hear him!' said Hira Smgh simply, pointing atthe crumpled figure that wept as though it would nevercease.

'He said, "My God!"' said little Mildred 'I heardhim say it.'

The colonel and the mess-room looked at the manin silence. It is a horrible thing to hear a man cry. Awoman can sob from the top of her palate, or her lips,or anywhere else, but a man must cry from his diaphragm,and it rends him to pieces.

'Poor devil!' said the colonel, coughing tremendously.'We ought to send him to hospital. He's been man-handled.'

Now the adjutant loved his carbines. They wereto him as his grandchildren, the men standing in thefirst place. He grunted rebeUiously: ' I can understandan Afghan steahng, because he's built that way. ButI can't understand his crying. That makes it worse.'

The brandy must have affected Dirkovitch, for helay back in his chair and stared at the ceiling. There^as nothing special in the ceiling beyond a shadow

as of a huge black coffin. Owing to some peculiarityin the construction of the mess-room this shadow wasalways thrown when the candles were lighted. Itnever disturbed the digestion of the White Hussars.They were in fact rather proud of it.

'Is he going to cry ail night?' said the colonel, 'orare we supposed to sit up with little Mildred's guestuntil he feels better?'

The man in the chair threw up his head and staredat the mess. 'Oh, my God!' he said, and every soulin the mess rose to his feet. Then the Lushkar captaindid a deed for which he ought to have been given theVictoria Cross—distinguished gallantry in a fight againstoverwhelming curiosity. He picked up his team with hiseyes as the hostess picks up the ladies at the opportunemomxcnt, and pausing only by the colonel's chair to say,'This isn't our affair, you know, sir,' led them into theverandah and the gardens. Hira Singh was the last togo, and he looked at Dirkovitch. But Dirkovitch haddeparted into a brandy-paradise of his own. His lipsmoved without sound and he was studying the coffin onthe ceihng.

'White—white all over,' said Basset-Hohner, theadjutant. 'What a pernicious renegade he must be!I wonder where he came from?'

The colonel shook the man gently by the arm, and'Who are you?' said he.

There was no answer. The man stared round themess-room and smiled in the colonel's face. LittleMildred, who was always more of a woman than a mantill' Boot and saddle' was sounded, repeated the questionin a voice that would have drawn confidences from ageyser. The man only smiled. Dirkovitch at the farend of the table slid gently from his chair to the floor.

No son of Adam in this present imperfect world can mixthe Hussars' champagne with the Hussars' brandy by fiveand eight glasses of each without remembering the pitwhence he was digged and descending thither. Theband began to play the tune with which the White Hus-sars from the date of their formation have concluded alltheir functions. They would sooner be disbanded thanabandon that tune; it is a part of their system. Theman straightened himself in his chair and drummed onthe table with his fingers.

^I don't see why we should entertain lunatics,' saidthe colonel. ' Call a guard and send him off to the cells.We'll look into the business in the morning. Give him aglass of wine first though.'

Little Mildred filled a sherry-glass with the brandyAnd thrust it over to the man. He drank, and the tunerose louder, and he straightened himself yet more. Thenhe put out his long-taloned hands to a piece of plateopposite and fingered it lovingly. There was a mysteryconnected with that piece of plate, in the shape of aspring which converted what was a seven-branchedcandlestick, three springs on each side and one in themiddle, into a sort of wheel-spoke candelabrum. Hefound the spring, pressed it, and laughed weakly. Herose from his chair and inspected a picture on the wall,then moved on to another picture, the mess watching himwithout a word. When he came to the mantelpiecehe shook his head and seemed distressed. A piece ofplate representing a mounted hussar in full uniformcaught his eye. He pointed to it, and then to the man-telpiece with inquiry in his eyes.

' What is it—Oh what is it?' said little Mildred. Thenas a mother might speak to a child, 'That is a horse.Yes, a horse.'

Very slowly came the answer in a thick, passionlessguttural—' Yes, I—have seen. But—where is the horse?'

You could have heard the hearts of the mess beatingas the men drew back to give the stranger full room in hiswanderings. There was no question of calling the guard.

Again he spoke—very slowly, 'Where is our horse?'

There is but one horse in the White Hussars, andhis portrait hangs outside the door of the mess-room.He is the piebald drum-horse, the king of the regimentalband, that served the regiment for seven-and-thirtyyears, and in the end was shot for old age. Half themess tore the thing down from its place and thrust itinto the man's hands. He placed it above the mantel-piece, it clattered on the ledge as his poor hands droppedit, and he staggered towards the bottom of the table,falling into Mildred's chair. Then all the men spoke toone another something after this fashion, 'The drum-horse hasn't hung over the mantelpiece since '67."How does he know?' 'Mildred, go and speak to himagain.^ 'Colonel, what are you gomg to do?' 'Oh,dry up, and give the poor devil a chance to pull himselftogether.' 'It isn't possible anyhow. The man's alunatic'

Little Mildred stood at the colonel's side talking in hisear. ' Will you be good enough to take your seats please,gentlemen!' he said, and the mess dropped into the chairs.Only Dirkovitch's seat, next to little Mildred's, wasblank, and little Mildred himself had found Hira Singh'splace. The wide-eyed mess-sergeant filled the glassesin deep silence. Once more the colonel rose, but hishand shook and the port spilled on the table as he lookedstraight at the man in little Mildred's chair and saidhoarsely,' Mr. Vice, the Queen.' There was a little pause,but the man sprung to his feet and answered without hesi-

tation, 'The Queen, God bless her!' and as he emptiedthe thin glass he snapped the shank between his fingers.

Long and long ago, when the Empress of India was ayoung woman and there were no unclean ideals in theland, it was the custom of a few messes to drink theQueen's toast in broken glass, to the vast delight of themess-contractors. The custom is now dead, becausethere is nothing to break anything for, except now andagain the word of a Government, and that has been bro-ken already.

'That settles it,' said the colonel, with a gasp. 'He'snot a sergeant. What in the world is he?'

The entire mess echoed the word, and the volley ofquestions would have scared any man. It was no wonderthat the ragged, filthy invader could only smile and shakehis head.

From under the table, calm and smiling, rose Dirko-vitch, who had been roused from healthful slumber byfeet upon his body. By the side of the man he rose,and the man shrieked and grovelled. It was a horriblesight coming so swiftly upon the pride and glory of thetoast that had brought the strayed wits together.

Dirkovitch made no offer to raise him, but littleMildred heaved him up in an instant. It is not goodthat a gentleman who can answer to the Queen's toastshould lie at the feet of a subaltern of Cossacks.

The hasty action tore the wretch's upper clothingnearly to the waist, and his body was seamed with dryblack scars. There is only one weapon in the world thatcuts: in parallel lines, and it is neither the cane nor thecat. Dirkovitch saw the marks, and the pupils of hiseyes dilated. Also his face changed. He said somethingthat sounded like Skto ve takete, and the man fawning an-swered, Cketyre,

* What's that?' said everybody together.

* His number. That is number four, you know.* Dirko-vitch spoke very thickly.

' What has a Queen's officer to do with a qualified num-ber?' said the Colonel, and an unpleasant growl ranround the table.

'How can I tell?' said the affable Oriental with a sweetsmile. 'He is a—how you have it?—escape—run-a-way,from over there.' He nodded towards the darkness ofthe night.

'Speak to him if he'll answer you, and speak to himgently,' said little Mildred, settling the man in a chair. It seemed most improper to all present that Dirkovitch should sip brandy as he talked in purring, spitting Rus-sian to the creature who answered so feebly and with such evident dread. But since Dirkovitch appeared to understand no one said a word. All breathed heavily, leaning forward, in the long gaps of the conversation. The next time that they have no engagements on hand the White Hussars intend to go to St. Petersburg in a body to learn Russian.

'He does not know how many years ago,' said Dirko-vitch, facing the mess, 'but he says it was very long ago in a war. I think that there was an accident. He says he was of this glorious and distinguished regiment in the war.'

'The rolls! The rolls! Holmer, get the rolls!' said little Mildred, and the adjutant dashed off bare-headed to the orderly-room, where the muster-rolls of the regiment were kept. He returned just in time to hear Dirkovitch conclude, 'Therefore, my dear friends, I am most sorry to say there was an accident wliich would have been repa-rable if he had apologised to that our colonel, which he had insulted.'

Then followed another growl which the colonel tried to beat down. The mess was in no mood just then to weigh insults to Russian colonels.

'He does not remember, but I think that there was an accident, and so he was not exchanged among the prisoners, but he was sent to another place—how do you say?—the country. So, he says, he came here. He does not know how he came. Eh? He was at Chepany'—the man caught the word, nodded, and shivered—^at Zhigansk and Irkutsk. I cannot understand how he escaped. He says, too, that he was in the forests for many years, but how many years he has forgotten—that with many things. It was an accident; done because he did not apologise to that our colonel. Ah!'

Instead of echoing Dirkovitch's sigh of regret, it is sad to record that the White Hussars liveHly exhibited un-christian delight and other emotions, hardly restrained by their sense of hospitahty. Holmer flung the frayed and yeUow regimental rolls on the table, and the men flung themselves at these.

'Steady! Fifty-sk—fifty-five—fifty-four,' said Hol-mer. 'Here we are. "Lieutenant Austin Limmason. Missing." That was before Sebastopol. What an infernal shame! Insulted one of their colonels, and was quietly shipped off. Thirty years of his life wiped out.'

'But he never apologised. Said he'd see him damned first,' chorused the mess.

' Poor chap! I suppose he never had the chance after-wards. How did he come here?' said the colonel.

The dingy heap in the chair could give no answer.

'Do you know who you are?'

It laughed weakly.

'Do you know that you are Limmason—^Lieutenant Limmason of the White Hussars?'

Swiftly as a shot came the answer, in a slightly surprised tone, 'Yes, I'm Limmason, of course.' The light died out in his eyes, and the man collapsed, watch-ing every motion of Dirkovitch with terror. A flight from Siberia may fix a few elementary facts in the mind, but it does not seem to lead to continuity of thought. The man could not explain how, like a homing pigeon, he had found his way to his own old mess again. Of what he had suffered or seen he knew nothing. He cringed before Dirkovitch as instinctively as he had pressed the spring of the candlestick, sought the picture of the drum-horse, and answered to the toast of the Queen. The rest was a blank that the dreaded Russian tongue could only in part remove. His head bowed on his breast, and he giggled and cowered alternately.

The devil that lived in the brandy prompted Dir-kovitch at this extremely inopportune moment to make a speech. He rose, swaying slightly, gripped the table-edge, while his eyes glowed like opals, andbegan:

' Fellow-soldiers glorious—true friends and hospitables.It was an accident, and deplorable—most deplorable.'Here he smiled sweetly all round the mess. 'But youwall think of this little, little thing. So little, is it not?The Czar! Posh! I slap my fingers—I snap my fingersat him. Do I believe in him? No! But in us Slavwho has done nothing, him I beHeve. Seventy—howmuch—millions peoples that have done nothing—notone thing. Posh! Napoleon was an episode.' Hebanged a hand on the table. 'Hear you, old peoples,we have done nothing in \hQ world—out here. Allour work is to do; and it shall be done, old peoples.Get a-way!' He waved his hand imperiously, andpointed to the man. *You see him. He is not good to

see. He was just one little—oh, so little—accident, thatno one remembered. Now he is That! So will you be,brother-soldiers so brave—so will you be. But youwill never come back. You will all go where he isgone, or'—he pointed to the great coffin-shadow on theceiling, and muttering, 'Seventy millions—get a-way,you old peoples,' fell asleep.

' Sweet, and to the point,' said little Mildred. ' What'sthe use of getting wroth? Let's make this poor devilcomfortable.'

But that was a matter suddenly and swiftly takenfrom the loving hands of the White Hussars. The Ueu-tenant had returned only to go away again three dayslater, when the wail of the Dead March, and the trampof the squadrons, told the wondering Station, who sawno gap in the mess-table, that an officer of the regimenthad resigned his new-found commission.

And Dirkovitch, bland, supple, and always genial,went away too by a night train. Little Mildred andanother man saw him off, for he was the guest of themess, and even had he smitten the colonel with the openhand, the law of that mess allowed no relaxation of hos-pitality.

' Good-bye, Dirkovitch, and a pleasant journey,' saidlittle Mildred.

^Au revoir,^ said the Russian.

'Indeed! But we thought you were going home?'

*Yes, but I will come again. My dear friends, isthat road shut?' He pointed to where the North Starburned over the Khyber Pass.

'By Jove! I forgot. Of course. Happy to meetyou, old man, any time you like. Got everything youwant? Cheroots, ice, bedding? That's all right. Well,au revoir, Dirkovitch.'

^Um/ said the other man, as the tail-lights of thetrain grew small. ^ Of—all—the— unmitigated !'

Little Mildred answered nothing, but watched theNorth Star and hummed a selection from a recent Simlaburlesque that had much deHghted the White Hussars.It ran—

I'm sorry for Mister Bluebeard,I'm sorry to cause him pain;But a terrible spree there's sure to beWhen he comes back again.

There's a convict more in the Central Jail,

Behind the old mud wall;There's a lifter less on the Border trail,And the Queen's Peace over all,

Dear boysThe Queen's Peace over all.

For we must bear our leader's blame,

On us the shame will fall,If we lift our hand from a fettered landAnd the Queen's Peace over all.

Dear boys,The Queen's Peace over all!

The Running of Shindand.

The Indus had risen in flood without warning. Lastnight it was a fordable shallow; to-night five miles ofraving muddy water parted bank and caving bank, andthe river was still rising under the moon. A litter borne by six bearded men, all unused to the work, stopped in the white sand that bordered the whiter plain.

'It's God's will,' they said. 'We dare not cross to-night, even in a boat. Let us light a fire and cook food. We be tired men.'

They looked at the litter inquiringly. Within, the Deputy Commissioner of the Kot-Kumharsen district lay dying of fever. They had brought him across country, six fighting-men of a frontier clan that he had

won over to the paths of a moderate righteousness, when he had broken down at the foot of their inhos-pitable hills. And Tallantire, his assistant, rode with them, heavy-hearted as heavy-eyed with sorrow and lack of sleep. He had served under the sick man for three years, and had learned to love him as men asso-ciated in toil of the hardest learn to love—or hate. Drop-ping from his horse he parted the curtains of the litter and peered inside.

'Orde—Orde, old man, can you hear? We have to wait till the river goes down, worse luck.'

'I hear,' returned a dry whisper. ^Wait till the river goes down. I thought w^e should reach camp before the dawn. Polly knows. She'll meet me.'

One of the litter-men stared across the river and caught a faint twinkle of light on the far side. He whispered to Tallantire, 'There are his camp-fires, and his wife. They will cross in the morning, for they have better boats. Can he live so long?'

Tallantire shook his head. Yardley-Orde was very near to death. What need to vex his soul with hopes of a meeting that could not be? The river gulped at the banks, brought down a cliff of sand, and snarled the more hungrily. The litter-men sought for fuel in the waste—dried camel-thorn and refuse of the camps that had waited at the ford. Their sword-belts clinked as they moved softly in the haze of the moonlight, and Tal-lantire's horse coughed to explain that he would like a blanket.

'I'm cold too,' said the voice from the litter. 'I fancy this is the end. Poor Polly!'

Tallantire rearranged the blankets. Khoda Dad Khan, seeing this, stripped off his own heav\'7d^-wadded sheepskin coat and added it to the pile. 'I shall be

warm by the fire presently/ said he. Tallantire took the wasted body of his chief into his arms and held it against his breast. Perhaps if they kept him very warm Orde might live to see his wife once more. If only blind Providence would send a three-foot fall in the river!

'That's better/ said Orde faintly. 'Sorry to be a nuisance, but is—is there anything to drink?'

They gave him milk and whisky, and Tallantire felt a little warmth against his own breast. Orde began to mutter.

'It isn't that I mind dying,' he said. 'It's leaving Polly and the district. Thank God! we have no chil-dren. Dick, you know, I'm dipped—awfully dipped—debts in my first five years' service. It isn't much of a pension, but enough for her. She has her mother at home. Getting there is the difficulty. And—and—you see, not being a soldier's wife '

'We'll arrange the passage home, of course,' said Tallantire quietly.

'It's not nice to think of sending round the hat; but, good Lord! how many men I lie here and remem-ber that had to do it! Morten's dead—he was of my year. Shaughnessy is dead, and he had children; I remember he used to read us their school-letters; what a bore we thought him! Evans is dead—Kot-Kum-harsen killed him! Ricketts of Myndonie is dead—and I'm going too. "Man that is born of a woman is small potatoes and few in the hill." That reminds me, Dick; the four Khusru Kheyi villages in our border want a one-third remittance this spring. That's fair; their crops are bad. See that they get it, and speak to Ferris about the canal. I should like to have lived till thatwas finished; it means so much for the North-Indusvillages—but Ferris is an idle beggar—wake him up.

You'll have charge of the district till my successor comes.I wish they would appoint you permanently; you knowthe folk. I suppose it will be Bullows, though. 'Goodman, but too weak for frontier work; and he doesn'tunderstand the priests. The blind priest at Jagai willbear watching. You'll find it in my papers,—in theuniform-case, I think. Call the Khusru Kheyl men up;I'll hold my last pubHc audience. Khoda Dad Khan!'

The leader of the men sprang to the side of the litter,his companions following.

*Men, I'm dying,' said Orde quickly, in the vernacular;'and soon there will be no more Orde Sahib to twistyour tails and prevent you from raiding cattle.'

'God forbid this thing!' broke out the deep basschorus. 'The Sahib is not going to die.'

'Yes, he is; and then he will know whether Mahomedspeaks truth, or Moses. But you must be good men,when I am not here. Such of you as live in our bordersmust pay your taxes quietly as before. I have spoken ofthe villages to be gently treated this year. Such of youas live in the hills must refrain from cattle-Hfting, andburn no more thatch, and turn a deaf ear to the voice ofthe priests, who, not knowing the strength of the Govern-ment, v/ould lead you into foolish wars, wherein you willsurely die and your crops be eaten by strangers. Andyou must not sack any caravans, and must leave yourarms at the pohce-post when you come in; as has beenyour custom, and my order. And Tallantire Sahib willbe with you, but I do not know who takes my place. Ispeak now true talk, for I am as it were already dead,my children,—for though ye be strong men, ye arechildren.'

'And thou art our father and our mother,' broke inKhoda Dad Khan with an oath. 'What shall we do<

now there is no one to speak for us, or to teach us togo wisely!'

'There remains Tallantire Sahib. Go to him; heknows your talk and your heart. Keep the young menquiet, listen to the old men, and obey. Khoda DadKhan, take my ring. The watch and chain go to thybrother. Keep those things for my sake, and I willspeak to whatever God I may encounter and tell himthat the Khusru Kheyl are good men. Ye have myleave to go.'

Khoda Dad Khan, the ring upon his finger, chokedaudibly as he caught the well-known formula that closedan interview. His brother turned to look across theriver. The dawn was breaking, and a speck of whiteshowed on the dull silver of the stream. 'She comes,'said the man under his breath. ' Can he live for anothertwo hours?' And he pulled the newly-acquired watchout of his belt and looked uncomprehendingly at thedial, as he had seen Englishmen do.

For two hours the bellying sail tacked and blunderedup and down the river, Tallantire still clasping Orde inhis arms, and Khoda Dad Khan chafing his feet. Hespoke now and again of the district and his wife, but,as the end neared, more frequently of the latter. Theyhoped he did not know that she was even then risk-ing her life in a crazy native boat to regain him. Butthe awful foreknowledge of the dying deceived them.Wrenching himself forward, Orde looked through thecurtains and saw how near was the sail. 'That's Polly,'he said simply, though his mouth was wried with agony.* Polly and—the grimmest practical joke ever played on aman. Dick—you'll—have—to—explain.'

And an hour later Tallantire met on the bank awoman in a gingham riding-habit and a sun-hat who

cried out to him for her husband—her boy and her darling—while Khoda Dad Khan threw himself face-down onthe sand and covered his eyes.

II

The very simplicity of the notion was its charm. Whatmore easy to win a reputation for far-seeing statesman-ship, originality, and, above all, deference to the desiresof the people, than by appointing a child of the countryto the rule of that country? Two hundred millions ofthe most loving and grateful folk under Her Majesty'sdominion would laud the fact, and their praise wouldendure for ever. Yet he was indifferent to praise orblame, as befitted the Very Greatest of All the Viceroys.His administration w^as based upon principle, and theprinciple must be enforced in season and out of season.His pen and tongue had created the New India, teemingwith possibilities—loud-voiced, insistent, a nation amongnations—all his very own. Wherefore the Very Greatestof All the Viceroys took another step in advance, andwith it counsel of those who should have advised himon the appointment of a successor to Yardley-Orde.There was a gentleman and a member of the Bengal CivilService who had won his place and a university degreeto boot in fair and open competition with the sons ofthe English. He was cultured, of the world, and, ifreport spoke truly, had wisely and, above all, sympatheti-cally ruled a crowded district in South-Eastern Bengal.He had been to England and charmed many drawing-rooms there. His name, if the Viceroy recollected aright,was Mr. Grish Chunder De, M. A. In short, did any-body see any objection to the appointment, always onprinciple, of a man of the people to rule the people?The district in South-Eastern Bengal might with advan-

tage, he apprehended, pass over to a younger civilianof Mr. G. C. De's nationality (who had written a re-markably clever pamphlet on the political value ofsympathy in administration); and Mr. G. C. De couldbe transferred northward to Kot-Kumharsen. TheViceroy was averse, on principle, to interfering withappointments under control of the Provincial Govern-ments. He wished it to be understood that he merelyrecommended and advised in this instance. As regardedthe mere question of race, Mr. Grish Chunder De wasmore EngHsh than the EngHsh, and yet possessed of thatpecuHar sympathy and insight which the best among thebest Service in the world could only win to at the endof their service.

The stern, black-bearded kings who sit about theCouncil-board of India divided on the step, with the in-evitable result of driving the Very Greatest of All theViceroys into the borders of hysteria, and a bewilderedobstinacy pathetic as that of a child.

*The principle is sound enough,' said the weary-eyedHead of the Red Pro\'inces in which Kot-Kumharsenlay, for he too held theories. ' The only difficulty is '

'Put the screw on the District officials; brigade Dewith a very strong Deputy Commissioner on each sideof him; give him the best assistant in the Province;rub the fear of God into the people beforehand; and ifanything goes wrong, say that his colleagues didn't backhim up. All these lovely little experuents recoil onthe District-Officer in the end,' said the Knight of theDrawn Sword with a truthful brutahty that made theHead of the Red Provinces shudder. And on a tacitunderstanding of this kind the transfer was accomplished,as quietly as might be for many reasons.

It is sad to think that what goes for public opinion

in India did not generally see the wisdom of the Viceroy'sappointment. There were not lacking indeed hirelingorgans, notoriously in the pay of a tyrannous bureau-cracy, who more than hinted that His Excellency was afool, a dreamer of dreams, a doctrinaire, and, worst ofall, a trifler with the lives of men. 'The Viceroy's Ex-cellence Gazette,' pubhshed in Calcutta, was at pains tothank 'Our beloved Viceroy for once more and againthus gloriously vindicating the potentialities of th-^BengaH nations for extended executive and administra-tive duties in foreign parts beyond our ken. We do notat all doubt that our excellent fellow-townsman, Mr.Grish Chunder De, Esq., M. A., will uphold the prestigeof the Bengali, notwithstanding what underhand intrigueand peshhindi may be set on foot to insidiously nip hisfame and blast his prospects among the proud civilians,some of which will now have to serve under a despisednative and take orders too. How will you like that,Misters? We entreat our beloved Viceroy still to sub-stantiate himself superiorly to race-prejudice and colour-blindness, and to allow the flower of this now our CivilService all the full pays and allowances granted to hismore fortunate brethren.'

Ill

'When does this man take over charge? I'm alonejust now, and I gather that I'm to stand fast under him.'

'Would you have cared for a transfer?' said BuUowskeenly. Then, laying his hand on Tallantire's shoulder:'We're all in the same boat; don't desert us. And yet,why the devil should you stay, if you can get anothercharge?'

'It was Orde's,' said Tallantire simply.

'Well, it's De'.^ now. He's a Bengali of the BengaHs,

crammed with code and case law; a beautiful man so faras routine and deskwork go, and pleasant to talk to.They naturally have always kept him in his own homedistrict, where all his sisters and his cousins and hisaunts lived, somewhere south of Dacca. He did no morethan turn the place into a pleasant Httle family preserve,allowed his subordinates to do what they liked, and leteverybody have a chance at the shekels. Consequentlyhe's immensely popular down there.'

'I've nothing to do with that. How on earth am I toexplain to the district that they are going to be governedby a BengaH? Do you—does the Government, I mean—suppose that the Khusru Kheyl will sit quiet whenthey once know? What will the Mahomedan heads ofvillages say? How will the poKce—Muzbi Sikhs andPathans—how will they work under him? We couldn'tsay anything if the Government appointed a sweeper;but my people will say a good deal, you know that. It'sa piece of cruel folly!'

'My dear boy, I know all that, and more. I've rep-resented it, and have been told that I am exhibiting"culpable and puerile prejudice." By Jove, if theKhusru Kheyl don't exhibit something worse than thatI don't know the Border! The chances are that youwill have the district alight on your hands, and I shallhave to leave my work and help you pull through. Ineedn't ask you to stand by the BengaH man in everypossible way. You'll do that for your own sake.'

'For Orde's. I can't say that I care twopence per-sonally.'

'Don't be an ass. It's grievous enough, God knows,and the Government will know later on; but that's noreason for your sulking. You must try to run the dis-trict, you must stand between hini and as much insult a=

possible; you must show him the ropes; you must pacifythe Khusru Kheyl, and just warn Curbar of the Police tolook out for trouble by the way. I'm always at the endof a telegraph-wire, and wilHng to peril my reputationto hold the district together. You'll lose yours, of course.If you keep things straight, and he isn't actually beatenwith a stick when he's on tour, he'll get all the credit.If anything goes wrong, you'll be told that you didn'tsupport him loyally.'

'I know what I've got to do,' said TaUantire wearily,'and I'm going to do it. But it's hard.'

'The work is with us, the event is with Allah,—asOrde used to say when he was more than usually in hotwater.' And Bullows rode away.

That two gentlemen in Her Majesty's Bengal CivilService should thus discuss a third, also in that service,and a cultured and affable man withal, seems strangeand saddening. Yet Hsten to the artless babble of theBlind Mullah of Jagai, the priest of the Khusru Kheyl,sitting upon a rock overlooking the Border. Five yearsbefore, a chance-hurled shell from a screw-gun batteryhad dashed earth in the face of the Mullah, then urginga rush of Ghazis against half a dozen British bayonets.So he became bhnd, and hated the EngHsh none the lessfor the httle accident. Yardley-Orde knew his failing,and had many times laughed at him therefor.

'Dogs you are,' said the Blind Mullah to the Hsteningtribesmen round the fire. 'Whipped dogs! Becauseyou Hstened to Orde Sahib and called him father andbehaved as his children, the British Government haveproven how they regard you. Orde Sahib ye know isdead.'

'Ai! ai! ai!' said half a dozen voices.

'He was a man. Comes now in his stead, whom thirU

ye? A Bengali of Bengal—an eater of fish from theSouth/

'A lie!' said Khoda Dad Khan. 'And but for thesmall matter of thy priesthood, I'd drive my gun butt-first down thy throat.'

'Oho, art thou there, Hckspittle of the Enghsh? Goin to-morrow across the Border to pay service to OrdeSahib's successor, and thou shalt slip thy shoes at thetent-door of a BengaH, as thou shaJt hand thy offering tua Bengali's black fist. This I know; and in my youth>when a young man spoke evil to a Mullah holding thedoors of Heaven and Hell, the gun-butt was not rammeddown the Mullah's gullet. No!'

The Blind Mullah hated Khoda Dad Khan withAfghan hatred; both being rivals for the headship of thetribe; but the latter was feared for bodily as the other forspiritual gifts. Khoda D ad Khan looked at Orde's ringand grunted, ' I go in to-morrow because I am not an oldfool, preaching war against the Enghsh. If the Govern-ment, smitten with madness, have done this, then . . ."

'Then,' croaked the Mullah, 'thou wilt take out theyoung men and strike at the four villages within theBorder?'

'Or wring thy neck, black raven of Jehannum, for abearer of ill-tidmgs.'

Khoda Dad Khan oiled his long locks with great care,put on his best Bokhara belt, a new turban-cap and finegreen shoes, and accompanied by a few friends camedown from the hills to pay a visit to the new DeputyCommissioner of Kot-Kumharsen. Also he bore tribute'—four or five priceless gold mohurs of Akbar's time in awhite handkerchief. These the Deputy Commissionerwould touch and remit. The little ceremony used to bea sign tliat, so far as Khoda Dad Khan's personal influ-

igS LIFE'S IL\XDICAP

ence went, the Khusni Kheyl would be good boys,—tillthe next time; especially if Khoda Dad Khan hap-pened to lilve the new Deputy Commissioner. In Yardley-Orde's consulship his visit concluded with a sumptuousdinner and perhaps forbidden Kquors; certainly withsome wonderful tales and great good-felloy\^ship. ThenKhoda Dad Khan would swagger back to his hold, vow-ing that Orde Sahib v/as one prince and Tallantire Saliibanother, and that whosoever went a-raiding into Britishterritory would be flayed aHve. On this occasion hefound the Deputy Commissioner's tents looking much asusual. Regarding himself as pri^dleged he strode throughthe open door to confont a suave, portly Bengali inEnglish costume writing at a table. Unversed in theelevating influence of education, and not in the leastcaring for university degrees, Khoda Dad Khan promptlyset the man dov.Ti for a Babu—the native clerk of theDeputy Commissioner—a hated and despised animal.

'UghI' said he cheerfully. 'Wliere's your master,Babujee?'

'I am the Deputy Commissioner,' said the gentlemanin Enghsh.

Now he overvalued the effects of university degrees,and stared Khoda Dad Khan in the face. But if fromyour earliest infancy you have been accustomed to lookon battle, murder, and sudden death, if spilt blood affectsyour nerves as much as red paint, and, above all, if youhave faithfully believed that the BengaH was the servantof all Hindustan, and that all Hindustan was vastlyinferior to your own large, lustful self, you can endure,even though uneducated, a very large amount of lookingover. You can even stare down a graduate of an Oxfordcollege if the latter has been born in a hothouse, of stockbred in a hothousev ^nd fearing physical pain as some

men fear sin; especially if your opponent's mother hasfrightened him to sleep in his youth with horrible storiesof devils inhabiting Afghanistan, and dismal legends oithe black North. The eyes behind the gold spectaclessought the floor. Khoda Dad Khan chuckled, andswung out to find Tallantire hard by. 'Here,' said heroughly, thrusting the coins before him, 'touch andremit. That answers for my good behaviour. But, OSahib, has the Government gone mad to send a blackBengaH dog to us? And am I to pay service to such anone? And are you to work under him? What does itmean?'

'It is an order,' said Tallantire. He had expectedsomething of this kind. 'He is a very clever S-sahib.'

'He a Sahib! He's a kala admi—a black man—-unfit to run at the tail of a potter's donkey. All thepeoples of the earth have harried Bengal. It is written,Thou knowest when we of the North v/anted women orplunder whither went we? To Bengal—where else?What child's talk is this of Sahibdom—after Orde Sahibtoo! Of a truth the BKnd Mullah was right.'

'What of him?' asked Tallantire uneasily. He mis-trusted that old man witli his dead eyes and his deadlytongue.

'Nay, now, because of the oath that I sware to OrdeSahib when we watched him die by the river yonder, Iwill tell. In the first place, is it true that the EngHshhave set the heel of the BengaH on their own neck, andthat there is no more EngHsh rule in the land?'

'I am here,' said TaHantire, 'and I serve the Maha-ranee of England.'

'The Mullah said otherwise, and further that becausewe loved Orde Sahib the Government sent us a pig toshow that we were dog?, who till now have been held by

800 LIFE'S HA^miCAP

the strong hand. Also that they were taking away thewhite soldiers, that more Hindustanis might come, andthat all was changing.'

This is the worst of ill-considered handling of a verylarge country. What looks so feasible in Calcutta, soright in Bombay, so unassailable in Madras, is mis-understood by the North and entirely changes its com-plexion on the banks of the Indus. Khoda Dad Khanexplained as clearly as he could that, though he himselfintended to be good, he really could not answer for themore reckless members of his tribe under the leadershipof the BHnd Mullah. They might or they might notgive trouble, but they certainly had no intention what-ever of obeying the new Deputy Commissioner. WasTallantire perfectly sure that in the event of any system-atic border-raiding the force in the district could put itdown promptly?

'Tell the Mullah if he talks any more fool's talk,' saidTallantire curtly, 'that he takes his men on to certaindeath, and his tribe to blockade, trespass-fine, and blood-money. But why do I talk to one who no longer carriesweight in the counsels of the tribe?'

Khoda Dad Khan pocketed that insult. He hadlearned something that he much wanted to know, andreturned to his hills to be sarcastically comphmented bythe Mullah, whose tongue raging round the camp-fireswas deadlier flame than ever dung-cake fed.

IV

Be pleased to consider here for a moment the unknowndistrict of Kot-Kumharsen. It lay cut lengthways bythe Indus under the line of the Khusru liills—rampartsof useless earth and tumbled stone. It was seventymiles long by fifty broad, maintained a population of something less than two hundred thousand, and paid taxes to the extent of forty thousand pounds a year on an area that was by rather more than half sheer, hopeless waste. The cultivators were not gentle people, the miners for salt were less gentle still, and the cattle-breeders least gentle of all. A police-post in the top right-hand corner and a tiny mud fort in the top left-liand corner prevented as much salt-smuggHng and cittle-lifting as the influence of the civihans could not put down; and in the bottom right-hand corner lay Ju-mala, the district headquarters—a pitiful knot of lime-washed bams facetiously rented as houses, reeking with frontier fever, leaking in the rain, and ovens in the sum-mer.

It was to this place that Grish Chunder De was travelling, there formally to take over charge of the dis-trict. But the news of his coming had gone before. BengaHs were as scarce as poodles among the simple Borderers, who cut each other's heads open with their long spades and worshipped impartially at Hindu and Mahomedan shrines. They crowded to see him, point-ing at him, and diversely comparing him to a gravid milch-buffalo, or a broken-down horse, as their limited range of metaphor prompted. They laughed at his poHce-guard, and wished to know how long the burly Sikhs were going to lead Bengali apes. They inquired whether he had brought his women with him, and ad-vised him expKcitly not to tamper with theirs. It re-mained for a wrinkled hag by the roadside to slap her lean breasts as he passed, crying, 'I have suckled six that could have eaten six thousand of him. The Govern-ment shot them, and made this That a king!' Whereat a blue-turbaned huge-boned plough-mender shouted, *Have hope, mother o' mine! He may yet go the way

of thy wastrels.' And the children, the little brown puff-balls, regarded curiously. It was generally a good thing for infancy to stray into Orde Sahib's tent, where copper coins w^ere to be v/on for the mere wishing, and tales of the most authentic, such as even their mothers knew but the first half of. No! This fat black man could never tell them how Pir Prith hauled the eye-teeth out of ten devils; how the big stones came to Heall in a row on top of the Khusru hills, and what happened if you shouted through the village-gate to the gray wolf at even 'Badl Khas is dead.' Meantime Grish Chunder De talked hastily and much to Tallantire, after the manner of those who are 'more English than the Enghsh,'•—of Oxford and 'home,' with much curious book-knowl-edge of bump-suppers, cricket-matches, hunting-runs, and other unholy sports of the ahen. 'We must get these fellows in hand,' he said once or twice uneasily; *get them well in hand, and drive them on a tight rein. No use, you know, being slack with your district.'

And a moment later Tallantire heard Debendra Nath De, who brotherliwise had followed his kinsman's fortune and hoped for the shadow of his protection as a pleader, whisper in Bengali, 'Better are dried fish at Dacca than drawn swords at Delhi. Brother of mine, these men are devils, as our mother said. And you will always have to ride upon a horse!'

That night there was a pubKc audience in a broken-down little town thirty miles from Jumala, when the new Deputy Commissioner, in reply to the greetings of the subordinate native officials, delivered a speech. It was a carefully thought-out speech, which w^ould have been very valuable had not his third sentence begun with three innocent words, 'Hamara hookum hai—It is my order.' Then there was a laugh, clear and bell-Hke, from

the back of the big tent, where a few border landholders sat, and the laugh grew and scorn mingled with it, and the lean, keen face of Debendra Nath De paled, and Grish Chunder turning to Tallantire spake: ^You—you put up this arrangement.' Upon that instant the noise of hoofs rang without, and there entered Curbar, the Dis-trict Superintendent of PoHce, sweating and dusty. The State had tossed him into a comer of the province for seventeen weary years, there to check smuggling of salt, and to hope for promotion that never came. He had forgotten how to keep his white uniform clean, had screwed rusty spurs into patent-leather shoes, and clothed his head indifferently with a helmet or a turban. Soured, old, worn with heat and cold, he waited till he should be entitled to sufficient pension to keep him from starving.

'Tallantire,' said he, disregarding Grish Chunder De, 'come outside. I want to speak to you.' They withdrew. 'It's this,' continued Curbar. 'The Khusru Kheyl have rushed and cut up half a dozen of the coolies on Ferris's new canal-embankment; killed a couple of m.en and carried off a woman. I wouldn't trouble you about that—Ferris is after them and Hugonin, my as-sistant, with ten mounted police. But that's only the beginning, I fancy. Their fires are out on the Hassan Ardeb heights, and unless we're pretty quick there'll be a flare-up all along our Border. They are sure to raid the four Khusru villages on our side of the line; there's been bad blood between them for years; and you know the Blind Mullah has been preaching a holy war since Orde went out. What's your notion?'

'Damn!' said Tallantire thoughtfully. 'They've be-gun quick. Well, it seems to me I'd better ride off to Fort Ziar and get what men I can there to picket among

the lowland villages, if it's not too late. Tommy Dodd commands at Fort Ziar, I think. Ferris and Hugonin

ought to teach the canal-thieves a lesson, and No,

we can't have the Head of the Police ostentatiously guarding the Treasury. You go back to the canal. I'll wire Bullows to come into Jumala with a strong police-guard, and sit on the Treasury. They won't touch the place, but it looks well.'

'I—I—I insist upon knowing what this means,' said the voice of the Deputy Commissioner, who had followed the speakers.

' Oh!' said Curbar, who being in the Police could not understand that fifteen years of education must, on principle, change the Bengali into a Briton. 'There has been a fight on the Border, and heaps of men are killed. There's going to be another fight, and heaps more will be kiUed.'

'What for?'

'Because the teeming millions of this district don't exactly approve of you, and think that under your benign rule they are going to have a good time. It strikes me that you had better make arrangements. I act, as you know, by your orders. What do you advise?'

*I—I take you all to witness that I have not yet assumed charge of the district,' stammered the Deputy Commissioner, not in the tones of the 'more English.'

'Ah, I thought so. Well, as I was saying, Tallantire, your plan is sound. Carry it out. Do you want an escort?'

'No; only a decent horse. But how about wiring to headquarters?'

'I fancy, from the colour of his cheeks, that your superior officer will send some wonderful telegrams before the night's over. Let him do that, and we shall have

half the troops of the province coming up to see what's the trouble. Well, run along, and take care of yourself—the Khusru Kheyl jab upwards from below, remember. Ho! Mir Khan, give Tallantire Sahib the best of the horses, and tell five men to ride to Jumala with the Dep-uty Commissioner Sahib Bahadur. There is a hurry toward.'

There was; and it was not in the least bettered by Debendra Nath De cHnging to a poKceman's bridle and demanding the shortest, the very shortest way to Jumala. Now originality is fatal to the Bengali. Debendra Nath should have stayed vath his brother, who rode steadfastly for Jumala on the railway-line, thanking gods entirely unknov/n to the most cathoUc of universities that he had not taken charge of the district, and could still—happy resource of a fertile race!—fall sick.

And I grieve to say that when he reached his goal two poHcemen, not devoid of rude wit, who had been con-ferring together as they bumped in their saddles, arrangedan entertainment for his behoof. It consisted of first oneand then the other entering his room with prodigiousdetails of war, the massing of bloodthirsty and deviUshtribes, and the burning of towns. It was almost as good,said these scamps, as riding with Curbar after evasiveAfghans. Each invention kept the hearer at work forhalf an hour on telegrams which the sack of Delhi wouldhardly have justified. To every power that could movea bayonet or transfer a terrified man, Grish Chunder Deappealed telegraphically. He was alone, his assistantshad fled, and in truth he had not taken over charge ofthe district. Had the telegrams been despatched manythings would have occurred; but since the only signallerin Jumala had gone to bed, and the station-master, afterone look at the tremendous pile of paper, discovered that

railway regulations forbade the forwarding of imperialmessages, policemen Ram Singh and Nihal Singh werefain to turn the stuff into a pillow and slept on it verycomfortably.

Tallantire drove his spurs into a ramxpant skewbaldstallion v/ith china-blue eyes, and settled himself for theforty-mile ride to Fort Ziar. Knowing his district blind-fold, he wasted no tim.e hunting for short cuts, but headedacross the richer grazing-ground to the ford where Ordehad died and been buried. The dusty ground deadenedthe noise of his horse's hoofs, the moon threw his shadow,a restless gobHn, before him, and the heavy dew drenchedhim to the skin. Hillock, scrub that brushed against thehorse's belly, unmetalled road where the whip-like foHageof the tamarisks lashed his forehead, illimitable levels oflowland furred wdth bent and speckled with drowsingcattle, Vv^aste, and hullock anew, dragged themselves past,and the skewbald was labouring in the deep sand of theIndus-ford. Tallantire was conscious of no distinctthought till the nose of the dawdhng ferry-boat groundedon the farther side, and his horse shied snorting at thewhite headstone of Orde's grave. Then he uncovered,and shouted that the dead might hear, 'They're out, oldman! Wish me luck.' In the cliill of the dawn he washammering with a stirrup-iron at the gate of Fort Ziar,where fifty sabres of that tattered regimicnt, the BeloochBeshaklis were supposed to guard Her Majesty's interestsalong a few hundred miles of Border. This particularfort was commanded by a subaltern, vv^ho, born of theancient family of the Derouletts, naturally answered tothe name of Tommy Dodd. Him Tallantire found robedin a sheepskin coat, shaking with fever Uke an aspen, andtrying to read the native apothecary's hst of invalids.

'So you've come, too,' said he. 'Well, we're all sick here, and I don't think I can horse thirty men; but we'rebub—bub—bub blessed willing. Stop, does this im-press you as a trap or a He?' He tossed a scrap of paperto Tallantire, on which was written painfully in crabbedGurmukhi, 'We cannot hold young horses. They willfeed after the moon goes down in the four border villagesissuing from the Jagai pass on the next night.' Then inEnglish round hand—'Your sincere friend.'

'Good man!' said Tallantire. 'That's Khoda DadKhan's v/ork, I know. It's the only piece of EngHsh hecould ever keep in his head, and he is immensely proudof it. He is pla\'7ddng against the Blind Mullah for hisown hand—the treacherous young ruffian!'

'Don't know the poHtics of the Khusru Kheyl, but ifyou're satisfied, I am. That was pitched in over thegate-head last night, and I thought we might pull our-selves together and see what was on. Oh, but we're sickwith fever here and no mistake! Is this going to be abig business, tliink you?' said Tommy Dodd.

Tallantire gave him briefly the outlines of the case, andTommy Dodd whistled and shook with fever alternately.That day he devoted to strategy, the art of war, and theenlivenment of the invahds, tiU at dusk there stood readyforty-two troopers, lean, worn, and dishevelled, whomTommy Dodd surveyed with pride, and addressed thus:'0 men! If you die you ^^dll go to Hell. Thereforeendeavour to keep alive. But if you go to Hell thatplace cannot be hotter than this place, and we are nottold that we shall there suffer from fever. Consequentlybe not afraid of dying. File out there!' They grinned,and went.

V

It will be long ere the Khusru Kheyl forget theirjoight attack an the lovdaud villages, The Mullah had

promised an easy victory and unlimited plunder; butbehold, armed troopers of the Queen had risen out ofthe very earth, cutting, slashing, and riding down underthe stars, so that no man knew where to turn, and allfeared that they had brought an army about their ears,and ran back to the hills. In the panic of that flightmore men were seen to drop from wounds inflicted byan Afghan knife jabbed upwards, and yet more fromlong-range carbine-fire. Then there rose a cry of treach-ery, and when they reached their own guarded heights,they had left, with some forty dead and sixty wounded,all their confidence in the Blind Mullah on the plainsbelow. They clamoured, swore, and argued round thefires; the women wailing for the lost, and the Mullahshrieking curses on the returned.

Then Khoda Dad Khan, eloquent and unbreathed,for he had taken no part in the fight, rose to improve theoccasion. He pointed out that the tribe owed every itemof its present misfortune to the Blind Mullah, who hadlied in every possible particular and talked them into atrap. It was undoubtedly an insult that a Bengali, theson of a Bengali, should presume to administer theBorder, but that fact did not, as the Mullah pretended,herald a general time of license and liftmg; and the inex-plicable madness of the English had not in the least im-paired their power of guarding their marches. On thecontrary, the baffled and out-generalled tribe would now,just when their food-stock was lowest, be blockadedfrom any trade with Hindustan until they had senthostages for good behaviour, paid compensation fordisturbance, and blood-money at the rate of thirty-sLxEnglish pounds per head for every %illager that theymight have slain. 'And ye know that those lowlanddogs will make oath that we have slain scores. Will the

Mullah pay the fines or must we sell our guns?' Alow growl ran round the fires. 'Now, seeing that allthis is the Mullah's work, and that we have gained noth-ing but promises of Paradise thereby, it is in my heartthat we of the Khusru Kheyl lack a shrine whereat topray. We are weakened, and henceforth how shall wedare to cross into the Madar Klieyl border, as has beenour custom, to kneel to Pir Sajji's tomb? The Madarmen v/ill fall upon us, and rightly. But our Mullah is aholy man. He has helped two score of us into Paradisethis night. Let him therefore accompany his flock, andwe will build over his body a dome of the blue tiles ofMooltan, and burn lamps at his feet every Friday night.He shall be a saint: we shall have a shrine; and there ourwomen shall pray for fresh seed to fill the gaps in ourfighting-tale. How think you?'

A grim chuckle followed the suggestion, and the softwheep, wheep of unscabbarded knives followed the chuc-kle. It was an excellent notion, and met a long felt wantof the tribe. The Mullah sprang to his feet, glaring withwithered eyeballs at the drawn death he could not see,and calling down, the curses of God and Mahomed onthe tribe. Then began a game of blind man's buff roundand between the fires, whereof Khuruk Shah, the tribalpoet, has sung in verse that will not die.

They tickled him gently under the armpit with theknife-point. He leaped aside screaming, only to feel acold blade drawn lightly over the back of his neck, or arifle-muzzle rubbing his beard. He called on his ad-herents to aid him, but most of these lay dead on theplains, for Khoda Dad Khan had been at some pains toarrange their decease. Men described to him the gloriesof the shrine they would build, and the little childrenclapping their hands cried, ^Run, Mullah, run! There's

a man behind you!' In the end, when the sport wearied,-Khoda Dad Khan's brother sent a knife home betweenhis ribs. 'Vv^herefore/ said Khoda Dad Khan withcharming simphcity, 'I am now Chief of the KhusruKheyl!' No man gainsaid him; and they all went tosleep very stiff and sore.

On the plain below Tommy Dodd was lecturingon the beauties of a cavalry charge by night, and Tal-lantire, bowed on his saddle, was gasping hystericallybecause there was a sword danghng from his wristflecked with the blood of the Khusru Kheyl, the tribethat Orde had kept in leash so well. When a Rajpoottrooper pointed out that the skewbald's right ear hadbeen taken oif at the root by some bhnd slash of its un-skilled rider, Tallantire broke down altogether, andlaughed and sobbed till Tommy Dodd made him lie downand rest.

'We must wait about till the morning,' said he. 'Imred to the Colonel just before v/e left, to send a wingof the BeshakKs after us. He'll be furious with me formonopoHsing the fun, though. Those beggars in the hillswon't give us any more trouble.'

^ Then tell the Beshaklis to go on and see whathas happened to Curbar on the canal. We m.ust patrolthe whole hne of the Border. You're quite sure. Tommy,that—that stuff was—v/as only the skewbald's ear?'

'Oh, quite,' said Tommy. 'You just missed cuttingoff liis head. / saw you when we went into the mess.Sleep, old man.'

Noon brought two squadrons of Beshaklis and aknot of furious brother ofhcers demanding the court-martial of Tommy Dodd for 'spoiHng the picnic,' anda gallop across country to the canal-works where Ferris,Curbar, and Hugonin were haranguing the terror-strickeo

coolies on the enormity of abandoning good work andhigh pay, merely because half a dozen of their fellowshad been cut down. The sight of a troop of the Beshaklisrestored wavering confidence, and the police-huntedsection of the Khusru Kheyl had the joy of watching thecanal-bank humming with Hfe as usual, while such oftheir men as had taken refuge in the watercourses andravines were being dri\en out by the troopers. Bysundown began the remorseless patrol of the Border bypolice and trooper, most Uke the cow-boys' eternal rideround restless cattle.

*Now,' said Khoda Dad Khan to his fellows, pointingout a line of twinkling fires below, ^ye may see how farthe old order changes. After their horse will come thelittle devil-guns that they can drag up to the tops ofthe hills, and, for aught I know, to the clouds when wecrown the hills. If the tribe-council thinks good, I willgo to Tallantire Sahib—who loves me—and see if I canstave off at least the blockade. Do I speak for thetribe?'

*Ay, speak for the tribe in God's name. How thoseaccursed fires wink! Do the EngHsh send their troopson the wire—or is this the work of the BengaH?'

As Khoda Dad Khan went down the hill he wasdelayed by an interview with a hard-pressed tribes-man, which caused him to return hastily for some-thing he had forgotten. Then, handing himself overto the two troopers who had been chasing his friend,he claimed escort to Tallantire Sahib, then with Bul-lows at Jumala. The Border was safe, and the timefor reasons in writing had begun.

* Thank Heaven!' said Bullows, 'that the troublecame at once. Of course we can never put down thereason in black and ^/hite. but all India will under-

stand. And it is better to have a sharp short out-break than five years of impotent administration insidethe Border. It costs less. Grish Chimder De hasreported himself sick, and has been transferred to hisown province without any sort of reprimand. Hewas strong on not having taken over the district.'

'Of course,' said Tallantire bitterly. 'Well, what amI supposed to have done that was wrong?'

'Oh, you will be told that you exceeded all yourpowers, and should have reported, and written, andadvised for three weeks until the Khusru Kheyl couldreally come down in force. But I don't think theauthorities will dare to make a fuss about it. They'vehad their lesson. Have you seen Curbar's version ofthe affair? He can't write a report, but he can speakthe truth,'

'What's the use of the truth? He'd much bettertear up tlie report. I'm sick and heartbroken overit all. It was so utterly unnecessary—except in thatit rid us of that Babu.'

Entered unabashed Khoda Dad Khan, a stuffedforage-net in his hand, and the troopers behind him.

'May you never be tired!' said he cheerily. 'Well,Sahibs, that was a good light, and Naim Shah's mother isin debt to you, Tallantire Sahib. A clean cut, they tellme, through jaw, wadded coat, and deep into the collar-bone. Well done! But I speak for the tribe. Therehas been a fault—a great fault. Thou knowest that Iand mine, Tallantire Sahib, kept the oath we swareto Orde Sahib on the banks of the Indus.'

'As an Afghan keeps his knife—sharp on one side,blunt on the other,' said Tallantire.

'The better swing in the blow, then. But I speakGod's truth. Only the Blind Mullah carried the young

men on the tip of his tongue, and said that there was nomore Border-law because a Bengali had been sent, and weneed not fear the EngHsh at all. So they came down toavenge that insult and get plunder. Ye know what be-fell, and how far I helped. Now five score of us are deador wounded, and we are all shamed and sorry, and desireno further war. Moreover, that ye may better Ksten tous, we have taken off the head of the Blind Mullah,whose evil counsels have led us to folly. I bring it forproof,'—and he heaved on the floor the head. 'He willgive no more trouble, for / am chief now, and so I sit ina higher place at all audiences. Yet there is an offset tothis head. That was another fault. One of the menfound that black Bengali beast, through whom thistrouble arose, wandering on horseback and weeping.Reflecting that he had caused loss of much good hfe,Alia Dad Khan, whom, if you choose, I will to-miorrowshoot, whipped off this head, and I bring it to youto cover your shame, that ye may bury it. See, no mankept the spectacles, though they were of gold.'

Slowly rolled to Tallantire's feet the crop-haired headof a spectacled Bengali gentleman, open-eyed, open-mouthed—the head of Terror incarnate. Bullows bentdown. 'Yet another blood-fine and a heavy one, KhodaDad Khan, for this is the head of Debendra Nath, theman's brother. The Babu is safe long since. All but thefools of the Khusru Kheyl know that.'

'Well, I care not for carrion. Quick meat for me.The thing was under our hills asking the road to Ju-mala and Alia Dad Khan showed him the road toJehannum, being, as thou sayest, but a fooi. Remainsnow what the Government will do to us. As to theblockade '

'Who art thou, seller of dog's flesh,' thundered Tallan-tire, *to speak of terms and treaties? Get hence to thehills—go, and wait there starving, till it shall please theGovernment to call thy people out for punishment—children and fools that ye be! Count your dead, and bestill. Best assured that the Government will send you aman!^

^Ay,' returned Khoda Dad Khan, 'for we also bemen.'

As he looked Tallantire between the eyes, he added,*And by God, Sahib, may thou be that man!'

Before my Spring I garnered Autumn's gain.Out of her time my field was white with grain,

The year gave up her secrets to my woe.Forced and deflowered each sick season lay,In mystery of increase and decay;I saw the sunset ere men saw the day,

Who am too wise in that I shotdd not know.

BUter Waters,

'But if it be a girl?'

'Lord of my life, it cannot be. I have prayed forso many nights, and sent gifts to Sheikh Badl's shrine sooften, that I know God will give us a son—a man-childthat shall grow into a man. Think of this and be glad.My mother shall be his mother till I can take him again,and the mullah of the Pattan mosque shall cast hisnativity—God send he be born in an auspicious hour!—and then, and then thou wilt never weary of me, thyslave.'

'Since when hast thou been a slave, my queen?"Since the beginning—till this mercy came to me.How could I be sure of thy love when I knew that I hadbeen bought with silver?'

'Nay, that was the dowry. I paid it to thy mother.*

'And she has buried it, and sits upon it aU day long

like a hen. What talk is yours of dower! I was bought

as though I had been a Lucknow dancing-girl instead of a

child.'

'Art thou sorry for the sale? *

'I have sorrowed; but to-day I am glad. Thou wiltnever cease to love me now?—answer, my king/

' Never—never. No.'

'Not even though the ^nein-log—the white women ofthy own blood—love thee? And remember, I havewatched them driving in the evening; they are very fair.'

'I have seen fire-balloons by the hundred. I haveseen the moon, and—then I saw no more iire-balloons.*

Ameera clapped her hands and laughed. 'Very goodtalk,' she said. Then with an assumption of great state-liness, 'It is enough. Thou hast my permission to de-part,—if thou wilt.'

The man did not move. He was sitting on a lowred-lacquered couch in a room furnished only with ablue and white floor-cloth, some rugs, and a very com-plete collection of native cushions. At his feet sat a"woman of sixteen, and she was all but all the world in hiseyes. By every rule and law she should have been other-wise, for he was an Enghshman, and she a Mussulman'sdaughter bought two years before from her mother, who,being left without money, would have sold Ameerashrieking to the Prince of Darkness if the price had beensufficient.

It was a contract entered into with a Hght heart;but even before the girl had reached her bloom shecame to fill the greater portion of John Holden's Hfe.For her, and the withered hag her mother, he had takena Kttle house overlooking the great red-walled city, andfound,—when the marigolds had sprung up by the wellin the courtyard and Ameera had estabHshed herselfaccording to her own ideas of comfort, and her motherhad ceased grumbling at the inadequacy of the cooking-places, the distance from the daily market, and at matters

of house-keeping in general,—that the house was to himhis home. Any one could enter his bachelor's bungalowby day or night, and the Hfe that he led there was anunlovely one. In the house in the city his feet onlycould pass beyond the outer courtyard to the women'srooms; and when the big wooden gate was bolted behindhim he was king in his own territory, with Ameera forqueen. And there was going to be added to this king-dom a third person whose arrival Holden felt inclined toresent. It interfered with his perfect happiness. Itdisarranged the orderly peace of the house that was hisown. But Ameera was wild with delight at the thoughtof it, and her mother not less so. The love of a man, andparticularly a white man, was at the best an inconstantaffair, but it might, both women argued, be held fast bya baby's hands. 'And then,' Ameera would always say,*then he will never care for the white mem-log. I hatethem all—I hate them all.'

*He will go back to his own people in time,' saidthe mother; 'but by the blessing of God that time is yetafar off.'

Holden sat silent on the couch thinking of the future,and his thoughts were not pleasant. The drawbacks ofa double life are manifold. The Government, withsingular care, had ordered him out of the station for afortnight on special duty in the place of a man who waswatching by the bedside of a sick wife. The verbalnotification of the transfer had been edged by a cheerfulremark that Holden ought to think himself lucky in beinga bachelor and a free man. He came to break the newsto Ameera.

*It is not good,' she said slowly, 'but it is not allbad. There is my mother here, and no harm will cometo me—unless indeed I die of pure joy. Go thou to

thy work and think no troublesome thoughts. When thedays are done I believe . . . nay, I am sure. And—and then I shall lay him in thy arms, and thou wilt loveme for i ever. The train goes to-night, at midnight is itnot? Go now, and do not let thy heart be heavy bycause of me. But thou wilt not delay in returning?Thou wilt not stay on the road to talk to the bold whitemem-log. Come back to me swiftly, my Hfe.'

As he left the courtyard to reach his horse that wastethered to the gate-post, Holden spoke to the white-haired old watchman who guarded the house, and badehim under certain contingencies despatch the filled-uptelegraph-form that Holden gave him. It was all thatcould be done, and with the sensations of a man whohas attended his own funeral Holden went away by thenight mail to his exile. Every hour of the day hedreaded the arrival of the telegram, and every hour ofthe night he pictured to himself the death of Ameera.In consequence his work for the State was not of first-rate quality, nor was his temper towards his colleaguesof the most amiable. The fortnight ended mthout asign from his home, and, torn to pieces by his anxieties,Holden returned to be swallowed up for two precioushours by a dinner at the club, wherein he heard, as aman hears in a swoon, voices telling him how execrablyhe had performed the other man's duties, and how hehad endeared himself to all his associates. Then he fledon horseback through the night with his heart in hismouth. There was no answer at first to his blows onthe gate, and he had just wheeled his horse round tokick it in when Pir Khan appeared with a lantern andheld his stirrup.

*Has aught occurred?' said Holden.

*The news does not come from my mouth, Protector
of the Poor, but ' He held out his shaking hand
as befitted the bearer of good news who is entitled to areward.

Holden hurried through the courtyard. A light burnedin the upper room. His horse neighed in the gateway,and he heard a shrill Uttle wail that sent all the blood intothe apple of his throat. It was a new voice, but it did notprove that Ameera was alive.

'Who is there?' he called up the narrow brick stair-case. >

There was a cry of delight from Ameera, and thenthe voice of the mother, tremulous with old age andpride—'We be two women and—the—man—thy—son.'

On the threshold of the room Holden stepped on anaked dagger, that was laid there to avert ill-luck, and itbroke at the hilt under his impatient heel.

' God is great!' cooed Ameera in the half-Hght. ' Thouhast taken his misfortunes on thy head.'

'Ay, but how is it with thee, life of my life? Oldwoman, how is it with her?'

' She has forgotten her sufferings for joy that the childis born. There is no harm; but speak softly,' said the mother.

'It only needed thy presence to make me all well,' said Ameera. ' My king, thou hast been very long away. What gifts hast thou for me? Ah, ah! It is I that bring gifts this time. Look, my Hfe, look. Was there ever such a babe? Nay, I am too weak even to clear my arm from him.'

'Rest then, and do not talk. I am here, bachari [little woman].'

'Well said, for there is a bond and a heel-rope [pee-charee] between us now that nothing can break. Look—canst thou see in this light? He is without spot

or blemish. Never was such a man-chfld. Ya illah Jhe shall be a pundit—no, a trooper of the Queen. And, my life, dost thou love me as well as ever, though I am faint and sick and worn? Answer truly.'

'Yea. I love as I have loved, with all my soul. Lie still, pearl, and rest.'

'Then do not go. Sit by ray side here—so. Mother, the lord of this house needs a cushion. Bring it.' There was an almost imperceptible movement on the part of the new life that lay in the hollow of Ameera's arm. 'Aho!' she said, her voice breaking with love. 'The babe is a champion from his birth. He is kicking me in the side with mighty kicks. Was there ever such a babe! And he is ours to us—thine and mine. Put thy hand on his head, but carefully, for he is very young, and men are unskilled in such matters.'

Very cautiously Holden touched with the tips of his fingers the downy head.

'He is of the faith,' said Ameera; 'for lying here in the night-watches I whispered the call to prayer and the profession of faith into his ears. And it is most marvellous that he was born upon a Friday, as I w^as born. Be careful of him, my life; but he can almost grip mth his hands.'

Holden found one helpless little hand that closed feebly on his finger. And the clutch ran through his body till it settled about his heart. Till then his sole thought had been for Ameera. He began to reahse that there was some one else in the world, but he could not feel that it was a veritable son with a soul. He sat down to think, and Ameera dozed hghtly.

' Get hence, sahih,^ said her mother under her breath. *It is not good that she should find you here on waking. She must be still.'

I go, said Holden submissively. 'Here be rupees. See that my baba gets fat and finds all that he needs/

The chink of the silver roused Ameera. 'I am his mother, and no hireling,' she said weakly. 'Shall I look to him more or less for the sake of money? Mother, give it back. I have born my lord a son.'

The deep sleep of weakness came upon her almost before the sentence was completed. Holden went down to the courtyard very softly with his heart at ease. Pir Khan, the old watchman, was chuckhng with delight. 'This house is now complete,' he said, and without further comment thrust into Holden's hands the hilt of a sabre worn many years ago when he, Pir Khan, served the Queen in the poHce. The bleat of a tethered goat came from the well-kerb.

'There be two,' said Pir Khan, 'two goats of the best. I bought them, and they cost much money; and since there is no birth-party assembled their flesh will be all mine. Strike craftily, sahib I 'Tis an ill-balanced sabre at the best. Wait till they raise their heads from crop-ping the marigolds.'

'And why?' said Holden, bewildered.

'For the birth-sacrifice. What else? Otherwise the child being unguarded from fate may die. The Protector of the Poor knows the fitting words to be said.'

Holden had learned them once with little thought that he would ever speak them in earnest. The touch of the cold sabre-hilt in his palm turned suddenly to the clinging grip of the child upstairs—the child that was his own son—and a dread of loss filled him.

'Strike!' said Pir Khan. 'Never life came into theworld but life was paid for it. See, the goats have raisedtheir heads. Now! With a drawing cut!'

Hardly knowing what he did Holden cut twice as he

muttered the Mahomedan prayer that runs: 'Almighty!In place of this my son I offer Hfe for Hfe, blood for blood,head for head, bone for bone, hair for hair, skin for skin/The waiting horse snorted and bounded in his pickets atthe smell of the raw blood that spirted over Holden'sriding-boots.

'Well smitten!' said Pir Khan, wiping the sabre. 'Aswordsman was lost in thee. Go with a Hght heart,Heaven-born. I am thy servant, and the servant of thyson. May the Presence live a thousand years and . . .the flesh of the goats is all mine?' Pir Khan drew backricher by a month's pay. Holden swung himself into thesaddle and rode off through the low-hanging wood-smokeof the evening. He was full of riotous exultation, alter-nating with a vast vague tenderness directed towards noparticular object, that made him choke as he bent overthe neck of his uneasy horse. 'I never felt like thisin my life,' he thought. 'I'll go to the club and pullmyself together.'

A game of pool was beginning, and the room was fullof men. Holden entered, eager to get to the light and thecompany of his fellows, singing at the top of his voice—

In Baltimore a-walking, a lady I did meet!

'Did you?' said the club-secretary from his corner.'Did she happen to tell you that your boots were wringingwet? Great goodness, man, it's blood!'

'Bosh!' said Holden, picking his cue from the rack.'May I cut in? It's dew. I've been riding throughhigh crops. My faith! my boots are in a mess though!'

'And if it be a girl she shall wear a wedding-ring,And if it be a boy he shall fight for his king,With his dirk, and his cap, and his little jacket blue,He shall walk the quarter-deck—'

'Yellow on blue—green next player/ said the markermonotonously.

^He shall walk the quarter-deck,—Am I green, marker?He shall walk the quarter-deck,— eh! that's a bad shot,—As his daddy used to do!'

'I don't see that you have anything to crow about,'said a zealous junior civilian acidly. 'The Governmentis not exactly pleased with your work when you relievedSanders.'

'Does that mean a wigging from headquarters?' saidHolden with an abstracted smile. 'I think I can standit.'

The talk beat up round the ever-fresh subject of eachman's work, and steadied Holden till it was time to goto his dark empty bungalow, where his butler receivedhim as one who knew all his affairs. Holden remainedawake for the greater part of the night, and his dreamswere pleasant ones.

II

' How old is he now?'

^Ya Utah I What a man's question! He is all butsix weeks old; and on this night I go up to the house-top with thee, my life, to count the stars. For that isauspicious. And he was born on a Friday under thesign of the Sun, and it has been told to me that he willoutlive us both and get wealth. Can we wish for aughtbetter, beloved?'

'There is nothing better. Let us go up to the roof,and thou shalt count the stars—but a few only, for thesky is heavy with cloud.'

'The winter rains are late, and maybe they come outof season. Come, before all the stars are hid. I haveput on my richest jewels.'

* Thou hast forgotten the best of all.*

^Ail Ours. He comes also. He has never yet seenthe skies.'

Ameera climbed the narrow staircase that led to theflat roof. The child, placid and unwinking, lay in the hollow of her right arm, gorgeous in silver-fringed muslin with a small skull-cap on his head. Ameera wore all that she valued most. The diamond nose-stud that takes the place of the Western patch in drawing attention to the curv^e of the nostril, the gold ornament in; the centre of the forehead studded with tallow-drop emeralds and flawed rubies, the heavy circlet of beaten gold that was fastened round her neck by the softness of the pure metal, and the chinking curb-patterned silver anklets hanging low over the rosy ankle-bone. She was dressed in jade-green muslin as befitted a daughter of the Faith, and from shoulder to elbow and elbow to wrist ran bracelets of silver tied with floss silk, frail glass bangles slipped over the wrist in proof of the slendemess of the hand, and certain heavy gold bracelets that had no part in her country's ornaments but, since they were Holden's gift and fastened with a cunning European snap, dehghted her immensely.

They sat down by the low white parapet of the roof, overlooking the city and its lights.

'They are happy down there,' said Ameera. *But I do not think that they are as happy as we. Nor do I think the white mem-log are as happy. And thou?'

'I know they are not.'

'How dost thou know?'

*They give their children over to the nurses.'

^I have never seen that,' said Ameera with a sigh, 'nor do I wish to see. A hi!—she dropped her head on Holden's shoulder,—'I have counted forty stars, and I

am tired. Look at the child, love of my life, he is count-ing too.'

The baby was staring with round eyes at the dark of the heavens. Ameera placed him in Holden's arms, and he lay there without a cry.

'What shall we call him among ourselves?' she said. *Look! Art thou ever tired of looking? He carries thy very eyes. But the mouth '

*Is thine, most dear. Who should know better than I?'

* 'Tis such a feeble mouth. Oh, so small! And yet it holds my heart between its Hps. Give him to me now. He has been too long away.'

*Nay, let him he; he has not yet begun to cry.'

'When he cries thou wilt give him back—eh? What a man of mankind thou art! If he cried he were only the dearer to me. But, my life, what Uttle name shaUwe give him?'

The small body lay close to Holden's heart. It was utterly helpless and very soft. He scarcely dared to breathe for fear of crushing it. The caged green parrot that is regarded as a sort of guardian-spirit in most native households moved on its perch and fluttered a drowsy wing.

'There is the answer,' said Holden. 'Mian Mittu has spoken. He shall be the parrot. When he is ready he will talk mightily and run about. Mian Mittu is the parrot in thy—in the Mussulman tongue, is it not?'

'Why put me so far off?' said Ameera fretfully. 'Let it be like unto some EngHsh name— but not wholly, For he is mine.'

'Then call him Tota, for that is Hkest English.'

'Ay, Tota, and that is still the parrot. Forgive me, my lord, for a minute aeo, but in truth he is too little to

wear all the weight of Mian Mittu for name. He shall be Tota—our Tota to us. Hearest thou, O small one? Littlest, thou art Tota.' She touched the child's cheek, and he waking wailed, and it was necessary to return him to his mother, who soothed him with the wonderful rhyme of Are koko, J are koko I which says:

Oh crow! Go crow! Baby's sleeping sound,

And the wild plums grow in the jungle, only a penny a pound.

Only a penny a pound, baba, only a penny a pound.

Reassured many times as to the price of those plums,Tota cuddled himself down to sleep. The two sleek,white well-bullocks in the courtyard were steadily chew-ing the cud of their evening meal; old Pir Khan squattedat the head of Holden's horse, his police sabre across hisknees, pulling drowsily at a big water-pipe that croakedlike a bull-frog in a pond. Ameera's mother sat spinningin the lower verandah, and the wooden gate was shut andbarred. The music of a marriage-procession came to theroof above the gentle hum of the city, and a string offlying-foxes crossed the face of the low moon.

'I have prayed,' said Ameera after a long pause, 'Ihave prayed for two things. First, that I may die inthy stead if thy death is demanded, and in the secondthat I may die in the place of the child. I have prayedto the Prophet and to Beebee Miriam [the Virgin Mary]-Thinkest thou either will hear?'

'From thy lips who would not hear the lightestword?'

'I asked for straight talk, and thou hast given mesweet talk. Will my prayers be heard?'

'How can I say? God is very good.'

'Of that I am not sure. Listen now. When I die,or the child dies, what is thy fate? Living, thou wilt

return to the bold white mem-log, for kind calls tokind.'

'Not always.'

'With a woman, no; with a man it is otherwise.Thou wilt in this life, later on, go back to thine own folk.That I could almost endure, for I should be dead.But in thy very death thou wilt be taken away to astrange place and a paradise that I do not know.'

'Will it be paradise?'

'Surely, for who would harm thee? But we two—I and the child—shall be elsewhere, and we cannot cometo thee, nor canst thou come to us. In the old days,before the child was born, I did not think of these |things;but now I think of them always. It is very hard talk.'

'It will fall as it will fall. To-morrow we do notknow, but to-day and love we know well. Surely we arehappy now.'

'So happy that it were well to make our happinessassured. And thy Beebee Miriam should listen to me;for she is also a woman. But then she would envy me!It is not seemly for men to worship a woman.'

Holden laughed aloud at Ameera's Kttle spasm ofjealousy.

' Is it not seemly? Why didst thou not turn me fromworship of thee, then?'

'Thou a worshipper! And of me? My king, for allthy sweet words, well I know that I am thy servant andthy slave, and the dust under thy feet. And I wouldnot have it otherwise. See!'

Before Holden could prevent her she stooped forwardand touched his feet; recovering herself with a littlelaugh she hugged Tota closer to her bosom. Then,almost savagely—

'Is it true that the bold white m£m-log live for three

times the length of my life? Is it true that they maketheir marriages not before they are old women?'

'They marry as do others—when they are women/

• That I know, but they wed when they are twenty-five.Is that true?'

•That is true/

' Ya illah! At twenty-five! Who would of his ownwill take a wife even of eighteen? She is a woman—aging every hour. Twenty-five! I shall be an old

woman at that age, and Those mem-log remain

young for ever. How I hate them!'

'What have they to do with us?'

'I cannot tell. I know only that there may now be alive on this earth a woman ten years older than I who may come to thee and take thy love ten years after I am an old woman, gray-headed, and the nurse of Tota's son. That is unjust and evil. They should die too.'

' Now, for all thy years thou art a child, and shalt be picked up and carried down the staircase.'

'Total Have a care for Tota, my lord! Thou at least art as foolish as any babe!' Ameera tucked Tota out of harm's way in the hollow of her neck, and was carried downstairs laughing in Holden's arms, while Tota opened his eyes and smiled after the manner of the lesser angels.

He was a silent infant, and, almost before Holden could reaHse that he was in the world, developed into a small gold-coloured httle god and unquestioned despot of the house overlooking the city. Those were months of absolute happiness to Holden and Ameera—happiness withdrawn from the world, shut in behind the wooden gate that Pir Khan guarded. By day Holden did his work with Ian immense pity for such as were not so toi-

WITHOUT BENEFIT OF CLERGY sag

tunate as himself, and a sympathy for small children that amazed and amused many mothers at the little station-gatherings. At nightfall he returned to Ameera,—Ameera, full of the wondrous doings of Tota; how he had been seen to clap his hands together and move his fingers with intention and purpose—which was manifestly a miracle—how later, he had of his own initiative crawled out of his low bedstead on to the floor and swayed on both feet for the space of three breaths.

'And they were long breaths, for my heart stood still with delight,' said Ameera.

Then Tota took the beasts into his councils—the well-bullocks, the little gray squirrels, the mongoose that lived in a hole near the well, and especially Mian Mittu, the parrot, whose tail he grievously pulled, and Mian Mittu screamed till Ameera and Holden arrived.

'O villain! Child of strength! This to thy brother on the house-top! Tohah, tohah! Fie! Fie! But I know a charm to make him wise as Suleiman and Afla-toun [Solomon and Plato]. Now look,' said Ameera. She drew from an embroidered bag a handful of almonds. 'See! we count seven. In the name of God!'

She placed Mian Mittu, very angry and rumpled, on the top of his cage, and seating herself between the babe and the bird she cracked and peeled an almond less white than her teeth. 'This is a true charm, my Kfe, and do not laugh. See! I give the parrot one half and Tota the other.' Mian Mittu with careful beak took his share from between Ameera's Hps, and she kissed the other half into the mouth of the child, who ate it slowly with wondering eyes. 'This I will do each day of seven, and without doubt he who is ours will be a bold speaker and wise. Eh, Tota, what wilt thou be when thou art a man and I am gray-h©ad«d?' Tota tucked his fat legs into

adorable creases. He could crawl, but he was not going to waste the spring of his youth in idle speech. He wanted Mian Mittu's tail to tweak.

When he was advanced to the dignity of a silver belt•—which, with a magic square engraved on silver and hung round his neck, made up the greater part of his clothing—he staggered on a perilous journey down the garden to Pir Khan and proffered him all his jewels in exchange for one Uttle ride on Holden's horse, having seen his mother's mother chaffering with pedlars in the verandah. Pir Khan wept and set the untried feet on his own gray head in sign of fealty, and brought the bold adventurer to his mother's arms, vowing that Tota would be a leader of men ere his beard was grown.

One hot evening, while he sat on the roof between his father and mother watching the never-ending warfare of the kites that the city boys flew, he demanded a kite of his own with Pir

Khan to fly it, because he had a fear of dealing with anything larger than himself, and [when Holden called him a 'spark,' he rose to his feet and answered slowly in defence of his new-found individual-ity, ^ Hum "park nakin Imi. Hum admi hai [I am no spark, but a man].'

The protest made Holden choke and devote himself very seriously to a consideration of Tota's future. He need hardly have taken the trouble. The delight of that life was too perfect to endure. Therefore it was taken away as many things are taken away in India—suddenly and without warning. The little lord of the house, as Pir Khan called him, grew sorrowful and complained of pains who had never known the meaning of pain. Ameera, wild with terror, watched him through the night, and in the dawning of the second day the life was shaken out of

r

him by fever—the seasonal autumn fever. It seemed altogether impossible that he could die, and neither Ameera nor Holden at first believed the evidence of the little body on the bedstead. Then Ameera beat her head against the wall and would have flung herself down the well in the garden had Holden not restrained her by main force.

One mercy only was granted to Holden. He rode tG his office in broad daylight and found waiting him an unusually heavy mail that demanded concentrated atten-tion and hard work. He was not, however, alive to this kindness of the gods.

Ill

The first shock of a bullet is no more than a brisk pinch. The wrecked body does not send in its protest to the soul till ten or fifteen seconds later. Holden realised his pain slowly, exactly as he had reaHsed his happiness, and with the same imperious necessity for hiding all trace of it. In the beginning he only felt that there had been a loss, and that Ameera needed com-forting, where she sat with her head on her knees shiver-ing as Mian Mittu from the house-top called. Tola! Tota! Tota! Later all his world and the daily life of it rose up to hurt him. It was an outrage that any one of the children at the band-stand in the evening should be alive and clamorous, when his own child lay dead. It was more than mere pain when one of them touched him, and stories told by over-fond fathers of their children's latest performances cut him to the quick. He could not declare his pain. He had neither help, comfort, nor sympathy; and Ameera at the end of each weary day would lead him through the hell of self-questioning re-proach which is reserved for those who have lost a child,

and befieve that with a little—just a little—^more care it might have been saved.

* Perhaps/ Ameera would say, 'I did not take suf-ficient heed. Did I, or did I not? The sun on the roof that day when he played so long alone and I was—ahil braiding my hair—it may be that the sun then bred the fever. If I had warned him from the sun he might have lived. But, oh my Hfe, say that I am guiltless! Thou knowest that I loved him as I love thee. Say that there is no blame on me, or I shall die—I shall die!'

' There is no blame,—^before God, none. It was written and how could we do aught to save? What has been, has been. Let it go, beloved.'

'He was all my heart to me. How can I let the thought go when my arm tells me every night that he is not here? Ahi! Ahi! O Tota, come back to me—come back again, and let us be all together as it was before!'

'Peace, peace! For thine own sake, and for mine also, if thou lovest me—rest.'

'By this I know thou dost not care; and how shouldst thou? The white men have hearts of stone and souls of iron. Oh, that I had married a man of inine own people—though he beat me—and had never eaten the bread of an alien!'

'Am I an alien—mother of my son?'

'What else—Sahib? . . . Oh, forgive me—for-give! The death has driven me mad. Thou art thelife of my heart, and the Hght of my eyes, and tlie breathof my life, and—and I have put thee from me, though itwas but for a moment. If thou goest away, to whomshall I look for help? Do not be angry. Indeed, itwas the pain that spoke and not thy slave.'

'I know, I knov/. We be two who were three. Thegreater need therefore that we should be one.'

They were sitting on the roof as of custom. The nightwas a warm one in early spring, and sheet-Kghtning wasdancing on the horizon to a broken tune played by far-offthunder. Ameera settled herself in Holden's arms.

*The dry earth is lowing like a cow for the rain,and I—I am afraid. It was not like this when wecounted the stars. But thou lovest me as much asbefore, though a bond is taken away? Answer!'

'I love more because a new bond has come out ofthe sorrow that we have eaten together, and that thouknowest.'

'Yea, I knew,' said Ameera in a very small whisper.*But it is good to hear thee say so, my life, who art sostrong to help. I will be a child no more, but a womanand an aid to thee. Listen! Give me my sitar and Iwill sing bravely.'

She took the light silver-studded sitar and begana song of the great hero Rajah Rasalu. The hand failedon the strings, the tune halted, checked, and at a lownote turned off to the poor little nursery-rhyme aboutthe wicked crow—

And the wild plums grow in the jungle, only a penny a pound.Only a penny a pound, baba—only . . .

Then came the tears, and the piteous rebellion againstfate till she slept, moaning a little in her sleep, withthe right arm thrown clear of the body as though it pro-tected something that was not there. It was after thisnight that Hfe became a Httle easier for Holden. Theever-present pain of loss drove him into his work, andthe work repaid him by filling up his mind for nine orten hours a day. Ameera sat alone in the house and

brooded, but grew happier when she understood thatHolden was more at ease, according to the custom ofwomen. They touched happiness again, but this timewith caution.

'It was because we loved Tota that he died. Thejealousy of God was upon us,' said Ameera. 'I havehung up a large black jar before our window to turn theevil eye from us, and we must make no protestations ofdelight, but go softly underneath the stars, lest God findus out. Is that not good talk, worthless one?'

She had shifted the accent on the word that means* beloved,' in proof of the sincerity of her purpose. Butthe kiss that followed the new christening was a thingthat any deity might have envied. They went abouthenceforward saying, 'It is naught, it is naught;' andhoping that all the Powers heard.

The Powers were busy on other things. They hadallowed thirty million people four years of plenty whereinmen fed well and the crops were certain, and the birth-rate rose year by year; the districts reported a purelyagricultural population varying from nine hundred totwo thousand to the square mile of the overburdenedearth; and the Member for Lower Tooting, wanderingabout India in pot-hat and frock-coat, talked largely ofthe benefits of British rule and suggested as the onething needful the establishment of a duly qualified elec-toral system and a general bestowal of the franchise. Hislong-suffering hosts smiled and made him welcome, andwhen he paused to admire, with pretty picked words,the blossom of the blood-red dhak-tree that had flowereduntimely for a sign of what was coming, they smiled morethan ever.

It was the Deputy Commissioner of Kot-Kumharsen,staying at the club for a day, who lightly told a tale

that made Holden's blood run cold as he overheard theend.

'He won't bother any one any more. Never saw aman so astonished in my Hfe. By Jove, I thought hemeant to ask a question in the House about it. Fellow-passenger in his ship—dined next him—bowled over bycholera and died in eighteen hours. You needn't laugh,you fellows. The Member for Lower Tooting is awfullyangry about it; but he's more scared. I think he's goingto take his enlightened self out of India.'

'I'd give a good deal if he were knocked over. Itmight keep a few vestrymen of his kidney to their ownparish. But what's this about cholera? It's fuU earlyfor anything of that kind,' said the warden of an un-profitable salt-Hck.

'Don't know,' said the Deputy Commissioner reflect-ively. 'We've got locusts with us. There's sporadiccholera all along the north—at least we're calling itsporadic for decency's sake. The spring crops are shortin five districts, and nobody seems to know where therains are. It's nearly March now. I don't want toscare anybody, but it seems to me that Nature's going toaudit her accounts with a big red pencil this summer.'

'Just when I wanted to take leave, too!' said a voiceacross the room.

'There won't be much leave this year, but there oughtto be a great deal of promotion. I've come in to persuadethe Government to put my pet canal on the list of famine-relief works. It's an ill-wind that blows no good. Ishall get that canal finished at last.'

'Is it the old programme then,' said Plolden; 'famine,fever, and cholera?'

'Oh no. Only local scarcity and an unusual preva-lence of seasonal sickness. You'll find it all in the

reports if you live till next year. You're a lucky chap.You haven't got a wife to send out of harm's way. Thehill-stations ought to be full of women this year.'

'I think you're incHned to exaggerate the talk in thebazars,* said a young civilian in the Secretariat. 'Now Ihave observed '

'I daresay you have/ said the Deputy Commissioner,'but you've a great deal more to observe, my son. Inthe meantime, I wish to observe to you——' and hedrew him aside to discuss the construction of the canalthat was so dear to his heart. Holden went to his bun-galow and began to understand that he was not alone inthe world, and also that he was afraid for the sake ofanother,—which is the most soul-satisfying fear knownto man.

Two months later, as the Deputy had foretold, Naturebegan to audit her accounts with a red pencil. On theheels of the spring-reapings came a cry for bread, and theGovernment, which had decreed that no man should dieof want, sent wheat. Then came the cholera from allfour quarters of the compass. It struck a pilgrim-gather-ing of half a million at a sacred shrine. Many died atthe feet of their god; the others broke and ran over theface of the land carrying the pestilence with them. Itsmote a walled city and killed two hundred a day. Thepeople crowded the trains, hanging on to the footboardsand squatting on the roofs of the carriages, and thecholera followed them, for at each station they""draggedout the dead and the dying. They died by the roadside,and the horses of the Englishmen shied at the corpses inthe grass. The rains did not come, and the earth turnedto iron lest man should escape death by hiding in her.The Enghsh sent their wives away to the hills and wentabout their work, coming forward as they were bidden to

fill the gaps in the fighting-line. Holden, sick with fearof losing his chiefest treasure on earth, had done his bestto persuade Ameera to go away with her mother to theHimalayas.

'Why should I go?' said she one evening on theroof.

'There is sickness, and people are dying, and all thewhite mem-log have gone.'

'All of them?'

'All—unless perhaps there remain some old scald-head who vexes her husband's heart by running risk ofdeath.'

'Nay; who stays is my sister, and thou must notabuse her, for I will be a scald-head too. I am glad allthe bold mem-log are gone.'

'Do I speak to a woman or a babe? Go to the hillsand I will see to it that thou goest like a queen's daughter.Think, child. In a red-lacquered bullock-cart, veiledand curtained, with brass peacocks upon the pole andred cloth hangings. I will send two orderlies for guard,and '

'Peace! Thou art the babe in speaking thus. Whatuse are those toys to me? He would have pattedthe bullocks and played with the housings. For hissake, perhaps,—thou hast made me very EngHsh—Imight have gone. Now, I will not. Let the mem-logrun.'

'Their husbands are sending them, beloved.'

'Very good talk. Since when hast thou been myhusband to tell me what to do? I have but borne theea son. Thou art only all the desire of my soul to me.How shall I depart when I know that if evil befall theeby the breadth of so much as my littlest finger-nail-is that not small?—I should be aware of it though I

were in paradise. And here, this summer thou mayestdie—at, janee, die! and in dying they might call to tendthee a wliite woman, and she would rob me in the last ofthy love!'

' But love is not born in a moment or on a death-bed!'

'What dost thou know of love, stoneheart? Shawould take thy thanks at least and, by God and theProphet and Beebee Miriam the mother of thy Prophet,that I v/ill never endure. My lord and my love, letthere be no more foolish talk of going away. Wherethou art, I am. It is enough.' She put an arm roundhis neck and a hand on his mouth.

There are not many happinesses so complete as thosethat are snatched under the shadow of the sword. Theysat together and laughed, calling each other openly byevery pet name that could move the wrath of the gods.The city below them was locked up in its own torments.Sulphur fires blazed in the streets; the conches in theHindu temples screamed and bellowed, for the gods wereinattentive in those days. There was a service in thegreat Mahomedan shrine, and the call to prayer from theminarets was almost unceasing. They heard the wailingin the houses of the dead, and once the shriek of amother who had lost a child and was caUing for its re-turn. In the gray dawn they saw the dead borne outthrough the city gates, each litter with its own littleknot of mourners. Wherefore they kissed each otherand shivered.

It was a red and heavy audit, for the land was verysick and needed a little breathing-space ere the torrentof cheap life should flood it anew. The children ofimmature fathers and undeveloped mothers made noresistance. They were cowed and sat still, waiting tillthe sword should be sheathed in November if it were

SO willed. There were gaps among the English, butthe gaps were filled. The work of superintending famine-relief, cholera-sheds, medicine-distribution, and whatlittle sanitation was possible, went forward because itwas so ordered.

Holden had been told to keep himself in readiness tomove to replace the next man who should fall. Therewere twelve hours in each day when he could not seeAmeera, and she might die in three. He was consideringwhat his pain would be if he could not see her for threemonths, or if she died out of his sight. He was absolutelycertain that her death would be demanded—so certainthat when he looked up from the telegram and saw PirKhan breathless in the doorway, he laughed aloud.'And?' said he,

'When there is a cry in the night and the spirit flut-ters into the throat, who has a charm that will restore?Come swiftly, Heaven-born! It is the black cholera.'

Holden galloped to his home. The sky was heavywith clouds, for the long-deferred rains were near and theheat was stifling. Ameera's mother met him in thecourtyard, whimpering, 'She is dying. She is nursingherself into death. She is all but dead. What shall I do,sahib ?'

Ameera was lying in the room in which Tota hadbeen born. She made no sign when Holden entered,because the human soul is a very lonely thing and, whenit is getting ready to go away, hides itself in a mistyborderland where the living may not follow. The blackcholera does its work quietly and without explanation.Ameera was being thrust out of Hfe as though the Angelof Death had liimself put his hand upon her. The quickbreathing seemed to show that she was either afraid or inpainj but neither eyes nor mouth gave any answer to

Holden's kisses. There was nothing to be said or done.Holden could only wait and suffer. The first drops ofthe rain began to fall on the roof, and he could hearshouts of joy in the parched city.

The soul came back a little and the lips moved.Holden bent down to listen. 'Keep nothing of mine/said Ameera. 'Take no hair from my head. Slie wouldmake thee bum it later on. That flame I should feel.Lower! Stoop lower! Remember only that I was thineand bore thee a son. Though thou wed a white womanto-morrow, the pleasure of receiving in thy arms thy firstson is taken from thee for ever. Remember me when thyson is bom—the one that shall carry thy name before allmen. His misfortimes be on my head. I bear witness—I bear witness'—the lips were forming the words on hisear—'that there is no God but—thee, beloved!'

Then she died. Holden sat still, and all thought wastaken from him,—till he heard Ameera's mother lift thecurtain.

' Is she dead, sahib ?'

'She is dead.'

'Then I will mourn, and afterwards take an inventoryof the fumiture in this house. For that will be mine.The sahib does not mean to resume it? It is so Httle, sovery little, sahib, and I am an old woman. I would liketo lie softly.'

'For the m.ercy of God be silent a while. Go out andmourn where I cannot hear.'

'Sahib, she will be buried in four hours.'

'I know the custom. I shall go ere she is taken away.That matter is in thy hands. Look to it, that the bed onwhich—on which she lies '

'Aha! That beautiful red-lacquered bed. I havelong de«red '

^That the bed is left here untouched for my disposal.AH else in the house is thine. Hire a cart, take every-thing, go hence, and before sunrise let there be nothingin this house but that wliich I have ordered thee torespect.'

'I am an old woman. I would stay at least for thedays of mourning, and the rains have just broken.Whither shaU I go?'

'What is that to me? My order is that there is agoing. The house-gear is worth a thousand rupees andmy orderly shall bruig thee a hundred rupees to-night.'

'That is very Httle. Think of the cart-hire.'

'It shall be nothing unless thou goest, and with speed.O woman, get hence and leave me with my dead!'

The mother shuffled down the staircase, and in heranxiety to take stock of the house-fittings forgot tomourn. Holden stayed by Ameera's side and the rainroared on the roof. He could not think connectedlyby Reason of the noise, though he made many attempts todo so. Then four sheeted ghosts ghded dripping into theroom and stared at him through their veils. They werethe washers of the dead. Holden left the room and wentout to his horse. He had come in a dead, stifling calmthrough ankle-deep dust. He found the courtyard a rain-lashed pond ahve with frogs; a torrent of yellow water ranunder the gate, and a roaring wind drove the bolts of therain like buckshot against the mud-walls. Pir Khan was.shivering in his Httle hut by the gate, and the horse wasstamping uneasily in the water.

'I have been told the sahib's order,' said Pir Khan.'It is well. This house is now desolate. I go also, formy monkey-face would be a reminder of that which hssbeen. Concerning the bed, I will bring that to thyhouse yonder in the morning; but remember, sakib,

it will be to thee a knife turning in a green wound,I go upon a pilgrimage, and I will take no money*I have grown fat in the protection of the Presencewhose sorrow is my sorrow. For the last time I holdlixs stirrup.'

He touched Holden's foot with both hands and thehorse sprang out into the road, where the creakingbamboos were whipping the sky and all the frogs werechuckHng. Holden could not see for the rain in hisface. He put his hands before his eyes and muttered—

' Oh you brute! You utter brute!'

The news of his trouble was already in his bungalow.He read the knowledge in his butler's eyes when AhmedKhan brought m food, and for the first and last time inhis life laid a hand upon his master's shoulder, saying,'Eat, sahih, eat. Meat is good against sorrow. I alsohave known. Moreover the shadows come and go,sahih; the shadows come and go. These be curriedeggs.'

Holden could neither eat nor sleep. The heavenssent down eight inches of rain in that night and washedthe earth clean. The waters tore down walls, brokeroads, and scoured open the shallow graves on theMahomedan burying-ground. All next day it rained,and Holden sat still in his house considering his sorrow.On the morning of the third day he received a telegramwhich said only, 'Ricketts, Myndonie. Dying. HoldenreUeve. Immediate.' Then he thought that before hedeparted he would look at the house wherein he had beenmaster and lord. There was a break in the weather,and the rank earth steamed with vapour.

He found that the rains had torn down the mudpillars of the gateway, and the heavy wooden gate thathad guarded his life hung hjzjly from one hinge. There

was grass three inches high in the courtyard; Pir Khan^slodge was empty, and the sodden thatch sagged betweenthe beams. A gray squirrel was in possession of tlieverandah, as if the house had been untenanted for thirtyyears instead of three days. Ameera's mother hadreinoved everything except some mildewed matting.The tick-tick of the little scorpions as they hurried acrossthe floor was the only sound in the house. Ameera'sroom and the other one where Tota had lived were heavywith mildew; and the narrow staircase leading to theroof was streaked and stained with rain-borne mud.Holden saw all these things, and came out again to meetin the road Durga Dass, his landlord,—portly, affable,clothed in white muslin, and driving a Cee-spring buggy.He was overlooking his property to see how the roofsstood the stress of the first rains.

'I have heard,' said he, 'you will not take this placeany more, sahih ?'

' What are you going to do with it?'

* Perhaps I shall let it again.'

'Then I will keep it on while I am away.'

Durga Dass was silent for some time. 'You shallnot take it on, sahib," he said. 'When I was a youngman I also , but to-day I am a member of the Munic-ipality. Ho! Ho! No. When the birds have gonewhat need to keep the nest? I will have it pulled down—the timber will sell for something always. It shall bepulled down, and the MunicipaKty shall make a roadacross, as they desire, from the burning-ghat to thecity wall, so that no man may say where this housestood.'

AT THE END OF THE PASSAGE

The sky is lead and our faces are red,

And the gates of Hell are opened and riven,And the winds of Hell are loosened and driven.

And the dust flies up in the face of Heaven,And the clouds come down in a fiery sheet,

Heavy to raise and hard to be borne.And the soul of man is turned from his meat,

Turned from the trifles for which he has strivenSick in his body, and heavy hearted,And his soul flies up like the dust in the sheetBreaks from his flesh and is gone and departed.

As the blasts they blow on the cholera-horn.

Himaiayan,

Four men, each entitled to 'life, liberty, and the pursuitof happiness,' sat at a table playing whist. The thermom-eter marked—for them—one hundred and one degreesof heat. The room was darkened till it was only justpossible to distinguish the pips of the cards and the verywhite faces of the players. A tattered, rotten punkah ofwhitewashed calico was puddling the hot air and whiningdolefully at each stroke. Outside lay gloom of a Novem-ber day in London. There was neither sky, sun, norhorizon,—nothing but a brown purple haze of heat. Itw^as as though the earth were dying of apoplexy.

From time to time clouds of tawny dust rose fromthe ground without wind or warning, flung themselvestablecloth-wise among the tops of the parched trees,and came down again. Then a whirling dust-devil wouldscutter across the plain for a couple of miles, break, and

244

fall outward, though there was nothing to check its flightsave a long low line of piled railway-sleepers white withthe dust, a cluster of huts made of mud, condemned rails,and canvas, and the one squat four-roomed bungalowthat belonged to the assistant engineer in charge of asection of the Gaudhari State line then under construc-tion.

The four, stripped to the thinnest of sleeping-suits,played whist crossly, with wranglings as to leads andreturns. It was not the best kind of whist, but they hadtaken some trouble to arrive at it. Mottram of theIndian Survey had ridden thirty and railed one hundredmiles from his lonely post in the desert since the nightbefore; Lowndes of the Civil Service, on special duty inthe poHtical department, had come as far to escape for a,ninstant the miserable intrigues of an impoverished nativeState whose king alternately fawned and blustered formore money from the pitiful revenues contributed byhard-wrung peasants and despairing camel-breeders;Spurstow, the doctor of the line, had left a cholera-stricken camp of coolies to look after itself for forty-eighthours while he associated with white men once more.Hummil, the assistant engineer, was the host. He stoodfast and received his friends thus every Sunday if theycould come in. When one of them failed to appear, hewould send a telegram to his last address, in order thathe might know whether the defaulter were dead or alive.There are very many places in the East where it is notgood or kind to let your acquaintances drop out of sighteven for one short week.

The players were not conscious of any special regardfor each other. They squabbled whenever they met; butthey ardently desired to meet, as men mthout waterdesire to drink. They were lonely folk who understood

the dread meaning of loneliness. They were all underthirty years of age,—which is too soon for any man topossess that knowledge.

'Pilsener?' said Spurstow, after the second rubber,mopping his forehead.

* Beer's out, I'm sorry to say, and there's hardlyenough soda-water for to-night,' said Hummil.

'What filthy bad management!' Spurstow snarled.

'Can't help it. I've written and wired; but the trainsdon't come through regularly yet. Last week the ice ranout,—as Lowndes knows.'

'Glad I didn't come. I could ha' sent you some if I had known, though. Phew! it's too hot to go on playing bumblepuppy.' This with a savage scowl at Lowndes, who only laughed. He was a hardened offender.

Mottram rose from the table and looked out of a chink in the shutters.

'What a sweet day!' said he.

The company yawned all together and betook them-selves to an aimless investigation of all Hummil's pos-sessions,—guns, tattered novels, saddlery, spurs, and the like. They had fingered them a score of times before, but there was really nothing else to do.

' Got anything fresh?' said Lowndes.

'Last week's Gazette oj India, and a cutting from a home paper. My father sent it out. It's rather amusing.'

'One of those vestrymen that call 'emselves M.P.'s again, is it?' said Spurstow, who read his newspapers when he could get them.

'Yes. Listen to this. It's to your address, Lowndes. The man was making a speech to his constituents, and he piled it on. Here's a sample: "And I assert unhesita-tingly that the Civil Service in India is the preserve—

the pet preserve—of the aristocracy of England. What does the democracy—what do the masses—get from that country, which we have step by step fraudulently an-nexed? I answer, nothing whatever. It is farmed with a single eye to their own interests by the scions of the aristocracy. They take good care to maintain their lavish scale of incomes, to avoid or stifle any inquiries into the nature and conduct of their administration, while they themselves force the unhappy peasant to.pay with the sweat of his brow for all the luxuries in which they are lapped."' Hummil waved the cutting above his head. ' 'Ear! 'ear!' said his audience.

Then Lowndes, meditatively: 'I'd give—I'd give three months' pay to have that gentleman spend one month with me and see how the free and independent native prince works things. Old Timbersides'—this was his flippant title for an honoured and decorated feudatory prince—' has been wearing my life out this week past for money. By Jove, his latest performance was to send me one of his women as a bribe!'

' Good for you! Did you accept it?' said Mottram.

*No. I rather wish I had, now. She was a pretty little person, and she yarned away to me about the hor-rible destitution among the king's women-folk. The darlings haven't had any new clothes for nearly a month, and the old man wants to buy a new drag from Calcutta,—solid silver raihngs and silver lamps, and trifles of that kind. I've tried to make him understand that he has played the deuce with the revenues for the last twenty years and must go slow. He can't see it.'

'But he has the ancestral treasure-vaults to draw on. There must be three millions at least in jewels and coin under his palace,' said Hummil.

Xatch a native king disturbing the family treasure!

The priests forbid it except as the last resort. Old Timbersides has added something like a quarter of a million to the deposit in his reign.'

'Where the mischief does it all come from?' said Mottram.

'The country. The state of the people is enough to make you sick. I've known the tax-men wait by a milch-camel till the foal was born and then hurry off the mother for arrears. And what can I do? I can't get the court clerks to give me any accounts; I can't raise anything more than a fat smile from the commander-in-chief when I find out the troops are three months in arrears; and old Timbersides begins to weep when I speak to him. He has taken to the King's Peg heavily,—liqueur brandy for whisky, and Heidsieck for soda-water.'

' That's what the Rao of Jubela took to. Even a native can't last long at that,' said Spurstow.

* He'll go out.'

'And a good tiling, too. Then I suppose we'll have a council of regency, and a tutor for the young prince, and hand liim back his kingdom with ten years' accu-mulations.'

* Whereupon that young prince, having been taught all the vices of the English, will play ducks and drakes with the money and undo ten years' work in eighteen months. I've seen that business before,' said Spurstow. 'I should tackle the king with a Hght hand, if I were you, Lowndes. They'll hate you quite enough under any circumstances.'

'That's all very well. The man who looks on can talk about the light hand; but you can't clean a pig-stye with a pen dipped in rose-water. I know my risks; but nothing has happened yet. My servant's an old Pathan, and he cooks for me. They are hardly likely to bribe him, and I don't accept food from my true friends, as they call themselves. Oh, but it's weary work! I'd

sooner be with you, Spurstow. There's shooting near your camp.'

* Would you? I don't think it. About fifteen deaths a day don't incite a man to shoot anything but himself. And the worst of it is that the poor devils look at you as though you ought to save them. Lord knows, I've tried everything. My last attempt was empirical, but it pulled an old man through. He was brought to me ap-parently past hope, and I gave him gin and Worcester sauce with cayenne. It cured him; but I don't recom*mend it.'

'How do the cases run generally?' said Hummil.

'Very simply indeed. Chlorodyne, opium pill, chloro-dyne, collapse, nitre, bricks to the feet, and then—the burning-ghat. The last seems to be the only thing that stops the trouble. It's black cholera, you know. Poor devils! But, I will say, little Bunsee Lai, my apothe-cary, works like a demon. I've recommended him for promotion if he comes through it all alive.'

'And what are your chances, old man?' said Mottram.

'Don't know; don't care much; but I've sent the letter in. What are you doing with yourself generally?'

'Sitting under a table in the tent and spitting on the sextant to keep it cool,' said the man of the survey. 'Washing my eyes to avoid ophthalmia, which I shall certainly get, and trying to make a sub-surveyor under-stand that an error of five degrees in an angle isn't quite so small as it looks. I'm altogether alone, y' know, and shall be till the end of the hot weather,'

'Hummil's the lucky man,' said Lowndes, flinging himself into a long chair. 'He has an actual roof—tornas to the ceiling-cloth, but still a roof—over his head. He sees one train daily. He can get beer and soda-water and ice 'em when God is good. He has books, pictures,'

—they were torn from the Graphic,—' and the society of the excellent sub-contractor Jevins, besides the pleasure of recemng us weekly.'

Hummil smiled grimly. 'Yes, I'm the lucky man, I suppose. Je\'ins is luckier.'

^How? Not '

'Yes. Went out. Last Monday.'

'By his own hand?' said Spurstow quickly, hinting the suspicion that was in everybody's mind. There was no cholera near Hummil's section. Even fever gives a man at least a week's grace, and sudden death generally implied self-slaughter.

'I judge no man this weather,' said Hummil. 'He had a touch of the sun, I fancy; for last week, after you fellows had left, he came into the verandah and told me that he was going home to see his wife, in Market Street, Liverpool, that evening.

'I got the apothecary in to look at him, and we tried to make him He dowm. After an hour or two he rubbed his eyes and said he believed he had had a fit,—hoped he hadn't said anything rude. Jevins had a great idea of bettering himself socially. He was very like Chucks in his language.'

'Well?'

'Then he went to his own bungalow and began clean-ing a rifle. He told the serv^ant that he was going toshoot buck in the morning. Naturally he fumbled withthe trigger, and shot himself through the head—accident-ally. The apothecary sent in a report to my chief, andJevins is buried somewhere out there. I'd have wired toyou, Spurstow, if you could have done anything.'

'You're a queer chap,' said Mottram. 'If you'd killedthe man yourself you couldn't have been more quiet aboutthe business.'

^Good Lord! what does it matter?' said Hummilcalmly. 'I've got to do a lot of his overseeing work inaddition to my own. I'm the only person that suffers.Jevins is out of it,—by pure accident, of course, but outof it. The apothecary was going to write a long screed onsuicide. Trust a babu to drivel when he gets the chance.'

'Why didn't you let it go in as suicide?' said Lowndes.

'No direct proof. A man hasn't many privileges inthis country, but he might at least be allowed to mis-handle his own rifle. Besides, some day I may need aman to smother up an accident to myself. Live andletKve. Die and let die.'

'You take a pill,' said Spurstow, who had been watch-ing Hummil's white face narrowly. 'Take a pill, anddon't be an ass. That sort of talk is skittles. Anyhow,suicide is shirking your work. If I were Job ten timesover, I should be so interested in what was going tohappen next that I'd stay on and watch.'

'Ah! I've lost that curiosity,' said Hummil.

'Liver out of order?' said Lowndes feelingly.

'No. Can't sleep. That's worse.'

'By Jove, it is!' said Mottram. 'I'm that way everynow and then, and the fit has to wear itself out. Whatdo you take for it?'

'Nothing. What's the use? I haven't had ten min-utes' sleep since Friday morning.'

'Poor chap! Spurstow, you ought to attend to this,'said Mottram. 'Now you mention it, your eyes arerather gummy and swollen.'

Spurstow, still watching Hummil, laughed lightly.' I'll patch him up, later on. Is it too hot, do you think,to go for a ride?'

'Where to?' said Lowndes wearily. 'We shall haveto go away at eight, and there'll be riding enough for us

then. I hate a horse, when I have to use him as a

necessity. Oh, heavens! what is there to do?'

* Begin whist again, at chick points ['a chick' is sup-posed to be eight shillings] and a gold mohur on the rub,'said Spurstow promptly.

'Poker. A month's pay all round for the pool,—nolimit,—and fifty-rupee raises. Somebody would bebroken before we got up,' said Lowndes.

' Can't say that it would give me any pleasure to breakmy man in this company,' said Mottram. 'There isn'tenough excitement in it, and it's fooHsh.' He crossedover to the worn and battered little camp-piano,—wreck-age of a married household that had once held thebungalow,—and opened the case.

'It's used up long ago,' said Hummil. 'The servantshave picked it to pieces.'

The piano was indeed hopelessly out of order, butMottram managed to bring the rebellious notes into a sortof agreement, and there rose from the ragged keyboardsomething that might once have been the ghost of apopular music-hall song. The men in the long chairsturned with evident interest as Mottram banged themore lustily.

'That's good!' said Lowndes. 'By Jove! the lasttime I heard that song was in '79, or thereabouts, justbefore I came out.'

' Ah!' said Spurstow with pride, * I was home in '80.' Andhe mentioned a song of the streets popular at that date.

Mottram executed it roughly. Lowndes criticisedand volunteered emendations. Mottram dashed into an-other ditty, not of the music-hall character, and madeas if to rise.

' Sit down,' said Hummil. ' I didn't know that you hadany music in your composition. Go on playing until you

can't think of anything more. I'll have that piano tunedup before you come again. Play something festive.'

Very simple indeed were the tunes to which Mottram'sart and the limitations of the piano could give effect, butthe men hstened with pleasure, and in the pauses talkedall together of what they had seen or heard when theywere last at home. A dense dust-storm sprung up out-side, and swept roaring over the house, enveloping it inthe choking darkness of midnight, but Mottram continuedunheeding, and the crazy tinkle reached the ears of thelisteners above the flapping of the tattered ceiling-cloth.

In the silence after the storm he ghded from themore directly personal songs of Scotl'and, half hummingthem as he played, into the Evening Hymn.

* Sunday,' said he, nodding his head.

' Go on. Don't apologise for it,' said Spurstow.

Hummil laughed long and riotously. ' Play it, by allmeans. You're full of surprises to-day. I didn't knowyou had such a gift of finished sarcasm. How does thatthing go?'

Mottram took up the tune.

*Too slow by half. You miss the note of gratitude,'said Hummil. 'It ought to go to the "Grasshopper'sPolka,"—this way.' And he chanted, prestissimo,—

'Glory to thee, my God, this nighLFor all the blessings of the light.

That shows we really feel our blessings. How does it goon?—

'If in the night I sleepless lie,My soul with sacred thoughts supply;May no ill dreams disturb my rest,'—

Quicker, Mottram!—

*0r powers of darkness me molest!'

* Bah! what an old hypocrite you are!'

'Don't be an ass/ said Lowndes. 'You are at fullliberty to make fun of anything else you like, but leavethat hymn alone. It's associated in my mind with themost sacred recollections '

'Summer evenings in the country,—stained-glasswindow,—hght going out, and you and she jamming yourheads together over one h\'7dTnn-book,' said Mot tram.

'Yes, and a fat old cockchafer hitting you in the eyewhen you v/alked home. Smell of hay, and a moon asbig as a bandbox sitting on the top of a haycock; bats,—roses,—milk and midges,' said Lowndes.

'Also mothers. I can just recollect my mother singingme to sleep with that when I was a Httle chap,' saidSpurstow.

The darkness had fallen on the room. They couldhear Hummxil squirming in his chair.

'Consequently,' said he testily, 'you sing it when youare seven fathom deep in Hell! It's an insult to theintelligence of the Deity to pretend we're anything buttortured rebels.'

'Take two pills,' said Spurstow; 'that's torturedliver.'

'The usually placid Hummil is in a vile bad temper.I'm sorry for his coolies to-morrow,' said Lowndes, as theservants brought in the hghts and prepared the table fordinner.

As they were settHng into their places about the miser-able goat-chops, and the smoked tapioca pudding, Spur-stow took occasion to whisper to Mottram, 'Well done,David!'

'Look after Saul, then,' was the reply.

'What are you two whispering about?' said Hummilsuspiciously.

' Only saying that you are a damned poor host. Thisfowl can't be cut/ returned Spurstow with a sweet smile.* Call this a dinner?'

' I can't help it. You don't expect a banquet, do you?'

Throughout that meal Hummil contrived laboriouslyto insult directly and pointedly all his guests in succession,and at each insult Spurstow kicked the aggrieved personsunder the table; but he dared not exchange a glance ofintelligence with either of them. Hummil's face waswhite and pinched, while his eyes were unnaturally large.No man dreamed for a moment of resenting his savagepersonalities, but as soon as the meal was over they madehaste to get away.

'Don't go. You're just getting amusing, you fellows.I hope I haven't said anything that annoyed you.You're such touchy devils.' Then, changing the noteinto one of almost abject entreaty, Hummil added, 'Isay, you surely aren't going?'

'In the language of the blessed Jorrocks, where Idines I sleeps,' said Spurstow. 'I want to have a look atyour cooHes to-morrow, if you don't mind. You cangive me a place to He down in, I suppose?'

The others pleaded the urgency of their severalduties next day, and, saddling up, departed together,Hummil begging them to come next Sunday. As theyjogged off, Lowndes unbosomed himself to Mottram—

' . . . And I never felt so like kicking a man at hisown table in my Hfe. He said I cheated at whist, and re-minded me I was in debt! 'Told you you were as goodas a liar to your face! You aren't half indignant enoughover it.'

'Not I,' said Mottram. 'Poor devil! Did you everknow old Hummy behave like that before or within ahundred miles of it?'

' That's no excuse. Spurstow was hacking my shin all thetime, so I kept a hand on myself. Else I should have '

'No, you wouldn't. You'd have done as Hummy didabout Je\ins; judge no man this weather. By Jovelthe buckle of my bridle is hot in my hand! Trot out abit, and 'ware rat-holes.'

Ten minutes' trotting jerked out of LowTides one verysage remark when he pulled up, sweating from everypore—

' 'Good thing Spurstow's with him to-night.'

'Ye-es. Good man, Spurstow. Our roads turn here.See you again next Sunday, if the sun doesn't bowl meover.'

'S'pose so, unless old Timbersides' finance ministermanages to dress some of my food. Good-night, and—God bless you!'

'What's wrong now?'

'Oh, nothing.' Lowndes gathered up his whip, and,as he flicked Mottram's mare on the flank, added,'You're not a bad little chap,—that's all.' And themare bolted half a mile across the sand, on the word.

In the assistant engineer's bungalow Spurstow andHummil smoked the pipe of silence together, each nar-rowly watching the other. The capacity of a bachelor'sestablishment is as elastic as its arrangements are simple.A servant cleared away the dining-room table, broughtin a couple of rude native bedsteads made of tapestrung on a light wood frame, flung a square of coolCalcutta matting over each, set them side by side, pinnedtwo towels to the punkah so that their fringes shouldjust sweep clear of the sleepers' nose and mouth, andannounced that the couches were ready.

The men flung themselves down, ordering the punkah-coolies by all the powers of Hell to pull. Every door

and window was shut, for the outside air was that ofan oven. The atmosphere within was only 104°, asthe thermometer bore witness, and heavy with the foulsmell of badly-trimmed herosene lamps; and this stench,combined with that of native tobacco, baked brick, anddried earth, sends the heart of many a strong man downto his boots, for it is the smell of the Great IndianEmpire when she turns herself for six months into ahouse of torment. Spurstow packed his pillows craftilyso that he recHned rather than lay, his head at a safeelevation above his feet. It is not good to sleep on alow pillow in the hot weather if you happen to be otthick-necked build, for you may pass with lively snoresand gugghngs from natural sleep into the deep slumberof heat-apoplexy.

^Pack your pillows,' said the doctor sharply, as hesaw Hummil preparing to He down at full length.

The night-light was trimmed; the shadow of thepunkah wavered across the room, and the 'flick' of thepunkah-towel and the soft whine of the rope throughthe wall-hole followed it. Then the punkah flagged,almost ceased. The sweat poured from Spurstow'sbrow. Should he go out and harangue the coolie? Itstarted forward again with a savage jerk, and a pin cameout of the towels. When this was replaced, a tomtom inthe coolie-lines began to beat with the steady throb of aswollen artery inside some brain-fevered skull. Spur-stow turned on his side and swore gently. There wasno movement on Hummil's part. The man had com-posed himself as rigidly as a corpse, his hands clinchedat his sides. The respiration was too hurried for anysuspicion of sleep. Spurstow looked at the set face. Thejaws were dinched, and there was a pucker round tb^quivering eyelids.

'He^s holding himself as tightly as ever he can/ thoughtSpurstow. * What in the world is the matter with him ?—Hummil!'

'Yes/ in a tliick constrained voice.

'Can't you get to sleep?'

'No.'

' Head hot? 'Throat feeling bulgy? or how?'

' Neither, thanks. I don't sleep much, you know/

"Feel pretty bad?'

'Pretty bad, thanks. There is a tomtom outside, isn'tthere? I thought it was my head at first. . . . Oh,Spurstow, for pity's sake give me something that willput me asleep,—sound asleep,—if it's only for six hours!'He sprang up, trembHng from head to foot. 'I haven'tbeen able to sleep naturally for days, and I can't stand it!—I can't stand it!'

' Poor old chap!'

' That's no use. Give me something to make me sleep.I tell you I'm nearly mad. I don't know what I sayhalf my time. For three weeks I've had to think andspell out every word that has come through my lipsbefore I dared say it. Isn't that enough to drive a manmad? I can't see things correctly now, and I've lost mysense of touch. My skin aches—my skin aches! Makeme sleep. Oh, Spurstow, for the love of God make mesleep sound. It isn't enough merely to let me dream.Let me sleep!'

'All right, old man, all right. Go slow; you aren'thalf as bad as you think.'

The flood-gates of reserve once broken, Hummil wasclinging to him like a frightened child. 'You're pinchingmy arm to pieces.'

'I'll break your neck if you don't do something forme. No, I didn't mean that. Don't be angry, old

fellow.' He wiped the sweat off himself as he foughtto regain composure. ' I'm a bit restless and off my oats,and perhaps you could recommend some sort of sleepingmixture,—bromide of potassium.'

'Bromide of skittles! Why didn't you tell me thisbefore? Let go of my arm, and I'll see if there's any-thing in my cigarette-case to suit your complaint.'Spurstow hunted among his day-clothes, turned up thelamp, opened a Httle silver cigarette-case, and advanced onthe expectant Hummil with the daintiest of fairy squirts.

'The last appeal of civiUsation,' said he, 'and a thing Ihate to use. Hold out your arm. Well, your sleepless-ness hasn't ruined your muscle; and what a thick hide itis! Might as well inject a buffalo subcutaneously. Nowin a few minutes the morphia will begin working. Liedown and wait.'

A smile of unalloyed and idiotic dehght began to creepover Hummil's face. 'I think,' he whispered,—'I thinkI'm gomg off now. Gad! it's positively heavenly! Spur-stow, you must give me that case to keep; you '

The voice ceased as the head fell back.

'Not for a good deal,' said Spurstow to the uncon-scious form. 'And now, my friend, sleeplessness of yourkind being very apt to relax the moral fibre in Httlematters of Hfe and death, I'll just take the liberty ofspiking your guns.'

He paddled into Hummil's saddle-room in his barefeet and uncased a twelve-bore rifle, an express, and arevolver. Of the first he unscrewed the nipples andhid them in the bottom of a saddlery-case; of the secondhe abstracted the lever, kicking it behind a big ward-robe. The third he merely opened, and knocked thedoll-head bolt of the grip up with the heel of a riding-boot.

'That's settled/ he said, as he shook the sweat off hishands. 'These little precautions will at least give youtime to turn. You have too much sympathy with gun-room accidents.'

And as he rose from his knees, the thick muffled voiceof Hummil cried in the doorway,' You fool!'

Such tones they use who speak in the lucid intervals ofdelirium to their friends a little before they die.

Spurstow started, dropping the pistol. Hummil stoodin the doorway, rocking with helpless laughter.

'That was awf'ly good of you, I'm sure,' he said, veryslowly, feeling for his words. ' I don't intend to go out bymy own hand at present. I say, Spurstow, that stuffwon't work. What shall I do? What shall I do?'And panic terror stood in his eyes.

' Lie down and give it a chance. Lie down at once.'

' I daren't. It will only take me half-way again, and Ishan't be able to get away this time. Do you know it wasall I could do to come out just now? Generally I am asquick as lightning; but you had clogged my feet. I wasnearly caught.'

'Oh yes, I understand. Go and lie down.'

*No, it isn't delirium; but it was an awfully mean trickto play on me. Do you know I might have died?'

As a sponge rubs a slate clean, so some power unknownto Spurstow had wiped out of Hummil's face all thatstamped it for the face of a man, and he stood at thedoorway in the expression of his lost innocence. He hadslept back into terrified childhood.

'Is he going to die on the spot?' thought Spurstow.Then, aloud, 'AH right, my son. Come back to bed, andtell me all about it. You couldn't sleep; but what was allthe rest of the nonsense?'

^'A place,—a place down there/ said Hummil, with

simple sincerity. The drug was acting on him by waves, and he was flung from the fear of a strong man to the fright of a child as his nerves gathered sense or were dulled.

*Good God! I've been afraid of it for months past, Spurstow. It has made every night hell to me; and yet I'm not conscious of having done anything wrong.'

'Be still, and I'll give you another dose. We'll stop your nightmares, you unutterable idiot!'

'Yes, but you must give me so much that I can't get away. You must make me quite sleepy,—not just a little sleepy. It's so hard to run then.'

'I know it; I know it. I've felt it myself. The symp-toms are exactly as you describe.'

'Oh, don't laugh at me, confound you! Before this awful sleeplessness came to me I've tried to rest on my elbow and put a spur in the bed to sting me when I fell back. Look!'

'By Jove! the man has been rowelled like a horse! Ridden by the nightmare with a vengeance! And we all thought him sensible enough. Heaven send us under-standing! You like to talk, don't you?'

' Yes, sometimes. Not when I'm frightened. Then I want to run. Don't you?'

'Always. Before I give you your second dose try to tell me exactly what your trouble is.'

Hummil spoke in broken whispers for nearly ten minutes, whilst Spurstow looked into the pupils of his eyes and passed his hand before them once or twice.

At the end of the narrative the silver cigarette-case was produced, and the last words that Hummil said as he fell back for the second time were, *Put me quite to sleep; for if I'm caught I die,—I die!'

'Yes, yes; we all do that sooner or later,—thank

Heaven who has set a term to our miseries/ said Spur-stow, settling the cushions under the head. 'It occurs to me that unless I drink something I shall go out before my time. I've stopped sweating, and—I wear a seven teen-inch collar.' He brewed himself scald-ing hot tea, which is an excellent remedy against heat-apoplexy if you take three or four cups of it in time. Then he watched tlie sleeper.

*A blind face that cries and can't wipe its eyes, a blind face that chases him down corridors! H'm! Decidedly, Hummil ought to go on leave as soon as possible; and, sane or otherwise, he undoubtedly did rowel himself most cruelly. WeU, Heaven send us understanding!'

At mid-day Hummil rose, with an evil taste in his mouth, but an unclouded eye and a joyful heart.

'I was pretty bad last night, wasn't I?' said he.

'I have seen healtliier men. You must have had a touch of the sun. Look here: if I write you a swingeing medical certificate, will you apply for leave on the spot?'

'No.'

'Why not? You want it.'

'Yes, but I can hold on till the weather's a little cooler.'

'Why should you, if you can get relieved on the spot?'

'Burkett is the only man who could be sent; and he's a born fool.'

'Oh, never mind about the line. You aren't so im-portant as all that. Wire for leave, if necessary.'

Hummil looked very uncomfortable.

'I can hold on till the Rains,' he said evasively.

' You can't. Wire to headquarters for FJurkett.'

'I won't. If you want to know why, particularly, Burkett is married, md his wile's just had a kid, and she's up at Simla, in the cool, and Burkett has a verynice billet that takes him into Simla from Saturday toMonday. That little woman isn't at all well. If Burkettwas transferred she'd try to follow him. If she left thebaby behind she'd fret herself to death. If she came,—and Burkett's one of those selfish little beasts whoare always talking about a wife's place being with herhusband,— she'd die. It's murder to bring a woman herejust now. Burkett hasn't the physique of a rat. If hecame here he'd go out; and I know she hasn't anymoney, and I'm pretty sure she'd go out too. I'm saltedin a sort of way, and I'm not married. Wait till theRains, and then Burkett can get thin down here. It'll dohim heaps of good.'

*Do you mean to say that you intend to face^—whatyou have faced, till the Rains break?'

'Oh, it won't be so bad, now you've shown me a wayout of it. I can always wire to you. Besides, now I'veonce got into the way of sleeping, it'll be all right. Any-how, I shan't put in for leave. That's the long and theshort of it.'

'My great Scott! I thought all that sort of thing wasdead and done with.'

'Bosh! You'd do the same yourself. I feel a newman, thanks to that cigarette-case. You're going overto camp now, aren't you?'

'Yes; but I'll try to look you up every other day, if Ican.'

'I'm not bad enough for that. I don't want you tobother. Give the coolies gin and ketchup.'

' Then you feel all right?'

'Fit to fight for my Hfe, but not to stand out in thesun talking to you. Go along, old man, and bless you!'

Hummil turned on his heel to face the echoing deso-lation of his bungalow, and the first thing he saw stand-ing in the verandah was the figure of himself. He hadmet a similar apparition once before, when he was suffer-ing from overwork and the strain of the hot weather.

'This is bad,—already,' he said, rubbing his eyes. 'Ifthe thing slides away from me all in one piece, like aghost, I shall know it is only my eyes and stom.ach thatare out of order. If it walks—my head is going.'

He approached the figure, which naturally kept at anunvarying distance from him, as is the use of all spectresthat are born of overwork. It slid through the houseand dissolved into swimming specks within the eyeballas soon as it reached the burning fight of the garden.Hummil went about his business till even. When hecame in to dinner he found himself sitting at the table.The vision rose and walked out hastily. Except thatit cast no shadow it was in all respects real.

No living man knov/s what that week held for Hum-mil. An increase of the epidemic kept Spurstow incamp among the coolies, and all he could do was totelegraph to Mottram, bidding him go to the bungalowand sleep there. But Mottram was forty miles awayfrom the nearest telegraph, and knew nothing of anythingsave the needs of the survey till he met, early on Sundaymorning, Lowndes and Spurstow heading towards Hum-mil's for the weekly gathering.

'Hope the poor chap's in a better temper,' said theformer, swinging himself off his horse at the door. 'Isuppose he isn't up yet.'

'I'll just have a look at him,' said the doctor. 'Ifhe's asleep there's no need to wake him.'

And an instant later, by the tone of Spurstow's voicecaUing upon them to enter, the men knew what hadhappened. There was no need to wake him.

The punkah was still being pulled over the bed, butHummil had departed this life at least three hours.

The body lay on its back, hands clinched by the side,as Spurstow had seen it lying seven nights previously.In the staring eyes was written terror beyond the ex-pression of any pen.

Mottram, who had entered behind Lowndes, bent over the dead and touched the forehead Hghtly with his hps.'Oh, you lucky, lucky devil!' he whispered.

But Lowndes had seen the eyes, and withdrew shud-dering to the other side of the room.

'Poor chap! poor old chap! And the last time I met him I was angry. Spurstow, we should have watched him. Has he ?'

Deftly Spurstow continued his investigations, ending by a search round the room.

'No, he hasn't,' he snapped. 'There's no trace of anything. Call the servants.'

They came, eight or ten of them, whispering and peer-ing over each other's shoulders.

'When did your Sahib go to bed?' said Spurstow.

'At eleven or ten, we think,' said Hummil's personal servant.

' He was well then? But how should you know?'

'He was not ill, as far as our comprehension extended. But he had slept very httle for three nights. This I know, because I saw him walking much, and specially in the heart of the night.'

As Spurstow was arranging the sheet, a big straight-necked hunting-spur tumbled on the ground. The doctor groaned. The personal servant peeped at the body.

'What do you think, Chuma?' said Spurstow, catching the look on the dark face.

'Heaven-born, in my poor opinion, this that was my master has descended into the Dark Places, and there has been caught because he was not able to escape with sufficient speed. We have the spur for evidence that he fought with Fear. Thus have I seen men of my race do with thorns when a spell was laid upon them to overtake them in their sleeping hours and they dared not sleep.'

Xhuma, you're a mud-head. Go out and prepare seals to be set on the Sahib's property.'

' God has made the Heaven-born. God has made me. Who are we, to inquire into the dispensations of God? I will bid the other servants hold aloof while you are reckoning the tale of the Sahib's property. They are all thieves, and would steal.'

*As far as I can make out, he died from—oh, any-thing; stoppage of the heart's action, heat-apoplexy, or some other visitation,' said Spurstow to his com-panions. 'We must make an inventory of his effects, and so on.'

'He was scared to death,' insisted Lowndes. 'Look at those eyes! For pity's sake don't let him be buried with them open!'

'Whatever it was, he's clear of all the trouble now,' said Mottram softly.

Spurstow was peering into the open eyes.

'Come here,' said he. 'Can you see anything there?'

'I can't face it!' whimpered Lowndes. 'Cover up the face! Is there any fear on earth that can turn a man into that likeness? It's ghastly. Oh, Spurstow, cover it up!'

'No fear—on earth,' said Spurstow. Mottram leaned over his shoulder and looked intently.

'I see nothing except some gray blurs in the pupil, lliere can be nothing there, you know.'

'Even so. Well, let's think. It'll take half a day to knock up any sort of coffin; and he must have died at midnight. Lowndes, old man, go out and tell the coolies to break ground next to Jevins's grave. Mot-tram, go round the house with Chuma and see that the seals are put on things. Send a couple of men to me here, and I'll arrange.'

The strong-armed servants when they returned to their own kind told a strange story of the doctor Sahib vainly trying to call their master back to Ufe by magic arts,—to wit, the holding of a Httle green box that clicked to each of the dead man's eyes, and of a be-wildered muttering on the part of the doctor Sahib, who took the httle green box away with him.

The resonant hammering of a coffin-lid is no pleasant thing to hear, but those who have experience main-tain that much more terrible is the soft swish of the bed-Hnen, the reeving and unreeving of the bed-tapes,when he who has fallen by the roadside is apparelled forburial, sinking gradually as the tapes are tied over, tillthe swaddled shape touches the floor and there is noprotest against the indignity of hasty disposal.

At the last moment Lowndes was seized with scruplesof conscience. 'Ought you to read the service,—frombeginning to end?' said he to Spurstow.

'I intend to. You're my senior as a civilian. Youcan take it if you like.'

*I didn't mean that for a moment. I only thought ifwe could get a chaplain from somewhere,—I'm willing toride anywhere,—and give poor Hummil a better chance.That's all.'

'Bosh!' said Spurstow, as he framed his lips to thetremendous words that stand at the head of the burialservice.

After breakfast they smoked a pipe in silence to thememory of the dead. Then Spurs tow said absently—

' Tisn't in medical science.'

*What?'

^Things in a dead man's eye.'

'For goodness' sake leave that horror alone!' saidLowndes. 'I've seen a native die of pure frightwhen a tiger chivied him. I know what killed Hum-mil.'

'The deuce you do! I'm going to try to see.' Andthe doctor retreated into the bath-room with a Kodakcamera. After a few minutes there was the sound ofsomething being hammered to pieces, and he emerged,very white indeed.

' Have you got a picture?' said Mottram. ' What doesthe thing look like?'

'It was impossible, of course. You needn't look,Mottram. I've torn up the films. There was nothingthere. It was impossible.'

'That,' said Lowndes, very distinctly, watching theshaking hand striving to relight the pipe,' is a damnedUe.'

Mottram laughed uneasily. 'Spurstow's right,' hesaid. 'We're all in such a state now that we'd believeanything. For pity's sake let's try to be rational.'

There was no further speech for a long time. Thehot wind whistled without, and the dry trees sobbed.Presently the daily train, winking brass, burnished steel,and spouting steam, pulled up panting in the intenseglare. 'We'd better go on on that,' said Spurstow.'Go back to work. I've written my certificate. Wecan't do any more good here, and work'll keep our witstogether. Come on.'

No one moved. It is not pleasant to face railway

journeys at mid-day in June. Spurstow gathered up hishat and whip, and, turning in the doorway, said—

•There may be Heaven,—there must be Hell.Meantime, there is our life here. We-ell?'

Neither Mottram nor Lowndes had any answer to thequestion.

THE MUTINY OF THE MAVERICKS

!^ • ' I (in forces j Regular forces,

^,^^^^r^l^ mutinyj belonging (Reserve forces,""ersons to('^'^'^"" to Her rAuxiliary forces,^Tuse J (Majesty'sJ Navy.

When three obscure gentlemen in San Francisco arguedon insufficient premises they condemned a fellow-creatureto a most unpleasant death in a far country, which hadnothing whatever to do with the United States, Theyforegathered at the top of a tenement-house in TehamaStreet, an unsavoury quarter of the city, and, there callingfor certain drirxks, they conspired because they were con-spirators by trade, officially known as the Third Three ofthe I.A.A.—an institution for the propagation of purelight, not to be confounded with any others, though it isaffiliated to many. The Second Three live in Montreal,and work among the poor there; the First Three havetheir home in New York, not far from Castle Garden,and write regularly once a week to a small house nearone of the big hotels at Boulogne. What happensafter that, a particular section of Scotland Yard knowstoo well, and laughs at. A conspirator detests ridicule.More men have been stabbed with Lucrezia Borgia dag-gers and dropped into the Thames for laughing at HeadCentres and Triangles than for betraying secrets; forthis is human nature.The Third Three conspired over whisky cocktails

270

and a clean sheet of notepaper against the British Empireand all that lay therein. This work is very like whatmen without discernment call poHtics before a generalelection. You pick out and discuss, in the company ofcongenial friends, all the weak points in your opponents'organisation, and unconsciously dwell upon and exagger-ate all their mishaps, till it seems to you a miracle thatthe hated party holds together for an hour.

'Our principle is not so much active demonstration—that we leave to others—as passive embarrassment, toweaken and unnerve,' said the first man. 'Wherever anorganisation is crippled, wherever a confusion is throwninto any branch of any department, we gain a stepfor those who take on the work; we are but the forerun-ners.' He was a German enthusiast, and editor of anewspaper, from whose leading articles he quoted fre-quently.

'That cursed Empire makes so many blunders of herown that unless we doubled the year's average I guessit wouldn't strike her anything special had occurred,'said the second man. 'Are you prepared to say that allour resources are equal to blowing off the muzzle of ahundred-ton gun or spiking a ten-thousand-ton ship ona plain rock in clear daylight? They can beat us at ourown game. 'Better join hands with the practicalbranches; we're in funds now. Try a direct scare in acrowded street. They value their greasy hides.' He wasthe drag upon the wheel, and an Americanised Irish-man of the second generation, despising his own raceand hating the other. He had learned caution.

The third man drank his cocktail and spoke no word.He was the strategist, but unfortunately his knowledgeof life was limited. He picked a letter from his breast-pocket and threw it across the table, That epistle to the

heathen contained some very concise directions from theFirst Three in New York. It said—

* The boom in black iron has already affected the easternmarkets, where our agents have been forcing down th^English-held stock among the smaller buyers who watch theturn of shares. Any immediate operations, such as westernbears, would increase their willingness to unload. This,Itowever, cannot be expected till they see clearly that foreigniron-masters are willing to co-operate. Mulcahy shouldbe dispatcJted to feel the pulse of tJte market, and act accord-ingly. Mavericks are at present the best for our purpose.—P.D.Q.'

As a message referring to an iron crisis in Penn-sylvania, it was interesting, if not lucid. As a newdeparture in organised attack on an outl>Tng EngHshdependency, it was more than interesting.

The second man read it through and murmured—

'Already? Surely they are in too great a hurry. Allthat DhuUp Singh could do in India he has done, downto the distribution of his photographs among the peas-antry. Ho! Ho! The Paris firm arranged that, andhe has no substantial money backing from the OtherPower. Even our agents in India know he hasn't.What is the use of our organisation wasting men on workthat is already done? Of course the Irish regiments inIndia are half mutinous as they stand.'

This shows how near a lie may come to the truth.An Irish regiment, for just so long as it stands still, isgenerally a hard handful to control, being reckless andrough. When, however, it is moved in the direction ofmusketry-firing, it becomes strangely and unpatrioticallycontent with its lot. It has even been heard to cheer theQueen with enthusiasm on these occasions.

But the notion of tampering with the army was, from

the point of view of Tehama Street, an altogether soundone. There is no shadow of stability in the policy ofan English Government, and the most sacred oaths ofEngland would, even if engrossed on vellum, find very fewbuyers among colonies and dependencies that have suf-fered from vain beliefs. But there remains to Englandalways her army. That cannot change except in thematter of uniform and equipment. The officers maywrite to the papers demanding the heads of the HorseGuards in default of cleaner redress for grievances; themen may break loose across a country town and seriouslystartle the pubKcans; but neither officers nor men have itin their composition to mutiny after the continentalmanner. The English people, when they trouble to thinkabout the army at all, are, and with justice, absolutelyassured that it is absolutely trustworthy. Imagine for amoment their emotions on realising that such and such aregiment was in open revolt from causes directly due toEngland's management of Ireland. They would prob-ably send the regiment to the polls forthwith and exam-ine their own consciences as to their duty to Erin; butthey would never be easy any more. And it was thisVague, unhappy mistrust that the I. A. A. were labouringto produce.

^Sheer waste of breath,' said the second man aftera pause in the council, 'I don't see the use of tamperingwith their fool-army, but it has been tried before andwe must try it again. It looks well in the reports.If we send one man from here you may bet your lifethat other men are going too. Order up Mulcahy.'

They ordered him up—a slim, slight, dark-hairedyoung man, devoured with that blind rancorous hatredof England that only reaches its full growth across theAtlantic. He had sucked it from his mother's breast in

the little cabin at the back of the northern avenues ofNew York; he had been taught his rights and his wrongs,in German and Irish, on the canal fronts of Chicago; andSan Francisco held men who told him strange and awfulthings of the great blind power over the seas. Once,when business took him across the Atlantic, he hadserved in an EngHsh regiment, and being insubordinatehad suffered extremely. He drew all his ideas of Eng-land that v/ere not bred by the cheaper patriotic printsfrom one iron-fisted colonel and an unbending adjutant.He would go to the mines if need be to teach his gospel.And he went as his instructions advised p.d.q.—whichmeans ^with speed'—to introduce embarrassment intoan Irish regiment, ^already half-mutinous, quarteredamong Sikh peasantry, all wearing miniatures of HisHighness Dhulip Singh, Maharaja of the Punjab, nexttheir hearts, and all eagerly expecting his arrival.'Other information equally valuable was given him by hismasters. He was to be cautious, but never to grudgeexpense in winning the hearts of the men in the regiment.His mother in New York would supply funds, and hewas to write to her once a month. Life is pleasant for aman who has a mother in New York to send him two hun-dred pounds a year over and above his regimental pay.

In process of time, thanks to his intimate knowledgeof drill and musketry exercise, the excellent Mulcahy,wearing the corporal's stripe, went out in a troopship andjoined Her Majesty's Royal Loyal Musketeers, commonlyknown as the 'Mavericks,' because they were masterlessand unbranded cattle—sons of small farmers in CountyClare, shoeless vagabonds of Kerry, herders of Bally-vegan, much wanted 'moonhghters' from the bare rainyheadlands of the south coast, officered by 0'Mores,Bradys, Hills, Kilreas, and the like. Never to outward seeming was there more promising material to work on. The First Three had chosen their regiment well. It feared nothing that moved or talked save the colonel and the regimental Roman Catholic chaplain, the fat Father Dennis, who held the keys of heaven and hell, and blared like an angry bull when he desired to be con-vincing. Him also it loved because on occasions of stress he was used to tuck up his cassock and charge with the rest into the merriest of the fray, where he always found, good man, that the saints sent him a revolver when there was a fallen private to be protected, or—but this came as an afterthought—his own gray head to be guarded.

Cautiously as he had been instructed, tenderly and with much beer, Mulcahy opened his projects to such as he deemed fittest to Hsten. And these were, one and all, of that quaint, crooked, sweet, profoundly irrespon-sible and profoundly lovable race that fight Uke fiends, argue like children, reason like women, obey like men, and jest like their own goblins of the rath through rebellion, loyalty, want, woe, or war. The underground work of a conspiracy is always dull and very much the same the world over. At the end of six months—the seed always falling on good ground—Mulcahy spoke almost explicitly, hinting darkly in the approved fashion at dread powers behind him, and advising nothing more nor less than mutiny. Were they not dogs, evilly treated? had they not all their own and their national revenges to satisfy? Who in these days would do aught to nine hundred men in rebel Hon? Who, again, could stay them if they broke for the sea, Hcking up on their way other regiments only too anxious to join? And afterwards . . . here followed windy promises of gold and preferment, office, and honour, ever dear to a certain type of Irishman.

As he finished his speech, in the dusk of a twilight, to his chosen associates, there was a sound of a rapidly unslung belt behind him. The arm of one Dan Grady flew out in the gloom and arrested something. Then said Dan—

'Mulcahy, you're a great man, an' you do credit to whoever sent you. Walk about a bit while we think of it.' Mulcahy departed elate. He knew his words would sink deep.

*Why the triple-dashed asterisks did ye not let me belt him?' grunted a voice.

'Because I'm not a fat-headed fool. Boys, 'tis what he's been dri\ing at these six months—our superior corpril with his education and his copies of the Irish papers and his everlasting beer. He's been sent for the purpose and that's where the money comes from. Can ye not see? That man's a gold-mine, which Horse Egan here would have destroyed \with a belt-buckle. It would be throwing away the gifts of Pro\idence not to faU in with his little plans. Of coorse we'll mut'ny till all's dry. Shoot the colonel on the parade-ground, massacree the company officers, ransack the arsenal, and then—Boys, did he tell you what next? He told me the other night when he was beginning to talk wild. Then we're to join with the niggers, and look for help from DhuHp Singh and the Russians!'

'And spoil the best campaign that ever was this side of Hell! Danny, I'd have lost the beer to ha' given him the belting he requires.'

'Oh, let him go this awhile, man! He's got no—no constructiveness, but that's the egg-meat of his plan, and you must understand that I'm in with it, an' so are you. We'll want oceans of beer to convince us—firma-ments full. We'll give him talk for his money, and one

by one all the boys '11 come in and he'll have a nest of nine hundred mutineers to squat in an' give drink to.'

'What makes me killing-mad is his wanting us to do what the niggers did thirty years gone. That an' hispig's cheek in saying that other regiments would come along/ said a Kerry man.

* That's not so bad as hintin' we should loose off on the colonel.'

'Colonel be sugared! I'd as soon as not put a shot through his helmet to see him jump and clutch his old horse's head. But Mulcahy talks o' shootin' our comp'ny orf'cers accidental.'

'He said that, did he.^' said Horse Egan.

'Somethin' like that, anyways. Can't ye fancy ouldBarber Brady wid a bullet in his lungs, coughin' Kke asick monkey, an' sayin', "Bhoys, I do not mind yourgettin' dhrunk, but you must hould your liquor Hke men.The man that shot me is dbrunk. I'll suspend in-vestigations for six hours, while I get this bullet cut out,an' then "'

'An' then,' continued Horse Egan, for the pepperyMajor's peculiarities of speech and manner were as wellknown as his tanned face; "'an' then, ye dissolute, half-baked, putty-faced scum o' Connemara, if I find a man somuch as lookin' confused, begad, I'll coort-martial thewhole company. A man that can't get over his liquorin six hours is not fit to belong to the Mavericks!'"

A shout of laughter bore witness to the truth of thesketch.

'It's pretty to think of,' said the Kerry man slowly.* Mulcahy would have us do all the devilmint, and getclear himself, someways. He wudn't be takin' all thisfool's throuble in shpoilin' the reputation of the regi-ment-—'

'Reputation of your grandmother's pig!' said Dan.

'Well, an' he had a good reputation tu; so it's all right.Mulcahy must see his way to clear out behind him, orhe'd not ha' come so far, talkin' powers of darkness.'

'Did you hear anything of a regimental court-martialamong the Black Boneens, these days? Half a companyof 'em took one of the new draft an' hanged him by hisarms with a tent-rope from a third story verandah.They gave no reason for so doin', but he was half dead.I'm thinking that the Boneens are short-sighted. It wasa iriend of Mulcahy's, or a man in the same trade.They'd a deal better ha' taken his beer,' returned Danreflectively.

* Better still ha' handed him up to the Colonel,' saidHorse Egan, ' onless—but sure the news wud be all overthe counthry an' give the reg'ment a bad name.'

'An' there'd be no reward for that man—he but wentabout talkin',' said the Kerry man artlessly.

'You speak by your breed,' said Dan with a laugh.'There was never a Kerry man yet that wudn't sell hisbrother for a pipe o' tobacco an' a pat on the back froma p'liceman.'

'Praise God I'm not a bloomin' Orangeman,' was theanswer.

'No, nor never will be,' said Dan. 'They breed menin Ulster. Would you like to thry the taste of one?'

The Kerry man looked and longed, but forbore. Theodds of battle were too great.

'Then you'll not even give Mulcahy a—a strike for hismoney,' said the voice of Horse Egan, who regarded whathe called ' trouble' of any kind as the pinnacle of felicity.

Dan answered not at all, but crept on tip-toe, withlarge strides, to the mess-room, the men following. Theroom was empty. In a corner, cased like the King of

Dahomey's state umbrella, stood the regimental Colours,Dan lifted them tenderly and unrolled in the light of thecandles the record of the Mavericks—tattered, worn, andhacked. The white satin was darkened everywhere withbig brown stains, the gold threads on the crowned harpwere frayed and discoloured, and the Red Bull, the to-tem of the Mavericks, was coffee-hued. The stiff, em-broidered folds, whose price is human life, rustled downslowly. The Mavericks keep their colours long andguard them very sacredly.

*Vittoria, Salamanca, Toulouse, Waterloo, Moodkee,Ferozshah, an' Sobraon—that was fought close next doorhere, against the very beggars he wants us to join. In-kermann, The Alma, Sebastopol! What are those Httlebusinesses compared to the campaigns of General Mul-cahy? The Mut'ny, think o' that; the Mut'ny an' somedirty little matters in Afghanistan; an' for that an'

thesean' those'—Dan pointed to the names of glorious bat-tles—'that Yankee man with the partin' in his haircomes an'says as easy as"have a drink." . . . HolyMoses, there's the captain!'

But it was the mess-sergeant who came in just as themen clattered out, and found the colours uncased.

From that day dated the mutiny of the Mavericks, tothe joy of Mulcahy and the pride of his mother in NewYork—the good lady who sent the money for the beer.Never, so far as words went, was such a mutiny. Theconspirators, led by Dan Grady and Horse Egan, pouredin daily. They were sound men, men to be trusted, andthey all wanted blood; but first they must have beer.They cursed the Queen, they mourned over Ireland, theysuggested hideous plunder of the Indian country side, andthen, alas—some of the younger men would go forth andwallow on the ground in spasms of wicked laughter.

The genius of the Irish for conspiracies is remarkable.None the less they would swear no oaths but those oftheir o\\ti making, which were rare and curious, and theywere always at pains to impress Mulcahy with the risksthey ran. Naturally the flood of beer wrought demoral-isation. But Mulcahy confused the causes of things, andwhen a very muzzy Maverick smote a sergeant on thenose or called his commanding officer a bald-headed oldlard-bladder and even worse names, he fancied that re-bellion and not Hquor was at the bottom of the outbreak.Other gentlemen w^ho have concerned themselves inlarger conspiracies have made the same error.

The hot season, in which they protested no man couldrebel, came to an end, and Mulcahy suggested a visiblereturn for liis teachings. As to the actual upshot of themutiny he cared nothing. It would be enough if theEnglish, infatuatedly trusting to the integrity of theirarmy, should be startled with news of an Irish regimentrevolting from political considerations. His persistentdemands would have ended, at Dan's instigation, in aregimental belting which in all probability would havekilled him and cut off the supply of beer, had not he beensent on special duty somie fifty miles away from the can-tonment to cool his heels in a mud fort and dismountobsolete artillery. Then the colonel of the Mavericks,reading his newspaper dihgently, and scenting Frontiertrouble from afar, posted to the army headquarters andpled with the Commander-in-chief for certain privileges,to be granted under certain contingencies; which con-tingencies cam^e about only a week later, when the an-nual Kttle v/ar on the border developed itself and thecolonel returned to carry the good news to the Mavericks.He held the promise of the Chief for active service, andthe men must get ready.

On the evening of the same day, Mulcahy, an uncon-sidered corporal—yet great in conspiracy—returned tocantonments, and heard sounds of strife and howlingsfrom afar off. The mutiny had broken out and thebarracks of the Mavericks were one white-washedpandemonium. A private tearing through the barrack-square, gasped in his ear, * Service! Active service. It'sa burnin' shame.' Oh joy, the Mavericks had risen onthe eve of battle! They would not—noble and loyalsons of Ireland—serve the Queen longer. The newswould flash through the country side and over to Eng-land, and he—Mulcahy—the trusted of the Third Three,had brought about the crash. The private stood in themiddle of the square and cursed colonel, regiment, ofScers,and doctor, particularly the doctor, by his gods. Anorderly of the native cavalry regiment clattered throughthe mob of soldiers. He was half Hfted, half draggedfrom his horse, beaten on the back with mighty hand-claps till his eyes watered, and called all manner of en-dearing names. Yes, the Mavericks had fraternisedwith the native troops. Who then was the agent amongthe latter that had blindly wrought with Mulcahy sowell?

An oflicer slunk, almost ran, from the mess to a bar-rack. He was mobbed by the infuriated soldiery, whoclosed round but did not kill him, for he fought his wayto shelter, flying for the life. Mulcahy could have weptwith pure joy and thankfulness. The very prisoners inthe guard-room were shaking the bars of their cells andhowling like wild beasts, and from every barrack pouredthe booming as of a big war-drum.

Mulcahy hastened to his own barrack. He couldhardly hear himself speak. Eighty men were poundingwith fist and heel the tables and trestles—eighty men,

flushed with mutiny, stripped to their shirt sleeves, theirknapsacks half-packed for the march to the sea, made thetwo-inch boards thunder again as they chanted to a tunethat Mulcahy knew well, the Sacred War Song of theMavericks—

Listen in the north, my boys, there's trouble on the wind;Tramp o' Cossack hooves in front, gray great-coats behind,Trouble on the Frontier of a most amazin' kind,Trouble on the waters o' the Oxus!

Then, as a table broke under the furious accompani-ment—

Hurrah! hurrah! it's north by west we go;Hurrah! hurrah! the chance we wanted so;Let 'em hear the chorus from Umballa to Moscow,As we go marchin' to the Kremling.

'Mother of all the saints in bliss and all the devilsin cinders, where's my fine new sock widout the heel?'howled Horse Egan, ransacking everybody's valise buthis own. He was engaged in making up deficienciesof kit preparatory to a campaign, and in that work hesteals best who steals last. 'Ah, Mulcahy, you're ingood time,' he shouted. 'We've got the route, and we'reoff on Thursday for a pic-nic wid the Lancers nextdoor.'

An ambulance orderly appeared with a huge basketfull of lint rolls, provided by the forethought of theQueen for such as might need them later on. HorseEgan unrolled his bandage, and flicked it under Mulcahy'snose, chanting—

' Sheepskin an' bees' wax, thunder, pitch, and plaster,The more you try to pull it oft, the more it sticks the faster.As I was goin' to New Orleans—

'You know the rest of it, my Irish American-Jewboy. By gad, ye have to fight for the Queen in the insideav a fortnight, my darlin'.'

A roar of laughter interrupted. Mulcahy lookedvacantly down the room. Bid a boy defy his father whenthe pantomime-cab is at the door; or a girl develop awill of her own when her mother is putting the lasttouches to the first ball-dress; but do not ask an Irishregiment to embark upon mutiny on the eve of acampaign; when it has fraternised with the nativeregiment that accompanies it, and driven its officers intoretirement with ten thousand clamorous questions, andthe prisoners dance for joy, and the sick men stand inthe open, calHng down aU kno^vn diseases on the head ofthe doctor, who has certified that they are "medicallyunfit for active service." At even the Mavericks mighthave been mistaken for mutineers by one so unversedin their natures as Mulcahy. At dawn a girls' schoolmight have learned deportment from them. They knewthat their colonel's hand had closed, and that he whobroke that iron disciphne would not go to the front:nothing in the world will persuade one of our soldierswhen he is ordered to the north on the smallest of affairsthat he is not immediately going gloriously to slay Cos-sacks and cook his kettles in the palace of the Czar. Afew of the younger men mourned for Mulcahy's beer,because the campaign was to be conducted on stricttemperance principles, but as Dan and Horse Egan saidsternly, 'We've got the beer-man with us. He shalldrink now on his own hook.'

Mulcahy had not taken into account the possibility ofbeing sent on active service. He had made up his mindthat he would not go under any circumstances, but for-tune was against him.

'Sick—you?' said the doctor, who had served anunholy apprenticeship to his trade in

Tralee poorhouses.'You're only home-sick, and what you call varicose veinscome from over-eating. A Httle gentle exercise will curethat.' And later, 'Mulcahy, my man, everybody isallowed to apply for a sick-certificate once. If he tries ittwice we call him by an ugly name. Go back to yourduty, and let's hear no more of your diseases.'

I am ashamed to say that Horse Egan enjoyed thestudy of Mulcahy's soul in those days, and Dan took anequal interest. Together they would communicate totheir corporal all the dark lore of death which is the por-tion of those who have seen men die. Egan had thelarger experience, but Dan the finer imagination. Mul-cahy shivered when the former spoke of the knife as anintimate acquaintance, or the latter dwelt with lovingparticularity on the fate of those who, w^ounded andhelpless, had been overlooked by the ambulances, andhad fallen into the hands of the Afghan women-folk.

Mulcahy knew that the mutiny, for the present atleast, was dead; knew, too, that a change had comeover Dan's usually respectful attitude towards him, andHorse Egan's laughter and frequent allusions to abortiveconspiracies emphasised all that the conspirator hadguessed. The horrible fascination of the death-stories,however, made him seek the men's society. He learntmuch more than he had bargained for; and in this man-ner: It was on the last night before the regiment en-trained to the front. The barracks were stripped ofeverything movable, and the men were too excited tosleep. The bare walls gave out a heavy hospital smell ofchloride of lime.

'And what,' said Mulcahy in an awe-stricken whisper,after some conversation on the eternal subject, 'are

you going to do to me, Dan?' This might have been thelanguage of an able conspirator conciliating a weak spirit.

'You'll see,' said Dan grimly, turning over in hiscot, 'or I rather shud say you'll not see.'

This was hardly the language of a weak spirit. Mul-cahy shook under the bed-clothes.

'Be easy with him,' put in Egan from the next cot.'He has got his chanst o' goin' clean. Listen, Mulcahy;all we want is for the good sake of the regiment thatyou take your death standing up, as a man shud. Therebe heaps an' heaps of enemy—plenshus heaps. Gothere an' do all you can and die decent. You'll die witha good name there. 'Tis not a hard thing considerin'.'

Again Mulcahy shivered.

'An' how could a man wish to die better than fightin'? *added Dan consoKngly.

'And if I won't?' said the corporal in a dry whisper.

'There'll be a dale of smoke,' returned Dan, sittingup and ticking off the situation on his fingers, 'sure to be,an' the noise of the firin' '11 be tremenjus, an' we'll berunning about up and down, the regiment will. But we,Horse and I—we'll stay by you, Mulcahy, and never letyou go. Maybe there'll be an accident.'

'It's playing it low on me. Let me go. For pity'ssake let me go. I never did you harm, and—and Istood you as much beer as I could. Oh, don't be hardon me, Dan! You are—you were in it too. You won'tkill me up there, will you?'

'I'm not thinkin' of the treason; though you shudbe glad any honest boys drank with you. It's for theregiment. We can't have the shame o' you bringin'shame on us. You went to the doctor quiet as a sickcat to get and stay behind an' live with the women atthe depot—you that wanted us to run to the sea in

wolf-packs like the rebels none of your black blooddared to be! But we knew about your goin' to thedoctor, for he told in mess, and it's all over the regiment.Bein', as we are, your best friends, we didn't allowany one to molest you yet. We will see to you our-selves. Fight which you will—us or the enemy—you'llnever lie in that cot again, and there's more glory andmaybe less kicks from fightin' the enemy. That's fairspeakin'.'

'And he told us by word of mouth to go and joinwith the niggers—you've forgotten that, Dan,' saidHorse Egan, to justify sentence.

'What's the use of plaguin' the man? One shot paysfor all. Sleep ye sound, Mulcahy. But you onderstand,do ye not?'

Mulcahy for some weeks understood very little ofanything at all save that ever at his elbow, in camp,or at parade, stood two big men with soft voices ad-juring him to commit hari-kari lest a worse thing shouldhappen—to die for the honour of the regiment in decencyamong the nearest knives. But Mulcahy dreadeddeath. He remembered certain things that priests hadsaid in his infancy, and his mother—not the one at NewYork—starting from her sleep with shrieks to pray for ahusband's soul in torment. It is well to be of a culturedintelHgence, but in time of trouble the weak humanmind returns to the creed it sucked in at the breast, andif that creed be not a pretty one trouble follows. Also,the death he would have to face would be physicallypainful. Most conspirators have large imaginations.Mulcahy could see him.self, as he lay on the earth in thenight, dying by various causes. They were all horrible;the mother in New York was very far away, and theRegiment, the engine that, once you fall in its grip, moves

you forward whether you will or won't, was daily comingcloser to the enemy!

They were brought to the field of Marzun-Katai, andwith the Black Boneens to aid, they fought a fight thathas never been set down in the newspapers. In response,many beheve, to the fervent prayers of Father Dennis,the enemy not only elected to fight in the open, but madea beautiful fight, as many weeping Irish mothers knewlater. They gathered behind walls or flickered acrossthe open in shouting masses, and were pot-vaHantin artillery. It was expedient to hold a large reserveand wait for the psychological moment that was beingprepared by the shrieking shrapnel. Therefore theMavericks lay down in open order on the brow of a hillto watch the play till their call should come. FatherDennis, whose duty was in the rear, to smooth thetrouble of the wounded, had naturally managed to makehis way to the foremost of his boys and lay like a blackporpoise, at length on the grass. To him crawled Mul-cahy, ashen-gray, demanding absolution.

'Wait till you're shot,' said Father Dennis sweetly.* There's a time for everything.'

Dan Grady chuckled as he blew for the fiftieth timeinto the breech of his speckless rifle. Mulcahy groanedand buried his head in his arms till a stray shot spokelike a snipe immediately above his head, and a generalheave and tremour rippled the line. Other shots fol-lowed and a few took effect, as a shriek or a grunt attested.The officers, who had been lying down with the men, roseand began to walk steadily up and down the front of theircompanies.

This manoeuvre, executed, not for publication, but as a

guarantee of good faith, to soothe men, demands nerve.You must not hurry, you must not look nervous, thoughyou know that you are a mark for every rifle withinextreme range, and above all if you are smitten youmust make as little noise as possible and roll inwardsthrough the files. It is at this hour, when the breezebrings the first salt whiff of the powder to noses rathercold at the tip, and the eye can quietly take in theappearance of each red casualty, that the strain on thenerves is strongest. Scotch regiments can endure forhalf a day and abate no whit of their zeal at the end;English regiments sometimes sulk under punishment,while the Irish, like the French, are apt to run forwardby ones and twos, which is just as bad as running back.The truly wise commandant of highly strung troopsallows them, in seasons of waiting, to hear the sound oftheir own voices uplifted in song. There is a legend of anEnglish regiment that lay by its arms under fire chaunting' Sam Hall,' to the horror of its newly appointed and piouscolonel. The Black Boneens, who were suffering morethan the Mavericks, on a hill half a nule away, beganpresently to explain to all who cared to listen—

We'll sound the jubilee, from the centre to the sea.And Ireland shall be free, says the Shan-van Vogh.

'Sing, boys,* said Father Dennis softly. 'It looks asif we cared for their Afghan peas.'

Dan Grady raised himself to his knees ajid opened hismouth in a song imparted to him, as to m.ost of his com^rades, in the strictest confidence by Mulcahy—theMulcahy then lying limp and fainting 0£l the grass, thechill fear of death upon him.

Company after company caught up^ fjig words which,

the I. A. A. say, are to herald the general rising of Erin,and to breathe which, except to those duly appointedto hear, is death. WHierefore they are printed in thisplace.

The Saxon in Heaven's just balance is weighed,His doom like Belshazzar's in death haLS been cast,

And the hand of the venger shall never be stayedTiU his race, faith, and speech are a dream of the past.

They were heart-filling lines and they ran with aswirl; the I. A. A. are better served by their pens thantheir petards. Dan clapped Mulcahy merrily on theback, asking him to sing up. The officers lay downagain. There was no need to walk any more. Theirmen were soothing themselves thunderously, thus—

St. Mary in Heaven has written the vowThat the land shall not rest till the heretic blood,

From the babe at the breast to the hand at the plough,Has rolled to the ocean like Shannon in flood!

*I'll speak to you after all's over,' said Father Dennisauthoritatively in Dan's ear. 'What's the use of con-fessing to me when you do this foolishness? Dan, you'vebeen playing with fire! I'll lay you more penance in aweek than '

' Come along to Purgatory with us, Father dear. TheBoneens are on the move; they'll let us go now!'

The regiment rose to the blast of the bugle as oneman; but one man there was who rose more swiftly thanall the others, for half an inch of bayonet was in thefleshy part of his leg.

* You've got to do it,' said Dan grimly. ' Do it decent,anyhow;' and the roar of the rush drowned his words,

for the rear companies thrust forward the first, still sing-ing as they swung down the slope—

From the child at the breast to the hand at the ploughShall roll to the ocean like Shannon in flood!

They should have sung it in the face of England, notof the Afghans, whom it impressed as much as did thewild Irish yell.

'They came down singing,' said the unofficial report ofthe enemy, borne from village to village the next day.'They continued to sing, and it was written that our mencould not abide when they came. It is beheved thatthere was magic in the aforesaid song.'

Dan and Horse Egan kept themselves in the neigh-30urhood of Mulcahy. Twice the man would havebolted back in the confusion. Twice he was heaved,kicked, and shouldered back again into the unpaintableinferno of a hotly contested charge.

At the end, the panic excess of his fear drove himinto madness beyond all human courage. His eyes star-ing at nothing, his mouth open and frothing, and breath-ing as one in a cold bath, he went forward demented, whileDan toiled after him. The charge checked at a high mudwall. It was Mulcahy who scrambled up tooth and nailand hurled down among the bayonets the amazed Afghanwho barred his way. It was Mulcahy, keeping to thestraight Hne of the rabid dog, who led a collection of ardentsouls at a newly unmasked battery and flung himself onthe muzzle of a gun as his companions danced among thegunners. It was Mulcahy who ran wildly on from thatbattery into the open plain, where the enemy were retir-ing in sullen groups. His hands were empty, he had losthehnet and belt, and he was bleeding from a wound in

the neck. Dan and Horse Egan, panting and distressed,had thrown themselves down on the ground by thecaptured guns, when they noticed Mulcahy's charge.

'Mad/ said Horse Egan critically. 'Mad with fear!He's going straight to his death, an' shouting's no use.'

'Let him go. Watch now! If we fire we'll hit him,maybe.'

The last of a hurrying crowd of Afghans turned at thenoise of shod feet behind him, and shifted his knife readyto hand. This, he saw, was no time to take prisoners.Mulcahy tore on, sobbing; the straight-held blade wenthome through the defenceless breast, and the body pitchedforward almost before a shot from Dan's rifle broughtdown the slayer and still further hurried the Afghanretreat. The two Irishmen went out to bring in theirdead.

'He was given the point and that was an easy death,'said Horse Egan, viewing the corpse. 'But would youha' shot him, Danny, if he had Hved?'

'He didn't Uve, so there's no sayin'. But I doubt Iwud have bekase of the fun he gave us—let alone thebeer. Hike up his legs. Horse, and we'll bring him in.Perhaps 'tis better this way.'

They bore the poor limp body to the mass of theregiment, lolling open-mouthed on their rifles; and therewas a general snigger when one of the younger subalternssaid, ' That was a good man!'

'Phew,' said Horse Egan, when a burial-party hadtaken over the burden. 'I'm powerful dhry, and thisreminds me there'll be no more beer at all.'

'Fwhy not?' said Dan, with a twinkle in his eye ashe stretched himself for rest. 'Are we not conspirin' allwe can, an' while we conspire are we not entitled to freedhrinks? Sure his ould mother in New York would not

let her son's comrades perish of drouth—^if she can bereached at the end of a letter.'

'You're a janius,' said Horse Egan. 'O' coorse shewill not. I wish this crool war was over an' we'd getback to canteen. Faith, the Commander-in-Chief oughtto be hanged in his own Httle sword-belt for makin' uswork on wather.'

The Mavericks were generally of Horse Egan's opinion.So they made haste to get their work done as soon aspossible, and their industry was rewarded by unexpectedpeace. 'We can fight the sons of Adam,' said the tribes-men, 'but we cannot fight the sons of EbHs, and thisregiment never stays still in one place. Let us thereforecome in.' They came in and 'this regiment' withdrewto conspire under the leadership of Dan Grady.

Excellent as a subordinate Dan failed altogether as achief-in-command—possibly because he was too muchswayed by the advice of the only man in the regiment whocould manufacture more than one kind of handwriting.The same mail that bore to Mulcahy's mother in NewYork a letter from the colonel telling her how valiantlyher son had fought for the Queen, and how assuredly hewould have been recom.mended for the Victoria Cross hadhe survived, carried a communication signed, I grieveto say, by that same colonel and all the of&cers of theregiment, explaining their willingness to do 'anythingwhich is contrary to the regulations and all kinds ofrevolutions' if only a httle money could be forwardedto cover incidental expenses. Daniel Grady, Esquire,would receive funds, vice Mulcahy, who 'was unwell atthis present time of writing.'

Both letters were forwarded from New York to TehamaStreet, San Francisco, with marginal comments as briefas thev were bitter. The Third Three read and looked

at each other. Then the Second Conspirator—he whobelieved in ^joining hands with the practical branches'—began to laugh, and on recovering his gravity said,' Gentlemen, I consider this will be a lesson to us. We'releft again. Those cursed Irish have let us down. I knewthey would, but'—here he laughed afresh—'I'd giveconsiderable to know what was at the back of it all.'

His curiosity would have been satisfied had he seenDan Grady, discredited regimental conspirator, trying toexplain to his thirsty comrades in India the non-arrivalof funds from New YorL

THE MARK OF THE BEAST

Your Gods and my Gods—do you or I know which are the stronger?
Native Proverb.

East of Suez, some hold, the direct control of Providenceceases; Man being there handed over to the power of theGods and Devils of Asia, and the Church of EnglandProvidence only exercising an occasional and modifiedsupervision in the case of EngHshmen.

This theory accounts for some of the more unnecessaryhorrors of life in India: it may be stretched to explainmy story.

My friend Strickland of the PoHce, who knows asmuch of natives of India as is good for any man, can bearwitness to the facts of the case. Dumoise, our doctor,also saw what Strickland and I saw. The inferencewhich he drew from the evidence was entirely incorrect.He is dead now; he died, in a rather curious manner,which has been elsewhere described.

When Fleete came to India he owned a Httle moneyand some land in the Himalayas, near a place calledDharmsala. Both properties had been left him by anuncle, and he came out to finance them. He was a big,heavy, genial, and inoffensive man. His knowledge ofnatives was, of course, Hmited, and he complained of thedifficulties of the language.

He rode in from his place in the hills to spend NewYear in the station, and he stayed with Strickland. OnNew Year's Eve there was a big dinner at the club, and

294

the night was excusably wet. When men foregatherfrom the uttermost ends of the Empire, they have a rightto be riotous. The Frontier had sent down a contingento' Catch-'em-Alive-0's who had not seen twenty whitefaces for a year, and were used to ride fifteen miles todinner at the next Fort at the risk of a Khyberee bulletwhere their drinks should He. They profited by their newsecurity, for they tried to play pool with a curled-uphedgehog found in the garden, and one of them carriedthe marker round the room in his teeth. Half a dozenplanters had come in from the south and were talking'horse' to the Biggest Liar in Asia, who was tr\'7ddng tocap all their stories at once. Everybody was there, andthere was a general closing up of ranks and taking stockof our losses in dead or disabled that had fallen duringthe past year. It was a very wet night, and I rememberthat we sang ' Auld Lang Syne' with our feet in the PoloChampionship Cup, and our heads among the stars, andswore that we were all dear friends. Then some of uswent away and annexed Burma, and some tried to openup the Soudan and were opened up by P'uzzies in thatcruel scrub outside Suakim, and some found stars andmedals, and some v/ere married, which was bad, and somedid other things which were worse, and the others of usstayed in our chains and strove to make money oninsufficient experiences.

Fleete began the night with sherry and bitters, drankchampagne steadily up to dessert, then raw, raspingCapri with all the strength of whisky, took Benedictinewith his coffee, four or five whiskies and sodas to im-prove his pool strokes, beer and bones at half-past two,winding up with old brandy. Consequently, when hecame out, at half-past three in the morning, into four-teen degrees of frost, he was very angry with his horse

for coughing, and tried to leapfrog into the saddle. Thehorse broke away and went to his stables; so Stricklandand I formed a Guard of Dishonour to take Fleete home.

Our road lay through the bazaar, close to a Kttletemple of Hanuman, the Monkey-god, who is a leadingdivinity worthy of respect. All gods have good points,just as have all priests. Personally, I attach muchimportance to Hanuman, and am kind to his people—thegreat gray apes of the hills. One never knows when onemay want a friend.

There was a light in the temple, and as we passed, wecould hear voices of men chanting hymns. In a nativetemple, the priests rise at all hours of the night to dohonour to their god. Before we could stop him, Fleetedashed up the steps, patted two priests on the back, andwas gravely grinding the ashes of his cigar-butt into theforehead of the red stone image of Hanuman. Strickland tried to drag him out, but he sat down and saidsolemnly:

'Shee that? 'Mark of the B—beashtl / made it.Ishn'titfine?'

In half a minute the temple was alive and noisy, andStrickland, who knew what came of polluting gods, saidthat things might occur. He, by virtue of his officialposition, long residence in the country, and weakness forgoing among the natives, was known to the priests andhe felt unhappy. Fleete sat on the ground and refusedto move. He said that 'good old Hanuman' made a verysoft pillow.

Then, without any warning, a Silver Man came out ofa recess behind the image of the god. He was perfectlynaked in that bitter, bitter cold, and his body shone likefrosted silver, for he was what the Bible calls 'a leper aswhite as snow.' A^so he had no face, because he was a

leper of some years' standing and his disease was heavyupon him. We two stooped to haul Fleete up, and thetemple was filling and filling with folk who seemed tospring from the earth, when the Silver Man ran in underour arms, making a noise exactly like the mewing of anotter, caught Fleete round the body and dropped his headon Fleete's breast before we could wrench him away.Then he retired to a corner and sat mewing while thecrowd blocked all the doors.

The priests were very angry until the Silver Mantouched Fleete. That nuzzHng seemed to sober them.

At the end of a few minutes' silence one of the priestscame to Strickland and said, in perfect English, 'Takeyour friend away. He has done with Hanuman, butHanuman has not done with him.' The crowd gaveroom and we carried Fleete into the road.

Strickland was very angry. He said that we might allthree have been knifed, and that Fleete should thank hisstars that he had escaped without injury.

Fleete thanked no one. He said that he wanted to goto bed. He was gorgeously drunk.

We moved on, Strickland silent and wrathful, untilFleete was taken with violent shivering fits and sweating.He said that the smells of the bazaar were overpowering,and he wondered why slaughter-houses were permitted sonear English residences. 'Can't you smell the blood?'said Fleete.

We put him to bed at last, just as the dawn wasbreaking, and Strickland invited me to have anotherwhisky and soda. While we were drinking he talkedof the trouble in the temple, and admitted that it baffledhim completely. Strickland hates being mystified bynatives, because his business in life is to overmatch themwith their own weapons. He has not yet succeeded m

doing this, but in fifteen or twenty years he will havemade some small progress.

'They should have mauled us/ he said, * instead ofmewing at us. I wonder what they meant. I don'tlike it one little bit.'

I said that the Managing Committee of the templewould in all probability bring a criminal action againstus for insulting their religion. There was a section ofthe Indian Penal Code which exactly met Fleete's offence.Strickland said he only hoped and prayed that they woulddo this. Before I left I looked into Fleete's room, andsaw him lying on his right side, scratching his left breast.Then I went to bed cold, depressed, and unhappy, atseven o'clock in the morning.

At one o'clock I rode over to Strickland's house toinquire after Fleete's head. I imagined that it wouldbe a sore one. Fleete was breakfasting and seemed un-well. His temper was gone, for he was abusing the cookfor not supplying him with an underdone chop. A manwho can eat raw meat after a wet night is a curiosity. Itold Fleete this and he laughed.

'You breed queer mosquitoes in these parts,' he said.* I've been bitten to pieces, but only in one place.'

'Let's have a look at the bite,' said Strickland. 'Itmay have gone down since this morning.'

While the chops were being cooked, Fleete openedhis shirt and showed us, just over his left breast, a mark,the perfect double of the black rosettes—the five or sixirregular blotches arranged in a circle—on a leopard's hide.Strickland looked and said, 'It was only pink this morn-ing. It's grown black now.'

Fleete ran to a glass.

' By Jove!' he said,' this is nasty. What is it?'

We could not answer. Here the chops came in, all

red and juicy, and Fleete bolted three in a most offensivemanner. He ate on his right grinders only, and threwhis head over his right shoulder as he snapped the meat.When he had finished, it struck him that he had beenbehaving strangely, for he said apologetically, 'I don'tthink I ever felt so hungry in my hfe. I've bolted likean ostrich.'

After breakfast Strickland said to me, 'Don't go.Stay here, and stay for the night.'

Seeing that my house was not three miles from Strick-land's, this request was absurd. But Strickland insisted,and was going to say something when Fleete interruptedby declaring in a shamefaced way that he felt hungryagain. Strickland sent a man to my house to fetch overmy bedding and a horse, and we three went down toStrickland's stables to pass the hours until it was timeto go out for a ride. The man w^ho has a weakness forhorses never wearies of inspecting them; and when twomen are killing time in this way they gather knowledgeand lies the one from the other.

There were five horses in the stables, and I shall neverforget the scene as we tried to look them over. Theyseemed to have gone mad. They reared and screamedand nearly tore up their pickets; they sweated andshivered and lathered and were distraught with fear.Strickland's horses used to know him as well as his dogs;which made the matter more curious. We left the stablefor fear of the brutes throwing themselves in their panic.Then Strickland turned back and called m.e. The horseswere still frightened, but they let us 'gentle' and makemuch of them, and put their heads in our bosoms.

'They aren't afraid of its,' said Strickland. 'D'youknow, I'd give three months' pay if Outrage here couldtalk.'

But Outrage was dumb, and could only cuddle up tohis master and blow out his nostrils, as is the custom ofhorses when they wish to explain things but can't. Fleetecame up when we were in the stalls, and as soon as thehorses saw him, their fright broke out afresh. It wasall that we could do to escape from the place imkicked.Strickland said, 'They don't seem to love you, Fleete.'

'Nonsense,' said Fleete; 'my mare will follow melike a dog.' He went to her; she was in a loose-box;but as he shpped the bars she plunged, knocked himdown, and broke away into the garden. I laughed, butStrickland was not amused. He took his moustache inboth fists and pulled at it till it nearly came out. Fleete, instead of going off to chase his property, yawned, saying that he felt sleepy. He went to the house to he down, which was a foolish way of spending New Year's Day.

Strickland sat with me in the stables and asked if I had noticed anything peculiar in Fleete's manner. I said that he ate his food like a beast; but that this might have been the result of living alone in the hills out of the reach of society as refined and elevating as ours for instance. Strickland was not amused. I do not think that he listened to me, for his next sentence referred to the mark on Fleete's breast, and I said that it might have been caused by blister-flies, or that it was possibly a birth-mark newly born and now visible for the first time. We both agreed that it was unpleasant to look at, and Strickland found occasion to say that I was a fool.

'I can't tell you what I tliink now,' said he, 'because you would call me a madman; but you must stay with me for the next few days, if you can. I want you to watch Fleete, but don't tell me what you think till I have made up my mind.'

'But I am dining out to-night,' I said.

So am I,' said vStrickland, 'and so is Fleete. At least if he doesn't change his mind/

We walked about the garden smoking, but saying nothing—because we were friends, and talking spoils good tobacco—till our pipes were out. Then we went to wake up Fleete. He was wide awake and fidgeting about his room.

'I say, I want some more chops,' he said. 'Can I get them?"

We laughed and said, 'Go and change. The ponies will be round in a minute.'

'All right,' said Fleete. 'I'll go when I get the chops—underdone ones, mind.'

He seemed to be quite in earnest. It was four o'clock, and we had had breakfast at one; still, for a long time, he demanded thos» underdone chops. Then he changed into riding clothes and went out into the verandah. His pony—the mare had not been caught—would not let him come near. All three horses were unmanageable—^mad w^ith fear—and finally Fleete said that he would stay at home and get something to eat. Strickland and I rode out wondering. As we passed the temple of Hanuman, the Silver Man came out and mewed at us.

'He is not one of the regular priests of the temple/said Strickland. 'I think I should pecuKarly like to lay my hands on him.'

There was no spring in our gallop on the racecourse that evening. The horses were stale, and moved as though they had been ridden out.

'The fright after breakfast has been too much for them,' said Strickland.

That was the only remark he made through the re-mainder of the ride. Once or twice I think he swore to himself; but that did not count.

We came back in the dark at seven o'clock, and saw that there were no Kghts in the bungalow. 'Careless ruffians my servants are!' said Strickland.

My horse reared at something on the carriage drive, and Fieete stood up under its nose.

'What are you doing, grovelling about the garden?'said Strickland.

But both horses bolted and nearly threw us. We dismounted by the stables and returned to Fieete, who was on his hands and knees under the orange-bushes.

'What the devil's wrong with you?' said Strickland.

'Nothing, nothing in the world,' said Fieete, speaking very quickly and thickly. 'I've been gardening—botan-ising you know. The smell of the earth is delightful. I think I'm going for a walk—a long walk—ail night.'

Then I saw that there was something excessively out of order somewhere, and I said to Strickland, ' I am not dining out.'

'Bless you!' said Strickland. 'Here, Fieete, get up. You'll catch fever there. Come in to dinner and let'shave the lamps lit. We '11 all dine at home.'

Fieete stood up unwillingly, and said, 'No lamps—nolamps. It's much nicer here. Let's dine outside andhave some more chops—lots of 'em and underdone—bloody ones with gristle.'

Now a December evening in Northern India is bit-terly cold, and Fleete's suggestion was that of a maniac.

'Come in,' said Strickland sternly. 'Come in atonce.'

Fieete came, and when the lamps were brought, wesaw that he was literally plastered with dirt from headto foot. He must have been rolling in the garden. Heshrank from the Kght and went to his room. His eyeswere horrible to look at. There was a green light behind

them, not in them, if you understand, and the man'slower Kp hung down.

Strickland said, 'There is going to be trouble—bigtrouble—to-night. Don't you change your riding-things.'

We waited and waited for Fleete's reappearance, andordered dinner in the meantime. We could hear himmoving about his own room, but there was no Hght there.Presently from the room came the long-drawn howl of awolf.

People write and talk lightly of blood running coldand hair standing up and things of that kind. Bothsensations are too horrible to be trifled with. My heartstopped as though a knife had been driven through it,and Strickland turned as white as the tablecloth.

The howl was repeated, and was answered by anotherhowl far across the fields.

That set the gilded roof on the horror. Stricklanddashed into Fleete's room. I followed, and we sawFleete getting out of the window. He made beast-noises\n the back of his throat. He could not answer us whenvN^e shouted at him. He spat.

I don't quite remember what followed, but I thinkthat Strickland must have stunned him with the longboot-jack or else I should never have been able to sit onhis chest. Fleete could not speak, he could only snarl,and his snarls were those of a wolf, not of a man. Thehuman spirit must have been giving way all day andhave died out \vith the twihght. We were dealing witha beast that had once been Fleete.

The affair was beyond any human and rational ex-perience. I tried to say 'Hydrophobia,' but the wordwouldn't come, because I knew that I was lying.

We bound this beast with leather thongs of the punkah-rope, and tied its thumbs and big toes together, and

gagged it with a shoe-horn, which makes a very efficientgag if you know how to arrange it. Then we carried itinto the dining-room, and sent a man to Dumoise, thedoctor, telling him to come over at once. After we haddespatched the messenger and were drawing breath,Strickland said, 'It's no good. This isn't any doctor'swork.' I, also, knew that he spoke the truth.

The beast's head was free, and it threw it about fromside to side. Any one entering the room would have be-lieved that we were curing a woli's pelt. That was themost loathsome accessory of all.

Strickland sat with his chin in the heel of his fest,watching the beast as it wriggled on the groimd, but say-ing nothing. The shirt had been torn open in the scuffleand showed the black rosette mark on the left breast. Itstood out like a blister.

In the silence of the watchmg we heard somethingwithout mewing like a she-otter. We both rose to ourfeet, and, I answer for myself, not Strickland, felt sick-actually and physically sick. We told each other, as didthe men in Pinafore, that it was the cat.

Dumoise arrived, and I never saw a Httle man sounprofessionaUy shocked. He said that it was a heart-rending case of hydrophobia, and that nothing couldbe done. At least any paihative measures would onlyprolong the agony. The beast was foaming at themouth. Fleete, as we told

Dumoise, had been bitten by dogs once or twice. Any man who keeps half a dozen terriers must expect a nip now and again. Du-moise could offer no help. He could only certify that Fleete was dying of hydrophobia. The beast was then how^ling, for it had managed to spit out the shoe-horn. Dumoise said that he would be ready to certify to the cause of death, and that the end was certain. He was

a good little man, and he offered to remain with us; but Strickland refused the kindness. He did not wish to poison Dumoise's New Year. He would only ask him not to give the real cause of Fleete's death to the public.

So Dumoise left, deeply agitated; and as soon as the noise of the cart-wheels had died away, Strickland told me, in a whisper, his suspicions. They were so wildly improbable that he dared not say them out aloud; and I, who entertained all Strickland's beliefs, was so ashamed of owning to them that I pretended to disbelieve.

^Even if the Silver Man had bewitched Fleete for polluting the image of Hanuman, the punishment could not have fallen so quickly.'

As I was whispering this the cry outside the house rose again, and the beast fell into a fresh paroxysm of struggling till we were afraid that the thongs that held it would give way.

'Watch!' said Strickland. 'If this happens six times I shall take the law into my own hands. I order you to help me.'

He went into his room and came out in a few minutes with the barrels of an old shot-gun, a piece of fishing-line, some thick cord, and his heavy wooden bedstead. I reported that the convulsions had followed the cry by two seconds in each case, and the beast seemed percepti-bly weaker.

Strickland muttered, 'But he can't take away the life! He can't take away the Hfe!'

I said, though I knew that I was arguing against my-self, 'It may be a cat. It must be a cat. If the Silver Man is responsible, why does he dare to come here?'

Strickland arranged the wood on the hearth, put the gun-barrels into the glow of the fire, spread the twine on

the table and broke a walking stick in two. There was one yard of fishing line, gut, lapped with wire, such as is used for mahseer-^ishing, and he tied the two ends together in a loop.

Then he said, 'How can we catch him? He must be taken alive and unhurt.'

I said that we must trust in Providence, and go out softly with polo-sticks into the shrubbery at the front of the house. The man or animal that made the cry was evidently moving round the house as regularly as a night-v/atchman. We could wait in the bushes till he came by and knock him over.

Strickland accepted this suggestion, and we sUpped out from a bath-room window into the front veranda and then across the carriage drive into the bushes.

In the moorJight we could see the leper coming round the corner of the house. He was perfectly naked, and from time to time he mewed and stopped to dance with his shadow. It was an unattractive sight, and thinking of poor Fleete, brought to such degradation by so foul a creature, I put av/ay all my doubts and resolved to help Strickland from the heated gun-barrels to the loop of twine—from the loins to the head and back again—with all tortures that might be needful.

The leper halted in the front porch for a moment and we jumped out on him with tlie sticks. He was wonder-fully strong, and we were afraid that he might escape or be fatally injured before we caught him. We had an idea tliat lepers were frail creatures, but this proved to be incorrect. Strickland knocked his legs from under him and I put my foot on his neck. He mewed hideously, and even through my riding-boots I could feel that his flesh was not the flesh of a clean man.

He struck at us with his hand and feet-stumps. We looped the lash of a dog-whip round him, under the arm-pits, and dragged him backwards into the hall and so into the dining-room where the beast lay. There we tied him with trunk-straps. He made no attempt to escape, but mewed.

When we confronted him with the beast the scene was beyond description. The beast doubled backwards into a bow as though he had been poisoned with styrch-nine, and moaned in the most pitiable fashion. Several other things happened also, but they cannot be put down here.

'I think I was right,' said Strickland. 'Now we will ask him to cure this case.'

But the leper only mewed. Strickland wrapped a towel round his hand and took the gun-barrels out of the fire. I put the half of the broken walking stick through the loop of fishing-line and buckled the leper comfortably to Strickland's bedstead. I understood then how men and women and little children can endure to see a witch burnt alive; for the beast was moaning on the floor, and though the Silver Man had no face, you could see horrible feelings passing through the slab that took its place, exactly as waves of heat play across red-hot iron—gun-barrels for instance.

Strickland shaded his eyes with his hands for a mo-ment and we got to work. This part is not to be printed.

The dawn was beginning to break when the leper spoke. His mewings had not been satisfactory up to that point. The beast had fainted from exhaustion and the house was very still. We unstrapped the leper and told him to take away the evil spirit. He crawled to the beast and laid his hand upon the left breast. That was all. Then he fell face down and whined, drawing in his breath as he did so.

We watched the face of the beast, and saw the soul of Fleete coming back into the eyes. Then a sweat broke out on the forehead and the eyes—they were human eyes—closed. We waited for an hour but Fleete still slept. We carried him to his room and bade the leper go, giving him the bedstead, and the sheet on the bedstead to cover his nakedness, the gloves and the towels with which we had touched him, and the whip that had been hooked round his body. He put the sheet about him and went out into the early morning without speaking or mewing.

Strickland wiped his face and sat down. A night-gong, far away in the city, made seven o'clock.

'Exactly four-and-twenty hours!' said Strickland. 'And I've done enough to ensure my dismissal from the service, besides permanent quarters in a lunatic asyliun. Do you beheve that we are awake?'

The red-hot gun-barrel had fallen on the floor and was singeing the carpet The smell was entirely real.

That morning at eleven we two together went to wake up Fleete. We looked and saw that the black leopard-rosette on his chest had disappeared. He was very drowsy and tired, but as soon as he saw us, he said,' Oh! Confound you fellows. Jlappy New Year to you. Never mix your liquors. I'm nearly dead.'

'Thanks for your kindness, but you're over time,' said Strickland. 'To-day is the morning of the second. You've slept the clock round with a vengeance.'

The door opened, and little Dumoise put his head in. He had come on foot, and fancied that we were laying out Fleete.

' IVe brought a nurse/ said Dumoise. ' I suppose that she can come in for . . . what is necessary.'

*By all means,' said Fleete cheerily, sitting up in bed.^Bring on your nurses.'

Dumoise was dumb. Strickland led him out andexplained that there must have been a mistake in thediagnosis. Dumoise remained dumb and left the househastily. He considered that his professional reputationhad been injured, and was inclined to make a personalmatter of the recovery. Strickland went out too. Whenhe came back, he said that he had been to call on theTemple of Hanimian to offer redress for the pollution ofthe god, and had been solemnly assured that no whiteman had ever touched the idol and that he was an incar-nation of all the virtues labouring under a delusion.'What do you think?' said Strickland.

I said,'" There are more things . . ."'

But Strickland hates that quotation. He says that Ihave worn it threadbare.

One other curious thing happened which frightenedme as much as anything in all the night's work. WhenFleete was dressed he came into the dining-room andsniffed. He had a quaint trick of moving his nose whenhe sniffed. 'Horrid doggy smell, here,' said he. 'Youshould really keep those terriers of yours in better order.Try sulphur, Strick.'

But Strickland did not answer. He caught hold ofthe back of a chair, and, without warning, went into anamazing fit of hysterics. It is terrible to see a strongman overtaken \with hysteria. Then it struck me thatwe had fought for Fleete's soul with the Silver Man inthat room, and had disgraced ourselves as Englishmenfor ever, and I laughed and gasped and gurgled just asshamefully as Strickland, while Fleete thought that we

had both gone mad. We never told him what we haddone.

Some years later, when Strickland had married andwas a church-going member of society for his wife's sake,we reviev/ed the incident dispassionately, and Stricklandsuggested that I should put it before the pubHc.

I cannot myself see that this step is likely to clearup the mystery; because, in the first place, no one willbelieve a rather unpleasant story, and, in the second, itis well known to every right-minded man that the godsof the heathen are stone and brass, and any attempt todeal with them otherwise is justly condemned.

The doors were wide, the stoiy saith,Out of the night came the patient wraith,He might not speak, and he could not stirA hair of the Baron's minniver—Speechless and strengthless, a shadow thin,He roved the castle to seek his kin.And oh, 'twas a piteous thing to seeThe dumb ghost follow his enemy!

TJie Baron.

Imeay achieved the impossible. Without warning, fov.no conceivable motive, in his youth, at the threshold ofhis career he chose to disappear from the world—whichis to say, the Httle Indian station where he lived.

Upon a day he was aUve, well, happy, and in greatevidence among the bilHard-tables at his Club. Upona morning, he was not, and no manner of search couldmake sure where he might be. He had stepped out ofhis place; he had not appeared at his office at the propertime, and his dogcart was not upon the public roads.For these reasons, and because he was hampering, in amicroscopical degree, the administration of the IndianEmpire, that Empire paused for one microscopical mo-ment to make inquiry into the fate of Imray. Pondswere dragged, wells were plumbed, telegrams were de-spatched down the Hues of railways and to the nearestseaport town—twelve hundred miles away; but Imraywas not at the end of the drag-ropes nor the telegraphwires. He was gone, and his place knew him no more.

311

Then the work of the great Indian Empire swept for-ward, because it could not be delayed, and Imray frombeing a man became a mystery—such a thing as men talkover at their tables in the Club for a month, and thenforget utterly. His guns, horses, and carts were sold tothe highest bidder. His superior officer wrote an alto-gether absurd letter to his mother, saying that Imrayhad imaccountably disappeared, and his bungalow stoodempty.

After three or four months of the scorching hotweather had gone by, my friend Strickland, of the Police,saw fit to rent the bungalow from the native landlord.This was before he was engaged to Miss Youghal—anaffair which has been described in another place—andwhile he was pursuing his investigations into native life.His own life was sufficiently peculiar, and men com-plained of his manners and customs. There was alwaysfood in his house, but there were no regular times formeals. He ate, standing up and walking about, whateverhe might find at the sideboard, and this is not good forhuman beings. His domestic equipment was limited tosix rifles, three shot-guns, five saddles, and a collectionof stifi'-jointed mahseer-rods, bigger and stronger than thelargest salmon-rods. These occupied one-half of hisbungalow, and the other half was given up to Stricklandand his dog Tietjens—an enormous Rampur slut whodevoured daily the rations of two men. She spoke toStrickland in a language of her own; and whenever, walk-ing abroad, she saw things calculated to destroy thepeace of Her Majesty the Queen-Empress, she returnedto her master and laid information. Strickland wouldtake steps at once, and the end of his labours was troubleand fine and imprisonment for other people. The nativesbeh'eved that Tietjens was a familiar spirit, and treated

her with the great reverence that is born of hate andfear. One room in the bungalow was set apart for heropecial use. She owned a bedstead, a blanket, and adrinking-trough, and if any one came into Strickland'sroom at night her custom was to knock down the invaderand give tongue till some one came with a light. Strick-land owed his life to her, when he was on the Frontier,in search of a local murderer, who came in the gray dawnto send Strickland much farther than the AndamanIslands. Tietjens caught the man as he was crawlinginto Strickland's tent with a dagger between his teeth;and after his record of iniquity was established in theeyes of the law he was hanged. From that date Tietjenswore a collar of rough silver, and employed a monogramon her night-blanket; and the blanket was of doublewoven Kashmir cloth, for she was a delicate dog.

Under no circumstances would she be separated fromStrickland; and once, when he was ill with fever, madegreat trouble for the doctors, because she did not knowhow to help her master and would not allow anothercreature to attempt aid. Macarnaght, of the IndianMedical Service, beat her over her head ^vith a gun-buttbefore she could understand that she must give room forthose who could give quinine.

A short time after Strickland had taken Imray'sbungalow, my business took me through that Station,and naturally, the Club quarters being full, I quarteredmyself upon Strickland. It was a desirable bungalow,eight-roomed and hea\dly thatched against any chanceof leakage from rain. Under the pitch of the roof ran aceiling-cloth which looked just as neat as a white-washedceiling. The landlord had repainted it when Stricklandtook the bungalow. Unless you knew how Indian bunga-lows were built you would never have suspected that

above the cloth lay the dark three-cornered cavern of theroof, where the beams and the underside of the thatchharboured all manner of rats, bats, ants, and foul things.Tietjens met me in the verandah with a bay like theboom of the bell of St. Paul's, putting her paws on myshoulder to show she was glad to see me. Stricklandhad contrived to claw together a sort of meal which hecalled lunch, and immediately after it was finished wentout about his business. I was left alone with Tie tj ensand my own affairs. The heat of the summer had brokenup and turned to the warm damp of the rains. Therewas no motion in the heated air, but the rain fell likeramrods on the earth, and flung up a blue mist when itsplashed back. The bamboos, and the custard-apples,the poinsettias, and the mango-trees in the garden stoodstill while the warm water lashed through them, and thefrogs began to sing among the aloe hedges. A littlebefore the Hght failed, and when the rain was at its worst, I sat in the back verandah and heard the water roar from the eaves, and scratched myself because I was covered with the thing called prickly-heat. Tietjens came out with me and put her head in my lap and was very sor-rowful; so I gave her biscuits when tea was ready, and I took tea in the back verandah on account of the little coolness found there. The rooms of the house were dark behind me. I could smell Strickland's saddlery and the oil on his guns, and I had no desire to sit among these things. My own servant came to me in the twihght, the muslin of his clothes clinging tightly to his drenched body, and told me that a gentleman had called and wished to see some one. Very much against my will, but only because of the darkness of the rooms, I went into the naked drawing-room, telling my man to bring the lights. There might or might not have been a caller waiting—it

seemed to me that I saw a figure by one of the windows—but when the lights came there was nothing save the spikes of the rain without, and the smell of the drinking earth in my nostrils. I exj.'^lained to my servant that he was no wiser than he ought to be, and went back to the verandah to talk to Tietjens. She had gone out into the wet, and I could hardly coax her back to me; even with biscuits with sugar tops. Strickland came home, dripping wet, just before dinner, and the first thing he said was.

*Has any one called?'

I explained, with apologies, that my servant had summoned me into the drawing-room on a false alarm; or that some loafer had tried to call on Strickland, and thinking better of it had fled after giving his name. Strickland ordered dinner, without comment, and since it was a real dinner with a white tablecloth attached, we sat down.

At nine o'clock Strickland wanted to go to bed, and I was tired too. Tietjens, who had been lying under-neath the table, rose up, and swung into the least exposed verandah as soon as her master moved to his own room, which was next to the stately chamber set apart for Tietjens. If a mere wife had wished to sleep out of doors in that pelting rain it would not have mattered; but Tietjens was a dog, and therefore the better animal. I looked at Strickland, expecting to see him flay her with a whip. He smiled queerly, as a man would smile after telling some unpleasant domestic tragedy. 'She has done this ever since I moved in here,' said he. 'Let her
go.'

The dog was Strickland's dog, so I said nothing, but I felt all that Strickland felt in being thus made Hght of. Tietjens encamped outside my bedroom window, and storm after storm came up, thundered on the thatch,

and died away. The lightning spattered the sky as a thrown egg spatters a barn-door, but the Hght was pale blue, not yellow; and, looking through my spHt bamboo blinds, I could see the great dog standing, not sleeping, in the verandah, the hackles aHft on her back and her feet anchored as tensely as the drawn wire-rope of a suspension bridge. In the very short pauses of the thunder I tried to sleep, but it seemed that some one wanted me very urgently. He, whoever he was, was trying to call me by name, but his voice was no more than a husky whisper. The thunder ceased, and Tiet-jens went into the garden and howled at the low moon. Somebody tried to open my door, walked about and about through the house and stood breathing heavily in the verandahs, and just when I was falling asleep I fancied that I heard a wild hammering and clamour-ing above my head or on the door.

I ran into Strickland's room and asked him whether he was ill, and had been calling for me. He was lying on his bed half dressed, a pipe in his mouth. 'I thought you'd come,' he said. 'Have I been walking round the house recently?'

I explained that he had been tramping in the dining-room and the smoking-room and two or three other places, and he laughed and told me to go back to bed. I went back to bed and slept till the morning, but through all my mixed dreams I was sure I was doing some one an injustice in not attending to his wants. What those wants were I could not tell; but a fluttering, whispering, bolt-fumbling, lurking, loitering Someone was reproach-ing me for my slackness, and, half awake, I heard the howling of Tietjens in the garden and the threshing of the rain.

I lived in that house lor iwo days. Strickland went

to his office daily, leaving me alone for eight or ten hours with Tietjens for my only companion. As long as the full light lasted I was comfortable, and so was Tietjens; but in the twilight she and I moved into the back verandah and cuddled each other for company. We were alone in the house, but none the less it was much too fully occupied by a tenant with whom I did not wish to inter-fere. I never saw him, but I could see the curtains between the rooms quivering where he had just passed through; I could hear the chairs creaking as the bamboos sprung under a weight that had just quitted them; and I could feel when I went to get a book from the dining-room that somebody was waiting in the shadows of the front verandah till I should have gone away. Tietjens made the twilight more interesting by glaring into the darkened rooms with every hair erect, and following the motions of something that I could not see. She never entered the rooms, but her eyes moved interestedly, that was quite sufficient. Only when my servant came to trim the lamps and make all Hght and habitable she would come in with me and spend her time sitting on her haunches, v/atching an invisible extra man as he moved about behind my shoulder. Dogs are cheerful compan-ions.

I explained to Strickland, gently as might be, that I would go over to the Club and find for myself quarters there. I admired his hospitahty, was pleased with his guns and rods, but I did not much care for his house and its atmosphere. He heard me out to the end, and then smiled very wearily, but without contempt, for he is a man who understands things. 'Stay on,' he said, 'and see what this thing means. All you have talked about I have known since I took the bungalow. Stay on and wait. Tietjens has left me. Are you going too?'

I had seen him through one little affair, connected with a heathen idol, that had brought me to the doors of a lunatic asylum, and I had no desire to help him through further experiences. He was a man to whom unpleasantnesses arrived as do dinners to ordinary people.

Therefore I explained more clearly than ever that T liked him immensely, and would be happy to see him in the daytime; but that I did not care to sleep under his roof. This was after dinner, when Tietjens had gone outto lie in the verandah.

' Ton my soul, I don't wonder,' said Strickland, with his eyes on the ceiling-cloth. 'Look at that!'

The tails of two brown snakes were hanging between the cloth and the cornice of the wall. They threw long shadows in the lampHght.

'If you are afraid of snakes of course ' said Strick-land.

I hate and fear snakes, because if you look into the eyes of any snake you \\all see that it knows all and more of the mystery of man's fall, and that it feels all the contempt that the Devil felt when Adam was evicted from Eden. Besides which its bite is generally fatal, and it twists up trouser legs.

'You ought to get your thatch overhauled,' I said. 'Give me a mahseer-rod, and we'll poke 'em down.'

'They'll hide among the roof-beams,' said Strickland. 'I can't stand snakes overhead. I'm going up into theroof. If I shake 'em down, stand by with a cleaning-rod and break their backs.'

I was not anxious to assist Strickland in his work, but I took the cleaning-rod and waited in the dining-room, while Strickland brought a gardener's ladder from the verandah, and set it against the side of the room.

The snake-tails drew themselves up and disappeared. We could hear the dry rushing scuttle of long bodies running over the baggy ceiling-cloth. Strickland took a lamp with him, while I tried to make clear to him the danger of hunting roof-snakes between a ceiling-cloth and a thatch, apart from the deterioration of property caused by ripping out ceiling-cloths.

* Nonsense!' said Strickland. * They're sure to hide near the walls by the cloth. The bricks are too cold for'em, and the heat of the room is just what they Hke.'He put his hand to the corner of the stuff and ripped it from the cornice. It gave with a great sound of tearing, and Strickland put his head through the opening into the dark of the angle of the roof-beams. I set my teeth and lifted the rod, for I had not the least knowledge of what might descend.

*H'm!' said Strickland, and his voice rolled and rvmibled in the roof. 'There's room for another set of rooms up here, and, by Jove, some one is occupying 'em!'

* Snakes?' I said from below.

'No. It's a buffalo. Hand me up the two last joints of a mahseer-rod, and I'll prod it. It's lying on the main roof-beam.'

I handed up the rod.

*What a nest for owls and serpents! No wonder the snakes live here,' said Strickland, chmbing farther into the roof. I could see his elbow thrusting with the rod. Xome out of that, whoever you are! Heads below there! It's falling.'

I saw the ceiling-cloth nearly in the centre of the room bag with a shape that was pressing it downwards and downwards towards the lighted lamp on the table. I snatched the lamp out of danger and stood back. Then the cloth ripped out from the walls, tore, split, swayed,

and shot down upon the table something that I dared not look at, till Strickland had sHd down the ladder and was standing by my side.

He did not say much, being a man of few words; but he picked up the loose end of the tablecloth and threw it over the remnants on the table.

'It strikes me,' said he, putting down the lamp, 'our friend Imray has come back. Oh! you would, would you?'

There was a movement under the cloth, and a little snake wriggled out, to be back-broken by the butt of the mahseer-rod. I was sufficiently sick to make no remarks worth recording.

Strickland meditated, and helped himseK to drinks. The arrangement under the cloth made no more signs of Hfe.

*Is it Imray?' I said.

Strickland turned back the cloth for a moment, and looked.

'It is Imray,' he said; 'and his throat is cut from ear to ear.'

Then we spoke, both together and to ourselves: 'That's why he whispered about the house.'

Tietjens, in the garden, began to bay furiously. A little later her great nose heaved open the dining-room door.

She sniffed and was still. The tattered ceiling-cloth hung down almost to the level of the table, and there was hardly room to move away from the discovery.

Tietjens came in and sat down; her teeth bared under her lip and her forepaws planted. She looked at Strick-land.

'It's a bad business, old lady,' said he. 'Men don't climb up into the roofs of their bungalows to die, and

they don't fasten up the ceiling cloth behind 'em. Let's think it out.'

* Let's think it out somewhere else,' I said.

'Excellent idea! Turn the lamps out. We'll get into my room.'

I did not turn the lamps out. I went into Strickland's room first, and allowed him to make the darkness. Then he followed me, and we lit tobacco and thought. Strickland thought. I smoked furiously, because I was afraid.

'Imray is back,' said Strickland. 'The question is—who killed Imray? Don't talk, I've a notion of my own. When I took this bungalow I took over most of Imray's servants. Imray was guileless and inoffensive, wasn't he?'

I agreed; though the heap under the cloth had looked neither one thing nor the other.

'If I call in all the servants they will stand fast in a crowd and He like Aryans. What do you suggest?'

'Call 'em in one by one,' I said.

'They'll run away and give the news to all their fellows,' said Strickland. 'We must segregate 'em. Do you suppose your servant knows anything about it?'

'He may, for aught I know; but I don't think it's Hkely. He has only been here two or three days,' I answered. 'What's your notion?'

'I can't quite tell. How the dickens did the man get the wrong side of the ceiling-cloth?'

There was a heavy coughing outside Strickland's bedroom door. This showed that Bahadur Khan, his body-servant, had waked from sleep and wished to put Strickland to bed.

'Come in,' said Strickland. 'It's a very warm night, isn't it?'

Bahadur Khan, a great, green-turbaned, six-foot

Mahomedan, said that it was a very warm night; but that there was more rain pending, which, by his Honour's favour, would bring reHef to the country.

'It will be so, if God pleases,' said Strickland, tugging off his boots. 'It is in my mind, Bahadur Khan, that I have worked thee remorselessly for many days—ever since that tune when thou first earnest into my service. What time was that?'

'Has the Heaven-born forgotten? It was when Imray Sahib went secretly to Europe without warning given; and I—even I—came into the honoured service of the protector of the poor.'

'And Imray Sahib went to Europe?'

'It is so said among those who were his servants.'

'And thou wilt take service with him when he re-turns? '

'Assuredly, Sahib. He was a good master, and cherished his dependants.'

'That is true. I am very tired, but I go buck-shooting to-morrow. Give me the httle sharp rifle that I use for black-buck; it is in the case yonder.'

The man stooped over the case; handed barrels, stock, and fore-end to Strickland, who fitted all together, yawn-ing dolefully. Then he reached down to the gun-case, took a sohd-drawn cartridge, and sKpped it into the breech of the '360 Express.

'And Imray Sahib has gone to Europe secretly! That is very strange, Bahadur Khan, is it not?'

'What do I know of the ways of the white man, Heaven-born?'

'Very Httle, truly. But thou shalt know more anon. It has reached me that Imray Sahib has returned from his so long journeyings, and that even now he Hes in the next room, waiting his servant.'

^Sahib!'

The lamplight slid along the barrels of the rifle as they levelled themselves at Bahadur Elhan's broad breast.

*Go and look!' said Strickland. 'Take a lamp. Thy master is tired, and he waits thee. Go!'

The man picked up a lamp, and went into the dining-room, Strickland following, and almost pushing him with the muzzle of the rifle. He looked for a moment at the black depths behind the ceiling-cloth; at the writhing snake under foot; and last, a gray glaze settling on hisface, at the thing under the tablecloth.

'Hast thou seen?' said Strickland after a pause.

'I have seen. I am clay in the white man's hands.What does the Presence do?'

'Hang thee within the month. What else?'

*For killing him? Nay, Sahib, consider. Walkingamong us, his servants, he cast his eyes upon my child,who was four years old. Him he bewitched, and in tendays he died of the fever—my child!'

'What said Imray Sahib?'

'He said he was a handsome child, and patted him onthe head; wherefore my child died. Wherefore I killedImray Sahib in the twihght, when he had come back fromoffice, and was sleeping. Wherefore I dragged him upinto the roof-beams and made all fast behind him. TheHeaven-born knows all things. I am the servant of theHeaven-born.'

Strickland looked at me above the rifle, and said, inthe vernacular, 'Thou art witness to this saying? Hehas killed.'

Bahadur ELhan stood ashen gray in the light of theone lamp. The need for justification came upon him veryswiftly. 'I am trapped,' he said, 'but the offence wasthat man's. He cast an evil eye upon my child, and I

killed and hid him. Only such as are served by devils,'he glared at Tietjens, couched stolidly before him, ^onlysuch could know what I did.'

*It was clever. But thou shouldst have lashed himto the beam with a rope. Now, thou thyself wilt hangby a rope. Orderly!'

A drowsy poHceman answered Strickland's call. Hewas followed by another, and Tietjens sat wondrous still.

'Take him to the poHce-station,' said Strickland.'There is a case toward.'

'Do I hang, then?' said Bahadur Khan, making noattempt to escape, and keeping his eyes on the ground.

'If the sun shines or the water runs—yes!' saidStrickland.

Bahadur Khan stepped back one long pace, quivered,and stood still. The two policemen waited furtherorders.

' Go!' said Strickland.

'Nay; but I go very swiftly,' said Bahadur Khan.'Look! I am even now a dead man.'

He Hfted his foot, and to the Httle toe there clung thehead of the half-ldlled snake, firm fixed in the agony ofdeath.

'I come of land-holding stock,' said Bahadur Khan,rocking where he stood. 'It were a disgrace to me togo to the public scaffold: therefore I take this way. Beit remembered that the Sahib's shirts are correctly enu-merated, and that there is an extra piece of soap in hiswashbasin. My child was bewitched, and I slew thewizard. Why should you seek to slay me with the rope?My honour is saved, and—and—I die.'

At the end of an hour he died, as they die who arebitten by the Httle brown karait, and the poHcemen borehim and the thing under the tablecloth to their appointed

places. All were needed to make clear the disappear-ance of Imray.

'This/ said Strickland, very calmly, as he climbedinto bed, 'is called the nineteenth century. Did youhear what that man said?'

' I heard,' I answered. ' Imray made a mistake.'

'Simply and solely through not knowing the natureof the Oriental, and the coincidence of a little seasonalfever. Bahadur Khan had been with him for four years.'

I shuddered. My own servant had been with me forexactly that lengtli of time. AVhen I went over to myown room I found my man waiting, impassive as thecopper head on a penny, to pull off my boots.

'What has befallen Bahadur Khan?' said I.

'He was bitten by a snake and died. The rest theSahib knows,' was the answer.

'And how much of tliis matter hast thou known?'

'As much as might be gathered from One coming inin the twihght to seek satisfaction. Gently, Sahib. Letme pull off those boots.'

I had just settled to the sleep of exhaustion when Iheard Strickland shouting from his side of the house—

'Tietjens has come back to her place!'

And so she had. The great deerhound was couchedstatelily on her own bedstead on her own blanket, while,in the next room, the idle, empty, ceiling-cloth waggledas it trailed on the table.

NAMGAY DOOLA

There came to the beach a poor exile of Erin,
The dew on his wet robe hung heavy and chill;
Ere the steamer that brought him had passed out of hearin',
He was Alderman Mike inthrojuicin' a bill!

American Song,

Once upon a time there was a King who lived on theroad to Thibet, very many miles in the Himalayas. HisKingdom was eleven thousand feet above the sea andexactly four miles square; but most of the miles stoodon end owing to the nature of the country. His revenueswere rather less than four hundred pounds yearly, andthey were expended in the maintenance of one elephantand a standing army of five men. He was tributary tothe Indian Government, who allowed him certain sumsfor keeping a section of the Himalaya-Thibet road inrepair. He further increased his revenues by sellingtimber to the railway-companies; for he would cut thegreat deodar trees in his one forest, and they fell thunder-ing into the Sutlej river and were swept down to theplains three hundred miles away and became railway-ties.Now and again this King, whose name does not matter,would mount a ringstraked horse and ride scores of milesto Simla-town to confer with the Lieutenant-Governor onmatters of state, or to assure the Viceroy that his swordwas at the service of the Queen-Empress. Then theViceroy would cause a ruffle of drums to be sounded, andthe ringstraked horse and the cavalry of the State—twomen in tatters—and the herald who bore the silver stick

326

before the King would trot back to their own place, whichlay between the tail of a heaven-climbing glacier and adark birch-forest.

Now, from such a King, always remembering that hepossessed one veritable elephant, and could count hisdescent for twelve hundred years, I expected, when it wasmy fate to wander through his dominions, no more thanmere license to Uve.

The night had closed in rain, and rolling cloudsblotted out the Hghts of the villages in the valley. Fortymiles away, untouched by cloud or storm, the whiteshoulder of Donga Pa— the Mountain of the Council ofthe Gods—upheld the Evening Star. The monkeys sangsorrowfully to each other as they hunted for dry roostsin the fern-wreathed trees, and the last puff of the day-wind brought from the unseen villages the scent of dampwood-smoke, hot cakes, dripping undergrowth, and rot-ting pine-cones. That is the true smell of the Hima-layas, and if once it creeps into the blood of a man, thatman will at the last, forgetting all else, return to the hillsto die. The clouds closed and the smell went away, andthere remained nothing in all the world except chillingwhite mist and the boom of the Sutlej river racing throughthe valley below. A fat-tailed sheep, who did not wantto die, bleated piteously at my tent door. He wasscuffing with the Prime Minister and the Director-General of Public Education, and he was a royal gift tome and my camp servants. I expressed my thanks suit-ably, and asked if I might have audience of the King.The Prime Minister readjusted his turban, which hadfallen off in the struggle, and assured me that the Kingwould be very pleased to see me. Therefore I despatchedtwo bottles as a foretaste, and when the sheep had enteredupon another incarnation went to the King's Palace

through the wet. He had sent liis army to escort me,but the army stayed to talk with my cook. Soldiers arevery much aUke all the world over.

The Palace was a four-roomed and whitewashed mudand timber house, the finest in all the hills for a day'sjourney. The King was dressed in a purple velvet jacket,white muslin trousers, and a saffron-yellow turban ofprice. He gave me audience in a little carpeted roomopening off the palace courtyard which was occupied bythe Elephant of State. The great beast was sheeted andanchored from trunk to tail, and the curve of his backstood out grandly against the mist.

The Prime Minister and the Director-General of PubHcEducation were present to introduce me, but all thecourt had been dismissed, lest the two bottles aforesaidshould corrupt their morals. The King cast a wreath ofheavy-scented flowers round my neck as I bowed, andinquired how my honoured presence had the feUcity tobe. I said that through seeing his auspicious counte-nance the mists of the night had turned into sunshine,and that by reason of his beneficent sheep his gooddeeds would be remembered by the Gods. He said thatsince I had set my magnificent foot in his Kingdom thecrops would probably yield seventy per cent more thanthe average. I said that the fame of the King hadreached to the four corners of the earth, and that thenations gnashed their teeth when they heard daily of theglories of his realm and the wisdom of his moon-likePrime Minister and lotus-like Director-General of PublicEducation.

Then we sat down on clean white cushions, and I wasat the King's right hand. Three minutes later he wastelling me that the state of the maize crop was somethingdisgraceful, and that the railway-companies would not

pay him enough for his timber. The talk shifted to andfro with the bottles, and we discussed very many statelythings, and the King became confidential on the subjectof Government generally. Most of all he dwelt on theshortcomings of one of his subjects, who, from all I couldgather, had been paralyzing the executive,

*In the old days,' said the King, 'I could have orderedthe Elephant yonder to trample him to death. Now Imust e'en send him seventy miles across the hills to betried, and his keep would be upon the State. TheElephant eats everything.'

^What be the man's crimes. Rajah Sahib?' said I.

'Firstly, he is an outlander and no man of mine ownpeople. Secondly, since of my favour I gave him landupon his first coming, he refuses to pay revenue. Am Inot the lord of the earth, above and below, entitled byright and custom to one-eighth of the crop? Yet thisdevil, establishing himself, refuses to pay a single tax; andhe brings a poisonous spawn of babes.'

'Cast him into jail,' I said.

'Sahib,' the King answered, shifting a Httle on thecushions, 'once and only once in these forty years sick-ness came upon me so that I was not able to go abroad,in that hour I made a vow to my God that I would neveragain cut man or woman from the hght of the sun andthe air of God; for I perceived the nature of the punish-ment. How can I break my vow? Were it only thelopping of a hand or a foot I should not delay. But even that is impossible now that the English have rule. One or another of my people'—he looked obliquely at the Director-General of Public Education—'would at once write a letter to the Viceroy, and perhaps I should be deprived of my ruffle of drums.'

He unscrewed the mouthpiece of his silver water-pipe, fitted a plain amber mouthpiece, and passed his pipe to me. 'Not content with refusing revenue,' he continued, 'this outlander refuses also the begar^ (this was the corv^ee or forced labour on the roads) 'and stirs my people up to the like treason. Yet he is, when he wills, an expert log-snatcher. There is none better or bolder among my people to clear a block of the river when the logs stick fast.'

'But he worships strange Gods,' said the Prime Minis-ter deferentially.

'For that I have no concern,' said the King, who was as tolerant as Akbar in matters of belief. ' To each man his own God and the fire or Mother Earth for us all at last. It is the rebellion that offends me.'

'The King has an army,' I suggested. 'Has not the King burned the man's house and left him naked to the night dews?'

'Nay, a hut is a hut, and it holds the life of a man. But once, I sent my army against him when his excuses became wearisome: of their heads he brake three across the top \\ith a stick. The other two men ran away. Also the guns would not shoot.'

I had seen the equipment of the infantry. One-third of it was an old muzzle-loading fowling-piece, with a ragged rust-hole where the nipples should have been, one-third a wire-bound matchlock with a worm-eaten stock, and one-third a four-bore flint duck-gun without a flint.

'But it is to be remembered,' said the King, reaching out for the bottle, ' that he is a very expert log-snatcher and a man of a merry face. What shall I do to him, Sahib?'

This was interesting. The timid hill-folk would as soon have refused taxes to their king as revenues to their Gods.

'If it be the King's permission/ I said, 'I will not strike my tents till the third day and I will see this man. The mercy of the King is God-like, and rebellion is like unto the sin of witchcraft. Moreover, both the bottles and another be empty.'

* You have my leave to go,' said the King.

Next morning a crier went through the state pro-claiming that there was a log-jam on the river and that it behoved all loyal subjects to remove it. The people poured down from their villages to the moist warm valley of poppy-fields; and the King and I went with them. Hundreds of dressed deodar-logs had caught on a snag of rock, and the river was bringing down more logs every minute to complete the blockade. The water snarled and wrenched and worried at the timber, and the popu-lation of the state began prodding the nearest logs with a pole in the hope of starting a general movement. Then there went up a shout of 'Namgay Doola! Namgay Doola!' and a large red-haired villager hurried up, stripping off his clothes as he ran.

'That is he. That is the rebel,' said the King. 'Now will the dam be cleared.'

'But why has he red hair?' I asked, since red hair among hill-folks is as common as blue or green.

'He is an outlander,' said the King. 'Well done! Oh well done!'

Namgay Doola had scrambled out on the jam and was clawing out the butt of a log with a rude sort of boat-hook. It slid forward slowly as an alligator moves, three or four others followed it, and the green water spouted through the gaps they had made. Then the vil-lagers howled and shouted and scrambled across the logs, pulling and pushing the obstinate timber, and there red head of Namgay Doola was chief among them all.

The logs swayed and chafed and groaned as fresh coii-signments from upstream battered the now weakemngdam. All gave way at last in a smother of foam, racinglogs, bobbing black heads and confusion indescribable.The river tossed everything before it. I saw the redhead go down with the last remnants of the jam anddisappear between the great grinding tree-trunks. Itrose close to the bank and blowing like a grampus.Namgay Doola wrung the water out of his eyes andmade obeisance to the King. I had time to observehim closely. The virulent redness of his shock headand beard was most startling; and in the thicket ofhair wrinkled above high cheek bones shone two verymerry blue eyes. He was indeed an outlander, but yeta Thibetan in language, habit, and attire. He spoke theLepcha dialect with an indescribable softening of thegutturals. It was not so much a lisp as an accent.

^Whence comest thou?' I asked.

'From Thibet.' He pointed across the hills andgrinned. That grin went straight to my heart. Mechani-cally I held out my hand and Namgay Doola shook it.No pure Thibetan would have understood the meaningof the gesture. He went away to look for his clothes, andas he climbed back to his village, I heard a joyous yellthat seemed unaccountably familiar. It was the whoop-ing of Namgay Doola.

*You see now,' said the King, 'why I would not killhim. He is a bold man among my logs, but,' and heshook his head like a schoohnaster, ' I know that beforelong there will be complaints of him in the court. Letus return to the Palace and do justice.' It was thatKing's custom to judge his subjects every day betweeneleven and three o'clock. I saw him decide equitably inweighty matters of trespass, slander, and a little \^dfe-

Stealing. Then his brow clouded and he summonedme.

'Again it is Namgay Doola/ he said despairingly.'Not content with refusing revenue on his own part, hehas bound half his village by an oath to the like treason.Never before has such a thing befallen me! Nor are mytaxes heavy.'

A rabbit-faced villager, with a blush-rose stuck behindhis ear, advanced trembling. He had been in the con-spiracy, but had told everything and hoped for the King'sfavour.

'O King,' said I, 'if it be the King's will let thismatter stand over till the morning. Only the Gods can doright swiftly, and it may be that yonder villager has lied.'

'Nay, for I know the nature of Namgay Doola; butsince a guest asks let the matter remain. Wilt thouspeok harshly to this red-headed outlander? He maylisten to thee.'

I made an attempt that very evening, but for the lifeof me I could not keep my countenance. NamgayDoola grinned persuasively, and began to tell me about abig brown bear in a poppy-field by the river. Would Icare to shoot it? I spoke austerely on the sin of con-spiracy, and the certainty of punishment. NamgayDoola's face clouded for a moment. Shortly afterwardshe withdrew from my tent, and I heard him singing tohimself softly among the pines. The words were unin-telligible to me, but the tune, like his liquid insinuatingspeech, seemed the ghost of something strangely familiar.

' Dir han6 raard-i-yemen dirTo weeree ala gee.'

sang Namgay Doola again and again, and I racked mybrain for that lost tune. It was not till after dinner

that I discovered some one had cut a square foot ofvelvet from the centre of my best camera-cloth. Thismade me so angry that I wandered down the valley inthe hope of meeting the big brown bear. I could hearhim grunting Hke a discontented pig in the poppy-field,and I waited shoulder deep in the dew-dripping Indiancom to catch him after his meal. The moon was at fulland drew out the rich scent of the tasselled crop. Then Iheard the anguished bellow of a

Himalayan cow, one of the little black crummies no bigger than Newfoundland dogs. Two shadows that looked like a bear and her cub hurried past me. I was in act to fire when I saw that they had each a brilliant red head. The lesser animal was trailing some rope behind it that left a dark track on the path. They passed within six feet of me, and the shadow of the moonlight lay velvet-black on their faces. Velvet-black was exactly the word, for by all the powers of moonlight they were masked in the velvet of my camera-cloth! I marvelled and went to bed.

Next morning the Kingdom was in uproar. Namgay Doola, men said, had gone forth in the night and with a sharp knife had cut off the tail of a cow belonging to the rabbit-faced villager who had betrayed him. It was sacrilege unspeakable against the Holy Cow. The State desired his blood, but he had retreated into his hut, barricaded the doors and windows with big stones, and defied the world.

The King and I and the populace approached the hut cautiously. There was no hope of capturing the man without loss of life, for from a hole in the wall projected the muzzle of an extremely well-cared-for gun—the only gun in the State that could shoot. Namgay Doola had narrowly missed a villager just before we came up. The Standing Army stood. It could do no more, for when it

advanced pieces of sharp shale flew from the windows. To these were added from time to time showers of scalding water. We saw red heads bobbing up and down in the hut. The family of Namgay Doola were aiding their sire, and blood-curdling yells of defiance were the only answers to our prayers.

* Never,' said the King, puffing, 'has such a thing befallen my State. Next year I will certainly buy a little cannon.' He looked at me imploringly.

*Is there any priest in the Kingdom to whom he will listen?' said I, for a fight was beginning to break upon me.

*He worships his own God,' said the Prime Minister. *We can starve him out.'

^Let the white man approach,' said Namgay Doola from within. ^All others I will kill. Send me the white man.'

The door was thrown open and I entered the smoky interior of a Thibetan hut crammed with children. And every child had flaming red hair. A raw cow's-tail lay on the floor, and by its side two pieces of black velvet—my black velvet—rudely hacked into the semblance of masks.

*And what is this shame, Namgay Doola?' said I.

He grinned more winningly than ever. 'There is no shame,' said he. 'I did but cut off the tail of that man's cow. He betrayed me. I was minded to shoot him, Sahib. But not to death. Indeed not to death. Only in the legs.'

'And why at all, since it is the custom to pay revenue to the King? Why at all?'

'By the God of my father I cannot tell,' said Namgay Doola.

*And who was thy father?'

*The same that had this gun.' He showed me his

weapon—a Tower musket bearing date 1832 and the stamp of the Honourable East India Company.

'And thy father's name?' said I.

'Timlay Doola/ said he. 'At the first, I being then a little child, it is in my mind that he wore a red coat.'

'Of that I have no doubt. But repeat the name of thy father thrice or four times.'

He obeyed, and I understood whence the puzzling accent in his speech came. 'Thimla Dhula,' said he excitedly. ' To this hour I worship his God.'

'May I see that God?'

*In a little while—at twilight time.'

'Rememberest thou aught of thy father's speech?'

*It is long ago. But there is one word which he saidoften. Thus "Shun." Then I and my brethren stoodupon our feet, our hands to our sides. Thus.'

* Even so. And what was thy mother?'

' A woman of the hills. We be Lepchas of Darjeeling, butme they call an outlander because my hair is as thou seest.'

The Thibetan woman, his wife, touched him on thearm gently. The long parley outside the fort had lastedfar into the day. It was now close upon twilight—thehour of the Angelus. Very solemnly, the red-headedbrats rose from the floor and formed a semicircle. Nam-gay Doola laid his gun against the wall, lighted a littleml lamp, and set it before a recess in the wall. Pullingaside a curtain of dirty doth, he revealed a worn brasscrucifix leaning against the helmet-badge of a long for-gotten East India regiment. 'Thus did my father,' hesaid, crossing himself clumsily. The wife and childrenfollowed suit. Then all together they struck up the wail-ing chant that I heard on the hillside—

Dir hane mard-i-yemen dirTo weeree ala gee.

I was puzzled no longer. Again and again they crooned,as if their hearts would break, their version of the chorusof the Wearing of the Green—

They're hanging men and women too,For the wearing of the green.

A diabolical inspiration came to me. One of the brats, aboy about eight years old, was watching me as he sang.I pulled out a rupee, held the coin between finger andthumb and looked—only looked—at the gun against thewall. A grin of brilliant and perfect comprehensionoverspread the face of the child. Never for an instantstopping the song, he held out his hand for the money,and then slid the gun to my hand. I might have shotNamgay Doola as he chanted. But I was satisfied. Theblood-instinct of the race held true. Namgay Dooladrew the curtain across the recess. Angelus was over.

*Thus my father sang. There was much more, but Ihave forgotten, and I do not know the purport of thesewords, but it may be that the God will understand. Iam not of this people, and I will not pay revenue.'

'And why?'

Again that soul-compelling grin. *What occupationwould be to me between crop and crop? It is betterthan scaring bears. But these people do not understand.'He picked the masks from the floor, and looked in myface as simply as a child.

'By what road didst thou attain knowledge to makethese devilries?' I said, pointing.

'I cannot tell. I am but a Lepcha of Darjeeling, andyet the stuff '

'Which thou hast stolen.'

'Nay, surely. Did I steal? I desired it so. The

338 LIFE'S HANDICAP

stuff—the stuff—what else should I have done with thestuff?' He twisted the velvet between his fingers.

'But the sin of maiming the cow—consider that.'

'That is true; but oh, Sahib, that man betrayed meand I had no thought—but the heifer's tail waved in themoonlight and I had my knife. What else should I havedone? The tail came off ere I was aware. Sahib, thouknowest more than I.'

'That is true,' said I. 'Stay within the door. I goto speak to the King.'

The population of the Scate were ranged on the hill-sides. I went forth and spoke to the King.

'O Eling,' said I. 'Touching this man there be twocourses open to thy wisdom. Thou canst either hanghim from a tree, he and his brood, till there remains nohair that is red within the lajid.'

'Nay,' said the King. 'Why should I hurt the littlechildren?'

They had poured out of the hut door and were mak-ing plump obeisance to everybody. Namgay Doolawaited with his gun across his arm.

'Or thou canst, discarding the impiety of the cow-mxaiming, raise him to honour in thy Army. He comiCS ofa race that mil not pay revt/iue. A red flame is in hisblood wliich comes out at the top of his head in thatglowing hair. Make him chief of the Army. Give himhonour as may befall, and full allowance of work, butlook to it, 0 King, that neithtr he nor his hold a footof earth from thee henceforward. Feed him with wordsand favour, and also Hquor from certain bottles that thouknowest of, and he will be a bulwark of defence. Butdeny him even a tuft of grass for his owti. This is thenature that God has given him. Moreover he hasbrethren '

The State groaned unanimously.

'But if his brethren come, they will surely j5ght witheach other till they die; or else the one will alwaysgive information concerning the other. Shall he be ofthy Army, O King? Choose.'

The King bowed liis head, and I said, 'Come forth,Namgay Doola, and command the King's Army. Thyname shall no more be Namgay in the mouths of men,but Patsay Doola, for as thou hast said, I know.'

Then Namgay Doola, new christened Patsay Doola,son of Timlay Doola, which is Tim Doolan gone verywrong indeed, clasped the King's feet, cufifed the Stand-ing Army, and hurned in an agony of contrition fromtemple to temple, making offerings for the sin of cattle-maiming.

And the King was so pleased with my perspicacity,that he offered to sell me a village for twenty poundssterling. But I buy no villages in the Himalayas solong as one red head flares between the tail of the heaven-climbing glacier and the dark birch-forest.

I know that breed.

BERTRAN AND BIMI

The orang-outang in the big iron cage lashed to thesheep-pen began the discussion. The night was stiflinglyhot, and as I and Hans Breitmann, the big-beamed Ger-man, passed him, dragging our bedding to the fore-peakof the steamer, he roused himself and chattered obscenely.He had been caught somewhere in the Malayan Archi-pelago, and was going to England to be exhibited at ashilHng a head. For four days he had struggled, yelled,and wrenched at the heavy bars of his prison withoutceasing, and had nearly slain a lascar, incautious enoughto come within reach of the great hairy paw.

'It would be well for you, mine friend, if you was aliddle seasick,' said Hans Breitmann, pausing by thecage. 'You haf too much Ego in your Cosmos.'

The orang-outang's arm slid out negligently frombetween the bars. No one would have beheved that itwould make a sudden snakelike rush at the German'sbreast. The thin silk of the sleeping-suit tore out;Hans stepped back unconcernedly to pluck a bananafrom a bunch hanging close to one of the boats.

'Too much Ego,' said he, peeKng the fruit and offeringit to the caged devil, who was rending the silk to tatters.

Then we laid out our bedding in the bows among thesleeping Lascars, to catch any breeze that the pace of theship might give us. The sea was like smoky oil, exceptwhere it turned to fire under our forefoot and whirledback into the dark in smears of dull flame. There was

a thunderstorm some miles away; we could see theglunmer of the lightning. The ship's cow, distressed bythe heat and the smell of the ape-beast in the cage, lowedunhappily from time to time in exactly the same key asthat in wliich the look-out man a,nswered the hourly callfrom the bridge. The trampling tune of the engines wasvery distinct, and the jarring of the ash-Hft, as it wastipped into the sea, hurt the procession of hushed noise.Hans lay down by my side and lighted a good-nightcigar. Tliis was naturally the beginning of conversation.He owned a voice as soothing as the wash of the sea,and stores of experiences as vast as the sea itself; forhis business in life was to wander up and down theworld, collecting orchids and wild beasts and ethnologicalspecimens for German and American dealers. I watchedthe glowing end of his cigar wax and wane in the gloom,as the sentences rose and fell, till I was nearly asleep.The orang-outang, troubled by some dream of the forestsof his freedom, began to yell like a soul in purgatory,and to pluck madly at the bars of the cage.

'If he was out now dere would not be much of usleft hereabout,' said Hans lazily. 'He screams goot.See, now, how I shall tame him when he stops liimself.'

There was a pause in the outcry, and from Hans'mouth came an imitation of a snake's hiss, so perfect thatI almost sprang to my feet. The sustained murderoussound ran along the deck, and the wrenching at the barsceased. The orang-outang was quaking in an ecstasy ofpure terror.

'Dot stopped him,' said Hans. 'I learned dot trickin Mogoung Tanjong when I was collecting liddlemonkeys for some peoples in Berlin. Efery one in derworld is afraid of der monkeys—except der snake. SoI blay snake against monkey, and he keep quite still.

'Dere was too much Ego in his Cosmos. Dot is der soul-custom of monkeys. Are you asleep, or will you listen,and I will tell a dale dot you shall not pelief?'

'There's no tale in the wide world that I can't believe/I said.

'If you haf learned pelief you haf learned somedings.Now I shall try your pelief. Goot! When I wascollecting dose liddle monkeys—it was in '79 or '80, undI was in der islands of der Archipelago—over dere in derdark'—he pointed southward to New Guinea generally—'Mein Gott! I would sooner collect life red devilsthan liddle monkeys. When dey do not bite off yourthumbs dey are always dying from nostalgia—home-sick—for dey haf der imperfect soul, which is mid-way arrested in defelopment—imd too much Ego. Iwas dere for nearly a year, und dere I found a man dotwas called Bertran. He was a Frenchman, und he wasgoot man—naturahst to his bone. Dey said he wasan escaped convict, but he was naturalist, und dot wasenough for me. He would call all der life beasts fromder forest, und dey would come. I said he was St.Francis of Assizi in a new dransmigration produced, undhe laughed und said he haf never preach to der fishes.He sold dem for tripang—beche'de-mer.

'Und dot man, who was king of beasts-tamer men, hehad in der house shust such anoder as dot devil-animalin der cage—a great orang-outang dot thought he was aman. He haf foimd him when he was a child—derorang-outang—und he was child und brother und operacomique all round to Betran. He had his room in dothouse—not a cage, but a room—mit a bed imd sheets,imd he would go to bed und get up in der morning undsmoke his cigar und eat his dinner mit Bertran, und wall:mit him hand in hand, which was most horrible. Herr

Gott! I haf seen dot beast throw himself back in hischair und laugh when Bertran haf made fun of me. Hewas not a beast; he was a man, und he talked to Bertran,imd Bertran comprehend, for I have seen dem. Und hewas always politeful to me except when I talk too longto Bertran und say nodings at all to him. Den he wouldpull me away—dis great, dark devil, mit his enormouspaws—shust as if I was a child. He was not a beast;he was a man. Dis I saw pefore I know him threemonths, und Bertran he haf saw the same; and Bimi,der orang-outang, haf understood us both, mit his cigarbetween his big dog-teeth und der blue gum.

'I was dere a year, dere und at dere oder islands—somedimes for monkeys und somedimes for butterflies undorchits. One time Bertran says to me dot he will bemarried, because he haf found a girl dot was goot, und heenquire if this marrying idee was right. I would notsay, pecause it was not me dot was going to be married.Den he go off courting der girl—she was a half-casteFrench girl—very pretty. Haf you got a new light formy cigar? Ouf! Very pretty. Only I say, "Haf youthought of Bimi? If he pull me away when I talk toyou, what will he do to your wife? He will pull her inpieces. If I was you, Bertran, I would gif my wife forwedding-present der stuff figure of Bimi." By dot timeI had learned some dings about der monkey peoples."Shoot him?" says Bertran. "He is your beast," I said;"if he was mine he would be shot now!"

'Den I felt at der back of my neck der fingers ofBimi. Mein Gott! I tell you dot he talked throughdose fingers. It was der deaf-and-dumb alphabet allgomplete. He slide his hairy arm round my neck, undhe tilt up my chui und looked into my face, shust to seeif I \mderstood his talk so well as he understood mine.

'"See now dere!" says Bertran, "und you wouldshoot him while he is cuddlin' you? Dot is der Teutoningrate!"

'But I kncw^ dot I had made Bimi a life's-enemy,pecause his fingers haf talk murder through the back ofmy neck. Next dime I see Bimi dere was a pistol inmy belt, und he touched it once, und I open der breech toshow him it was loaded. He haf seen der Hddle monkeyskilled in der woods: he understood.

'So Bertran he was married, and he forgot clean aboutBimi dot was skippin' alone on der beach mit der half ofa human soul in his belly. I was see him skip, und hetook a big bough und thrash der sand till he haf made agreat hole like a grave. So I says to Bertran, "For anysakes, kill Bimi. He is mad mit der jealousy."

'Bertran haf said "He is not mad at all. He haf obeyund lofe my wdfe, and if she speak he will get her slippers,"und he looked at his wife agross der room. She was avery pretty girl.

'Den I said to him, "Dost dou pretend to knowmonkeys und dis beast dot is lashing himself mad uponder sands, pecause you do not talk to him? Shoot himwhen he comes to der house, for he haf der light in hiseye dot means killing—und killing." Bimi come to derhouse, but dere was no Kght in liis eye. It was all putaway, cunning—so cunning—und he fetch der girl hersUppers, und Bertran turn to me und say, "Dost douknow him in nine months more dan I haf known him intwelve years? Shall a child stab his fader? I haffed him, und he was my child. Do not speak thisnonsense to my wife or to me any more."

'Dot next day Bertran came to my house to help memake some wood cases for der specimens, und he tell medot he haf left his wife a Hddle while mit Bimi in der

BERTRAN AND BIMI 345

garden. Den I linish my cases quick, und I say, 'Xet usgo to your houses und get a trink." He laugh and say," Come along, dry mans."

'His wife was not in der garden, und Bimi did notcome when Bertran called. Und his wife did not comewhen he called, und he knocked at her bedroom door unddot was shut tight—locked. Den he look at me, und hisface was white. I broke down der door mit my shoulder,und der thatch of der roof was torn into a great hole,und der sun came in upon der floor. Haf you ever seenpaper in der waste-basket, or cards at whist on der tablescattered? Dere was no wife dot could be seen. I tellyou dere was nodings in dot room dot might be a woman.Dere was stuff on der floor und dot was all. I looked atdese things und I was very sick; but Bertran looked ahddle longer at what was upon the floor und der walls,und der hole in der thatch. Den he pegan to laugh, softund low, und I knew und thank Gott dot he was mad.He nefer cried, he nefer prayed. He stood all still inder doorway und laugh to himself. Den he said, "Shehaf locked herself in dis room, and he haf torn up derthatch. Fi done! Dot is so. We will mend der thatchund wait for Bimi. He vv^ill surely com.e."

' I tell you we waited ten days in dot house, after derroom was made into a room again, und once or twice wesaw Bimi comin' a hddle way from der woods. He wasafraid pecause he haf done wrong. Bertran called himwhen he was come to look on the tenth day, und Bimicome skipping along der beach und making noises, mit along piece of black hair in his hands. Den Bertran laughand say, "Fi done!" shust as if it was a glass brokenupon der table; und Bimi come nearer, und Bertran washoney-sweet in his voice und laughed to himself. Forthree days he made love to Bimi, pecause Bimi would not

let himself be touched. Den Bimi come to dimier atder same table mit us, und the hair on his hands was allblack und thick mit—mit what had dried on der hands.Bertran gave him sangaree till Bimi was dnmk andstupid, und den '

Hans paused to puff at his cigar.

'And then?'said I.

*Und den Bertran he kill him mit his hands, und Igo for a walk upon der beach. It was Bertran's ownpiziness. When I come back der ape he was dead, undBertran he was dying abofe him; but still he laughedHddle und low und he was quite content. Now youknow der formula of der strength of der orang-outang—it is more as seven to one in relation to man. ButBertran, he haf killed Bimi mit sooch dings as Gott gifhim. Dot was der miracle.'

The infernal clamour in the cage recommenced. ' Aha!Dot friend of ours haf still too much Ego in his Cosmos.Be quiet, dou!'

Hans hissed long and venomously. We could hearthe great beast quaking in his cage.

'But why in the world didn't you help Bertran insteadof letting him be killed?' I asked.

'My friend,' said Hans, composedly stretching himselfto slumber, 'it was not nice even to mineself dot I shouldlive after I haf seen dot room mit der hole in der thatch.Und Bertran, he was her husband. Goot-night, und—sleep well.'

Once upon a time there was a coffee-planter in Indiawho wished to clear some forest land for coffee-planting.Whtn he had cut down all the trees and burned theunder-wood the stumps still remained. Dynamite isexpensive and slow-fire slow. The happy medium forstump-clearing is the lord of all beats, who is the elephant.He will either push the stump out of the ground withhis tusks, if he has any, or drag it out with ropes. Theplanter, therefore, hired elephants by ones and twosand threes, and fell to work. The very best of all theelephants belonged to the very worst of all the drivers ormahouts; and the superior beast's name was Moti Guj.He was the absolute property of his mahout, which wouldnever have been the case under native rule, for Moti Gujwas a creature to be desired by kings; and his name,being translated, meant the Pearl Elephant. Because theBritish Government was in the land, Deesa, the mahout,enjoyed his property undisturbed. He was dissipated.When he had made much money through the strength ofhis elephant, he would get extremely drunk and giveMoti Guj a beating with a tent-peg over the tender nailsof the forefeet. Moti Guj never trampled the Hfe out ofDeesa on these occasions, for he knew that after thebeating was over Deesa would embrace his trunk andweep and call him his love and his Hfe and the Hver ofhis soul, and give him some Hquor. Moti Guj was veryfond of liquor—arrack for choice, though he would drink

347

palm-tree toddy if nothing better offered. Then Deesawould go to sleep between Moti Guj's forefeet, and asDeesa generally chose the middle of the public road, andas Moti Guj mounted guard over him and would notpermit horse, foot, or cart to pass by, traffic was congestedtill Deesa saw fit to wake up.

There was no sleeping in the daytime on the planter'sclearing: the wages were too high to risk. Deesa sat on Moti Guj's neck and gave him orders, while Moti Guj rooted up the stumps—for he owned a magnificent pair of tusks; or pulled at the end of a rope—for he had a magnificent pair of shoulders, while Deesa kicked him behind the ears and said he was the king of elephants. At evening time Moti Guj would wash down his three hundred pounds' weight of green food with a quart of arrack, and Deesa would take a share and sing songs between Moti Guj's legs till it was time to go to bed. Once a week Deesa led Moti Guj down to the river, and Moti Guj lay on his side luxuriously in the shallows, while Deesa went over him with a coir-swab and a brick. Moti Guj never mistook the pounding blow of the latter for the smack of the former that warned him to get up and turn over on the other side. Then Deesa would look at his feet, and examine his eyes, and turn up the fringes of his mighty ears in case of sores or budding ophthalmia. After inspection, the two would come up with a song from the sea,' Moti Guj all black and shining, waving a torn tree branch twelve feet long in his trunk, and Deesa knotting up his own long wet hair.

It was a peaceful, well-paid life till Deesa felt the return of the desire to drink deep. He wished for an orgie. The little draughts that led nowhere were taking the manhood out of him.

He went to the planter, and 'My mother's dead/ said he, weeping.

*She died on the last plantation two months ago; and she died once before that when you were working for me last year,' said the planter, who knew something of the ways of nativedom.

^Then it's my aunt, and she was just the same as a mother to me,' said Deesa, weeping more than ever.'She has left eighteen small children entirely without bread, and it is I who must fill their Httle stomachs,' said Deesa, beating his head on the floor,

'Who brought you the news?' said the planter.

'The post,' said Deesa.

'There hasn't been a post here for the past week. Get back to your lines!'

'A devastating sickness has fallen on my village, and all my wives are dying,' yelled Deesa, really in tears this time.

'Call Chihun, who comes from Deesa's village,' said the planter. ' Chihun, has this man a wife?'

'He!' said Chihun. 'No. Not a woman of our village would look at him. They'd sooner marry the elephant.' Chihun snorted. Deesa wept and bellowed.

'You will get into a difficulty in a minute,' said the planter. ' Go back to your work!'

'Now I will speak Heaven's truth,' gulped Deesa, with an inspiration. 'I haven't been drunk for two months. I desire to depart in order to get properly drunk afar off and distant from this heavenly plantation. Thus I shall cause no trouble.'

A flickering smile crossed the planter's face. 'Deesa,'said he, 'you've spoken the truth, and I'd give you leave on the spot if anything could be done with Moti Guj while you're away. You know that he will only obey your orders.'

'May the Light of the Heavens live forty thousand years. I shall be absent but ten Httle days. After that, upon my faith and honour and soul, I return. As to the inconsiderable interval, have I the gracious permission of the Heaven-born to call up Moti Guj?'

Permission was granted, and, in answer to Deesa's shrill yell, the lordly tusker swung out of the shade of a clump of trees where he had been squirting dust over himself till his master should return.

'Light of my heart, Protector of the Drunken, Mountain of Might, give ear,' said Deesa, standing in front of him.

Moti Guj gave ear, and saluted with his trunk. 'I am going away,' said Deesa.

Moti Guj's eyes twinkled. He liked jaunts as well as his master. One could snatch all manner of nice things from the roadside then.

'But you, you fubsy old pig, must stay behind andwork.'

The twinkle died out as Moti Guj tried to look de-lighted. He hated stump-hauling on the plantation.It hurt his teeth.

'I shall be gone for ten days, 0 Delectable One. Holdup your near forefoot and I'll impress the fact upon it,warty toad of a dried mud-puddle.' Deesa took a tent-peg and banged Moti Guj ten times on the nails. MotiGuj grunted and shuiHed from foot to foot.

'Ten days,' said Deesa, 'you must work and haul androot trees as Chihun here shall order you. Take upChihun and set him on your neck!' Moti Guj curledthe tip of his trunk, Chihun put his foot there and wasswung on to the neck. Deesa handed Chihun the heavyanktis, the iron elephant-goad.

Chihun thumped Moti Guj's bald head as a paviourthumps a kerbstone.

Moti Guj trumpeted.

*Be still, hog of the backwoods. Chihun's yourmahout for ten days. And now bid me good-bye, beastafter mine own heart. Oh, my lord, my king! Jewel ofall created elephants, lily of the herd, preserve yourhonoured health; be virtuous. Adieu!'

Moti Guj lapped his trunk round Deesa and swunghim into the air twice. That was his way of bidding theman good-bye.

* He'll work now,' said Dessa to the planter. 'Havel leave to go?'

The planter nodded, and Deesa dived into the wt)ods.Moti Guj went back to haul stimips.

Chihun was very kind to him, but he felt unhappyand forlorn notwithstanding- Chihun gave him balls ofspices, and tickled him under the chin, and Chihun'slittle baby cooed to him after work was over, andChihun's wife called him a darling; but Moti Guj was abachelor by instinct, as Deesa was. He did not under-stand the domestic emotions. He v/anted the Ught of hisuniverse back again—the drink and the drunken slumber,the savage beatings and the savage caresses

None the less he worked well, and the planter won-dered. Deesa had vagabonded along the roads till hemet a marriage procession of his own caste and, drinking,dandng, and tippling, had drifted past all knowledge ofthe lapse of time.

The morning of the eleventh day dawned, and therereturned no Deesa. Moti Guj was loosed from his ropesfor the daily stint. He swung clear, looked round,shrugged his shoulders, and began to walk away, as onehaving business elsewhere.

'Hi! ho! Come back, you,' shouted Chihun. Tomeback, and put me on your neck, Misborn Mountain. Re-

352 LIFE'S HANDICAP

turn, Splendour of the Hillsides. Adornment of allIndia, heave to, or I'll bang every toe off your fat fore-foot!'

Moti Guj gurgled gently, but did not obey. Chihunran after him with a rope and caught him up. Moti Gujput his ears forward, and Chihun knew what that meant,though he tried to carry it off with high words.

'None of your nonsense with me,' said he. 'To yourpickets, Devil-son.'

'Hrrump!' said Moti Guj, and that was all—thatand the forebent ears.

Moti Guj put his hands in his pockets, chewed abranch for a toothpick, and strolled about the clearing,making jest of the other elephants, who had just set towork.

Chihun reported the state of affairs to the planter,who came out with a dog-whip and cracked it furiously.Moti Guj paid the white man the compliment of charginghim nearly a quarter of a mile across the clearing and'Hrrumping' him into the verandah. Then he stood out-side the house chuckling to himself, and shaking all overwith the fun of it, as an elephant will.

'We'll thrash him,' said the planter. 'He shall havethe finest thrashing that ever elephant received. GiveKala Nag and Nazim twelve foot of chain apiece, and tellthem to lay on twenty blows.'

Kala Nag—which means Black Snake—and Nazimwere two of the biggest elephants in the lines, and one oftheir duties was to administer the graver punishments,since no man can beat an elephant properly.

They took the whipping-chains and rattled them intheir trunks as they sidled up to Moti Guj, meaning tohustle him between them. Moti Guj had never, in allhis life of thirty-nine years, been whipped, and he did not

intend to open new experiences. So he waited, weavinghis head from right to left, and measuring the precisespot in Kala Nag's fat side where a blunt tusk wouldsink deepest. Kala Nag had no tusks; the chain washis badge of authority; but he judged it good to swingwide of Moti Guj at the last minute, and seem to appearas if he had brought out the chain for amusement.Nazim turned round and went home early. He did notfeel fighting-fit that morning, and so Moti Guj was leftstanding alone with his ears cocked.

That decided the planter to argue no more, and MotiGuj rolled back to his inspection of the clearing. Anelephant who will not work, and is not tied up, is notquite so manageable as an eighty-one ton gun loose in aheavy sea-way. He slapped old friends on the back andasked them if the stumps were coming away easily; hetalked nonsense concerning labour and the inalienablerights of elephants to a long 'nooning'; and, wanderingto and fro, thoroughly demoralized the garden till sun-down, when he returned to his pickets for food.

'If you won't work you shan't eat,' said Chihunangrily. 'You're a wild elephant, and no educatedanimal at all. Go back to your jungle.'

Chihun's Uttle brown baby, rolling on the floor of thehut, stretched its fat arms to the huge shadow in thedoorway. Moti Guj knew well that it was the dearestthing on earth to Chihun. He swung out his trunk witha fascinating crook at the end, and the brown baby threwitself shouting upon it. Moti Guj made fast and pulledup till the brown baby was crowing in the air twelve feetabove his father's head.

' Great Chief!' said Chihun. ' Flour cakes of the best,twelve in number, two feet across, and soaked in rumshall be yours on the instant, and two hundred pounds'

LIFE'S HANDICAP

weight of fresh-cut young sugar-cane therewith. Deignonly to put down safely that insignificant brat who is myhe-art and my Hfe to me.'

Moti Guj tucJced the brown baby comfortably betweenhis forefeet, that could have knocked into toothpicks allChihun's hut, and waited for his food. He ate it, and thebrown baby crawled away. Moti Guj dozed, and thoughtof Deesa. One of many mysteries connected with theelephant is that his huge body needs less sleep than any-thing else tliat Hves. Four or five hours in the nightsuffice—two just before midnight, lying down on one side;two just after one o'clock, lying down on the other.The rest of the silent hours are filled with eating andfidgeting and long grumbhng soliloquies.

At midnight, therefore, Moti Guj strode out of hispickets, for a thought had come to him that Deesa mightbe l\'7ddng drunk somewhere in the dark forest with noneto look after him. So all that night he chased throughthe undergrowth, blowing and trumpeting and shakinghis ears. He went down to the river and blared acrossthe shallows where Deesa used to wash him, but therewas no answer. He could not find Deesa, but he dis-turbed all the elephants in the fines, and nearly frightenedto death some gypsies in the woods.

At dawn Deesa returned to the plantation. He hadbeen very drunk indeed, and he expected to fall intotrouble for outsta>dng his leave. He drew a long breathwhen he saw that the bungalow and the plantation werestill uninjured; for he knew something of Moti Guj'stemper; and reported himself with many lies and salaams.Moti Guj had gone to his pickets for breakfast. Hisnight exercise had made hun hungry.

'Call up your beast,' said the planter, and Deesashouted in the mysterious elephant-language, that sonif?

mahouts believe came from China at the birth of theworld, when elephants and not men were masters. MotiGuj heard and came. Elephants do not gallop. Theymove from spots at varying rates of speed. If an ele-phant wished to catch an express train he could notgallop, but he could catch the train. Thus Moti Guj wasat the planter's door almost before Chihun noticed thathe had left his pickets. He fell into Deesa's armstrumpeting with joy, and the man and beast wept andslobbered over each other, and handled each other fromhead to heel to see that no harm had befallen.

*Now we will get to work,' said Deesa. 'Lift me up,my son and my joy.'

Moti Guj swung him up and the two went to thecoffee-clearing to look for irksome stumps.

The planter was too astonished to be very angry.

VENVOI

My new-ciU ashlar takes the light

Where crimson-blank the windows flare;

By my own work, before the night,Great Overseer, I make my prayer.

If there be good in that I wrought,

Thy hand compelled it, Master, Thine;

Where I have failed to meet Thy thoughtI know, through Thee, the blame is mine.

One instant's toil to Thee denied

Stands all Eternity's offence,Of that I did with Thee to guide

To Thee, through Thee, be eoccellence.

Who, lest all thought of Eden fade.

Bring'st Eden to the crajtsman's brain,

Godlike to muse o'er his owti tradeAnd Manlike stand with God again.

The depth and dream of my desire.The bitter paths wherein I stray.

Thou knowest Who hast made the Fire,Thou knowest Who hast made the CUy.

One stone the more swings to her place

In that dread Temple of Thy Worth-It is enough thai through Thy graceI saw naught common on Thy earth.

Take not that vision from my ken;

Oh whatso'er may spoil or speed,Edp me to need no aid from men

That I may help such men as need I

THE END

Printed in Great Britain
by Amazon